WHEAT AND TARES TOGETHER SOWN

Don Teviot

Illustrations from original watercolours by the author
ISBN 0 9534295 6 3

Also available with colour illustrations
ISBN 0 9534295 7 1

Published by and produced on demand by

Fairway Folio

Alsager, Cheshire
01270 874662

Contents

THE LAY OF THE LAND

After seven years of active service, and not long after the end of the Second World War, a certain young fighting soldier was 'demobbed'. He shed his khaki but still bore in his body, mind and soul the ineradicable marks of his oft-times exposure to the violence of that conflict. And yet, strange as it may seem, he had become imbued with a persistent notion of holy vocation. Subsequently judged worthy, he was committed to the rigours of a new discipline which involved, amongst other inconveniences, a highly specialized academic training. Thus completely re-equipped he was ecclesiastically ordained, formally presented with a special new Bible, and invested with an honoured courtesy title. He was then thrust otherwise raw into a circumstance which was calculated to complete his wondrous transformation into a full-blown Minister of the Church. Tradition would now require him to don 'the cloth', be constantly attired in sombre hue, and sport a peculiar style of neck gear. He would presume upon certain rights and privileges concomitant with the office, and at the same time attain validation of his 'call' by being content with working long hours for small pay. That Church, one of the major denominations, was surely richer in faith than in practical wisdom in entrusting the cure of souls to a tyro such as this, requiring him to guide and direct in all things pertaining to this life and the next, a sturdy people who by nature were infinitely more mature in the art of living than he was. It therefore becomes inevitable that the following selection of short stories, fashioned out of memories of certain of his initial encounters in this unfamiliar field of battle, may turn out to be but a comic catalogue of the mishaps, mistakes, misdemeanours and misjudgements of a misfit.

Ironically however, there is a sense in which this 'trial by ordeal' worked out for ultimate good. Whether by design, accident, or providence that stint of initiation which - one suspects - may well have been imposed (the posting was in an insignificant fringe of church life!) in order to bring a headstrong young aspirant down to size, actually had the effect of increasing him in worldly wisdom and moral stature. Albeit the process necessitated some drastic measures of rehabilitation, and exposure to awkward levels of cultural shock, all of which the kindly country folk administered with native tolerance and thoroughly good humour.

I was the young man in question, and was in need of complete re-direction in my thinking on life. Thus it was that I was destined to discover some astounding facts about human nature - particularly my own. I had to adjust to the knowledge that life in general is experienced as a compendium of anomaly and contradiction, wherein even the best regulated one is as prone to accident from within as from without. So it is that in the grand drama of living, mystery and farce, tragedy and comedy, right and wrong are curiously intermingled. I was to discover, often to my confusion and profound dismay, that there is not always ample scope for cold rationality in the life of faith to which I was now committed; idealism requires a fair degree of naivete, and therefore absolutes cannot always be credited with universal credence in any given human situation. Therefore in my new station in life I was constantly lured towards the easy options of dubious compromise or vain imprudence.

In the circumstance it may be deemed somewhat irregular for a parson to cherish shades of humour in his memories, the pastoral office being commonly associated with things solemn, sad and serious. These episodes however may betray a certain quirk in my constitution which causes me to initially evaluate a situation funny-side-up. It is perhaps a kind of emotional defence mechanism called up from the subconscious to offset shock, or resorted to as a necessary foil to an innate sense of inadequacy. As for any direct humour which may appear here and there, no disrespect nor disparagement is ever intended. Indeed it may be noted that the joke, whether stated or implied, is usually upon me. At the same time I have to make ready admission that there have been circumstances, often of my own doing, in which the only alternative to this proneness to look back and laugh would have been debilitating despair and irrevocable despondency.

It was inevitable that during this period of rehabilitation, some residue of orientation from my recent stressful past would colour some of my reaction to new and unfamiliar situations. Often to my utter dismay I found this not a little intrusive and unwelcome, sometimes wreaking havoc with my earnest pastoral intentions. Army logic should be confined to logistics! There would persist in me an indelicacy of application which would not only expose some of my basic ineptitudes, but also call forth my singular penchant for converting a perfectly ordinary situation into a near disaster. The soldier turned pastor needed to be rid of his too-ready instinct for self-defence.

Although what follows describes a period of crisis in a young man's life as he blundered through the vicissitudes of his early noviciate, it is not to be seen as autobiography in the strict sense of the term. It is crafted from an amalgam of personal impressions and illustrative material to represent real life situations in which I found myself seriously implicated. It is hoped that there is never any unwarranted trespass into the sacred preserve of pastoral confidence. Proper names and place names are inventions. Therefore any accidental similarity with any counterparts which they may have in any time or place is unintentional and regretted. Nevertheless it is hoped that this comment upon the early phase of the transition from fighting soldier to some semblance of a shepherd of souls, will leave room for some laughter as well as allowing ample scope for serious interest.

The setting is among the northern slopes of the Pennines. As a child I had been taught that this was the backbone of England. Here there dwelt a noble people such as is found at no other altitude and in no other terrain. Their character could not easily be defined within the elementary categories of black and white, for its hallmark was a unique blend of colours, tones and features intrinsically matched with their magnificent environment. I soon learned to love their plain manners, often quaint, sometimes brusque, always candid. I could but marvel at their practical down-to-earth philosophy, subtle deadpan humour, and that charming brand of kindly cunning which is indigenous to no other breed of man. I was fascinated by their delightful dialect with its rich open rounded vowel sounds, sharply clipped consonants, velvet soft aspirates and blunted sibilants. Obviously with strong Nordic roots it had its own peculiar syntax and highly specialized range of phonetic orientations. Therefore in order to preserve some measure of realism, I have endeavoured to render a literal approximation of the way it sounded in my untutored ears, whilst at the same time striving to affect sufficient modification to ensure that the dialogue will be intelligible to speakers of each variant of our glorious English tongue.

Now I look back in wonder and acknowledge my lifelong indebtedness to those splendid folk who set me on my way, ever mindful of their unwearied patience with my youthful bungling and misplaced exuberance. It became my privilege to serve them at the level of their joys and griefs, and my own, and to proffer what little I had to give in exchange for their trust, to smile at their idiosyncrasies and to see them marvel in disbelief at mine.

And that troublesome part of me which in those early days would oft-times slip in from my warlike past, and interfere in my pastoral affairs. That soldier - what of him? The truth is that he has never done the soldier-like thing and just faded away. No deserter he, for often as the circumstance of the hour has required, he has come forward and allied himself to my cause, reinforcing my puny efforts with qualities of courage, endurance, and self-discipline such as this minister of the church could never have mustered without him.

Wheat and Tares Together Sown

Don Teviot

The late summer of nineteen-forty-nine was one of the hottest in living memory. The afternoons were sweltering, and each evening the languid sun lingered long before sinking wearily to rest. It was on such a day, near the end of August that Gina and I, a pair of starry-eyed newly-weds with a certain amount of worldly wisdom, a wide range of naivete, and no money, set off on an auspicious journey. We had not chosen the posting; it had been imposed upon us. Nevertheless there was a strong element of adventure in the prospect, principally because this journey signalled the start of a new career which, so it was anticipated, would endure for the next forty years.

We had been provided in advance with some necessary statistics and fore-warnings, together with the proviso that ownership of a car was to be regarded as the top priority for the work of a parson in that remote area of the Northern Pennines for which we were heading. Accordingly we had pooled our meagre financial resources and blown the entire one-hundred-and-fifteen pounds on an 'unrepeatable bargain'. The car was beyond doubt a hybrid, various of its vital constituents having been cannibalized from noble ancestors, all of which had become obsolete before the year nineteen-thirty-seven; although how long before was not readily apparent. Even so, we were assured that the little Sportster before us added up to a genuine one-hundred-percent 8 hp MG Midget, and perhaps even more, just as the famous octagonal motif up front on the radiator and on the impressive wheel-hubs proclaimed and the tatty log-book testified. For reasons already stated, which particular Series, or Model, or Type could not be classified with any certainty, nor authoritatively defined. Gina suggested, appropriately in this case, that the letters 'MG' could be meant to represent 'Mixed Grill'. In spite of its dubious pedigree, this sprightly package of assorted automobility was quite a spectacle, some crazy previous owner having over-painted the original racing green livery with a garish yellow, making it reminiscent of Enid Blyton's 'Noddy' stories for children. During the few weeks of our possession, the little car had already established itself as our indispensable pride and joy, winning our tireless devotion, schooling us in the finer arts of self control and good temper, and ensuring our perpetual poverty. But banger though she was, this small jalopy was destined to feature significantly in many aspects of our subsequent career at Lyndassby, towards which destination she was presently hastening us with characteristic bluster.

A mountain of miscellaneous baggage, topped by a disorderly array of inevitable afterthoughts, gave the open two-seater a striking resemblance to a decrepit pack-horse assembled by a drunken drover. Amid all of this, my young wife, together with other of my precious and recently acquired belongings, and even more of her own, was crammed down into her allotted one half of the cockpit. Throughout the journey the precarious load, including that piled up to the rear, lurched and shifted, constantly threatening to ram us through the windscreen and deposit us out over the front of the long bonnet. I was always aware of a curious 'feel' about the overall trim of the car, and had some growing doubts as to the location of its centre of gravity. I sensed some fearful anxiety about the unfamiliar lightness at the steering wheel. All things considered however, our pint-sized heroine seemed to be singing along confidently; that is so long as we remained insensitive to ominous overtones of escaping internal combustion and dry clashing metal. Our own excited chatter eventually dried up, for we turned tired of shouting into each other's ear. Instead we each became pleasantly pre-occupied with sweet recollections and happy anticipation.

This day was the grand sequel to an eventful ten years in my own life. A programme of higher education had been rudely interrupted by the outbreak of war in nineteen-thirty-nine. There followed over six years of active service as a fighting soldier which had inflicted some indelible scars upon my body, mind, and soul. After the war ended, three years back at University had culminated in recent Ordination as a Non-Conformist minister, and brought me to this very time and place. Whilst in the Army I had met Gina, either by pure accident, inexplicable co-incidence, Divine providence, or sheer good fortune, and from that moment onwards our two lives had moved with delightful spontaneity towards this event. Georgina Graham, who had very recently qualified as a school teacher, was pretty, pert, and petite, a dark-haired, bright-eyed country girl, and six years my junior. We had been married for only a few weeks and were still in honeymoon mood. But from this day forward, for better or for worse, together we would have to face up to the practical realities of our new life, like setting up home, and not least to adjusting to the stringencies of the clerical office. Fully cognizant of this we pressed on with cheerful optimism, sceptical towards any minor misgivings which maybe still lurked in the obscure places of our minds. Today we would be taking possession of our first home. It was a church house, called a Manse, and therefore would be fully furnished, too large, perhaps somewhat pretentious, too costly to maintain and well nigh impossible to heat adequately; a legacy from former times when a clergyman's means were more realistically matched to the standard of living that was expected of him. Even yet parsons and their wives were looked upon as a race apart, and were thus required to keep up appearances consistent with the old status quo - although on a much leaner budget. The ethos of my denomination of the church endued every aspirant after Ordination with an inscrutable sense of 'Call', carrying with it a kind of built-in tolerance to the vicissitudes of the pastoral office, and implying some sort of mystical compensation for his pecuniary embarrassments and physical discomforts.

Our reverie came to an abrupt end with the appearance of the little sign-post poised at a rakish slant in the long grass by the left side of the main road. Rather shyly it proclaimed that magic legend for which our eyes had been scanning for mile after hectic mile - LYNDASSBY 9 MILES. Another board, rectangular and much larger was slung at a crazy angle beneath it. This one bore the ominous warning, 'Narrow Road, Weight Limit Max 3 Tons' causing us both to simultaneously cast an involuntary glance back over our shoulders towards our precariously perched load of goods and chattels. The acutely angled turn off the busy highway switched us with astonishing immediacy onto a narrow unclassified causeway. Wonder of wonders, for it felt as if we had digressed into another world, where other values pertained and every observation was tempered with a serene sense of spaciousness and peace. The transition was so startling that now I slowed down the car to walking pace, let it drift of its own accord until with snorts and jerks of protest it stopped and yielded to the silence. Not a word passed our lips as we stared awe-stricken upon our Promised Land spread out majestically before our eyes. A vast panorama of undulating moor, variegated in multiple shades of green, richly purpled with limitless acres of full-blown heather, beribboned with the deckle-edged narrow trail, twisting and turning, rising and dipping, and finally losing itself among the gentle folds of high hills in the grey-pink-hazed distance beyond. There were no fences by the road-sides, nor any kerbstones. At frequent intervals wide strips of vegetation had invaded long stretches of the centre and blossomed in defiance of assault by foot, hoof or tyre. In the near distance rugged dry-stone walls struck irregular patterns up and over the hills, giving the entire vista an aura of unorganised splendour. When we broke out of our entrancement and got back into motion, the coarse surface of the rustic road began to make harmonious music with the tyre tread, and the slip-stream whistled delightful ditties through the wire-spoked wheels. The melody was punctuated at intervals by a smooth swish through a shallow ford, or an alarming rattling percussion as we passed over a cattle grid. The only visible living creatures were the ubiquitous sheep, endlessly engrossed in sideways chewing, occasionally raising a head, twitching an ear, or casting a disdainful glance in our direction, and all without the slightest interruption to the movement of the mandible. At times our passing would raise a curlew, piping frantically, or give a pair of lapwings cause to harry us from overhead. Often a flurry of grouse would explode from out of a patch of bracken by the roadside with loud crucks and thrashing pinions. And there were the rabbits, scores of them to the mile, recklessly skittering over the road and about the verges in every direction, and taxing the driver's manoeuvring dexterity to the limit. It was all so exhilarating, exciting - casting over us a spell of rare wonder. And oddly, the little car seemed to become caught up in the spirit of the moment - purely subjective on our part of course but she seemed to be running with unprecedented goodwill and lack of noisy aggression. At the now leisurely and uncompetitive pace, even the exhaust discharge, normally delivered in evil smelling wafts of black and blue smoke, was coming clean. In this wise she hummed along merrily, filling us with that unique ecstasy of power and motion known to none but owners of mighty MG Midgets of absolutely any vintage, whatever their history, or colour... until... an ear-splitting screech of sudden braking... juddering scream of skidding tyres... a violent body twist... painful forward jolt... and a dull thud from somewhere up front.

"Honestly darling... I tried... I really did try... awfully hard too... somehow... well... I just couldn't miss... sorry."

The unfortunate rabbit's timing, or mine, had been slightly less than precise and we had coincided somewhere near the middle of the road. I leapt out of the car, picked up the poor creature and held it up by the ears, "It's not squashed or anything horrible Gina dear... well not really... I mean there's no blood running out or anything like that... just... well... I think it might be very... dead."

"But the poor little thing's eyes are wide open".

"And so would yours be if I held you up by the ears," I jested with a careless loss of tact. "Nice way to die anyway... wouldn't feel a thing would it? Just... BOOM... and that's it."

The lady was not amused, but the period of shocked silence which ensued not only helped to restore sensible equilibrium but also made us acutely aware of the approach of another vehicle, already quite close at hand. It was an incredibly audible motor-cycle, astride of which was perched an incredibly long policeman with an incredibly audible voice.

"Nowwwww... and what 'ave we got 'ere then? Nice yan an' all. Tellus lad, didst tha hit it apurpose, or wad ye say it was soort o' accidental leyke?"

Gina furtively receded into her small portion of the cockpit like melting wax, leaving me, incriminating evidence in hand, to face the dire consequences of the law alone. I fancied I could hear her killing herself with muffled laughter. The lone rider did not cut out his engine; with a voice like that he didn't need to, and judging by the state of its mechanics he probably didn't dare. He simply pitched his voice to a matching resonance. The resultant din made it extremely difficult for me to keep my mind upon formulating my defence.

"Didst tha knaw tha front numberplate's all bent back then? Nae number or owt tha can see."

The observation let loose some peptic panic in my members and sent me fumbling for words. But none would come. Mercifully none were needed for again the strident voice of the law boomed out,

"Tha should 'appen dae leyke t'lads on t'Posth vans and put tha plate on hinges, so't when tha cracks yan, stops it gittin' bent ower... keyeps t'rabbit nice and clean an' all."

At this the officer burst into a spate of raucous four-stroke laughter, concomitant with the heavy pounding of his machine which, although running on low revs, was dancing rhythmically under him. I might have conjured up some welcome relief for myself by reciprocating his amusement, had it not been that he was in the same instant slowly extricating from his breast pocket an ominous looking black note book.

"Now then, if I've got me facts reyght, I reckons tha'll be t'new parson fella that's cummin' ower tae Lyndassby... Reyght?" Here he gave a cursory flick at the peak of his cap, "Aye, and they telt us all abowet tha … tla'al car an' all... Gay bonnie yan that eh. Bet tha can nearly flee in that yan... pair o' wings 'appen, and tha'd be off." More thunderous laughter.

The conversation was still leaning uncomfortably to one side, until, after tremendous effort I managed to squeeze in, or out, with,

"Yes that's who I am actually... Don Teviot I'm called or if it has to be more precise or anything, The Reverend Gordon MacDonald Teviot... that's where the Don comes from actually... bit of a mouthful otherwise what... I mean... yes of course... this is my... the car actually... ghastly colour I know... and well... O yes, and this is my wife, this is her here... well somewhere around... amongst that lot I think. She's Gina Teviot... Georgina to be exact ...." At which point my fluster winded me.

"Now where ist-tha? Let's hev a good leyeke at tha lass... they said tha was a gayly youngun... Now tha's gittin' thesel' into a reyght scrow there hest tha not? Nae... just bide theesel' still now... din't disturb t'luggage or owt."

Gina, emerging cautiously from down amongst the stowage, issued one of her delightful chuckles, calculated to totally disarm even the most determined would-be aggressor, and doubtlessly in the present emergency, to compel the officer to modify any punitive intentions that he might be incubating.

"Onywey's, nice tae meet tha Missus Teviot, and tha man here... leyeke for'ad tae seein' mare on tha... And O aye... should've mentioned it afore... Littlejohn's t'name... tae be proper, Police Constable J. T. Littlejohn, North West Pennines Constabulary. See plenty o' tha bayeth nae doubt in days tae cum... us livin' in t'sayeme place and all that. O aye... t'name's Jack."

"We'll sure look forward to that," chortled the sweet voice from down in the depths... "er... Jack."

"And O aye," he continued, although now reverting to his navy-blue voice, "That rabbit tha's hoddin' there... tha'll not be wantin' it for owt, so I'll just tek it frae tha... for me dog. O aye... and another thing... In future, try not tae gaw squashing ower mony of them wilt tha. Messy business on t'roaads... and sic a waste o' good meyate an' all. So hit 'em clean if tha can in t'future... O aye, and fetchem intae t'Station... for me dog."

The policeman had never parted from his saddle throughout this bizarre encounter. But now in one single deft manoeuvre he shuffled his iron steed across in front of the car, stooped down and re-aligned the twisted number-plate, set the chin-strap of his cap firmly between his front incisors, clamped his ponderous goggles down over his eyes, and made to blast off. The violent rev-up stalled the engine. How deep and eerie was the sudden stillness; but not for long however. Treating the kick-start to five mighty thrusts from the long leg of the law, he got ignition, crash engaged the gears and shot off in a noisy commotion of sharp explosions and flailing metal.

Neither Gina nor I reacted in any positive way for some minutes, that is, until the departing policeman was completely out of sight, and a surprisingly long time afterwards, out of earshot, and until the oily fumes from his exhaust which engulfed us, had dispersed. Now that the slaughter of the odd rabbit had been passed off as legitimate, inevitable, and maybe even welcomed, and the recent interruption seen as nothing more sinister than an efficient country policeman's novel way of introducing himself, we happily resumed our journey. We soon settled back into a gentle wind-blown ecstasy, the car droning contentedly at a steady unhurried pace for mile after glorious mile.

The escarpment appeared before our eyes unexpectedly, round a sharp bend with high rocky sides. The car let out a piercing yelp of pain as she was brought to a slithering halt. The engine stalled. The abrupt shock to our senses and the strange sound vacuum which ensued left us gazing ahead, transfixed in enraptured delight. There, spread out before us and far beyond, lay the magnificent Lyndass Valley. In the middle distance, nestled about an acute curve in the glistening river, between two gentle massives shimmering in the pale mauve haze of the late summer afternoon, Lyndassby stood out bright, clear, and beckoning. Should we linger here gazing in awesome wonder, or should we press on with haste and claim it for our own? This was our first glimpse of Home; the moment was touched with the magic only known to youth, and there was the added ingredient of sacred destiny. The little car, put back into motion, seemed to catch the mood, for she trod softly, coasting without clamour all the way down the long final descent, the engine idling peacefully, and the tyres and wire-spoked wheels humming melodious overtones.

******

The house was larger than we had anticipated, was built in the local style of sombre mortarless grey stones, and the curtains in the bow windows were not smiling. The low boundary wall in front was surmounted by dark brown cast-iron spikes, and two rugged rusted stumps indicated where a gate had once been. In gold paint, on the inside of the glass pane above the front door, were the skeletal remains of a name which had originally ended with the letters 'SE'. In an instant we had conjectured so many grim possibilities terminating thus that we declined to give the matter utterance or second thought. My three indecisive raps on the heavy cast-iron knocker adorning the front door brought forth nought but a long anxious wait with no audible response from within.

"Hit it again dear, you won't break it." came a restrained voice from the hidden depths of the cockpit.

Three more clanks, slightly more determined this time, were followed almost immediately by the unmistakable sound of big boots moving along a hard floor. Maybe there were giants in this land - perhaps it was the enthusiastic approach of an official welcoming committee. Maybe it was an Army? Opening the door clumsily to its full extent, and a fraction more, the man simply stood there, not uttering a word, regarding me wide-eyed and rosy-faced. The said face was void of any significant expression, although occasionally its owner affected quaint nodding motions, alternating with long sniffs and staccato snorts from his long bony nose. Then there issued from out of him a strange husky sound, unaccompanied by any articulation of the facial muscles or any other bodily movement,

"Ayrrrghhhhhh... !"

This, I was subsequently to learn, was an extremely explicit, and common article of the local doric. It could mean almost anything, according to the inflexion of the voice, the angle of the eye, and various other complicated physical factors coincidental with the precise moment of utterance. This basic monosyllable was astonishingly versatile. Whether it came out with shattering velocity or, as was often the case, it was merely breathed, it invariably constituted a thoroughly definitive comment, or even substituted for an entire sentence.

"Ayrrrghhhhhh... !" it came again, and this swarthy descendent of the Viking race continued to stare at me, over me, around me, and through me. It was only then that it occurred to me that the poor man was but thoroughly bemused by the odd spectacle which stood before him, attired in a motley assortment of shabby leftovers from war-time days; a green beret, outsize goggles, voluminous bomber jacket, khaki trousers, knee-length boots, the whole supplemented by an ostentatiously draped university scarf. My swift removal of the facial camouflage seemed to worsen the situation, for the man's rigid features metamorphosed into a grimace of sheer incredulity. And no wonder, for except for that area which had been shielded by the goggles, the remainder of my face was covered in a layer of brown road dust and must have resembled the painted mask of a circus clown.

"Ayrrrghhhhh... Tha'll be t'new ministher I warrant?" said the man, in a deep velvet voice. And were his features really carved out of pink marble, or was this merely his way of suppressing a laugh? "Well, if I meyght say sae, nae offence meynd ye, tha din't leyeke leyke usual soort, does tha?"

"Well not actually... at the moment that is... what I mean is... anyway I'm so glad to mee..."

"Is yon tha la'al car then... yella yan eh... gayly flash a bit... aye... Now tellus, dost tha git intae it proper... or 'appen put it on leyke a slipper?" Here a morsel of wheezy laughter.

"Not a bad little bus actually... uncertain lineage and all that... but in spite o—"

"O aye now," he chopped in unsmiling, "Tha's got a bit wife hest that not - a new un an' all? Tha should hev browt her witha... tha 'appen hadn't plenty o' rooam this trip eh?"

As stated previously, by this stage most of the luggage which had been originally stacked over the rear portion of the car, had shaken itself loose during the rigours of the long journey Southward, and bit by bit transferred itself to the vicinity of the cockpit. When the item of luggage that was snugly swathed in a grey blanket began to move in a desperate effort to extricate itself from the mêlée, the poor man nearly threw a convulsion.

"Now tha's a bonny soort o' lass isn't tha. Onyweys we're reyght glad tae see tha beyeth, so just cum theesel's inside t'house, and we've got a la'al bite tae eyate all ready fo'tha."

After a quick clean-up and a bare modicum of conversation, we were unceremoniously ushered up to a large mahogany table which was spread with a gleaming white cloth and laden to the edges with an extravagant variety of home-made fare such as we had never seen for many a year, food rationing still being partially in operation. Lush scones heavily layered with what we assumed would be local farm butter, lean home-cured ham in massive slices, bloated apple pies accompanied by a great dish of thick cream; these were just some of the treats on offer. A furtive exchange of glances between Gina and I indicated that each was ruefully pondering as to whether we would ever again see this table burdened with such a repast. The long and hectic journey had left us with little immediate appetite for food, and we felt much intimidated by the sight of so lavish a feast. Presently we were joined by a lady, long and lean, maybe quite young, maybe not. She presided over the meal silently, yet displaying in one person the combined attributes of a highly proficient Martha and a meekly submissive Mary. She smiled perpetually, with a subtle half smile, like a low light behind lace curtains. Now and again she would gesture encouragement to us with a twist of the mouth and a vaguely discernible movement of her left hand. The man, who was either her husband, brother, father, or a distant acquaintance, after an initial "Now just tha git theesels stuck in," stood immobile for the entire duration of the meal, solemnly observing our performance from the open doorway with unsmiling approval, sporadically addressing comments to us, obliquely via the lady's ears, and usually merely to extol the much desirability of various items of the grand spread. He called her Doris; to which her lips responded with the shape of 'Yes Harry.'

An abrupt clatter from the front door knocker startled Gina, and caused me to bite my tongue halfway through a big ham sandwich.

"Tha'd better answer t'dooar Misther... s'your house ye knaw. It'll be summat for thee ony roaad." Harry moved slightly, for the first time, to make way for me.

"Wyatt's t'name Josh Wyatt fra' Brigham Gill are they tekin good care o' tha then fotherin' tha up alreyght - now howist-tha - gayly nice tae meet tha." All this came forth in one deep epiglottal explosion from the big tweedy man at the door. He had rugged, weathered features, and a smile like a mid-Summer dawn. Vigorously thrusting forward a pair of mighty hands, rough as half-sculpted granite, he deposited into mine with not even a pretence of gentleness, a large brown paper bag of eggs, so fresh that some of them still had feathers attached.

"Here Misther, these'll be nice for la'al wife's supper... and... wait a minute... now wheres't I've putten th...?" Here a spot of deep quarrying in his jacket pockets, "O aye, here they are. Now just tha tek these for theesel' - meyght find them usefu' eh?"

Praise be! Petrol coupons, more to be desired than fine gold, and sweeter than honey from the honeycomb.

"When tha gits a bit settled in, and tha can find tha way tae Ackensfield, just tha ca' and slip these in tae owd Charlie Tomlin at t'garage be t'crossroaads. Just tell him Josh sent tha and he'll fill tha up summat. Should keep tha a-goin' for a weyek or two." Josh chortled as with a mischievous wink, a swift turn and a brisk step he was gone, leaving me gasping and at the same time hating myself for hoping that he would call often.

Now it was back to continue with that sumptuous meal. Although it required strong will-power and considerable effort on our part, Gina and I deemed it a matter of elementary courtesy to affect the appearance of two famished travellers; at the same time continuing mindful of our customary genteel manners of course. Our two friends, whilst persisting throughout with their 'do have some more' gestures, seemed nevertheless satisfied with our performance, right up to the point when it was patently obvious that we were more than adequately sated. Then smiling broadly, they cleared the table with astonishing speed and dexterity, and prepared to take their leave of us.

"Now just tha meyek theesel's at hoame wiln't tha." Unbelievably this was the first time we had clearly heard the lady's voice, and certainly the first time that any communication from her had been addressed directly towards us. Her speech was low-pitched, deliberate and clear, and signalled to us beyond a doubt, that friendship was her forte, "And if there's owt else tha meyght want, well tha knaws where tae cum, and who tae ask for."

As a matter of fact we didn't, for so far neither Harry nor Doris had indulged themselves in the pleasantries of formal introduction, and indeed had responded shyly to ours with nothing more than flashed smiles aside. Now they left us, unobtrusively, as was their wont, Harry leading the way and the faithful Doris following on. Neither glanced back. The low moan and the loud 'thunk' of the front door indicated that now they would be disappearing from sight, and for the present, from our ken. Yet remarkably, in spite of their quiet reserve they had established us in a rich new bond of friendship, and in less than the space of one hour had given us cause to feel totally domiciled in this place. And we liked the sensation.

Up to this point we had been too pre-occupied with matters gastronomic to take note of the interior aspect of our new abode. We were not thrilled. On the contrary, for the decor was jaded and dingy, the air was musty, and our immediate predecessor must have kept a plurality of cats. Like most church houses at the time in question, its rooms were over-furnished with a motley mix-up of the shabby cast-offs and obsolete chattels of worthy members long since departed. Oddly however the grim sight elicited no sense of shock nor disgust, and no hollow feeling of anticlimax. Such sentiments had been totally neutralized by the lingering warmth of the welcome tendered to us so serenely by Harry and Doris. And so undemonstrably.

That first little drama ended, alone now in our very first home, initiated into our new life and new world of experience, we lovingly embraced, gripped in a mood of silent joy, a new zest for living, some trace elements of awe. But rather oddly, no sense of apprehension; even though we knew that from now on, everything that happened to us was for make or break.

Chapter 2

IN AT THE DEEP END

The hills were up bright and early, but the valley was reluctant to stir and tucked in tenaciously to its deep white blanket of downy mist. On the higher ground dark shadows picked out the rugged wet crags, which glistened with the crystal dew of that crisp September morning, whilst the rising sun promised to uncover fresh bejewelled delights with every passing moment. This was the new dawn of our first Sunday at Lyndassby, and the momentous start of a new life. It was sheer inspiration. The mood of eager expectancy in which I awoke matched the glory of it, and a keen spirit of high adventure, thrilling yet awesome, dispelled any lingering doubts as to the rightness of my choice of vocation.

The morning service however did not match up with the zest and zeal of the preacher. There was no mark of great moment or spirit of special occasion, no indication that this, for that church, was the beginning of a spectacular new era, and for me the initiation into a ministry which from here would span over forty years and lead me to the four corners. In my judgement the whole thing was a modest flop. My vanity had led me to expect that the people would turn up in great crowds, even if only out of curiosity. But they didn't. I had indeed anticipated, with bated breath, an event of considerable consequence. But it wasn't. What took place was another routine morning service within the normal run of things. This was the first lesson I had to learn about life in the dale. These latter day Norse were not adept at affording special deference to special events or personages, they did not readily display excitement, and worked everything into the weft and weave of the common round. My performance that morning was agonisingly subdued, and my struggles to break out from my frustration produced a hollow feeling inside, and heaven alone knows what sort of sound without. At last it was over, and little conversation passed between Gina and me as we walked slowly and dejectedly home, except for a few futile attempts to disown any disappointment.

"And yet... they were warm and friendly... so welcoming... but yet so... so... er... restrained," Gina broke in, over the drag of our footfalls.

"Just their peculiar way darling - take things like friendship, loyalty, and generosity for granted, both in the giving and in the receiving."

"Not very gushing you mean?"

"That's right - not very demonstrative - don't wear their hearts on their sleeves - too big for that - keep them in proper place. They don't express deep feelings readily. Perhaps those feelings are too deep to surface readily. S'pose it comes a bit hard at first with big-heads like us eh? But on the other hand just look at their eyes darling, searching, perceptive, sincere, loving even. Ah yes, we're going to be alright here, you and I, that's what those eyes told me." And with this we broke into a brisker pace.

"Whaat's all th'urry?" burst in a loud voice on heavy boots from immediately behind us, "Reckon t'man wants 'is dinner - heavy day for tha eh? Hev tae be gettin' off reyght sharp this efterneyen wiln't tha. Joe Netherick's me name. Well - Joe onyroaad. Leyeks efter t'chapel cleaning, and t'boiler. Hevn't lit up t'boiler yet... cum November 'appen, if it gits cawld enough. Gen'ly what leyghts it then."

Joe then treated us each to a rough hearty handshake which all but threw me onto my back, and threatened to send Gina into earth orbit. He then proceeded to inform us that he worked for the County Council on the roads as a lengthman, his wife was called Nellie, and she had stopped in bed a bit laanger than usual this morning and had missed chapel, he had four children, all fine bairns, although they were lasses, lived just a la'al bit farther down the road fra' us, and if ever there was owt we needed, just to gae him a call. Joe kept up this fascinating patter for as long as he was able, and yet never gave so much as a hint that the recent morning service had made the slightest impression upon him, or indeed had taken place at all. Maybe his silence was apt comment upon the subject.

"I sees tha's ower at Heston Fell this efterneyen. Reyght out in the wilds that yan, but ye'll enjoy t'run. Quiet a bit meynd ye, nowt much gits alaang in them parts - specially at weekends. Tha'll want tae gaw alang t'Slattersgill roaad as far as Yak Yat, and turn off sharp reyght yance tha gits there. There's only that yan roaad gaws up that way frae there - tha canna miss it."

I was soon to discover why the possession of a car was deemed to be the first priority for a Non-conformist minister working in these remote parts. My pastorate consisted of one fairly large church at Lyndassby and thirteen small satellite chapels scattered along the valley and the fellsides. Some of these places were so distant that my range of pastoral responsibility extended over an area of about fifteen miles square. Associated with each of the said small chapels were other obscure hamlets and isolated farmsteads, all remote from any main thoroughfare. I knew not what dark destiny had decreed that I should be sent out on my first day to the most distant and inaccessible extreme of my new domain. It was probably one of the curious quirks of local wisdom that any process of initiation is most effectively accomplished when accompanied by shock. And so it was that my introduction to the vagaries of rural Christianity should be thus.

The car refused to start. After twenty minutes of grinding and churning the ailing battery gave out, so that from then on it was down to the accursed starting handle, a long fearsome crank of cold steel which, inserted through a shaped hole in the middle of the front bumper, penetrated right through to the very bowels of the engine. Twenty more minutes of all-in wrestling which shook the little lady from end-to-end, side-to-side, up-and-down, and shook me in spasms of blind rage, painful sighs, subdued curses and muffled fury, brought from her nothing except brief contemptuous coughs.

"Sure you've got some petrol in it dear? Is it properly switched on dear? Turning that handle thing the right way dear? Maybe it's those plug what-nots again dear - they're a regular nuisance aren't they? I bet it's one of those bits of wire come loose again dear? Don't you think so dear? Is there anything I can hold for you dear? There simply must be something not working properly, mustn't there? I mean it was alright yesterday wasn't it? By the way are you keeping an eye on the time dear... I mean shouldn't you be ge—"

Gina was merely trying to be helpful, bless her, but this eager recital was building up dangerous pressure inside me, until - no I didn't speak, for the intended words rushed past my vocal chords at too great a force to permit them to vibrate. I froze into a senseless stare of total exasperation; so much indeed that I was not aware of the exact moment of Gina's hasty departure from the scene. Nor was I aware of the silent approach of the spindly rustic, silly grin on his face, and pushing a rusty old spindly bicycle,

"That's a gay la'al yan tha's gittin theesel there - bet it'll not gaw," said he in a rusty old spindly voice, "Aren't ye afeared on it fleein' off th'andle?"

That did it. In an instant my strength had become as the strength of ten. A ferocious growl, an almighty yank at the crank, a violent judder, ear-splitting bang, clouds of acrid black-and-blue smoke and I was deposited in a painful and undignified heap against the garden fence. The sudden shock seemed to have dislocated every joint of my frame. But it did even more for the car, which roaring at full throttle, stood there raring to go as though nothing had ever been amiss. And as for the spindly apparition, with the spindly bike, and the spindly voice, he had simply vanished into thin air or perhaps he had been taken up in the cloud, scriptural fashion.

All is well that ends well, so they say, and so far this journey was no exception to the rule. I had not proceeded far along the fell-side road before that thrilling sense of first day high adventure had overtaken me. Wide panoramic views from the high unfenced road evoked strong feelings of unfamiliar ecstasy. Moving along the lower reaches of the valley the dry-stone roadside walls flashing past me created the illusion of travelling at great speed, and the engine noise echoed back with an impression of immense reserves of power under the bonnet. There was so much here to excite a young adventurer's wild fancy, as we sped along carefree, with the cool bracing air streaming past, stroking my thick curly hair and caressing the skin of my face into an invigorating glow of calm delight. The chill air, refreshing and subtly scented with a rich blend of rural aromas, came at me in an overpowering profusion. So did the dung, suddenly and unexpectedly. One enormous, freshly minted round - there was perhaps no other for miles - and my front off-side wheel searched it out, picked it up, whirled a number of times before releasing it with tremendous force in the direction of the cockpit. And so it was that in one blinding splat, I was inundated with the disgusting contents of some fully fledged bovine bowel. Nor was this to be the entirety of my baptism into the finer pleasantries of country motoring. Before completing the next turning, the car spun into uncontrollable convulsions of slithering confusion as I braked to try and avoid making an over-intimate acquaintance with a solid phalanx of rump steak on the hoof. The huge creatures occupied the full width of the narrow road, the spaces at the sides, and I feared to contemplate how much of its length. Not only but also, in their ghastly wake they had laid a messy minefield with long trails of high intensity dung, rendering my brakes and steering mechanism completely redundant. By some rare and inexplicable providence, the animals parted in the middle of the closed ranks just at the dreadful moment of inevitable impact. Before I could say 'Moo' I was wedged solidly in their midst. I had never before realised that cows were so gigantic, ugly and ungainly, or that they possessed so much girth amidships. This seething, moaning mass of beef at close quarters was positively terrifying, and the minute proportions of the little open car put me at a serious disadvantage. The inquisitive beasts took turns at examining the car interior, making detailed checks on the dashboard data, getting alarmingly close to my ribs with raking horns, and too near to my face with slimy noses. Don't cows have rotten breath! Pushing, shoving, nudging, and some randy specimens actually mounting one another, they constantly threatened to stove in the car sides, or capsize her. They rocked her, kicked her, licked her, bawled at her, and buffeted her relentlessly. Sometimes fat bulging bellies would protrude too close to me for comfort, and muck- laden tails swish from several directions at once, executing a deft smearing job over paintwork, upholstery, and my face.

"Tha'll hev tae back 'er out," piped a thin small voice from somewhere among the beef-jam, "The've nivver seen owt the leykes o' that yan afore... we'll nivver shift the ba..."

"Ma-oooooooo." at precisely the right moment the entire herd voiced their agreement.

The little man with a crooked stick, equally crooked nose, and a very tatty trilby hat which he seemed to be wearing sideways on, bobbed up from the terrifying mass and made a relatively insignificant appearance. Of course he was absolutely correct regarding the kine, for cow curiosity is a formidable force, and especially when it's packed tight on all sides of you. And so the disgusting creatures continued their crescendo of mooing, bawling, coughing, shuffling and gawping, and looked as though nothing short of dynamite would move them on. The car engine had stopped of course - perhaps it had got dunged-up. I desperately hoped that just for this once, she would not put on one of her tantrums, and would respond kindly to the starter first pull. As it happened, she selected that moment to demonstrate one of her classical bursts of 'up-and-at-it'. I had but touched the starter switch, and I triggered off an earthquake. One tremendous bang, a rapidly rising cloud of thick blue-black smoke and a savage snarling roar momentarily dulled my senses. But certainly not those of the cattle. They shot off with amazing swiftness, higgledy-piggledying in individual stampedes in all directions. I didn't understand what it was that the little man was trying to communicate to me by word and gesture after that, and so I simply assumed that he was using some local adjectival phrases and body signs with which I was not yet fully familiar. A great pity really, for he seemed to be so emphatic about something.

The remainder of the journey was without incident, the narrow road becoming increasingly desolate, deserted, and interminable. Just when I was beginning to despair of ever arriving at my destination a fellow traveller came into view; a rather scrawny fellow, walking towards me with a slinky dog at heel. Clamped between his toothless gums he sported an enormous rough-hewn cherry wood pipe. Removing the said article of ordnance, he spat loudly onto the ground, studied me quizzically awhile, rasped his stubbly chin with horny fore-finger and thumb, and tilted back his cap,

"Heston eh? Aye... well now if tha turns sharp right as seyen as tha gits tae Yak Yat, it's not much on frae there, it'll not tek tha lang... Tha canna miss it." At which intelligence I carried on but still with some misgivings as to how the local folk might calculate distance, for I had once heard of, and experienced, the notorious 'Lincolnshire Mile' and was beginning to fear the worst. Eventually a small cluster of cottages and farm buildings appeared up ahead.

"Excuse me Madam," I enquired of a woman who was walking down the middle of the road, carrying a small can, and dragging an unwilling child by her side, "I'm looking for Yak Yat, and wondered if this is the place?"

"Yak Yat - Nay lad, tha's missed it proper - that tha has. T'other end o' village is whaat tha's wantin' - roaad gaws off and teks tha up tae Heston. Tha'll hev tae turn arownd an gaw back a bit. It's big enough 'appen... Tha canna miss it."

The other end of the village petered out all too soon, as likewise so did another half mile of desolate road, when (Good Lord deliver us) - more cows. With well-calculated discretion I parked the car off the road behind a conveniently situated small building, and with equally measured caution approached the elderly cowman on foot.

"Excuse me Sir, but I'm looking for Yak Yat - that's the place where I have to turn off for Heston Bank I believe?"

"Yak Yat... O Aye... ony amount o' them abowt here 'appen. Now which yan o' them would ye be wantin' ye reckon?"

Lord have mercy - more complications. There was more than one place of that name?

"Now then we doesn't want tae get tha all mixed up or owt leyke, but if it's t'yan that gaws off tae 'eston, then tha's cummed reyght past it... mile back... big un it is tha canna miss it."

The old man exhaled ostentatiously, and was just about to move on when an elderly brown Austin Twelve saloon drew up awkwardly. The sole occupant leaned out of the window and beckoned. He was wearing a cassock of off black with a greenish hue, indicating that it had originated a long way back in the Apostolic Succession. Hanging about his scraggy neck like an ill-fitting halter was the thickest, broadest, but certainly not the whitest clerical collar I had ever beheld. A rich bass diapason voice, culled from a heavy concentration of ecclesiastical culture, came to my aid from somewhere deep down in the man's spacious thorax,

"Yairk Yairt? O yes yes yes, of course. Most extraordinary pronunciation - strong Nordic connections airctually - vernacular for - Oak Gate. Ah yes yes yes - now let me see - there's a large and interesting specimen just at the point where this road has a turn off for Heston Fell - a little less than a mile from here but you'll have to turn about I'm afraid, you seem to have passed it by. O and by the way, that moor road's a mere track I'm afraid."

"Aye that's reyght, a canny bit back I'd say. Tha canna miss it," proffered the swarthy cowman, flashing his beady eyes wildly across to the clergyman for divine approval, "Tsappen-oppen-onywees." Which final comment left me with considerable food for thought.

And so, ever patient, ever speculative, I went back the prescribed distance, as speedily as the wheels would turn, with yak yats to the left of me, yak yats to the right of me, and many other species of yat as well. At last behold! There it stood, bold and clear in the bright sunshine, that elusive postern. Pointing nervously towards it from the opposite side of the road, and half-concealed in the long grass, was a battered old finger post bearing the welcome message 'To Heston Fell'. Across the top bar of the great yat was boldly inscribed the instruction 'Shut yat', to which some passing wit had appended 'PLEEZE'. It was said that no two gates in the whole of this area were fitted with the same fastening device, and the wire puzzle securing this particular gate had been devised with devilish cunning. I struggled frantically with the baffling contraption until my fingers became numbed in fumbling confusion. At the point of total despair I just happened to glance sideways and I instantly observed that the gate could easily be lifted off its pivot hinges, the rutted arc struck across the track indicating that this had long been the accepted *modus operandi.*

Greatly to my surprise, I arrived outside the little chapel at Heston Fell on time. Not that this mattered significantly, for 'We'll just mek a stairt when tha's ready' seemed to be the spirit in which most matters were conducted in these serene parts, and that was especially true of church services. Finishing time however, was critical and more strictly observed, being diligently regulated in terms of milking time and other essential farmyard chores. By any standard Heston Fell would be difficult to define as a village. For one thing, it was not easy to ascertain at what point it began, and where it ended, or where its centre was located. There seemed to be a marked prejudice against parallel lines. Small groups of old cottages huddled together at irregular intervals, and there were some sprawling farm buildings. The chapel itself, a severely austere little building of limited architectural merit, stood stark naked and isolated on a barren patch of sacred earth near the roadside. Vast sweeps of open fell stretched downward toward the valley and upwards on the other side right to the horizon. The entire grand vista was boldly criss-cross etched by an asymmetrical tracery of rough dry stone boundary walls.

A small cadre of people had assembled outside in front of the open doorway of the chapel, and this gave a certain boost to my presently rather shattered ego, and indeed a warm sense of satisfaction. Surely this must be some kind of official welcoming party, happily delegated to greet their new Minister on this auspicious occasion. The so-called greeting was, to say the least, restrained, unsmiling, and tendered without either word or action. It just had to be assumed. Eventually one very big man, who looked as though there may have been a grizzly bear somewhere in his ancestry, stirred vaguely and broke the impasse by declaring in a surprisingly gentle voice,

"Tha should've cummed ower t'top roaad... 'tslot sharper."

Now, without any further speeches, the group parted in the middle to facilitate my grand entry. This was for me an early lesson towards the knowledge that these hill folk were prone to giving voice only to the most rudimentary emotions, and certainly would not squander any excess of feeling or verbiage in the presence of strangers. My next lesson was to discover that implicit within this shy composure there is a warmth of acceptance which would be spoiled by anything so overt as formal speech. There was another surprise; no one seemed to react to the smears of cow dung on my face, jacket and trousers, nor to the browny-green stains on my brand new clerical collar. And they were totally impervious to the aromatics.

The little chapel, as plain inside as on the outside, was not blessed with such luxurious superfluity as a vestry. Consequently, I was ushered directly from the door to the pulpit, a lofty, disproportionate structure in unornate varnished red pine, standing dead centre up front in unsplendid isolation. It seemed to have been specifically designed for the discouragement of corybantics, its upper edge offering cramped accommodation for a massive pulpit bible, its slightly lesser companion the hymnbook, a large vase of assorted dahlias, and my elbows. Once I was installed therein, and had divested myself of my travelling accoutrements, an elderly gentleman in course tweeds approached me, held out a shaky hand, and whispered hoarsely,

"Yorrymns misther?"

To which I responded by handing to him the narrow slip of numbered paper so hallowed to non-Conformists. There now ensued an interval of patient waiting as with heavy breathing and fumbling fingers the frail old saint selected from a little wooden box the chosen hymn numbers, fitted them into the slotted board, which with considerable difficulty he then proceeded to hitch up onto a large nail which protruded from the wall just marginally out of reach. The dear old soul had probably faithfully fulfilled this weekly ritual every Sunday of his life from time immemorial. We were now ready to begin. This was amply indicated by the organist, who began to pedal her harmonium noisily and get up a good head of steam for the first hymn. Each day since I had begun my life's work in this locality had been fraught with some degree of cultural shock, but the singing of that hymn went further, and produced a shock to the nervous system; the opening up of a fresh new world of sound. The said organist, an immaculately groomed lady of vast proportions and voluminous headgear, continued to pound her instrument, obviously intent upon crushing every ounce of potential from its ancient bellows. The women of the congregation sang with shrill high-pitched voices in unrestrained rapture, while the men's vocal equipment, deeply resonant, was obviously fine tuned to match the heights, depths, and distances of the local terrain. The plain, unadorned interior of the building provided excellent acoustic properties, added a pleasing echo, and contributed significantly to the uniqueness of the grand rendition. In this vein the service proceeded, until it was time for the sermon, which, judging by the manner in which the people began to shuffle themselves into long-stay postures in their hard pine pews, was regarded as the main event, to be savoured, tolerated, or simply endured. For my own part, it was a disaster. For the whole of its duration I was upstaged by a large blue bottle with noisy engines, as it carried out wide reconnaissance sorties over every square inch of the chapel, and at the most inappropriate moments making dive-bombing attacks in my direction. Unlike my hearers, I was not immune from the nuisance of the bleating of sheep immediately outside. At one point, two shaggy, horned specimens would appear in the open doorway, gape at me incredulously for a few minutes, pip in with some muttered responses, then wander away, presumably to communicate to their friends some measure of the enlightenment they had received. There was also a very small boy with a snotty nose, who on occasion would interrupt some relatively impressive passage of the sermon with a long drawn out sigh and a very decisive ' Is he nearly done Muther?' He also was noticed by none but me. A gigantic, square-rigged man with black hair and heavy jowls, fixed on me with a furious scowl throughout the duration of the sermon, whilst his meagre wife sat self-consciously trying to compensate for the gesture with a supercilious smile. The man's somewhat unnerving expression was not uncommon in local congregations, but however, to my tremendous comfort and relief I was in time assured that these stoic stares bore no malice, and in reality were indeed a sure indication of attentive listening and intense mental activity. Otherwise everything proceeded with reasonable normality, until I was about to announce the final hymn, a gesture which moved several members of the congregation to glance furtively towards the spotty-faced old clock which was ticking it out like a ragged ratchet on the wall above my head. Abruptly an unsmiling fellow of middle years rose to his feet from a pew near to the door and called out,

"Clection... tha's forgettin' t'clection." Whereupon with big hobnailed boots he clanked back and forth along the scrubbed white boards of the uncarpeted aisle, thrusting before each of the faithful in turn a long-handled wooden device resembling a banjo, and extracting from them the Lord's due. Eventually arriving before the foot of the pulpit, he held out the contraption to me and in low key pronounced,

"Tha blesses it... wi prayer or summat leyke."

Meanwhile the lady organist had got herself carried away in an ecstatic bout of Handel, and thus kept us waiting with patient endurance until she had completed every note and stanza of her Interlude.

The service was terminated on time, and the younger men dashed away with urgent haste to the call of duty. Other people lingered to indulge in quiet pleasantries, which although none was addressed directly to me, nevertheless sufficed to make me feel deep within that I was already safely installed as part of this wonderful scene. I was to conclude without a doubt, that what may have been lacking in refinement was generously made up in simple sincerity.

"Me Gran allus teks Ministher hoame for 'is tea," piped in the shrill small voice of the little sermon-hating brat leaning up against my right leg. "I leykes it when Ministher cums 'cos Gran meyeks special cayekes and that... Well, cum on then."

Chapter 3

COME YE THANKFUL PEOPLE COME

The small fellside chapels were, in the main, plain, austere, grey structures of simple uncomplicated design, and utilitarian to a fault. In some examples they may have shown a hint of neo-Gothic in windows or doorway, but few were encumbered with such needless appendages as vestry or porch. The large heavy door located near to the middle of a long side wall was almost standard. Welsh or Lakeland slate was the preferred topping medium, although some older specimens had low roofs of large heavy flagstones, which gave them the appearance of minor fortresses. There were some exceptions however, and of such was the chapel at Fellsyke. The complicated instructions for locating the place which had been given to me included constant references to the 'Tin Yan', leading me to set off with a kind of replica of a Chinese temple in mind. My search, after a picturesque journey over hill and dale, culminated in a perilous ford through a fast-flowing stream by the edge of a vast undulating fell. And there on the other side, standing on the rising ground in isolated splendour, stood the object of my quest, a neat little building of brown painted corrugated iron, its cruciform lay-out, latticed windows, and the bell-less wooden contraption atop the roof at one end clearly indicating a place of worship. The Tin Yan! The mystery solved, the Tin One of course. The interior was true to form, with timber lined walls which were painted up to half-way in the same dull sienna as that on the outside, and the remainder, including the ceiling, was of a hue and texture reminiscent of flaky pastry. The rude backed forms (they could scarcely qualify as pews) also in that sombre chocolate tone, were regimented in closely packed rows right down to the edge of a formidable dais at the front. In the middle of the dais was a simple desk-cum-lectern which contrasted strongly with a large, over-ornate American organ of Victorian vintage, standing prominently behind. Presently my eye was attracted by a long length of black cast-iron piping which was dangling ominously from the ceiling at about the centre of the room and terminating at about seven feet from the floor.

"Chimli for t' stoave," came a husky voice from behind me, "We alweys gits a big crowd for th'Harvest... t's efterneyen'll be a gayly big crush as usual... allus teks out stoave aforehand and meks mare room for t'foalkes in t'middle."

"Tha'll be t'new Ministher I warrants?" boomed another, suddenly appearing adjacent to the first, "They telt us tha was nobbut a young un... Aye well tha's gawin' tae hev a mighty blessed teyme tae be sure... allus gits a blessed teyme at t'Harvest, din't we Bob?" With this inspiring intelligence he took my right hand into what felt like the grip of a giant clam and nearly dislocated my shoulder with an earthquake handshake.

"T'yan afore tha was a reyght grand fella, that he was," bewailed the first man, "Stopped here for t'whole o t'war he did... gat hissel fair settled aye. Ney preacher mind tha, but allus gat us a good sing - thats t'main thing - and not talkin ower much. Aye tha' din't git mony the leykes on 'im nowadays, dost tha... nay, not ony mare."

Under normal circumstances the interior of the chapel would be drab, almost to the point of ugliness, but on this special day it was quite different. Large bunches of grapes, and of onions, boxes and dishes of apples, and oranges, buckets of scrubbed potatoes, clusters of ripe bananas, and of Brussels sprouts, bundles of celery and of rhubarb, packets, bags, cans, jars, pots and basins, cabbages and chrysanthemums, leeks, carrots, and eggs, beetroot, marigolds, and some coal; the message of Harvest was thrust upon us in this overpowering display of super-abundance. Garlands of deftly woven straw, studded with hips and haws, hung from ceiling, walls, and windows, and there seemed to be bracken at every level, and a riot of bright flowers in every direction. Even the old black stovepipe, dangling grotesquely from the top, had not escaped the special treatment, and was festooned with a colourful spiral of mixed foliage and nasturtiums. A voluminous sheaf of long whiskered barley occupied more than its fair share of space on either side of the lectern, and an outsize bunch of deep purple grapes hung heavily from the centre of the reading desk. The morning sun had gone to work on the tin roof, and already the place was hot as a slow oven. The rich cocktail of powerful Harvest aromas was almost intoxicating.

Outside, the fields were already turning white onto harvest. From all directions they were coming, converging on the little shrine, families of farm folk on foot, some in cars, on motor cycles, push bikes, smoky oily old Fordson tractors, big blue Fordson Majors, and some sporting the new revolutionary grey Ferguson T20s. Some even arrived on horseback. This was definitely the big time for the Tin Yan, and indeed a significant date on the neighbourhood calendar.

"They say he's just a bit yungun' - Talks soort o' Scotch— Got gay bonny la'al wife they tellus... and nobbut a bairn 'appen— should've left her at scheyel... Hest tha seen la'al car stood yonther? Gayly lish yan so polliss telt us." These are but snippets of passing conversation that my keen ears picked up from my rather obscure position near the open doorway. I was unable to decipher the rest. Which suddenly reminded me - where was Gina? A detailed scan of the terrain eventually brought her into view, in happy receipt of the attentions of a group of handsome young men who appeared to be enthusiastically interested in the exquisite physical attributes of the car?

The place was filling up with frightening rapidity, and began to look as though it would, quite literally, burst at its many seams. The Tin Yan was but a single-roomed affair providing neither vestry nor any other place of refuge and strength for a besieged preacher. The dais, to which I now had to squeeze my way with an enforced lack of due dignity, was not without its limitations neither, for in addition to several agricultural exhibits, its available space had to be shared with the said barley-clad lectern, the flamboyant American organ with blue dummy pipes, and a high organ stool. This latter article was so situated that in position for their respective functions, organist and preacher would be closely juxtaposed, back-to-back. I was actually ruminating on these inevitabilities, when the lady organist presented herself from out of the heaving melee, and added some lively interest to my speculations. My platform mate was a curvocative concentration of delectable distractions, who needed to expend no greater effort than a coy half smile to lift me clean off the end of the organ stool where I had recently perched myself. Flushing slightly at my less than concealed reaction she coo-ed, in a voice the texture of velvet, low-pitched and melodious,

"Have you got me numbers please? I leykes to check ower tunes and mek sure we knaws them. T'name's Mabel... and nice tae meet you to be sure."

The winsome smile on the girl's face was like the rising sun on a perfect dawn, and sent out warmth in wistful waves. As she tilted her head to the side, as she always did when she smiled, I was mercifully distracted by the vivid floral accessories on her hat, which I suspected were deliberately contrived to match the adornment of the organ, and were no doubt by the same hand. Turning to look back over the assembled congregation, it crudely occurred to me that I had never before beheld bodies packed so closely together, except in the sheep pens at the mart, two days before. I felt myself blush inwardly with guilt and disgust, because the thought had amused me. O God, and they were all looking the same way, at me, passive, waiting.

"Time tha was mekin' a start", my sweet companion of the podium leaned over backwards on her stool and chimed the words into my ear. Before the effect had taken hold, I heard myself blurting forth in my grandest pulpit style,

"The hymn number eight-five-four - Come Ye Thankful Peop..."

Before the line could be completed, I was cut short by an excruciating wheeze from behind me as the little organ braced its lungs and thorax for the ordeal to come. Mabel executed her introductory stanza with tremendous aplomb, and the congregation rose as a single body. Right on the beat, the word 'Cum' blasted out with such mighty force that the courts of Heaven must have felt a sudden tremor. The celestial ten thousand times ten thousand could surely not have matched this vocal effort for sheer volume and vigour. With each succeeding verse, the great crescendo built up momentum. My earlier bout of claustrophobia developed into near panic, and I got the dreadful sensation of being shut up helplessly in a small, hot tin box with the combined vocal might of the entire National Farmers Union. Mercifully, in time I was able to adjust my raw senses to this new experience of rural thankfulness. Until - all too soon, the next hymn fell due; that one which bears the verse:-

Yes God is good, all nature says;
By God's own hand with speech endued,
And man in louder notes of praise
Should SHOUT for joy that God is good.

I begun to realise that this congregation was greatly disposed to obeying such pious injunctions with remarkable literalness. Some of the worshippers confessed to having saved up all their spiritual (and vocal?) resources for a whole year, to expend them on this one great occasion.

"Nivver misses t'Harvest," boasted one hill man to me in a voice which sounded as though he'd swallowed a corncrake live, "Gen'ly what cums this yance in t'year tae soort o' keyep things reyght and proper leyke wi' t'Almighty."

Mabel was carried away into realms of glory throughout her performance. Whether accompanying the singing or delivering one of her rousing voluntaries, her whole soul was put into the effort. So was her entire body. She rhythmically writhed and twisted, head back, legs full stretch and pedalling furiously in an ecstasy of high-pressure music making. Even at rest, she maintained this full stretch posture, often resulting in a preponderance of buttock protruding over the back edge of the narrow organ stool. This precipitated a minor incident during the sermon. At a critical point I required a clearer angle on my script, and in backing slightly to facilitate this, I initiated a gluteal collision of exquisite softness, bringing from Mabel an equally exquisite blush and scolding smile. Gina sitting below and to the side, had observed the incident and was now struggling valiantly with all the feints she knew for suppressing laughter, from repeatedly blowing her nose to hiding her face in a hymnbook, or stooping low down in the pretence of searching for a lost treasure on the floor. Such incidents apart however, the sermon was not the disaster I had feared it would be. Although of necessity brief, I was not totally aware that it was to the point, or indeed any point at all, or what the point was supposed to be. There was that typical unnerving stare from the congregation throughout. Assured as I had been, that this gesture was not an indication of fear of Hell, holy terror, utter incredulity or malicious intent, but normally signalled intense concentration, I blundered on regardless. I even resolved that here was a splendid test bed for some of the powerful oratorial skills in which I had been recently schooled. For example, there was the dramatic silence which when appropriately applied can be quite electric. Well, that might have been so, except that on this particular occasion the device short-circuited. Other tricks of the oratorial art suffered a similar fate. To keep them usefully occupied for the duration of the sermon the children had been provided with apples, at which they gnawed with noisy persistence, and that especially during my frequent dropouts. The nuisance incited further distraction in the shape of restrained sniggers from spindly youths occupying the standing-room only in the rear, and muffled giggles from over-dressed adolescent girls squeezed together in the nearby aisles. The taking up of the collection was a mammoth task, to which four hefty stewards sprang with unbridled enthusiasm. Sweeping their large wooden trays methodically over the congregation, so that none would be denied, and nothing missed, they diligently gathered in the Lord's portion, the rattle and clash of tumbling coins hardly offset by Mabel's *double-forte* rendering of 'He Shall Feed His Flock'.

At the end of what had been for me a gruelling one and a half hours, came the Benediction, which was followed promptly by a succession of uninhibited bronchial expirations from older men. This I presumed denoted either satisfaction or relief, or merely the physical exertion required in extricating themselves from the packed pews. For my own consolation I opted for 'satisfaction', a view reinforced by the comment from one good brother as he went out,

"Aye 'tsbeen a gayly good 'arvest this yan - tha's done us proud tha has," and I instantly felt guilty for suspecting that this was a reference to the quantity of the collection rather than to the quality of the service.

"Onyweys" he went on, "see tha tomorrow neyght then eh - for th'auction - tha'll leyke that yan tae be sure - hailf seven."

When the man had walked away I looked about me and saw that the multitude was dissolving into the surrounding fellsides, along the narrow lanes, and down the valley, as quickly as it had assembled. Then I remembered that it was afternoon still and postponed farmyard chores would be beckoning urgently. Within ten minutes I was left alone with the wide moor, the nearby rushing stream, the empty Tin Yan, a few curious sheep, the car, and Gina.

"See tha tomorrow neyght then," she mused, "We thankful people must come again, for there's more harvest to be safely gathered in."

As she leapt into the open car she chuckled merrily, "See tha tomorrow night– Hands, Knees and Bumps-a-Daisy– Whoopee," and she fell back into one of her spasms of chortling laughter, which continued all the way home.

******

There were many hallowed old customs which had remained intact among the fellside folk, whilst the rest of society had long since yielded to the inexorable pressures of time, change and decay. Amongst these ancient traditions, that which stood paramount was the Annual Harvest Thanksgiving Sale, better known in church parlance as the Sale of Fruit and Vegetable Etc. for Church Funds. This prestigious event took place on the evening of the Monday immediately following the Harvest Sunday, and was generally pursued with the same vigour and enthusiasm. When we arrived at Fellsyke on that Monday evening quite early, I was astounded to see that the Tin Yan had already filled up, to such an extent that it seemed to have expanded internally, even without affecting any of its external dimensions. Gina made the bright suggestion that perhaps the miracle had been achieved by the levelling out of the corrugated iron sheets of which the building was constructed. It did not require a very close inspection however to note the drastic transformation which had taken place on the inside. Except for leafy decorations and floral garlands which were temporarily out of reach, all the harvest produce had been stripped of any sacred symbolism, representative, liturgical, or otherwise, which it may have embodied on the previous day. The entire harvest store was graded, stacked and displayed unashamedly on a line of long tables across the front, after the manner of a market stall. The wooden forms had been marshalled into closer proximity so that the occupants, whilst still being afforded some small accommodation for their buttocks would have to make other arrangements for their knees, elbows, and feet. The arrangement had significantly increased the area of standing room at the back. Even that space was already filled, mainly with restless adolescents. As on the previous day, all faces were directed eagerly forward. But this time, not at me. And there were some other notable differences. There were no fine and colourful dresses or smart suits on show, from which I deduced that this present function was to be regarded as a working event. Did I imagine it, were not those faces wearing changed expressions since yesterday? It was not that they bore anything so vulgar as the mercenary leer of the bargain hunter. In truth those good folk were displaying the local version of the carnival spirit, coupled with a generous measure of rare abandon. They had come to give their 'la'al bit o' supoort for t'chapel', and to thoroughly enjoy themselves in doing so.

"Tha'd better be gittin' theesel up on t'platform Mr.Whaatsit, or tha'll be gettin' stuck in t'back and we'll hev to lift tha ower," advised a steward who had appointed himself to take care of me.

"But this is an auction sale is it not?" I protested. "You don't need me for anything. Buying and selling - I'd be useless."

"Nay lad, nowt like that. Just it's... well... you see we hev tae stairt things off proper... ye knaw... hymn and prayer and..."

"A kind of short service you mean?"

"Well soort of... nay not a proper service or owt... hymn and prayer and that... O aye and ye'll hev tae speak a few words... not ower lang mind ye... so I think tha'd better be gettin' up in tha pulpit, and get things stairted... t'foalkes are gettin' restless."

The distinction between matters sacred and matters secular was sharply defined in the minds of the local chapel folk. And so it was that various devices were invoked to bridge the conscience gap wherever there was any danger of engendering compromise or unwaringly slipping into transgression. The simple formula of hymn, prayer, short scripture reading and/or a 'few words' with a vaguely religious flavour worked miracles. It would settle the scruples of traditional piety and, by some mystical process was capable of transforming any otherwise 'secular' exercise into an event worthy of God's house; that is, so long as it concluded with the Benediction, and especially if the Minister was present to pronounce it.

As I mounted the small platform I suffered a strange premonition, a fundamental gut feeling that the stage was all set for a repetition of yesterday's calamities, served with interest. They actually began while I was still pondering the thought. My sugar-loaf organist had arrived at the step in the same instant as I, and obeying my instinct for chivalry, I deferred to the lady. Hardly a sensible gesture however, for the floor at that point was so cluttered with empty boxes, baskets, and other packing stuff as to cause her necessary squeeze past me to appear slightly less than decorous - for a Minister, that is. Mabel responded by treating me to one of her frowning smiles, carefully aimed at where it would produce optimum effect. The ploy worked, for charged with a bout of unusual gallantry, I set to carving a passage through to her organ stool with all the flustered flurry of an amateur Sir Galahad. As for myself, I was only able to secure a foothold at the reading desk after a clumsy display of further ungentlemanly contortions. So much for the 'devotional' start to the proceedings, for this exhibition had provided some intriguing entertainment for the assembled company and set the scene for anything but worship, in the strict sense of the term.

'We Plough The Fields And Scatter...' The opening hymn was a prolonged explosion, which must have sent up the moorland birds for miles around. According to the slip of a programme handed to me 'We will now call upon Brother Charlton to lead us in prayer.' And this he did, a very tall lean man with a stentorian voice that even Heaven couldn't ignore.

For a dreary, unpunctuated seventeen minutes he subjected the good Lord, and us, to much detailed thanksgiving for all these good gifts spread out here before us, confession (not so detailed) for our past ingratitude and present slothfulness, present sins - (not enumerated), and our utter meanness in all things pertaining to Thy house, and then with a final burst of prayerful exuberance beseeching the Lord to fill us all with a spirit of generosity at this here sale tonight, and make us all 'not afeared to dig our hands deep into our pockets.' My next humble task was to announce another hymn. 'O Lord of Heaven and Earth and Sea' was taken at a slow tempo, to allow the words and fine tones to be rolled around ecstatically in the mouth, each cadence sustained with obvious relish, but then fading into a drawn out slur at the point of discharge from the lips. The cause of this astounding change in musical mode very soon made its presence felt. The temperature of the little chapel was rising, alarmingly.

Either this dramatic surge, or vibrations set up by the singing, or maybe the search for air, had set up some frantic activity amongst the resident insects. Dazed bluebottles buzzed about aimlessly in a low key, loosing height and momentum as they came towards me, and often crash-landing with clammy feet on my face or neck. Blow flies, a disgusting species which lay eggs and infest living bodies with maggots, staggered through the air, sometimes seeking refuge or a place to start a family in my thick hair. Earwigs, carried in with the corn, crawled randomly about the reading desk, their primed fork tails raised high, and stupefied spiders dangled uncertainly above my head from long lifelines. It set up my itch. I develop it whenever I encounter creepy-crawlies. It may be totally irrational and purely psychosomatic, but I become afflicted with insufferable torments from patches of acute irritation upon areas of my anatomy where it is not possible to scratch inconspicuously. It just had to happen while I was saying my little piece, about everybody being welcome and the like, but it came, there was no mistake about the sensation, and with it the compulsive urge to search out and kill. One or more of those loathsome creatures, earwig, spider, some fearsome myriapod, centipede perhaps, or ants, but it, or they, had penetrated my defences and were moving in line down my spine and spreading outwards at the bottom end. I wriggled and spluttered my way through my futile speech, growing more desperately agitated with every sentence. Had I been positioned in closer proximity with the wall, I could have shuffled backward and crushed the menace to a grease spot, and nobody would ever have noticed the summary execution. This was a vain hope, for situated between me and that wall was the organ, with the result that Mabel's stool was placed less than the wag of an earwig's tail from where I was standing back-to-back from her. The pestilence was growing worse, and more concentrated, and likewise the urge to scratch. Neurotic or not, the intolerable itch had intensified far beyond the point of mere imagination, and consequently the remedy must needs be of equal tangibility. I would do it slyly; surreptitiously. No untoward movements or awkward jerks. A deceptive sham move. And throughout I would keep up the benign smile. The old hand in pocket ruse didn't work - slightly out of reach. Neither did the sly belt adjustment, or handkerchief search from both trouser pockets at once - a risky strain on my fly buttons. There was surely no other way but direct attack. With unhurried stealth, and feigned cool calm, whilst gesticulating purposefully with my left hand, I brought the right to creep slowly and unobtrusively toward my rear, and located the main trouble spot. In all my calculations, I had not reckoned on the over-hang; that is, that portion of the luscious Mabel's posterior anatomy which protruded beyond the width of the narrow-gauge organ stool. And so it was that, as with indescribable ecstasy I dug my fingernails deeply into my afflicted gluteals and scratched, my knuckles echoed a gentle rubbing contact with hers. The shock of Mabel's sudden freeze-up shot right up through my arm, nearly strangled me as it was conducted through my neck, and boiled my saliva dry when it reached my mouth en-route for my face, which instantly fell into total atrophy. I turned slightly towards Mabel, and she was not smiling. Her expression was a new and as yet unfamiliar one, and was definitely set at the red.

So overwhelmingly distracted was I by this crazy episode that I was not aware of the approach of the rotund fellow with polished red cheeks, as he battered his way towards the platform.

"I'll hev tae be changin' places wi'tha Mister, if ye please... Sid Hackthwaite it is - th'auctioneer."

The immediate problem concerned where to go, for already Sid's substantial bulk was blocking the only available exit point on the platform. The big man continued his resolute advance towards the rostrum, and I was thus obliged to aim myself at the only morsel of space in sight, that being a small portion of the organ stool that was not covered by Mabel but which was already partly occupied by a small brown paper bag. The squelch was not audible, but O what a hideous sensation!

“Them’s me grayeps... bought them afore we started.” Mabel’s spate of merry laughter bubbled bright and fresh as a mountain brook. For the next ten minutes the poor girl nearly asphyxiated herself in stifled giggles, her shaking with muffled mirth placing the dowels of her stool in some peril. And incidentally, the signal had returned to green.”

“Now let’s git younguns a-chowin’ fust - them big apples Charlie,” exploded Sid, coarsely scattering any vestige of reverent propriety that remained about the place, “Whattammabidda now? Cum on whattammabidda?”

Thanksgiving had ended, and business begun. The bidding came fast and furious, the good folk at times seeming to vie with one another, not for the acquisition of the best bargains, but in the application of the greatest generosity.

“Onybodybiddin for this yan now? Cum on, whaat’s hoddin’ tha all? Cum on then let’s hev some mare bids tha’s not startin’ tae tire alriddy are tha? That’s mare leyke it mare bids, cum on.” Most of Sid’s rapid firing gibberish was lost on me, but was clearly the acceptable mode of commercial communication among the rest of those here present. One factor however, continued to baffle me, and that was the period of deadly silence which followed immediately in the wake of each noisy cluster of ‘bids’.

“Whaatammabidda... reyght... ony advance... five an’ fowerpence. ...and five... six... six bob it is... Annie Barnes yonther... tha’ll be gettin’ theesel’ a reyght bellyache fra this lot lass. Mare Charlie... let’s hae them bunches o’ rhubarb up will tha.”

Another cacophonous interlude, interspersed with those strange silences. Then the sudden slam of Sid’s hammer (a large hymnbook actually) and another satisfied customer. By this time I had managed to move away from the vicinity of the platform and had taken up a less perilous position directly in front of it, but still within Sid’s spitting range. Nevertheless from this vantage point I could observe the ritual with greater intensity and perhaps fathom its mysterious workings. I was actually pondering this very thought when my insect adversaries spotted me, and struck again. A moribund bluebottle, an earwig seeking revenge, terror from the ceiling, a war party of ants on the march? Whatever it was, it was getting to work behind my left ear and along my collar. The clamour and tumult of the bidding served to divert my attention briefly. Then came that awful silence, only this time, in my estimation, it seemed to be unnecessarily prolonged. Perhaps the folk were growing weary? The evil abomination behind my left ear certainly was not, for it resumed work with terrible vengeance. I just had to do it, I could hold out no longer. I just had to raise my hand to my ear and give a brief, sharp rub.

“Minister yonther - fifteen bob - thankye sir - nice bag o’ tayties tha’s got... Archie Symes growed them... alweys mucks them well. ‘appen la’al wife’ll gae ye nowt but chips for a few months.”

This was my cruel introduction to the rural sign language devised for use at auction sales. I was subsequently warned that I had best keep my hands firmly jammed into my pockets, my eyelids battened down securely, and my features frozen solid whenever I ventured into the local livestock Mart. The evening wore on and my education continued without further mishap. Sid showed little sign of growing weary, and continued to harangue his bidders with relentless zeal. Meanwhile the interior of the chapel grew hotter and hotter. Sid had long since cast off his loud tweed jacket, removed his tie, loosed his neck studs, rolled up his shirt sleeves, and was now taking on the appearance of a deep-fried sausage. His voice, although losing nothing of its incredible velocity, was developing a slight croak. It was at this stage that he decided to have the necessary drink. After some blind fumbling about in front, which he never allowed to interrupt his patter, he located the pulpit water. Raising the glass slowly to his face, he was sharply cut short,

"Hailf-a-crowan"

"Three bob."

"And a tanner."

"Fower."

And so it went on and on, and up and up. I can solemnly declare that never before, and never since have I witnessed the sale of a glass of lukewarm pulpit water for the princely sum of seventeen shillings and sixpence. Eventually the stall was sold out, bidding ceased, and it was time to bring the grand event to a suitably formal close. It was with this in mind that I begun to scramble to my feet.

"Not yet Mister... bide on a la'al minute... we gat summat else here." and at this declaration a cool air of eager expectancy seemed to waft over the place. Or was it that someone at the back had just opened the door?

"Tommy's yow... fetch her streyght in Tommy," called out Sid, signalling the approach of much scuffing and scraping along the bare hardwood floor. Enter the said Tommy with his talons firmly clamped into the neck and rump of a fat 'Swardale' ewe which he proposed, as on many previous such occasions to 'donate for t'lord's good work here at Fellsyke.'

The bidding poured forth fast and furious, and the bids more recklessly extravagant with each call. The price finally arrived at for that blessed sheep was such that no auction mart in the whole kingdom would have dared to emulate it.

"Now then, we'll just ask t'Ministher here tae cum for'ard and pronounce t'Bened—" broke in a Steward, but was abruptly cut short by a shrill voice from the side,

"What abowt these... lyin' on t'winther sill here... hest tha forgotten them or summat?" A puny old lady was holding up a scraggy bunch of mixed flora.

"Tek them hoame for your Billie," came many voices in chorus, and my futile attempt at the Benediction (must end everything proper) was all but swamped in the exit hullabaloo.

The setting sun suffused the September evening with an aura of fluorescent pink, and a soft cool breeze brought welcome refreshment after the pyretic ordeal of the past ninety minutes. There seemed to be no urgent haste to return home, for the evening chores had been brought forward and completed beforehand. The people stood around in small groups on the green, about their transports, and by the chapel door. Here again we were witnessing another harvest time tradition which went back many generations. This social gathering unfortunately provided our delinquent MG Midget with a splendid opportunity to lay on one of her most spectacular shows to date. She coughed, wheezed, spluttered and popped, but stubbornly refused to start up. Within minutes all the amateur mechanics of the dale were gathered about her, bonnet up, and in full cry.

"Ney petrol."

"Whaat's t'smell then? Plenty petrol... s'runnin' all ower top of th'ingine... s'ignition A's tellin' tha ...ney spark or owt. Listen... hear owt? Clankin'...brokken valve stem I'd say." "Mare leyke a big end if tha asks me... knockin' leyke He—"

"Little end mare leyke... noise is cumin' fra top."

"Carbyretha... gittin' sum muck in't... meyne daes t'seyeme."

"Hest got her switched on... what abowt th'oil pressure?"

"Better away and fetch Andy ower... Andy'll leyek at it for tha... onybody seen Andy abowt?"

The great Andy duly appeared. He was an ungainly fellow, who looked as though he would be wearing the same clothes twenty-four hours a day for three hundred and sixty five days a year. That is, with the exception of this special occasion, the Harvest Festival, for here he was looking more like a gamekeeper than a tractor man. With no formal training, no recognised qualifications, but simply a natural flair and rare instinct for matters mechanical, Andy kept most of the local farm machinery, ancient and modern, in good practical working order, (they say his father was a goodun wi' horses).

"La'al canary here'll not stairt up Andy. Dust think tha can dae owt forra?"

"Got tae get this here minister fella hoame tae his bed 'appen."

"Tha should pedal it hoame ministher... s'lot cheyper..."

"Or mebees carry it... stick feet through t'bottom and shove it alang t'road."

"No... gey it sum bird seyed... that'll meyek it sing for tha."

"Bet la'al lass here could get it agoin... get me a goin' an' all for that matter." came a discarnate voice, soon to be swallowed an up in mock protestations.

Meanwhile the taciturn Andy had become fully absorbed in his diagnostic quest, and had transferred a fair quantity of greasy grime from the engine compartment onto his hands and protruding shirt cuffs. He then elected to examine the underbelly of the car, and was about to crawl underneath when a clarion voice split the air,

"Just get theesel' up... tha's got tha best suit on... ney wonder tha nivver hes owt deycent to gaw out wi'... now just tha get theesel' up." Mrs. Andy was furious and Andy was quick to honour and obey.

"I was just hevin' a sharp leyek at bottom, that's all, nowt else." he pleaded. "Hest tha got startin' handle onywhere?"

With much difficulty, and lots of unsolicited advice from enthusiastic bystanders, Andy eventually located the engine dogs. He gave the handle a violent turn which would have thrown a heavyweight. It worked, and the car roared into thunderous action, but soon to falter and peter out,

"Timing," drawled Andy, "Timing's wrang. Where's me screwdriver?"

So ended our little yellow jalopy's long-standing reputation for sensational starts. Meanwhile Gina, observing from what she would consider to be a safe distance away, had involuntarily gathered about her an admiring posse of handsome young agrifils, each apparently competing ardently for her undivided attention.

"What abowt me cumin' tae pick tha up sumtime Miss?" proffered one exeptionally bold specimen, obviously not being aware of her connections.

"Got big car... fast and all that... new un."

"Big head as well - and big gob what abowt me now?"

"Sorry," trilled the sweet lass, "Timing's wrang... where's me true driver?"

And little Gina laughed and laughed, all the way home.

Chapter 4

TO TAKE THE BULL BY THE HORNS

The mile and a half of narrow road between Lyndassby and Ettlegill was one of those rare stretches of local highway on which it was possible to ride a bicycle without having to make frequent dismounts and push uphill. For the most part it was bounded on either side by dry stone walling, continuous except at those crude interruptions which substituted for gateways. By local standards, the surface was reasonably level, although punctuated at regular intervals by short-notice potholes. A contrary camber would surprise you at many of the turns, around which a sprawl of loose chippings might threaten to snatch away your front wheel. All of which added to the necessity for proceeding with due caution. It was a warm afternoon anyway, and besides, I was in no particular hurry. So I rode along tranquilly, letting the sweet country air caress my thick curly hair, gently stroke my face, and fill me with beautiful thoughts that all was well with my little world. And so it was - up to a point.

That point arrived with startling abruptness, just round one of those hazardous blind turns. Which of us took the greater shock I cannot say, for both me and the young bovine that had been trotting along merrily in the opposite direction stopped dead in our tracks, and froze in mutual wide-eyed, terrified stares. I was, as yet, still fairly raw in matters of country lore and rural procedures. I did realise however, that a lone farm animal travelling on hoof along a public highway was an irregularity which must needs be dealt with at once by anyone who should chance upon it. Neither had I yet established any mode of rapport with farm animals, and didn't even know how to address them correctly.

"Now my young friend," I gasped nervously, "And where do you think you're off to eh?"

The only response was that soft lowing sound which young kine sometimes make, with their nose to the ground and eyes turned upward.

"Come along now little Moo, back home you trot, like a good— a good— a good—" A good what? Lad? Or lass? Or which? I was still appallingly weak in matters agricultural, and had not yet learnt to discriminate between the physical features which denoted the sex of young animals. Just then the sprightly maverick tossed its head and thrust into my face that sinister symbol which, in spite of the calf-like features and tender eyes, left no doubt as to its gender and status. A bright copper ring dangled ominously from its nostrils. He made that lowing sound again, and this time I fancied there was an undertone of menace in it. For the longest half minute I have ever endured we stood there transfixed, neither of us so much as batting an eyelid. It was nothing more definite than a slight twitch of the young bull's right ear, and a whispered snort from his nose, but it sent my arms flailing in panic, and my entire vocal capacity exploding into a tremendous screaming 'SHOOOOO'.

I should not have done that, for it broke the spell. The stripling drew back for a mere second, did a curious peg-legged performance of running on the spot, then just when I was sufficiently bemused bolted past me to continue the journey upon which it was resolutely bent before I so rudely interrupted it. Well, I had done my best to rescue the poor lost creature, but alas my noble effort had not been appreciated. No doubt he would encounter somebody else who would be more successful, farther back along the road. Farther back along the road? My goodness! The School - Lyndassby Infant School. It was near half-past three and the little ones would be coming out at that door at any minute. An unfamiliar sensation took hold on me - heroism I think - and in a flash I was back on the saddle, pedalling with all my might and main, pursuing that maverick like a latter day knight-errant. Soon I was up on him, level alongside him, past him, and waiting for him to appear behind the next turning. I was still leaning over the crossbar of the bike, panting painfully, in the middle of the road, when with shattering suddenness he came crashing into view. What was worse, he didn't seem to be noticing me. Which treated my nervous system to such a violent shock that some involuntary lightning reflex picked up the machine and threw it straight at him. The impact twisted the handlebars, bent the mudguards, and scratched the paint, but apparently made not the slightest impression upon the beast. He came on without a pause, trampling indecently over the bicycle, and brushing past me as though I was but a vague distraction. It was the sight of the crumpled machine lying on the road, coupled with the scornful indifference with which the animal regarded me that did it, setting up within my depths a storm of nasty emotions, compounded of anger, frustration, indignation, and pure blind rage. In a shaking fury, I picked up my bike, clamped the front wheel between my knees to re-align the handlebars, bounded into the saddle, and the chase was resumed with grim and dangerous determination. My rapid frenzied breathing was a match for any proud bovine bellowing, and those pedals had never turned faster. Soon I had overtaken my adversary again, turned about, and was waiting for him; this time with a few seconds in hand to work out a strategy. I took the precaution of leaving my bike well clear of the battle zone. At the exact moment the animal made his entry I was shocked to realise that I was facing him with my back close up against the wall. In less than a thousandth of a second, I mustered my total physical assets of eleven-stone-five-pounds and hurled them into a perfect flying tackle, clamping my arms like a vice about his neck. His head came down to ground alright, just as I had intended, but he merely shook it a little and slid me off the end of his nose in an unseemly heap on the road. I did not relish that situation one bit, and was therefore promptly back onto my feet with all the bouncing resilience of a circus acrobat. And still the bull had not turned, but rather was parading his indomitable intention of proceeding unhindered to Lyndassby. The school was in sight by now, and I could hear the happy sound of children's voices. Before I could think out my next move, I had his tail, coiled it into a good firm twist around my arm, and hung on. For a dozen yards or more, he dragged me, half on my knees and half on my toe-ends, before executing a violent swing at full circle which deposited me in an absurd pile of painful bruises and hurt pride against the wall. Now the young bull broke into a final frenzied dash for the village, still undeterred by my futile intervention. Why had I interfered in the first place, and not simply crept discreetly past the brute? But this was no time to sit by the roadside ruminating my regrets; that bull was running amok, and was in an ugly temper. Once more I found myself pedalling as fast and furiously as my battered limbs and severely daunted will would allow. I overtook him, gained a good lead on him, and was poised for... well I wasn't quite sure for what. Outside the school, infants were milling about all over the place, and a nearby clutch of young mothers waited to gather up their offspring. There was not a man in sight. I was the only male of the species on hand to administer the superior manly prerogative commensurate with this perilous situation. I became rather anxious as to what effect the frantic squealing and arm waving might have upon the animal, other than add to its confusion, but yet this behaviour of the women produced a singular reaction in me, in the shape of a hot surge of unprecedented bellicosity. For a few mighty seconds, I knew that I was invincible. Now riding alongside the maddened runaway, I sprang from the saddle with all the reckless agility of a seasoned rodeo performer, and hurled myself at his midriff with sufficient impetus to cave in a gable end. I bounced off of course. The impact being totally absorbed by the animal's belly, I was left to gather together from underneath him all that remained of the once proud me. Surely it was a good providence, that when District Nurse Mallinson went out on call, she habitually left her garage door wide open. Having finally shrugged me off as but a minor irritation, that young bull strolled nonchalantly towards the garage door, pausing on the way to crop a few tufts of lush green grass. Before my incredulous eyes, two of the young mothers walked resolutely up to him, whispered a few tender words into his ear, then gently ushered him into the garage, calmly closing the door behind him.

"Alreyght luv - not hurt or owt?" said the others to me without any obvious concern, "Tha's gettin' tha bike bent a la'al bit."

From which I realised that I had much to learn about young bulls, and young mothers.

Putting on a brave face, I set off to resume my slightly interrupted journey to Ettlegill, albeit secretly much shaken in body and mind and not a little bruised in both. There were no further complications, except that the bicycle now had an unfamiliar 'feel', and the sweet country air caressing my thick curly hair and stroking my face, no longer induced a sense of tranquillity nor invoked beautiful thoughts that all was well with my little world. For the remainder of that warm afternoon my obligatory pastoral duties entailed being pleasant, cheerful, polite, and tactfully optimistic in every circumstance, listening patiently to tales of woe and frustration, mediating concern for disappointments and disasters, and doling out impracticable advice in all manner of personal dilemmas. There would be the inevitable discussions on the state of the weather, the land, the market, and I would confidently tender my inexpert opinion on all three. Evening, much longed for was a long time in coming. Eventually it arrived, bringing with it the welcome prospect of a leisurely ride homeward. As it turned out, although the air was cool, the journey was by no means exhilarating. The machine seemed to have acquired several additional stones in weight during the course of the afternoon, all the bearings had tightened up or dried out, and the brakes were secretly binding. Some geological upheaval had inclined the entire length of the road uphill, and no matter in which direction I was facing the wind was always from my front. And what was worse; there persisted in me a dull foreboding that somewhere up ahead, just round one of those blind turns, right in the middle of the road, something would be waiting. It might be HIM - or perhaps, his dad.

And sure enough, just as I rounded that treacherous bend near Sleath Farm, there he stood dead centre in the road, arms held out at full stretch, beckoning wildly - Sandy Sneaston.

"I see'd tha cum ower t'top o' t'brae yonder... Missus's just gettin' nice pot o' tea a-brewin... tha's timed it just reyght hest tha not. Oneyweys, had tae stop tha ony road... got summat for that la'al wife or yorn... cum on in... leave t'beyke agin t'wall,"

Sandy was ageless, although he'd reputedly been in his seventieth year for as long as most people had known him, and that was a long time. He was long, lean, sinewy, and as sprightly as an antelope.

Sandy was loquacious to the point of overloading one's audio receptors, and that especially when he was effusing on how good the Lord had been to him. Sandy had certainly prospered materially, both on the land and in property dealing; from which one was led to presume that the same good and bountiful Lord had created him both an efficient husbandman and an astute speculator. The Lord had also given him a kind heart, and Sandy had a wide reputation for his acts of unbridled generosity. His good wife, a very large woman called Rachael, was of similar ilk, and was compelling in her good will. Predictably, the conversation at supper was largely one-sided. Therefore there being no opportunity for me to talk, except for the odd word of concurrence squeezed in here and there, I was better able to concentrate upon the demolition of a pile of Mrs. Sneaston's delicious pastries. The good lady took obvious delight in my display of *bon appetit* and was visibly flattered by it. For my own part therefore any feeling of gluttony was offset by the dubious reasoning that I did it purely for her pleasure and satisfaction. I over-stretched my flattery however when I complimented her specifically upon her superb seed cake. The result was that from thenceforth, each time the last morsel of the portion in hand was raised up to my mouth, my plate was swiftly replenished with another large block of the stuff, which in the cause of courtesy and face-saving I was obliged to consume with feigned delight.

"It's t'seed that meks it sae good," declared Sandy with his horse-size teeth half-way through a wadge like a mini hay bale, "stock thrives amain on t'seed onyweys... sayeme stuff as they puts in t'cattle cayke ye knaw."

The only way in which to escape from the Sneastons' exuberant hospitality was to devise a sudden emergency ('Good gracious - look at the time - O dear - I've just remembered - much as I hate to - but I'm afraid I'll have to make a quick dash...') adding a sharp shocked glance at the wrist watch for realism. Not that one was over anxious to withdraw, for these two kindly people had a tremendous capacity for making you feel good about yourself.

"Reight sorry tha hes to gaw se seyen - duty calls I suppose... but wait... see what I've got for t'bonny la'al wife... surprise!"

Sandy vanished into the larder, closely followed by Rachael. To keep up my ploy of urgent haste, I was already outside and standing astride my bike when they re-emerged. Sandy carried a potato sack which he carefully slung over the handlebars, hooking one corner under my right thumb. The contents had to remain a mystery until I got home where, Sandy assured me, it would be 'a nice treat for ye beyeth.'

"And this is special for Mrs.Teviot" called out Mrs. Sneaston out of breath, "nice bit o' farm butter for her scones... Hod it steady now... still runny a bit... basin's in t'bottom o t'bag... so din't gaw shekin' it or owt... din't pedal ower fast neither wiln't tha not or tha'll cowp it all ower tha."

"O aye... afore tha gets away," said Sandy in that tone of voice which heralded the commencement of another discourse, "there's summat else I was wantin' tae tell tha if tha hadn't been in sic a fash tae get hoame. Aye... the good and gracious Lord hes been partic'1ar good wi' me today and browt rich and special blessing."

"So glad to hear it Mr. Sneaston. In what particular way?" I had actually begun to move off when Sandy spoke, and so the jolt of my sudden stop certainly did not bring special blessing to the burden dangling from the handlebars, nor to that competing for space in my turbulent innards.

"Got ya lish young bull in t'bottom pasture yonder, and sum on these hiker foalkes musta left t'yat oppen, and he gat away see."

"Shameful isn't it," I pronounced, "the way these townspeople come out here, and are so totally ignorant of, and contemptuous towards the ways of our agricultural community."

"Ah well... aye... that's reyght... Onyweys he didn't get very far, only up t'Lyndassby Road a bit, afore some young lasses gat ahowd on 'im and shut 'im up in nurse's garage yonther. He's not teken ony hurt or owt, but I'll hev tae git mesel' up t'road and fetch him back afore that nurse meyght start pamperin' the thing 'appen."

That misty, pious look came into his eyes, and he cherished it for a time before continuing, "Isn't it a wondrous blessing that t'Lord gat t'Nurse called out t'sefterneyen, and stopped me bull awanderin' ower far, or gettin' hissel' into ony mischief of ony soort.'

Suddenly I felt pain in all my limbs at once, my stomach tried to break loose from its moorings, and my head went into a spiral. I made an inelegant move to remount, even though Sandy had a hand on the saddle.

"What's wrang wi' la'al yella car then? Hest tha gone off it?"

"No, not really... rest does it good now and again... pleasant day for cycling actually... leisurely... and the exercise does one good I suppose... always like plenty of exercise you know."

"Aye tha's very wise there. Good for t'body, mind, and soul, that it is. Canna git ower much o' that."

That last comment instigated a mood of mild depression as I set off, because the real reason for my use of the bike that day as on many other days, was a case of harsh economic expediency. Due to the rather difficult financial straits in which young clergy and their wives often found themselves, in those unenlightened days, sometimes the few shillings required for a gallon of petrol had to be directed towards more essential needs. This morbid train of thought however, was soon scotched by my necessary pre-occupation with balancing the bicycle, avoiding the frequent potholes and— 'Good grief. What if that garage door has swung open? Or Nurse has arrived home and turfed out my former acquaintance? Or he'd bulldozed his way to freedom, grown lonely or homesick, or in need of a fight, and was back onto this road?'

Arriving safely at home, I stumbled into the house, and presented the precious offerings to Gina. For obvious reasons she opened up the more delicate of the two bundles first. The dish of rich, creamy butter filled her with instant delight, but the sturdy package firmly wedged beneath it, which she had some difficulty in extricating from the bottom of the bag, seemed to cause her both surprise and consternation.

"It's... a bit er... solid... smells strongly of caraway seed I think... cake... or maybe a local pudding of some kind... perhaps meant to be served up in small quantities... with a sauce I would say... Tell you what dear, this should put some strong muscle into your legs for your cycling days."

For some reason or other, Gina elected to unravel the mystery of the large rough sack as though it was her own private province, and she transported it to the kitchen as if it contained a live serpent. The sudden spine-chilling shriek which followed her disappearance made me suspect that perhaps it did. Dashing to the rescue, I found Gina pinned back against the wall, pale-faced and totally aghast. I had never before realised that Gina had such big shiny eyes.

“Arrrrrggggghhhh... Darrrrrrrrghghlinggggggggg it’s a ddddo-o-o-o-ggggg... a poor little dead dog... all stiff... and cold... and... dead.”

As it turned out, the animal in the sack was a hare, which had been neatly shot through the temple. It was dead of course. Persuading Gina that the rare delicacy was meant for our consumption was but the first in a series of problems. There was for instance the matter of skinning the animal and preparing it for cooking. And not least how to eat our way through so large and substantial a morsel in the short time available to us, for these were the days before the domestic refrigerator was common currency. During the next few days we ate jugged hare, boiled hare, minced hare, hare stew. Incidentally, the dog refused to eat a portion offered to it, and the next door cat took one sniff at it and bolted in panic.

If ever I see a hare, in a field, or on the road, I will do the proverbial thing, and pass it by on the other side. And the same will apply to young bulls.

Chapter 5

CALLED TO HIGHER SERVICE

"And what's this I've been hearing on the grape vine?" I queried Ned Aitkin in that ebullient manner which I had developed as a foil to current misgivings. "Rebecca's had a short spell at the hospital they tell me. Glad she's home again now anyway, and no doubt feeling much better for it."

My sorry efforts at communicating solace and good cheer were still at a very amateur stage. In this particular case it might have been better to be as taciturn as Ned himself habitually was.

"Airgh," he sighed impatiently, 'She's in t'kitchen if tha's wantin' tae see her," Ned mumbled with scarcely a flicker of facial muscle.

"Good. And tell me, how's she feeling then? Just fine I bet, and jolly glad to be back home eh. Marvellous places hospitals I reckon and do some wonderful things when one needs them, but best place to be is home isn't it."

"Better gaw in and ask her theesel hadn't tha... tha knaws t'way, so din't let me keep tha... tha's a busy man." said Ned dismissively, and strode off in long skinny strides in the direction of the flight of stone stairs which led up to the hay loft.

It was invariably a difficult task to establish any measure of communication with Ned. He was undoubtedly most at home amid the lonely wastes which surrounded his remote hill farm. Whatever anxieties may have tormented him, they remained secret and unuttered; whatever surges of sorrow disturbed the mysterious depths of his soul, he suffered them alone. If guilty passions strove to possess him, he duelled with them without recourse to help from outside, and whatever happy contemplations may ever have delighted his fancy, he never deigned to share them. Ned's emotions never registered externally. The contours of his face were inflexible, and the expression was constantly set at neutral. His voice was pitched in a low, flat, unvarying monotone.

Gina had accompanied me on this call, and at first remained seated in the car whilst I went off into the yard to try and accost Ned. I presumed she had to recover her breath after the hectic trip up the lane. It was more likely however an example of her fine womanly intuition in spotting the opportunity to engage Rebecca woman to woman as soon as Ned and I were off the pitch.

"She's alright isn't she... I mean nothing bad nor anything is there?" I blurted out rather brashly whilst following Ned about his work. Ned would never allow such useless activity as conversation to interfere with whatever task he was engaged in, and one was always obliged to address the back of his neck.

"Nay, nay, nowt tha can speak of... nowt at all," the words had to squeeze their way through clenched teeth.

"Good... just thought, you know... being in hospital and all that... well... she hasn't been too good lately... has she?"

"Send them away tae them places for nowt these days din't they." mumbled Ned without so much as looking up from his chore, "Aye... as I says... send them in for nowt."

"What kind of nowt was it Ned?"

"Nowt... just nowt... that's all there's tae it... nowt."

I hung on precariously, yet following Ned like a hound, me by now feeling somewhat futile, and often at a loss for what to say next. Then Ned surprised me. Pausing, but not turning to face me, he propped his chin on the shaft of the hay-rake with which he had been tidying the loft floor, and volunteered,

"Woman's complaint 'appen... they gaws gittin' alsoorts of queer rumbles and whaat-nuts at that age... gits mowdy a bit an' all sumtimes... and summonem gaws gittin' theirsels all worrit tae dey-ath. Sheep's seyeme... once had an owd black-fayeced yow and she gat tae frettin' and scrattin' and mopin' abowt... vet said is was nat'ral or summat, nae worry or owt, so I ju—"

"Yes, yes, Ned, that's right. Perhaps Rebecca's just got a bit depressed and down in the dumps a bit. Glad she's having some attention anyway." Saying this I walked away, realising uncomfortably that if that final remark was intended to bring some consolation to the man, it was hardly of the essence. Young and inexperienced though I was in facing up to dire human situations, I nevertheless suspected that this untypical outburst of Ned's betrayed rather than concealed some stirrings of grave anxiety.

Rebecca Aitkin was a woman of quiet fortitude. She spoke with a soft voice which seemed to come from a long way off. She was particular in her choice of words, and these were always carefully measured out. And always, there was that sad, but beautiful smile, like the light of a full moon through and around a thin white cloud. On this day however, she was obviously making a very special effort to appear unharried, and carefree.

"O aye, had a few days holiday last week. Just a la'al bit of a check-up that's all. Got this bit pain... lang teyme in gawin' away... but nowt tae crack on really. Doctors were quite pleased wi' t'result I think... sent me back hoame onywey so they musn't be ower worrit must they."

"Well that's sure nice to know," said Gina sweetly and assuredly.

"Better try t'Vet next time eh," Rebecca chuckled.

In those days women, and more so the less sophisticated country women, did not discuss their bodily intimacies freely. Openness in respect of the reproductive functions was not yet in vogue. The term 'Woman's Complaint', whilst referring to a variety of complications, was usually uttered in a low voice, and as a rule brought a premature end to conversation on matters of feminine health. Doctors sometimes had to work against this background of reticence, and listen to a history of symptoms whispered through a mush of guilt, fear and embarrassment. The cervical smear, if known at all, was not common practice. Many women condemned themselves to needless anguish, suffered secretly, or died miserably in the prime of life. And Gina had culled sufficient information from her conversation with Rebecca to confirm our worst fears.

"Poor, poor Rebecca. I do hope I'm not letting my imagination run away with me Don... I really do hope. And poor Ned, in spite of those statuesque features I suppose he thinks. And those poor sweet bairns," said Gina once we were back to the car. "It musn't be dear, it just can't be."

For the next few weeks nobody noticed any significant change either in Ned's appearance or his demeanour. His unsmiling face, slow, ambling gate, and sparsity of conversation were fixtures, part of his stock in trade which were taken for granted by all who knew him. If indeed he was a worried man, the fact would never show up in the few modes of expression which were available to him. He went about his work with steady and unfailing regularity, and together with Rebecca and his four children, he made his weekly appearance at morning service in the little Naiston chapel. As more weeks went by, even if by pure observation alone, it became general knowledge that Rebecca Aitkin was 'a bit under t'weather', and yet when Ned and the children began to arrive on Sunday mornings without her, it was merely assumed that, as Ned said, she was temporarily off colour. Not unnatural at her time of life.

******

"O hello! This is Margaret Skelton here... yes Naiston Post Office, aye. Is that t'Minister then?" An unusual call, I thought, and at seven o'clock on a Monday morning at that.

"Hello! Are ye still there? Aye, sorry tae trouble tha sae early in t'mornin' but well... you see I've got Rebecca here... aye, Aitkin - Rebecca Aitkin. Nay she doesn't want tae speak on t'phone - not used tae these newfangled things she says --- nay. Well it's Ned ye see, Ned Aitkin, fra up at Nettle Brow aye. She says he's 'appen gone away. Nay he's naewhere abowt t'place, and she's nearly out o' her mind... doesn't knaw where he'll hev gone or owt... just gone away that's all. Poor Rebecca... and her not well an' all. O aye she's left t'bairns up at hoame."

"Listen Mrs. Skelton," I responded, with a promptness which startled me, yet in a low steady voice, "Listen carefully. Get her up home sharp will you please, and somebody to go with her if you can. I'll be over there as soon as I can. And by the way - not a word of this to anybody else mind you - alright. Thank you."

The first three miles along the road to Naiston was relatively easy going, and allowed me the opportunity to try and gather together my senses for whatever situation I would encounter at the Aitkin place. Ned's spread, Nettle Brow, was about the most inaccessible farm in the county, and to reach it would have strained the resources of an invasion force. The ascent from the road and over the fell began with an ancient gate which must have been fabricated by demons. The device which substituted for a latch required some ten minutes of finger-breaking, back-straining, nerve-racking frustration before one could perceive the vaguest notion as to how it worked. More by chance than by design, on this occasion the abomination fell loose of its own accord in my hand, and I was through. Now followed a half mile of farm track which presented almost every obstacle to wheeled traction known to man, and some not yet discovered. The final stretch would have provided a formidable testing ground for a Tiger tank. I worked long and arduously on the ingenious fastening device of the second gate, a wire puzzle which defied, distorted, and confounded every principle of practical logic, philosophy, common sense, or indeed whatever it is which enables man to unfasten things. Then, at the moment of triumph, on passing through, and returning to close the gate behind me, I observed that it would have been much simpler to have slipped over the post the loop of strong wire which sufficed as a hinge, even as it appeared that most users of the gate had done for generations past.

Why do sheep, with hundreds of acres of open fell available to them, choose to doss down in the middle of narrow roads and high-sided farm tracks? Ned's sheep were of a singularly awkward strain, with a strong affinity with the force of gravity in their breeding. They were undisturbed by the dust and noisy commotion set up by my little old MG sports car, and being as insensitive to colour as they were to most other stimuli, they didn't even react to its strident yellow paintwork. The said sheep were completely indifferent to my earnest entreaties, and sceptical towards my reasoning with them. They sat tight. Fortunately, the Almighty in His infinite wisdom had fitted the beasts with short horns, inclined downwards. These accessories were obviously intended as handles, for the sole purpose of facilitating the removal of obdurate animals from the path of country ministers upon urgent pastoral business. Those shaggy heaps of inanimate mutton weighed heavy, and smelled ghastly. As I got nearer to the farm, the track petered out into terrain so rough that I conceded to myself that horses were a great invention after all. I made no attempt to unravel the mystery that held the final gate in place, but leaving the car outside the farm-yard, I climbed over the wall. As I did so, I chanced to look back. The view almost took my breath away. Down below, the whole valley of the Lyndass was stretched out before me in an exquisite patchwork of mauves and greens, shades of rich brown woven in with clumps of trees, islands of maturing bracken, and scars of jagged rock. The entire vista was inter-laced with a tracery of dry stone walls, reaching far beyond to dissolve into the purple haze of the distant hills. Like a silver chain, the glistening river, flowing out from a remote nowhere, played hide-and-seek for miles along the valley before breaking out to saunter splendidly across the flat far below the rise upon which the farmstead was situated. The birds echoed the mood, and were singing an ode to beauty and peace. A warm breeze whispered soothing thoughts to the trees, and the morning sun poured forth life out of a cloudless sky.

The moment of ecstasy was shattered with a cruel jolt. The farm-house door was ajar, and I heard the sound of bitter sobbing, coming from within. I did not knock, nor wait, but quietly entered. Under normal circumstances a model of calm composure, now Rebecca was frantic with grief and despair. Never before had I seen her looking so unkempt, nor had I ever, during my short life, witnessed anyone so distraught with sorrow. Her rich black hair, slightly streaked with grey, her pride and joy, normally so immaculately groomed, hung down in a knotty shambles over her face. Her dark brown eyes were raw from many tears, and her thinning face looked like cold, wet, stone.

"He's left me... my Ned's gone away and left me... what have I done to him? Me and these poor bairns... what will we do?"

The two older children, Henry who was about eleven years old, and John less than one year younger, stood staring indifferently, seemingly fighting back whatever sparse emotions they may have inherited. The other two, Josie and May, mere infants, were clinging fearfully to their mother's skirt. At the tragic sight, my own emotions, like the colours of the spectrum when whirled at great speed, ran together into a turbid flux, and no words would come. I was striving hard to clutch at any delaying tactic which might conveniently come to hand, when Rebecca jerkily pushed a large sheet of lined note-paper towards me.

"Left this letter on t'table yonder. He cummed up tae bed rather layete last neyght so I thowt... stopped up a lang time readin' his bible... didn't hear him cum up... must've been gayly quiet. Sumtimes he forgets the time when he gets reading that bible of a neyght... sumtimes hae te gaw down the stairs and fetch him up tae bed. Him and that bib... Here! where' is it... where's his bible? It regular bides on t'shelf in t'corner... gone... musta tekken it away wi' him... he's not cumin' back"

Rebecca broke off into a spasm of unrestrained and agonised weeping. There was so much that I wanted to say, needed to say, but I knew not what. It was then that I made the important discovery that in a situation such as this, the best things to say are spoken with a strong enclosing arm, and a broad shoulder that is well able to absorb tears. And better without words.

Ned's cryptic note was difficult to decipher. Scrawled out by hands that were better adapted to the pulling of wurzels than to the production of legible script, it was a desultory diatribe of irregular lines, irregular verbs, and even more irregular notions. Ned Aitken had received a 'call' from God, who had lately spoken to him through the medium of his bible. Notwithstanding so short a period thus far in the ministry of the church, I was beginning to suffer considerable dismay regarding well-meaning people who spoke and acted as though the bible had been created specifically for them. It was a treasure chest of instant instructions for immediate application to any circumstance that required decision making. They would speak in familiar terms of God 'leading' them to a certain page, or passage, or text, even though they made their selection as randomly as cutting a pack of playing cards. A bible falling open, or discovered lying open, was a boon not to be passed over. Isolated words of holy writ, divorced from their original historic setting, and even whole passages, were culled from any part of the Book and applied with literal exactness to present situations. Obscure scriptural references, lifted clean out of context, and sometimes with some devious verbal modification, would give divine sanction to a decision already conceived or a judgement already established in the mind. And therefore a single word, a whole line, or passage, with a pleasing sound would be sufficient to authenticate a plan already formulated subconsciously. The hill farmers lived very practical down-to-earth lives of course, and their philosophy was maybe neither complicated nor sophisticated but they were by no means simple people, and there was much of life that could be learned from them. Unfortunately however, in matters religious, some were at times overtly simplistic, and suffered themselves an irrational guilt sense should they inadvertently apply a modicum of intelligent thought to matters of the spirit. To do so would be to run counter to the exercise of that most prized of all virtues, simple faith.

The Lord had indeed spoken to Ned. He had led His faithful servant by means of guided page selection, first to Saint Matthew, chapter 28, verse 19: 'Go ye therefore, and teach all nations, baptizing them in the name of the Father, and of the Son, and of the Holy Ghost; teaching them to observe all things whatsoever I have commanded you: And lo, I am with you always, even unto the end of the world.'

A further shuffle through the hallowed pages had turned up Saint Luke, chapter 18, verse 29, 'There is no man that hath left house, or parents, or brethren, or wife, or children, for the kingdom of God's sake, who shall not receive manifold more in this present time, and in the world to come, life everlasting.' Yet another delve into this manual of divine instruction had landed Ned upon Saint Luke, chapter 10, verse 4, 'Carry neither purse, nor scrip, nor shoes; and salute no man in the way.' The implications of the remainder of that passage alone were frightening, especially when one considered that one such as Ned may be using his Bible as a kind of religious Russian Roulette. It is surely dangerous to gamble with sacred things; a text out of context provides a perilous pretext; distorted spirituality holds terrible potential.

Ned however, retained no doubts as to the validity of his 'call', and was clearly set to obey his instructions to the letter. Furthermore, he had subjected his momentous decision to some unbiased reasoning. By a process of simple deduction and uninspired logic he had arrived at the happy conclusion that in reality, he was not forsaking his farm to ruin, nor leaving his wife and family comfortless, nor, in any wise abdicating his earthly responsibilities. On the contrary; he was entrusting them to the loving care of their Heavenly Father, which was far better, for He never failed a soul which trusted in Him. He rejoiced in the sure knowledge that his family were indeed honoured and richly blest in what he was doing. And they would be glad, for his wife was the faithful handmaiden of the Lord, and thus she was loyal and obedient to her husband. His four children were loving, and therefore fully acquiesced in all his opinions. It was maybe a matter of some significance that Ned's farewell letter made no mention of Rebecca's current state of health, nor did it make as much as a hint of anxiety for her on his part. The final page tailed off into an unintelligible rigmarole of warped notions and growing confusion. Not however before delivering a dreadful dissertation on the evil powers that had been let loose upon the world, warnings and forebodings concerning the inevitable wrath to come, most terrible prophecies of unimaginable doom, and evil portents soon to descend upon the whole of mankind. All of this, one might add, with thoroughgoing exegetical support, and relevant quotes supplied.

There was no time to lose, nor to waste over trying to analyses or to deduce some thread of reason out of this tragic diatribe of delusion. We must seek, and find Ned with the utmost urgency. But how? Where? He had no doubt got a good start by now. But in which direction? Over which desolate moor, or lonely mountain track? There was one mischievous thought, that if Ned was obeying his instruction to the letter, he might be bare-foot, and would be carrying neither food, money, nor scrip, in which case he would not have travelled very far. It would seem he had taken his Bible with him, and so unless he had discovered some hitherto unknown means of deriving physical as well as spiritual sustenance from it, he might even be faltering from hunger and exhaustion. And sore feet of course. A conglomeration of hideous calculations came over me all at once which, try as I may, I was unable to reduce to a single line of rational thought. Out of it the name of Lyndy Brigg suddenly hit me like the harsh resounding clang of a cracked gong. The thought seemed to come out of nowhere, and it refused to go away. Lyndy Brigg, the old hump-backed stone bridge, spanning the Lyndy Gorge high up over the roaring falls, the jagged rocks, and the spectacular drop. Local folk lore contained many tales of the deranged for whom Lyndy Brigg had held a fascinating and fatal attraction.

A good road led to within a half mile of Lyndy Brigg, and so if my intuition was leading me in the right direction, I should be able to gain some ground on the crazy wanderer. In my swift resolve to be up and going, I had omitted from my reckoning that tortuous track which led down from Ned's farm to the road. But my little yellow car turned mountain goat. She slithered and slid, leapt and lurched, bucked and bounced, and yet always managed to get her wheels back onto the ground, although not necessarily all at the same time. And by some strange contradiction of the law of gravity, I actually stayed on board. Unfastening those two devil cursed gates almost unhitched all of my finger joints, as well as my reason. Once onto the road, that miniscule, bright yellow MG Midget, of unknown vintage, and rare specifications, streaked like a frantic comet with trailing tail of dust and smoke, as this young divine dashed with hysterical haste to the rescue of a soul in peril. Eventually a sharp left incline, and through a gap between two isolated stone posts from which every vestige of gate had long since departed, and I came to a thumping halt at the start of the grassy lane which led up to Lindy Brigg. The front off-side tyre was down hard on the rim. Several seasons of University sport, and my Army training and experience as a commando during the recent war were not lost on me, for I sprinted up that long winding track like a young gazelle. The empty cigarette packet on the grass at the side could not possibly have been dropped by a passing Ned, for to him, smoking was a deadly vice reserved exclusively for the apprentices of Hell. Maybe, after all, I was pursuing another than he; some sensible walker perhaps, a fisher, or a shepherd rounding up some strays. Happy thought! Some mild compunction made me go back a few yards and take another look at that coloured card. It was not a cigarette packet. Closer examination showed it to be a book mark, and it bore an obscure scriptural text in heavy Gothic print. Out of Ned's bible?

Sure enough when I got within sight of the Brigg, I spotted Ned, gaunt and crazed, standing ominously astride the low wall, waving his arms about, and wringing his hands. As I came stealthily up behind him, I heard that he was frantically muttering some throaty gibberish. For the most part it was unintelligible, except for the frequent recurrence of a word which sounded like 're-baptism'. In the circumstances and to my suspicious mind, that precluded almost every possibility but one, more especially as Ned was now leaning forward perilously, and addressing his remarks to the swirling torrent down below. My panic surfaced with a sudden jar, and before I could take control of my actions I had rushed forward to grasp Ned from behind in a suffocating bear hug. Then a violent wrench, and I threw him sideways onto the ground. Quickly regaining his breath and his feet, Ned laid into me with all the fiery fervour of an Old Testament prophet. Hurling scriptural quotations at me like envenomed darts, he savagely designated me and my miserable kind for everlasting torment. Had not the Lord God called him from the plough, and the field, and the cattle shed? Had not the Almighty himself set him apart for a great mission to all mankind, predestined from the very beginning of time? The former things were passed away, a new age was dawning, which he Ned was to herald. This was his calling, his re-baptism. Had not God set it all down in here, to be revealed unto him in this latter day? Here Ned treated the cover of his tattered Bible to a resounding slap with the back of his hand, then vigorously reshuffled the pages from Genesis to Revelation.

"But He's set more great things than these in his blessed word Ned... He caused it to be wri-"

"Fain to bring your high sounding doctrines to me Priest, for thou art anti-Christ... I know thee, who thou art," Ned fiercely interjected, his lips trembling with emotion, and the muscles of his narrow face distorted and quivering.

"But Ned my friend, Ned, listen to me, for I've g—"

"Away with you and your modern science, your corrupt learning, your crafty wiles, your worldly wisdom... your... you... your—"

"Ned, Ned, if only you will listen, just for a sec—"

"Thy master the devil hath verily sent thee unto me to tempt me sore... get thee behind me... away with thee... away...awwwww—" Ned's voice worked its way up to a screaming crescendo through a disgusting surfeit of saliva.

"Ned, listen to me, you're unwell and I've come to hel—"

"Again I command thee... get thee behind me Satan... get..." Ned's mouth was completely awash in spit, and his eyes were blurred with passion. "Get thee hence... hence... hence... for I must be on my way."

"Ned... Ned... Rebecca... your wife... your bairns... they're crying... they need you back to them... Ned"

"No man hath left house, or wife, or children... hast thou not read the scriptures O man... Dost thou not hearken unto the command of God? Lo thou art a grievous burden unto me... away with you."

Another fluctuation in mood and Ned's speech became pontifical. I began to fear that if there was indeed a way of breaking into this tragic paranoiac circle, I had already squandered it miserably. Nevertheless I resolved to make yet another attempt to breach the facade of biblical literalism within which Ned's mind and soul were held. Perhaps I could penetrate through to where some lovelier sentiment could still be aroused.

"Your dear wife loves you Ned... loves you... do you hear? She's missing you... she needs you... God gave her to you for you to care for... Rebecca is br—"

"My wife is a God-fearing woman and an obedient servant of her Lord," snapped Ned with incredible pomposity, " She knows the way I take and rejoices in it, and is exceedingly glad... My wife... my wife... my—"

"Your wife is... dying." I swear I do not know where the words came from, for they slipped out involuntarily.

For some interminable seconds Ned stood erect and rigid, observing me blankly, his features having suddenly reverted to their natural format. Had I inadvertently touched a vital nerve? The moment of quiet respite was brief. Without warning, except for a sinister hissing sound emitting from behind his tightly clenched teeth, Ned hurled his lanky frame at me with what looked like murderous intent. Five-feet-eight-inches may not seem a very practical height for a combatant, except perhaps when he is young, energetic, strong, and in panic. And when certain arts from a former career come readily to hand as if by instinct. Before Ned realised what was happening, he was squirming on the ground in pain and shock. Overcome with pity and shame I turned away ruefully regretting the readiness with which I had resorted to violent action. Whilst I stood off guard, the tough tall hill man got back to his feet and was on me again, flailing and grappling like some great cephalopod. I was forced to reciprocate in kind, although not in degree, so presenting a bizarre spectacle of two mismatched men pushing and pummelling each other like a pair of winded game cocks. So encumbered was I in this futile contest that I did not notice the stealthy approach of the big game keeper type. I did however feel the impact of his straight right upon my rib cage, and I heard the resounding crack of that same straight right as it made contact with the side of Ned's face.

"Awah wi' ye... sully bastarrrrds. Now what the hell arrre ye up tae?"

Stuart MacKraghan held us apart by our collars as though wickedly contemplating the banging together of our heads. Then releasing his hold, the massive

Scot stood before us like a highland chieftain in his moment of triumph, and delivered to us an impromptu lecture on the folly of childishness, and other personality defects.

"I warrrant ye'll be feichtin' ourrre some wee lassie or itherrr. Ye should be awah and drrroon yerrrsels in that burrrn yonder, and leave the lassies aleyn. Scrrratchin' and scrrrappin' like a pairrr of wee bairrrns. Noo awah tae yourrr mitherrrs the pairrr o' ye, will ye, aforrre I kick the hell oot o' ye."

I was too shattered to respond immediately, or to explain. Although gasps of breath passed through my larynx, they arrived at my mouth with no words in them. Which was most fortuitous, for it gave the moment to Ned.

"Rebecca... my poor Rebecca," he wailed, "Ministher 'ere says she's a-dying."

"Ministerrr?" gasped Stuart, in that same instant spotting the grimy remains of my clerical collar.

"Says she's a-dying, that's what he says... that's what he—"

"I didna ken ye werrre a ministerrr sirrr," Stuart beseeched, re-tuning his voice and modifying his manner to indicate the traditional Scottish reverence for the cloth. "And what's this evil rrrogue been up tae? Feichtin' with ye leyke that...'tis surrrely an abominable thing tae dae."

Before Stuart could direct all his righteous wrath towards the hapless Ned, I was able to call him aside and explain the sad situation to him. Let it suffice to say that it broke the big man. Ned had by now moved further along the track, and was sitting on the grass at the side, with his head buried deeply in his hands, whimpering pitifully, and Stuart's faithful Labrador doing its best to comfort him in doggie fashion. Ned had become more composed and rational, and I began to wonder which feature of this sorry episode had restored him thus. The physical blow to his face, which is a well-known corrective for hysteria? Perhaps the shock of my frenzied outburst about the seriousness of Rebecca's illness had driven home some notion which Ned's mind had perceived but was unwilling, or unable, to evaluate. And of course the intervention of Stuart MacKraghan must have played a large part in the working of the miracle. We joined Ned on the grass, and talked long and patiently, before walking with him back to the little two-seater near the gateway to the road.

There was the small matter of the punctured front tyre. With big MacKraghan substituting for the wheel jack I did not possess, we fitted the spare, and with hardly a word passing between us, I drove Ned home to Rebecca and the children. The scene which ensued after my arrival was too touching for words, and I would prefer to leave my description of those hallowed moments at just that. Within a few days, with tactful pastoral care, the patient skill of a brilliant and dedicated country doctor, and always Rebecca at his side, Ned made a good recovery. Eventually he seemed to become quietly resigned to whatever inevitability the future held in store. I was now to be presented with a dilemma the like of which would become a regular feature of the whole of my subsequent ministry as a Minister of the church. The bilateral confidence is a heavy burden to bear, and one which requires the good pastor to possess rich resources of discretion and fortitude. For so it was, that in this case, Rebecca realised that she was dying, but did not wish for Ned to know or suspect the truth. Ned realised that Rebecca was dying, but did not wish for her to know it, nor suspect it. And the minister intimately knew both sides.

Rebecca's health deteriorated with alarming rapidity. Soon the scandalous rumour which ignorance feeds began to spread it abroad that Ned's habitual indifference to his wife's feelings, together with his recent misdemeanour, had accelerated her decline. For my part, I had to manage the balancing act of protecting Ned's sullied reputation, and at his request, guarding the presumed secret of Rebecca's terminal cancer. The truth however, surfaced sooner than anticipated, as Rebecca was observed to grow more listless, and to age unnaturally.

She died serenely on a lovely afternoon, when the sun poured streams of warmth and light over the rugged hill-top on which the old farm stood, and bathed it in glory. The cattle gathered in a lowing huddle at the gate of the adjacent field, and the rooster refrained from crowing as his dames clucked quietly as they went about their farmyard chores. Old Gyp, lazing peacefully outside his kennel, whined, and didn't give a reason why. The gentle breeze whispered words of love amongst the trees, and the birds sang of peace and joy. And all was beautiful down in the valley below.

I feared for Ned. Under normal circumstances he was as introversive as a retreating snail, and as aforesaid, neither his countenance, speech, nor outward demeanour bore any obvious clue as to his emotions. This was his great misfortune, for if any of his neighbours and friends had detected any sign of repressed anxiety concerning Rebecca's state of health, or had been permitted to share it, they may indeed have been able to ward off his tragic slide into the neurosis which so nearly brought him to an untimely end.

On the day of the funeral Ned was a model of quiet dignity. The heartless ones however interpreted this as evidence of his habitual stolidity, and of his reputed insouciance towards Rebecca's wants and needs. As we sadly turned away from the graveside at that bleak fell-side cemetery, Ned paused for a moment, as though profoundly reflecting. With his children clutching closely to his fore-arms, he turned toward me, with the semblance of a smile upon his face. and the man who had once vehemently denounced me as an evil emissary of Satan himself, slowly held out his hand,

"Alreight minister --- brother --- friend --- ivrything's gawn tae be alreight - I've got t'victory."

I reluctantly confess that the gesture both troubled and confused me. Coming from Ned it contained, to my mind at any rate, so many possible implications, theological and otherwise, that I wasn't quite sure how to react. I dodged the issue, putting it to the back of my mind, and submitting it to the wise criticism of the pre-conscious.

When we reached the gate leading out of the cemetery, we saw a very large man standing by. He was wearing a kilt in the tartan of the Royal House of Scotland.

Chapter 6

MIND THA BOOT LACES

Emerson Slack was a delightful scandal monger. Originally an immigrant from the towns, an 'off-comer', he regarded the local populace with cynical objectivity. But for amusement only, for there was never so much as a trace of malice in his reflections. He made laughter out of scurrilous tales, traded gleefully in reports of human errors, misdeeds, and eccentricities, basing his logic upon the safe and sound dictum that things are never quite what they seem. His mischief however, never got very far, for Emerson was a chronic invalid, confined to the house, and for the most part, to his bed. Bolstered in a semi-recumbent position, he would greet your arrival with the outburst of hearty laughter which invariably preceded his opening gambit of. "Say, 'ave ye heard about this one then?" For the remainder of your stay he would entertain you, and amuse himself, with a selection of items from his seemingly inexhaustible stock of seamy information. Incidents of dubious notoriety, rumours incontrovertible, and spicey anecdotes were cited from past, present, and even future, for Emerson would often speculate as to where a particular train of events would inevitably end up. He was an expert on human nature, especially in the raw, well versed in the wiles of men and women of all ages, classes, and stations, and an able exponent of the facts, and otherwise, of local social history. At times he would veer, only slightly, towards the hypothetical, when a touch of extra colour was required to bring up the details of an otherwise plain account. His ready judgements usually bore a bias towards frivolity. It might be 'that black-feyced tup Willie Nettleton bowt fra Ned Nixon', the supposed marital status of 'them two that's cummed tae live ower at Fenny Beck.' Then there was that 'young heifer Charlie Mace sowld Bob Stourton, that was an all rowan yan, until haff-way frae t'mart, shower o' rain cummed and weshed t'brown boot polish off t'white patches.' Emerson cherished a choice supply of speculations regarding the doubtful pedigree of certain people of prominence, or a local ill-esteemed snob. Emerson unmaliciously culled his stories from a dream world, where although imperfect, everything was designed to be funny.

I was always welcomed to spend an hour at his bedside; longer if I could stand it. When I entered the room I would be initially greeted by a small, shaggy brown mongrel dog, which would leap up onto the bed, from which position it would spit out fierce invective toward me or anyone else who should venture too close to its master. For the parson there were other perils, such as becoming so deeply engrossed in Emerson's humorous tales as to overlook the fact that the visit was primarily pastoral, that is, for the benefit of his soul. There were the choicer moments, such times when Emerson would bring out and display some jewels of memory and emotion which were of rare worth. He laughed a great deal, but he could cry quite as readily. He had just cause to have cried much more, and perhaps may have done so, but for his ability to counter his afflictions with his obsessional interest in the proclivities of others more fortunate than him. He had a unique fund of pithy sayings, which he invariably accredited to one Confucius, whom he insisted was a notoriously mixed-up Oxford professor. Take for instance the time when Emerson had a visit from an extremely bald-headed bore, who excused his cranial aridity with the usual "Grass nivver grows on a busy street." To which, in a flash, Emerson gave the tart reply, "Aye, and tha nivver thatches empty barns neither." On one occasion when he and I had been discussing the perils of prevarication, he rounded off with "You must nivver tie tha bootlace in a field of strawberries." I pondered long over the implications of that wisdom. I eventually realised that the simple moral is that it is unwise to be seen doing anything which, although perfectly innocent, may have the appearance of evil.

A sad incident once brought the lesson home to me. It was in an afternoon, and I was walking up the long main street of the village. I cannot now remember where I was going, nor for what purpose, but I can well remember the sequence of events which followed. I was not moving very fast, but I nevertheless overtook a lady who was rather clumsily holding to her hip a large laden laundry basket, and seemed to be walking with some difficulty. Chivalrous to the hilt I called out,

"Carry your luggage Madam?"

"I manage on me own thankye - used tae it." the lady replied coldly.

"Far too heavy... come on... hand it over."

"Now look, why don't you just bugger off, and leave me alone…"

"But we're going the same way aren't we... and anyway, I can't walk straight past a lady struggling with a load like that."

"Lady! The bloody cheek... bloody washer woman mare leyke... there's nae ladies in this hole... gentlemen neither for that matter... and look, just leave me alone will tha... and pi— Hey mister, I'm reyght sorry... didn't knaw tha was a vicar... wouldn't hev said anything bad, leyke bloody and that, if I'd— Good God!"

The sight of the clerical collar put paid to all conversation, but I continued to walk alongside the lady. I had observed that the heavy basket was slipping slowly downward, and realised that sooner or later she would have to let go her precarious hold. When eventually the basket slid to the ground, I took my chance to resume the conversation.

"Now may I lift it up, and put it back under your arm for you?"

"Nae Vicar... it's alright... I can get it up... often drops it you knaw... and picks it up mesel."

"All the more reason why you should let me carry it for you."

"Very kind of you sir... I do appreciate it to be sure... but couldn't let a vicar dae that... wouldn't be proper or owt."

"Listen dear lady, vicars have everything that other men have, and that includes strong backs, and strong muscles, and some even have strong wills... And I've got the full quota."

"Nice tae hear that," she gurgled with a mischievous twinkle, "But all t'sayeme it wouldn't be reyght... I mean you being a... proper gentleman leyke. Onyweys, I don't gaw tae church or owt ye knaw, and I'm pretty strong mesel... most things onywey."

"Then that's a pair of us, so you grab one handle, me t'other and we'll make a twosome shall we."

Before she could respond to this suggestion I had stooped down, taken hold of one handle of the basket and begun to raise it slowly from the ground. Fearing that the contents would be spilled, the lady hastily seized the other handle, laughing apologetically. And so it was, that almost the entire population of Lyndassby, more especially the eminent, elderly, or spinsterly members of my church, witnessed the spectacle of their minister bearing half the burden of a basket of soiled linen up the main street. Not only was I sore tempted to muse on the subtle symbolism embodied in the act, but thought on the relevance of the good apostle's injunction to the Church. Mind you he probably didn't have dirty washing in mind - not literally I mean. Gradually the woman began to familiarise herself with the bizarre situation, and we even got round to gently swinging the basket to-and-fro as we walked.

"Live in Jubilee Row - Council houses - end of t'village. Look Mister, tha doesn't need tae cum t'whole way... manage mesel' fra here."

"Sorry Madam, but what I start, I always like to finish, and not stop in the middle of things. So let's go the whole hog you and I, eh."

Methought the sudden outburst of harsh laughter with which the woman responded to this suggestion betokened a very warped sense of humour, to say the least. However charity being charity, I was checked in any peremptory judgement by the warning that perhaps the misconstruction was purely subjective.

"Out of condition I reckon... what I mean is... well it's a long time since I helped to carry a load of soiled linen uphill you know. And you do it every day don't you?"

"Not exactly," she said quizzically, now trying to stifle a fresh fit of naughty mirth, "But say - bet you could make good use of a nice hot cuppa tea. Damn...

what am I thinking about... the leykes o' you wouldn't be wantin' tae cum intae my place would tha? Nivver gaws tae Church or Chapel nor nowt leyke... nivver been very religious or owt leyke that. Just keeps tae mesel' most o' the time these days. Din't git intae a lot o'mischief when tha keeps tae theesen, does tha?"

"In that case you probably wouldn't mind bothering with me," I said, in another bad attempt at choosing my words discreetly, now that I recognised her warpish turn of mind. "Yes... well... what I mean is... what about that cuppa tea eh."

The place was neat, tidy, and well ordered, in spite of an excess of novelty nick-nacks, and a generous scattering of magazines, distributed over every available flat top. There was a gallery of numerous photographs, small portraits mainly, displayed in one corner of the room. Flowers were there, in plenty, exquisitely arranged, and some obviously picked from the wild. No sooner had we entered than the lady busied herself with a swift superficial tidy-up, in the manner of women when greeting 'unexpected' visitors. She completed the process with a flourish, by ostentatiously fluffing up the cushions of a large easy chair, for my personal use.

"O by the way... should have told you, my name's Don Teviot. O yes, and I am a parson. I'm minister along at the local Methodist Church... you call it chapel don't you. In fact I'm minister of all the chapels in the dale, whole bang lot of them. But look, you haven't told me your name neither, have you."

"Liz - Liz Makin... Elizabeth Mary if tha'd leyke it posh."

"Well now Mrs. Makin—"

"Not Missus... just call me Liz leyke everybody else does... it's Miss onywey."

Splendidly enthroned on the large plush chair, I consumed one cup of tea, then another, and another, and eventually entered upon a second brewing. Liz simply talked, and talked, and talked, and, (so I flattered myself into thinking) she unburdened herself a great deal. As she became more and more relaxed, she became increasingly talkative. Liz was a simple soul whom, in consequence, life had pushed around somewhat. She had never travelled very far, nor moved outside a very narrow spectrum of experience. She was past the first flush of youth, and could be coming up fortyish. The traces of greying at root level hinted at an amateur tinting job on dark hair. The indiscreet application of cheap make-up to her well-worn features only served to highlight a sad lacking of sophistication. Her facial movements, like her speech, were slow and cumbersome, and the expressions didn't always match over well with the sense of the words she was speaking. And yet there was about this woman a strong brand of femininity which was uncanny in its attraction.

"You married then?" Liz queried over the top of her third cup of tea.

"Yes, only last year... wife Gina... school teacher before we married... from way up North... Borders."

"Think I've seen her... nice neat figure... shoulder length dark hair... always dressed so smart...talks swanky a bit. Seen her in t'Post Office. Hey, She's nowt but a la'al bairn is she not... 'bout sixteen... tha musta stolen her frae scheyel or summat."

"Quite a mature and wise young woman actually... twenty four."

Liz had never married - the war you know - so unsettling. Mind you, she had sported a substantial number of boy friends in her time, but none of them had stuck for very long. Noting my interest in a framed photograph which was set apart from the others, she coughed a little, and said pathetically,

"That was t'nearest I think - Charlie - poor owld Charlie."

"Very special?" I said, only then noticing that all the photos were of servicemen.

"In a way, yes... sailor... Scotchman... lost in t'Meddi... torpedoed I think... nivver got tae knaw owt efter his letters stopped cuming. Then one o' his mates wrote me... lang time afterward... said he thowt Charlie would be deyad. Nivver heard nae mare."

"What about Charlie's family? Didn't they contact you?"

"Nivver knew owt about them. Nivver knew exactly where he cummed fra or owt. Just... well, as I says, he was Scotch, and I didn't knaw him for very lang... short leaves... you knaw how it was in them days din't tha. But I miss 'im all t'sayeme."

"Sad and terrible days Liz - the war - and some of us, I fear, will never really get them out of our system."

"Had its laughs though, 'adn't it. Had sum real good times."

"In the forces? ATS? WAAF? WRENS?"

"Nay, not me. Wouldn't 'ave me in that lot. Worked a bit in WVS canteen... lived in t'town then... cummed back here efter t'war."

"Made a lot of friends though?"

"Ye can say that again - soldiers mainly - did me bit for the boys ye knaw, darnin', mendin', knittin' socks and scarfs and socks and things... soldiers' cumforts they called them... summonem called me t'sayeme. O aye, and I did alsoorts o' other things for the war effort as well, and the boys... happy days."

"You'd be greatly appreciated I assure you."

"O aye, I was that.. ..every little helps they used tae say didn't they. They'd move in, stop for a few days or weeks, then all on a sudden they'd be moved on. Naebody ivver knew where they went, or what would happen tae them. Then streight away another lot would move in and tek their place, stop a bit, then... well ye knaw how it was."

"I was a soldier Liz, for seven years. Went through the whole lot."

"Well I be damned! Thowt there was summat queer about thee - summat diff'rent tae this lot round this dump. Bet tha was a bit of a reight lad an' all... I can just see tha...in tha uniform. I say, it's just like owld times this is... seems gayly lang time syne I had a soldier in me house, I tells tha."

"And now?" I queried, suspecting that the conversation was in need of some deflection.

"Tried me hand at lots o? things, but nivver stuck tae any for very lang. Not much gawin' up here is there. On for mesel' now...teks in other foalk's weshin'... keeps me a-goin' leyke... and best thing is, I'm me own boss...that's t'main thing... me own boss."

"By the looks of things around the place, you still do a fair amount of knitting Liz."

"For me bairns," Liz replied with marked enthusiasm, "Me bairns... little coats and 'ats, socks and booties and things, and stuff for t'bigger yans as well."

"But you said you weren't married," I said with a stupid abandonment of tact.

"Plenty o' bairns all t'sayeme. Knits for 'em all... wiles away t'time on lang nights on me own... specially in t'Winter, and keeps me out o'mischief an' all."

"Your bairns?"

"Aye, Barnado's an' that. Nivver seen ony o' them... orphans they are fra all ower t'place. Din't belang tae naebody poor la'al darlins. Sumbody hes tae luv them hasn't they."

"That's simply magnificent Liz. You must surely be—"

"Nivver been very clever or owt. But I can knit. And I knits and knits away, and luvs them all t'time while I'm at it."

My wayward mind drifted off into a fatuous fantasy of psychoanalysis and I set up an assessment in terms of unrequited love, frustrated maternal instinct, lingering war-time trauma and the like. For a brief period I allowed myself to be carried away by such senseless ruminations. Then the sound of Liz's voice smashed in like a clanging bell, in precisely the same instant as my brain had stumbled upon some weird theory of sublimation, backed up by an extensive pastoral experience - one year.

"Hest tha ivver luvved onybody that naebody else wants?"

It was clearly time for me to take my leave. My delicate ego-system was not conditioned to dealing with shocks like that, and I felt myself becoming a little confused. At any rate, my visit had already exceeded the time limit of a casual call, and the duration of a cup of tea. Liz accompanied me down the four steps from her front door to the gate, calling cheerily after me as I departed,

"Nice 'aving you... be sure tae call back again... seyen mebees."

Although Liz was soon out of sight, and earshot, this was not to be the end of the matter. In the first place, that poignant phrase haunted me, and taunted me, with every step I took; "Hest tha ivver luved onybody that naebody else wants?" So deeply did it burn into my thoughts, that I was not fully cognizant of passers by. I was therefore totally impervious to the manner in which some of them were observing me.

"I sees tha's stairted tekkin' in weshin' Minister," Archie Roathe startled me back to conscious reality, calling out to me without looking up from the rails of his front gate which he was painting, "Sumonem teks in a lot mare than weshin tha knaws."

"Late a bit darling," chided Gina when I arrived back at home, "Bet you're ready for a nice cup of tea... but your jam and bread's got a bit cold I'm afraid."

"No dear, not tea. Something else if you please. I've nearly drowned in the stuff this afternoon," I pleaded, and followed on with my story of helping the lady with the laundry basket.

"Ravishing young blonde I bet... couldn't tear yourself away and all that... well worn tactic that one," she teased, "Sorry my hair's so dark, dark, dark, and my tea's so cold, cold, cold."

"I wish I could laugh at it too darling, but you see there's a rather tragic side to this one. Besides, she wasn't a blonde, nor was she ravishing. In fact she wasn't quite a brunette neither. She was - well - neither so to speak. Bit of a mixture."

I went on to tell a very patient Gina about this simple soul, possibly forgotten, neglected, maybe despised, or just downright lonely. And about the unseen host of little children who benefit from her charity.

"Friend of the friendless again eh," Gina softly cooed.

"O yes, she's certainly that alright."

"No, I mean you darling. You see, I suspect the heavy basket of soiled linen was not the only burden you've helped her to carry. There was more, far more, wasn't there?" Gina's big brown eyes were welling up with tenderness.

"Yes there was more; far, far more. Much of it was unuttered and unexpressed I'm afraid. But how's this one? 'Hest tha ivver luvved onybody that naebody else wants?'"

The meeting at the church on that evening was sparsely attended, and was, I fancied, somewhat off-key. I responded, unintentionally, by falling short a little in disguising my usual boredom with such inane institutions as routine church business. There were other matters on my mind which seemed to be distancing me from the immediate affairs of the moment. The meeting was less prolonged than usual. Fewer people than the usual inner core elected to remain for the tea and biscuits session at the close, and those who did addressed me with uncharacteristic coldness, and each other in low voices. Morning service on the following Sunday was in similar vein. Although, as was normal, the place was filled to near capacity, the service itself was a lack lustre occasion all through. Neither did the drabness end at the Benediction. It seemed to spill out into the vestibule, where I took up my customary position as the worshippers departed. The exchange of greetings was less than spontaneous. Granted, the fell-side people were of sober manners, never gushing, nor hail-fellow-well-met. They were like the rugged crags which jutted out from the edges of their native fells, steadfast and changeless, constant in their attitudes, and not noticeably prone to inexplicable variations of mood. Yet I was troubled, not because there was any detectable animosity anywhere, but because I sensed those surface ripples which denoted deep and silent undercurrents. The regular patterns of life in the village had not altered in any way, and yet an irrational sense of alienation was gradually taking hold of me. In a rare moment of selfless insight, I calculated that all of this was purely subjective, and at worst was but a trick of my hypersensitive imagination. I was reacting to the strains imposed by these early stages of my ministry - nothing more. In spite of my valiant efforts to brace myself with such pleasant reasoning however, the exercise only served to exacerbate my problem. I was thus constrained to share it with Gina.

"Nothing wrong with you darling," she consoled. "Indeed if there is, then I've got the same bug. Nothing's quite right out there... the very atmosphere is wrong. But it's them, not us. Nobody seems to be as friendly as they used to be, and even those who are, seem so terribly patronising with it. And I'm sure this isn't the work of my own imagination neither."

"Then I'm right. I feel a coldness, especially in the church... among the older folk mainly. And in the village in general. I had considered that it was maybe only in my own mind. But no. In fact in the Post Office this afternoon, those dear Miss Bowran sisters, old fuss pots who are usually all over me with sickening adulation, were decidedly distant, and just a wee bit acidic I thought."

"The kids are still OK though bless 'em. Had a great time with them all at youth club tonight," said Gina. "So, whatever's the trouble it certainly isn't with us, or the kids would spot it for sure."

One day at about that time, my senior colleague from the town chanced to call on us. He told me that he had seen old Tom Jenkins at the mart recently, and that the old man was sore troubled. "It's yon young minister of ours - sic a gayly la'al wife an' all... should keyep betther company, that's what. Nowt agin 'im mind ye grand fella in lots o' ways. Just, well, nivver smoke wi'out fire is there."

"The old chap was no more specific than that mind you, and I'm afraid I failed to draw him further. But, well, you will know by now what they're like around here for inuendo I suppose. Perhaps you yourself may have some idea what's eating the old boy."

"Honestly John, I just haven't a clue," I replied. "But mind you, if there were any reputed publicans and sinners about, whether inside or outside the pale of the church, I would feel it incumbent upon me to follow the Master's example and befriend them, despite the odds, or risks. And if there were any special ones, I wou—"

"But surely brother, all so-called publicans and sinners are special in our book. We simply cannot be selective if we are to be of any assistance to those who may slip and fall." Which reminds me... something else the old codger said, and I couldn't sort out. Something about the kind of houses you keep going in and out of. 'Rubs off you know'. I wondered if there might be plague in the village.

That clinched it. The lady with the laundry basket of course. The class-ridden snobs. The self-righteous hypocrites. I had offended against their unholy law, and there was no health in me. The dignity of my office required me to leave no room for common compassion, and the maintenance of religious respectability precluded any concern for the outcast or despised. No smoke without fire indeed. Did they not know that the quenchless fires of Hell give off no smoke, and even if on occasion they do, that smoke may have the alluring scent of incense. With such nasty thoughts I worked myself up into such a pitch of rage and indignation that it became urgent for me to sound off to somebody. And, in the circumstances, who better than my old friend Emerson? The old rascal responded to my furious outburst with a paroxism of constricted, wheezy laughter, which for some time looked as though it would finish him off. Sobering up at last, he gasped,

"Alright lad, alright, now just calm thaself. I knaws all about it. I misses nowt around here tha knaws - absolutely nowt. Gettin' them all a-worried te de-ath tha has. Liz Meakin! Fizzie Lizzie! Tha sure picks tha lasses doesn't tha. Very special off-comer that'n. Very special. In fact very very special. Tha's picked theesen' a proper trollop this time me lad."

"And what's wrong with that, might I ask? I tell you Emerson, everybody's the same in my book, and I don't intend to pick and choose. What I mean is - we're all alike sinners, and in need of th—"

"Aye, sinners. Now tha's hit t'nail right on th'ead that time, specially as far as Lizzie's concerned anyway. Right sinner that'n, by local standards that is - or judgements should I say?"

"What's wrong with the lady? What's so objectionable? What's so iniquitious about taking in washing to try and earn a modest living?"

"Nowt - nowt at all. Only, as they say round here, weshin's not the only thing she's supposed te tek in for an immodest living. That's all that's matter. Look, I'd better tell tha a bit moore I think, 'cos to be frank, tha really surprizes me tha knaws."

Liz had not lived at Lyndassby for very long before news of her erstwhile notoriety had followed her, gathering extra colour and spicy detail along the way. She was alleged to have quite a distinguished war record. The bare facts alone however, were sufficient to make a meal out of. Fizzie Lizzie (would drink nothing but lemonade) had not only been known as the local nympholite at the place of her former abode, but her house there had acquired a certain reputation among a long succession of servicemen during the recent world war. Being an ex-soldier myself I would, of course, fully understand what he meant, so Emerson obviously assumed.

"Well I for one, don't find it very amusing old friend. It's not all one big joke out there, and I've got to live with it."

"It'll soon pass by, tha'll see. They gets like that wi' owt that's a bit new fangled tha knaws, or different fra what they're used tey, or folks that acts a bit different fra theirsels," said Emerson, soberly. "You see, it's just that tha's done summit they've nivver done afore, and they just din't knaw what te mak on it."

"Don't know what to make of me you mean." I felt the rage beginning to build up again, but was checked by Emerson,

"Could be that... could be. Tha's a bit younger, and a lot different from owt they've ivver had afore you see. They'll get used te tha in time I reckon. But tha'll hev te be patient wi' them. If I was you I wouldn't worry ower much. They're all grand folks at heart, most on them. Sum's a bit queer in their ways, but they mean well. Sum's reet bad'ns mind ye, but only a few."

"I agree wholeheartedly, but they do seem to have got me wrong a wee bit, don't they."

"Nay lad, neybody's suspicious o' thee or owt like. Ney distrust nor owt like that. More likely sum on them on th'outside o' t'church that passes rotten judgement on owt tha does. Them on th'inside is mare critical on owt tha doesn't do. All that's happened is maybees a little indiscretion on your part, and you've knocked a bit hole in their pride or summat. When they've had time te chow it ower for a bit, they'll cu—"

"Pride? But Emerson, that's the cardinal sin. It's at once the seed and the disgusting precursor of every transgression there is."

"Aye, and specially when it shows up ower much respectability, and we've all gotten ower much o' that nowadays."

"Same thing... makes us too ready to pass rash judgement."

"Isn't there yan in t'good book about tekkin' up t'fust stone? Sum on this lot carries them ready in their pockets." Again Emerson rocked with laughter, "Don my young friend, dinna thou mind me... just I always sees t'funny side o' owt that happens. Got te laugh, or I'd bloomin' well cry." And Emerson's little dog leapt up onto the bed and barked, barked, and barked.

I was unable to share Emerson's optimistic philosophy. For one thing, lingering echoes of his habitual facetiousness rendered his good sense less than convincing. I did not fully appreciate his over-simplistic hypothesis; namely that I had merely run up against the passing prejudices of a bunch of silly old wives (of both sexes) within the church in whose pious eyes I had committed a dire affront to ordinary decency. Neither could I digest the alternative theory that the mischief was nothing more than the harmless observations of a few common cynics on the outside to whom 'Once a soldier, always a soldier' was a current maxim. The hour spent with Emerson did nothing for me, except to exacerbate my feelings of righteous indignation. Or was it injured pride?

On leaving the house I was nevertheless fully resolved to go out there and risk all in an unambiguous bid to set the record straight. Fortunately the long, slow, uphill walk home gave me time for further reflection, and perchance, cooling off. On second thoughts, was it not part and parcel of a parson's appointed lot to suffer in silence? Was it not for him to accept the inevitability of being misjudged and misrepresented? Should not he be praying for those who despitefully used him? Did not his divine Master pronounce as 'blessed' those who were persecuted for righteousness, and reviled for His sake? I suddenly began to feel unhealthily virtuous. Surely, one who deigns to help the fallen, must seek and find them where they are, for the truly lost knows no way back. And although it is not imperative for him to share their contagion, he must be prepared to join them in suffering their rejection. It is surely a risky business, being a pastor of souls. And yet my anger, indignation, hurt pride, fear, or whatever it was, painfully persisted, insinuating itself into every facet of my thinking for the whole of the subsequent week.

It is not acceptable clerical ethics for a preacher to utilise the invulnerability of his pulpit for the purpose of hanging out his congregation's dirty linen, the public airing of his private pre-occupations, nor the free exercise of any of his personal animosities. But what of it when the Lection for that following Sunday just happened to be part of the Gospel of Saint Luke, chapter 15; the part concerning the pharisees' complaint over Christ's habit of frequenting the houses of known publicans and sinners? And was it a like co-incidence, that in my sermon on that theme it became expedient to have recourse to several cross-references to Mary the Magdelene, and to the woman taken in the very act of adultery? As age-old custom dictates, I ought therefore to have selected my Text from the Bible itself, for Heaven knows there is an abundance of highly appropriate and sufficiently sleazy material on the theme to be had from that source. But for once, and for no conscious reason, I did not conform to the custom. Instead, I elected to quote old Emerson's very apt quip for starters, "Nivver tie tha boot-lace in a field of strawberries". Whatever cause I had subconsciously intended to serve by my presentation of this fortuitous lectionary selection, it fell conspicuosly flat. Not even the sermon, which I had endeavoured to render more pointedly than was my wont, brought forth any spectacular response. I was met with the usual incredulous stare from the congregation. The bombshell came towards the end of the service, as I read out the weekly church notices. I found myself half-way through the following intimation, tucked in amongst the rest, before its import took a hold on me:

> 'The young people of Mrs. Gina Teviot's Youth Group are assisting in a voluntary knitting project, to help to provide small garments for war-orphaned children in Dr. Barnardo's Homes. Gifts of wool, and practical help from more willing knitters, of all ages, are urgently needed. Please help. Some of the young people will be waiting in the vestibule after this service to receive offers.'

And there was something familiar about the writing in which the note was penned.

Chapter 7

MUTHER THERE'S A MAN AT T'DOOR

The four year old laboriously prised open the big rough farmhouse door, only wide enough to permit him to poke through a startled face before hastily retreating back down the long echoing passage,

"Muther! Muther! There's a queer soort o' man at dooer... got funny white thing on t'neck... think it's God or summat."

Like so many of the sporadic comments of children, this one spoke volumes. In addition to the error of mistaken identity, the kid had actually confirmed my own suspicions concerning that age-old church institution known as pastoral visitation. Within the local tradition it seemed to be invested with a mystique which, in my particular case, would tend to inhibit conversation and natural social intercourse. It was as though I had suddenly and unexpectedly descended upon a household directly out of Heaven or some other grand estate equally remote from experiential life.

To my mind, this phenomenon bore traces of the crass clericalism of the Middle Ages, and fostered the perilous prerogatives of priestly authority, privilege, and inviolability. The parson's pedestal could thereby become a throne, his personal opinions accorded the status of divine wisdom, and his momentarily conceived judgements fraught with eschatological implications. Notwithstanding my undeniable proof of vocation, it was not within my forte to communicate at that level. It was, as yet, early days however, and I had much to learn - not least about myself. These were the reactionary post-war days of inevitable readjustments in social attitudes, structures, and comparisons, when people were tending to become less formal, and were sending tradition to the wind. Progress was the order of the day and, although with some predictable resistance, and slower pace, the process was beginning to operate within the church. It remained necessary however for me to take cognizance of the fact, that in a rural setting such as was my present sphere of activity, one was working with stout material which, although by no means brittle, needs to be warmed a little before it becomes flexible.

Pastoral visitation, or as I preferred to term it, meeting the people, was by no means an anachronism. It would indeed occupy a fair proportion of my time, energy, and ingenuity. I thereupon decided that cultivation of open friendship would be my *modus operandi*. In such a relationship as that, one has to reach neither upward nor downward, but always outward and across. I would not under any circumstance take parsonic prestige for granted. If I had to have respect, I would wish to earn it by personal merit. At the same time I would be ever watchful of giving the appearance of easy familiarity, unwarranted brashness, kindly condescension, or sickly patronisation. I would strive to meet the people just where they were, and always to fall into line with their immediate pre-occupations. Thus I issued forth with my well-laid plan to achieve a fresh dimension of pastoral care.

The best-laid plans of mice and men being what they are, things did not turn out quite as I had expected. Old habits die hard, and ancient attitudes turn into stone. Consequently some of my early pastoral excursions landed me into situations of unmentionable absurdity which, far from enhancing my humility, did a great deal towards devastating my self-esteem. In the first place, I could never fathom the reason why it was generally assumed that my call on a household was for the purpose of ministering solely to the women. And why was it that my arrival at a farmstead usually coincided with the men-folk having to scuttle away in pursuit of some urgent agricultural task which had just at that very moment sprung to mind? Or they were always just on the way out anyway?

"Nae disrespect or owt leyke Minister... just there's this coo up in t'far medda... droppin' t'fust calf ony teyme now... well ye knaws what they're leyke these coos din't tha. Nice o' ye te call onywey... sorry canna stop... mebees ye'll still be arownd when I cums back in. Onywey see tha it t'chapel yan Suntha 'appen—" A quick flip of the cap, a crashing exit, and gone.

Soon I had devised the habit when visiting farms, of making directly for the fields, outbuildings, or wherever I perceived the sound or sight of men at work. I began to dress less formally, for more than one good practical reason. After a few weeks of experimenting with this technique, I noticed that I was beginning to be made welcome by all members of the establishment. I had also acquired a reputation as the minister who always carried a pair of wellies, some overalls, and a set of tools in his car locker, who could talk with the best (and the worst) of them about football, fighting, farming, dogs, cows, sheep, poultry, women, or God, yet nivver tried to convert you when you were trapped with him in the cow-byre or out in the field spreading muck or owt. And he'd nivver gaw all red in t'face or owt if tha let a blast, or bugger, or bloody hell or owt leyke slip out be accident. The women of course were more amenable (why are they so considerate of parsons?) and kindly receptive of my pastoral attentions. In most cases however, they simply had to be, for my visit would often entrap them in their kitchens, or about some other indoor domestic task.

The hill farmers and their wives were, in their own inimitable way warm, homely, and hospitable people. Invariably the ladies would greet my arrival with, "Now tha's just cummed reyght for cuppa tea and a la'al bite te eyate... tha musta knawn I'd just put t'kettle on." The truth of the matter was that the said kettle was never off, but sat perpetually crooning comfortably on the hob by the side of the open fire place or on the top of the stove. My arrival would send mother, and/or daughters of the household into an instant flurry of industry, leaving grandma if one was present, to chat up the minister. In an astonishingly short time the dashing about would culminate in the presentation of a substantial spread of wholesome goodies. This was the 'La'al bite' or, to their generous minds, but a snack to set me on my way happy and amply refreshed. Unfortunately the imbibing of this 'snack', some necessary socialising, and polite conversation could cost me the best part of an afternoon. Over a period of many months I experimented with various dodges to try and avoid this time consuming distraction before I realised that it was I indeed who was the trapped one. I tried putting out the rumour that I was not very fond of tea, or coffee, or cocoa, or milk. This ruse however, was scotched at the very outset one hot Summer's afternoon by the jolly Sarah Broomfield.

"Nae use askin' tha if tha'll hev a cuppa tea or owt when tha doesn't like t'stuff is it. But tha's got te hev summat 'appen hest tha not.. All that sweatin' aridin' that owld bike tha's got, or shekin up in that la'al car. But wait, I've got summat as'll suit tha I bet."

A ponderous swirl of voluminous skirt, and Sarah was out of the parlour and into the kitchen. She returned within minutes, bearing a large tray upon which sat a monolithic pie, a large lump of cake which looked as though it was fresh from the baler, an enormous mug and a more enormous enamel jug.

"Eyate tha fill now... and here, just tha try a pot o' this... tha'll leyke it to be sure... brew it mesel' for Ernest and t'lads ivry haytime... gits through gallons o' stuff... keeps them agawn."

I couldn't find it in me to enquire as to what were its basic ingredients, and besides, as it was approximately the colour of soapsuds I had notions of my own. Judging from the overpowering gas emitting from its surface I suspected that it might have been brewed from neat silage - well matured. The pie was good, the cake was better, and the fluid was seductive. As soon as it touched the lips, this farmhouse plonk took hold and pulled itself powerfully down the oesophagus, like some vital elixir which the whole body craved for in order to survive.

"I sees tha leykes it... knawed tha would... here 'ave another pot... dae tha a world o' good."

It was all so innocent and innocuous, at least I had assumed it was, until on my way home my legs began to turn into soft rubber, my knee-joints seemed to work backwards, I rang my cycle bell continuously, and hailed every field gate en route with a vigorous Nazi salute. I assumed that the mood had worn off by the time I had reached home. Teatime seemed to be proceeding with reasonable normality when Gina suddenly paused, threw up her hands and startlingly observed,

"Darling! Whatever's got into you? You're actually leering at me."

This might be the appropriate point to mention the fact that to the fell-side non-conformists, total abstinence was a matter of strict and unbending principle. Intoxicating liquor was of the very essence of Hell, and the very thought of it was anathema to the faithful. By some queer quirk of reasoning however, any substance brewed at home did not suffer this devilish stigma but acquired a firm status of respectability and unquestioned acceptance. And this more especially when it had been manufactured specifically for necessary consumption during harvest or hay times.

It would happen on occasion that my call on a farmstead would coincide with the mid-afternoon snack, or indeed what passed off as teatime proper. Sometimes I got firmly ensconced before the men had been able to make their urgent scramble for the outbuildings with the remains of an interrupted meal clasped in their hands, or stuffed hurriedly into their mouths. My arrival at such inconvenient times appeared to cause them some embarrassment, but it gave me a great deal more. Within the normal course of events these practical, down-to-earth farm folk did not always recognise any clear-cut distinction between working hours and daily meal times. The women may have had certain social aspirations, but largely due to the nature of their work the men were not always able to concur. They did not require regular recourse to habits of refinement, and did not always find it easy to switch over at short notice to a special level of table etiquette. That was something which usually accompanied the wearing of their Sunday suits. Their afternoon chores and stringent demands upon their time meant that such a meal would be hurried through with the bare minimum of ceremony, and little semblance of organisation. Therefore my unexpected appearance could find the men perched or lounging at all manner of quaint angles about a large table which was either scrubbed spotlessly white, or covered with a square of floral leather cloth. They would be hastily imbibing large morsels of good wholesome food from well-stocked plates, and pulling noisy draughts of hot strong tea from pint-size mugs, some of which were cracked, chipped, or minus handle, but each bearing some notable feature which identified it as personal property. Within seconds of my entering the room, the men, by now trapped at table, would be nudged toward one side, made to remove their caps from their heads or knees, and their elbows off the table. Mother would then spread out a crisp white cloth, assemble the best bone china, recharge the table with a rich variety of more dainty fare, swiftly accomplishing an astonishing transformation befitting the occasion of the Minister to tea. As for my own part, the consideration, whilst flattering, was somewhat misplaced, and the situations sometimes produced by it could turn out to become bizarre in the extreme. Some hapless male would be sure to commit an unwitting table manners offence, slurp his tea, hiccup with hurry, jam a big rough forefinger in the minuscule handle of a dainty china tea-cup, clamp a massive two-handed grip on a meagre cucumber sandwich, consume a slushy confection in the manner of loading a hopper, accidentally burp, or nearly asphyxiate himself with a crumb down the wrong way. Or - worst of all - he could have his once ravenous appetite seize up while his mouth was still chock full to over-spill. Alternatively, or as well as, some precocious juvenile at table would select a particularly opportune moment to blurt out,

"By gum Muther, these cayekes is champion... wish t'minister'd cum ivry day."

A little girl might explode into a fit of giggles, sending a cascade of pre-digested fragments in every direction, whilst a younger sister would publicly announce in a shrill voice her intention of going off to the toilet, being careful to proclaim in detail for what purpose.

After a number of such experiences, I resolved that I must make some tactful bid to forestall any such predicaments of mutual embarrassment. After all it was I who was the intruder, and therefore it was surely I who must accommodate. It would be quite simple really, so long as I got the timing right, and could apply the correct touch of boldness without appearing too brash or unduly vulgar. So it was subsequently, that if ever I strayed into certain places at tea time (accidentally of course) I would sound off blatantly, and all in one breath with,

"Ah great. Teatime... aren't I lucky... timed it well eh. Oh yes, I could sure put away a la'al bite o' summat, and a big mug of extra strong tea... big yan... like the lads here please."

Whether or not my little scheme was successful was a matter for the folk themselves to judge. Needless to add, the early reactions were both mixed and unexpected. The very art of taking down one of those whopping mugs of tea without drowning took a considerable time to master, and the effort to emulate the men's' gargantuan appetites nearly damaged my personality beyond repair. In the meantime it no doubt provided them with an interesting source of entertainment sufficient to offset their former tea break inhibitions. All in all, my efforts seemed to work wonders. They revealed, I hoped, a willing spirit which was gradually becoming kindred and did much to establish a strong rapport with those wonderful hill-farming folk. Some of the details I have set down here may seem a trifle crude, or might suggest an attitude of mean condescension. This is by no means intentional; on the contrary. They are intended to illustrate the essence of a culture of warm domesticity and unmatched homeliness, best to be shared and enjoyed on equal terms.

Not all pastoral visits turned out to be futile, amusing, or simply embarrassing. Many indeed produced rare jewels of friendship, fellowship and mutual trust, and would even reveal trials, struggles and triumphs of the human spirit which can only be disclosed and shared at depth, and best in a context of deep faith. It was awesome at first to try and come to terms with the knowledge that to these good people you were the man of God, and therefore the means and manner by which you conducted yourself rendered you not only responsible to them but also answerable to Him.

Chapter 8

MAN OF SORROWS

Old Daniel Quinton was different. True, he was accepted as a local resident of long standing, but different. He was markedly void of any indigenous family resemblances or native attributes. For one thing, he retained a tacit refinement in his general demeanour which had been little affected by his long exposure to his present rural environment. Even though he had made some early attempts to vulgarize his speech he had never mastered the pure vernacular of the dale, and the characteristic Southern rounding off of the vowel sounds marked him out as a refugee from some very distant place. Despite some bold efforts to appear 'local', traces of an alien cultural background were still clearly discernible. The popular opinion throughout the dale was that he had gone to college in his young days and got some special sort of education. But of course that was a very long time ago. And there the matter rested, for this enigmatic man's earlier history was by now far too remote in time and place to be of any immediate consequence. As to why, at the age of eighty-three years he was content to remain resident in this moorland backwater, living the miserable life of a solitary, no-one ever chanced to speculate, for he had been about the place for so long that his personal and private affairs were beyond question. There was no knowledge of any relatives, dependants, or distant acquaintances, and it was thus assumed that if ever there had been such, they also would be forgotten or lost in the long years gone by. In some quiet quarters it was rumoured that he had taken a wrong turning in his early life, way back beyond the reach of retrievable memory, and from there the lonely road had led him on through an aimless and fruitless life, to fritter away his days in insignificance in this obscure little hamlet of Swarsgill.

Daniel Quinton was, as a matter of fact, trained in the law, and had gained a handsome first at Oxford before embarking upon what had held promise of a very distinguished career in his profession. That promise had soon evaporated however, for openly profligate he had squandered his vital early years in reckless abandon. There had been a serious drinking problem, a catastrophic professional error, and an irrevocable breech of confidence. In addition to these woes, he had accumulated some crippling debts, largely aided and abetted by his several injudicious platonic adventures. There had once been a seductively attractive young woman whom he had entrusted with his confidence and love, but she had turned out to be a slick and heartless deceiver. Then there was Gwendoline, dear sweet Gwendoline. She was his cousin, on his mother's side, and they fell deeply in love. To the great delight of the family, the pair early announced their engagement, and planned their marriage. For a time it seemed that young Daniel's wanderings had ceased and his life was restored in poise and direction. That was, until that fateful holiday together in the Swiss Alps, but a month before their wedding day. The avalanche came unannounced and with devastating fury. Among its many victims was dear Gwendoline. It was surely but a poor part of Daniel Quinton which survived the disaster, for from thenceforth he never succeeded in mustering sufficient moral resolve to pull his shattered life together again. Gradually he sank into a dark mood of self-rebuke, and finally retreated Northwards to this secluded place to while away his morbid regrets past the point of no return. This was all so long ago that Daniel would often confess his doubts as to whether any of these things had in fact really happened, or were but impressions from out of his copious reading which had accidentally slipped over into the memory compartment of his brain. He would sometimes try and deflect the conversation by brushing the matter off as 'a clear case of chronic cryptamnesia'. For my own part I had no doubt whatever regarding the authenticity and consistency of his disclosures. They were sparsely worded, and unlike the enhanced editions of erstwhile insignificances so characteristic of old men's tales. They came over as vividly and sharp as on the day they were burned into his soul. The deep pain of remembrance was obvious, for he would invariably terminate his story abruptly. His speech would falter at some crucial point as he encountered trouble with his saliva. Then he would go through a routine of clacking his tongue and pouting his lips, as though trying to discharge something odious which had come up into his mouth.

Truly, I was more than fascinated by Daniel's ramblings, yet one factor has always remained a mystery to me. Why was it that this man, normally so secretive about the past and reserved in the present, should elect to confide his life story in me, who must at best have appeared to him as a pompous young upstart? Was it that the dear old man had no desire to die misunderstood, or that for some strange reason he had perceived in my youth a vague empathy with the errors of his own? At any rate, the thought provided me with a useful foil to the pride which sometimes accompanies the receipt of pastoral confidences.

It was assumed locally that Daniel possessed money. For as long as he had lived in Swarsgill, he had never found it necessary to go out to work, and had never been prone to accepting gifts or unpaid service. He had always been known to spend a great deal of time fishing, usually below the falls at nearby Bleastone Force. On the rare occasion when he made a significant catch, he would give the fish to the first person whom he met as he strolled slowly home to his cottage at the edge of the village. He had no close acquaintances, nor particular friends, but exuded an exquisite blend of benevolence and charm towards anyone who came within his immediate range, invariably promoting an impression of well-matured contentment. On some evenings he would turn up in the humble Cuddy's Lowp and treat himself to a pint of his favourite, but he always contrived to arrive near to 'time' so as not to find it necessary to linger for long.

Daniel did have money of course. There was a small income from an invested legacy, a meagre annuity from some obscure source, and the state old age pension. None of these amounted to very much, but his needs were few and his living was frugal. His life here had not been spent entirely in idleness, for there had been some attempts to break free from his bondage to self-pity. He had tried journalism once, and then writing novels. But for this amiable man with a built-in faculty for failure, both ventures had gone the way of every other endeavour. He read avidly, and kept a large and splendid selection of books. A casual perusal of the titles in the well-stocked shelves revealed that they were mainly fiction, and aroused the suspicion that they were maybe intended to provide a bright fantasy world to which Daniel could escape when something of his real world came up at him from out of the grim and distant past. And so it was, that for more years than most of the local folk could recall, Daniel Quinton had chosen to remain marooned with his morbid memories in this lonely place. Here, over the long years he had ambled aimlessly along a lone monotonous trail which had no time marks, and led to nowhere.

Now the silent pursuer had crept up on Daniel unnoticed, laying upon his weary shoulders the full weight of his eighty-three years, and for good measure had added the consummate miseries of a long lost life. His health was deteriorating rapidly, and his once steady gait became a painful shuffle. He breathed in noisy agonised wheezes and long drawn-out gasps, as though each intake of air had to be sought and won at tremendous cost. His speech, once so well refined, eloquent, and clear, was now becoming slurred and garbled. Having lost the time key, his mind was a conglomeration of confused yesterdays. Once so immaculately attired, and fastidious in the smallest detail of personal turnout, he had now become unkempt and dirty. Old Daniel was but the blurred shadow of a life far spent, and the pathetic parody of a man that might have been. The genial old gentleman was now but a disgusting recluse, seldom seen, and rarely sought out.

******

True to instinct, the little car chose a particularly desolate stretch of rough road, high up on Callanby Moor, to begin to splutter, cough, and jerk, and finally come to a shuddering halt with an ominous rattle of loose working parts. For more than an hour I struggled alone with her on that bleak and silent moor, bruising and blacking my hands, face, and character in the process.

"You blasted ramshackle old mule... you loathsome heap of scrap iron... you bl—" Mercifully the crescendo of corruption was abruptly checked by the sight of a large car, coming rapidly towards me.

"That wee thing wants kicked into Hell I tell ye. Ye meyght hae been stuck out herrrre for a whole week if I hadnae come this way. Get yerrrsel a prroper motor-carr man."

Doctor Fergus MacLoughlin was what might be termed one of the local characters, meaning, that amongst other sterling qualities, he possessed a high degree of originality. Some would describe him as the archetypal country physician. He habitually dressed in heavy tweeds, a soft deerstalker hat worn at a rakish angle, riding breeches, and highly polished light brown tall boots. His complexion was ruddy, and his manner brusque. There was a cultured coarseness about this jolly Scot, which far from causing offence, actually served to endear him to all who knew him well. When first introduced to him, I mistook him for the local Squire, or the Vet, an incident which he would often recall with magnanimous amusement.

"Let's hae a wee look now... bonnet up... both sides... now turn yon handle contraption... slowly... ever so slow... in... out... in... hold it... out. Is there a cough of any sorrrt... over-heating maybe... firrst thing in the morrning maybe... bad starrt... liverish a wee bit?"

"No, but there's plenty of movement in the bowels... loose a bit...free metal flying about somewhere deep down."

"Oh aye... keep on turrrning a wee bit more. Aye... looks like a job for the old guessing tubes... now where the Hell have I hung them... wipe the top o' this rocker cover will ye." crooned the good doctor in his best professional style, proceeding to subject the machinery to a thorough clinical check-up.

"Aye, we'll need tae have her in. I'll tow ye back to town to Jack Sisterson's place - he'll soon get her back on the road. Rope?"

"But that's in the wrong direction. How ever do I get home?"

"Och well now, we'll just tackle that problem when we come tae it won't we. Come on then, don't just stand there looking lost... in ye jump... out o' gear... handbrake off... and hang on like H—"

After a breath-taking trip reminiscent of a ride on a fairground big dipper, we arrived safely at Sisterson's place. Jack soon located the trouble spot, which of course was perfectly obvious anyway. It would take about an hour to fix it, and require a spare part provided by a scrap vehicle lying in the yard.

"Which gives me an idea," said my Good Samaritan, "One guid turrn deserrves another they say, and you Ministerrr, are just the man for the job I have in mind, the very man, indeed I'd say ye must have been laid on tae order."

"Anything to oblige... just spell it out Doctor."

"Now ye mind o' old Daniel Quinton, ye'll ken him no doubt, way over at Swarsgill... bloody god-forsaken place."

"I haven't been over in that direction for some weeks. Yes I do know old Daniel. Sad case. Is he not so well then?"

"Aye - the auld senility bug's caught up on him at last... aye and lots o' other bugs as well, in a manner of speaking. Dirty he is, filthy, crawling all over. I've got tae get him away from there man, get him somewhere else, get him in somewhere."

The doctor's habitually jovial tone did not conceal his genuine sad concern for old Daniel. He had a brand of compassion all of his own, and it rang true, like a blacksmith's anvil.

"But Doctor, even you can't just go barging into a house where a man has lived for most of his life, and, well, just turf him out."

"That's not exactly what I have in mind. Not turf him out or kick him out, or anything drastic like that. Just, shall we say, help him out. I'm prescribing a move for him, and it's pretty urgent I tell ye. What's more, I'm asking you Mr. Minister to come along with me and give such help as you're able."

"Not my province Doctor," I protested, "This is a thoroughly medical matter, you'd best leave me out of this one."

"Och I see you're thinking you're some kind o' specialist eh. My boy, before you get much older in your job you're going tae find the boundaries between health of body, mind, and soul are not as clearly defined as you'd like tae think. This one's a clear case of a soul in peril, and ye ken that as well as I do. There's sorrow, shame, fear, remorse, despair, hopelessness is there not. These are all symptoms of a sickness in the soul man."

"Sickness in the soul." The timely rebuke of the gruff country doctor immediately began to resound in my heart and mind as a divine 'call', and I was planning my parsonic ministrations accordingly. I would fashion choice words of comfort and consolation, tell the old man of that goodness and mercy which followeth us all the days of our life, extol the love which never lets us go, point him to the peace which passeth understanding, and above all instruct him that everything worketh together for good to them that love God. This charming compendium of inspired quotations just needed this one crowning touch to seal its authority and efficacy, 'We know that if the earthly house of our tabernacle be dissolved, we have a building from God, a house not made with hands, eternal in the heavens.' - Wow!

"Ye've turned very quiet I obserrrve. Thinking of something maybe. Yon wee car I bet," teased the doctor.

Yes I was thinking, but not in the way the doctor had surmised. I was revelling in delight at my rapid recall of those delectable gems of scriptural truth. I was now ready, willing, able, and keen to administer my sacred medicine to this dear old soul in distress. We were soon on our way to Swarsgill, the doctor driving his car like a lifeboat in a storm.

"The stench'll rot your lungs I'm telling ye," the doctor's voice broke in, shattering my private euphoria, "The place is filthy man... filthy... so don't you go throwing up or anything sae disgusting. And by the way, watch your woollies... wee beasties... old man must be crawling in them frae head tae foot, I'm telling ye."

"We've really got to do something quite positive to help him, haven't we," I contributed, beginning to relish the importance of my role, and actually enjoying the feeling of the term 'We'.

"Now firrrst and forrremost, listen," enjoined the doctor as we walked briskly up the narrow footpath towards the cottage door, "We've simply got tae get him out of this place, ye hear. Somewhere where he can get cleaned up a bit, and aye, given some elementary creature comfort. We're taking him to The Maples... by hook or by crook. Ye hearrd what I said?"

The low door opened with an inhospitable creak, as though the movement had caused it pain. Inside the house the light was poor, and the air was foul with the pungent odour of dirt and decayed food. Old Daniel's flare for orderliness had deserted him, and when I drew back a jaded curtain at the misty window, I let in some light upon a disgusting, reeking chaos. Daniel hardly as much as raised an eye to greet us, and yet even his dulled senses seemed to perceive that the purpose of our visit was less than benevolent.

"Now then Mr. Quinton, how arre you today? It's MacLoughlin, aye the doctor, MacLoughlin. O now ye'll ken this braw fellow here won't ye. The Minister, Teviot, aye Teviot. He's just popped in tae see ye too. Now look, I want ye tae sit very still for a minute... I'm just going to gae ye a wee prick... it'll no hurrt ye at all... and it'll make ye feel a lot better. Alright? Then we'll take ye for a trip tae yon wee hospital place at Kirton Bridge eh... just for a wee while tae get ye sorrted out a bit."

Before MacLoughlin had laid as much as a finger on him, the old man stiffened out, with every muscle, sinew, and joint locked rigid, and every inch of his skin drawn up taut as a drum. He was a very large man, and merely to sit motionless was sufficient to thwart any trespass upon his person. He made no sound, but welded himself to his big chair with an obduracy as fixed as Gibraltar. There was no practical way of getting the hypodermic needle anywhere near to his arms, for he had clasped his hands tightly together across his midriff; nor to his thighs, for his legs were locked fast around the legs of the chair. The agony staring out of his eyes was painful to behold. The good doctor continued his urgent pummelling and pulling and I fancied that he was beginning to lose hold on his self-control.

"Hell man - it'll ha'e tae be his backside come on Minister dinna just stand there man - gimme a hand and get him over will ye - right over on his side - or better still— Whoops!"

The poor old man was too slow in his reactions to counter the quick flip by which I sent him rolling over. The removal of his smelly trousers to expose a suitable area of buttock presented no problem, his fly buttons being already undone, after the habit of very old men.

My feeling of self-satisfaction and power on breaking down this ancient mountain of resistance survived for but a brief moment ere it was overtaken by a massive backlash of remorse and disgust. The sheer indignity! Like a flash of lightning the syringe appeared, and with deadly precision one-and-a-half inches of hypodermic steel found its target deep in the *gluteus maximus*. Then we got old Daniel pulled together, after a fashion, and sat him upright in his chair fortress. And still he uttered never a word, but set upon us a glassy gaze of steadfast defiance.

"There now Mr. Quinton, that should make you feel a lot better," sighed the doctor, and then aside to me, "That'll settle him a wee bit I warrrant... just a few minutes, and he'll be no trouble at all ye'll see."

I suddenly remembered that I once mistook this man for a vet, and, come to think of it, this poor old gentleman once mistook me for a minister. Only two days before, I had seen a frantic beast brought down and sedated at the mart. For another loathsome moment I suffered the awful sensation of slipping helpless and headlong into the woeful divide between heartless professionalism and elementary compassion. As predicted Daniel was soon subdued, and docile was he as we ushered him out of his cottage and into MacLoughlin's car. He occupied the whole of the back seat, where he sat silent and motionless. I was grateful for the doctor's interminable chatter, for it distracted my attention from our captive behind me.

"You're no feeling it draughty Mr. Quinton arre ye?" called out the doctor as though the rear seat was a mile back down the road. In the same instant he was turning down his front side window, and motioning for me to do likewise; for very obvious reasons.

It was about at that point when, to my utter dismay, it occurred to me that having actively participated in the whole of this regrettable episode thus far, I had not yet delivered my words of pious comfort to Daniel, as had been my earnest intention. It would be useless now however, for Daniel was in a daze. My sense of ineptitude was becoming quite unbearable. Then the doctor created a powerful diversion by priming his enormous pipe, almost igniting his copious moustache in the process, and then proceeding to belch forth obnoxious clouds of blue smoke, which must surely have originated from a compound of minerals extracted from Vesuvius and the basic ingredient of chloroform.

"Ye did a damn guid job back there laddie. Say, wherre did ye lairrn that throw?" he squeezed through a small gap at the free corner of his mouth.

And so, onward to The Maples. Perhaps I would have an opportunity in that place to catch up on my official ministrations. Once the old man had been cleaned up and settled in peace and comfort he would be more amenable to receiving the words of divine wisdom which it was yet my duty and privilege to impart. On arrival my first observation was to wonder where the place had got its name, for there was not a single Maple tree in sight, the whole place being almost surrounded by a sombre screen of pines. The building itself was not an object of high architectural merit. It had been built in Victorian times, originally as the Workhouse, and was thoroughly functional to the last rough grey stone. Times had radically changed however, social progress dictating the necessity for some change of name, status, and purpose; for which cause, some minor modifications had been carried out within the building in recent years. Nevertheless, in the minds of the aged, the old stigma remained, as indelible as the humiliating prospect of having to end their days in that place. The harsh paved floors of the entrance hall, long monotonous corridors, heavy oaken doors with ornate brass knobs, bland paintwork and high crazed ceilings induced an immediate feeling of fearful foreboding. There was the dreadful sepulchral echo from footfalls on hard floors, and garbled voices escaping from distant rooms and cavernous halls, playing chase along the labyrinth of passages, reverberating from wall to wall so that when they reached you they sounded like the long drawn out wailing of lost souls in torment.

There were various odours which seemed to move along the corridors in distinguishable wafts; carbolic, lysol, bleach, and nauseating culinary smells. Combining with them all and pervading the whole atmosphere of the place, was that vague hue of urea that is common wherever very old people are institutionalised. The day rooms were painted from top to bottom in the insipid green of thin pea soup, and had spacious floors of highly polished unstained boards. An assortment of small tables and unmatched easy chairs added a slight touch of rudimentary homeliness, and every massive cast-iron radiator was enclosed within an equally massive fireguard. The rooms were warm, somewhat short on ventilation, and oppressive. There were other large rooms, long and narrow, and more Spartan, where, backed along every wall, sat the grim grey shadows of lives that had decayed into unpublic insignificance. Expressionless eyes peered out of nothing towards nowhere. Occasionally someone would break into a spasm of contorted facial movements, or unintelligible mumblings, in a vain attempt to communicate. Others struggled up from their seats to hobble, shuffle or jerk about the room aimlessly, or swayed incongruously in large wooden chairs. A pitiful row filed past, each member staring blankly into empty space, an assembly line of ignominy being led to the next stage of their daily routine. The sight set my mind into a painful whirl. Did each of these pathetic figures represent a life which had once had a simple dignity all of its own? Did each one have a name, a unique identity, reputation, or even notoriety? Had the long road which had ended here once entailed pride, purpose, resolve, creativeness, fulfilment? When these were real lives, had they loved and been loved, married, fondled their own children? And do they still retain somewhere amongst their confusion, blissful memories of friendship, family, and the common joys and sorrows of ordinary living? Are these indeed but transient entities which must expire with the spent years, and is there nothing left but to be cast aside like empty, screwed-up, disposable cartons? 'Good God,' I felt myself praying, ' if this is the price to be paid for longevity, let me die at a ripe young age, but pray spare me from a geriatric purgatory.'

It must be said, that these were early days and a period of transition in the process of making care for the elderly infirm a major social issue. It must also be said, that the staff of The Maples were wonderful. For the most part they were not young, and few, if any, had been specifically trained for this type of nursing and care. They were however singularly blessed with special qualities of compassion, and patient endurance. They worked with a sparseness of suitable equipment, whilst funding and organisation still tended to linger within the old charitable sector.

I shuddered at the realisation that Dr. MacLoughlin and I had just committed Daniel Quinton LLB. to share with these others this final but inevitable indignity. The doctor's voice crashed in like the clang of a cracked cymbal,

"Used tae be the worrkhouse this lot. Still is ye ken, nae matter what fresh name they give the damned place, or what fancy job they expect it tae carry out. It's fixed for every generation afore ours as the workhouse, the bloody total failure at the end of every life that's had nae chance but tae fail. Time they pulled it down, with all it stands for, and started afresh. Sores like this never heal up, I tell ye."

It was now five hours since the doctor had rescued me and my stricken car on the desolate moorland road. Leaving The Maples, and walking over to the garage at the opposite end of town, I found that Sisterton had completed the repair of the car, and also drawn up a frightening bill to be paid within twenty-eight days.

"Time tha thowt o' gettin' rid o' this yan ye knaw. Gittin' ower owld it is... ower much bother te keyep it gawin'... be startin te git a bit expensive afore lang an' all. Ivrything should 'appen be tossed on t'scrap-heyap when it stairts gittin' owld leyke this ye knaw... scrap-heyap... best place for them... nae mare bother tae onybody yance they're there."

Jack's poignant words came back at me with a harsh double ring as I drove back to The Maples to see how my old friend was faring before I ventured back over the moors for home. Old Daniel was cleaned up by now, tucked snugly into a soft warm bed, and the effects of the sedative had worn off. He seemed to be fully rational again. Perhaps I could say my little piece after all, add the sacred finale to the events of this momentous day, put his mind at rest, and who knows, perhaps help to make his predicament more acceptable. With a confident and mature pastoral air I prepared to launch into my platitudes. But Daniel had other ideas, and before I could utter one word, he forestalled me.

"Ah there you are... so nice to see you, Minister."

"And so nice to see you too Mr.Quinton," I politely returned.

"I just wanted to say, that I'm somewhat surprised at you... nay disappointed in you - a man of God, and Minister of our most holy religion—"

Here his voice faltered and for a moment it seemed as though his period of rationality was alas going to be short-lived. But taking a deep laboured breath he continued,

"You young man aided and abetted that monstrous fiend who so heartlessly threw me into this place. You who called yourself my friend have become an accessory after the fact. You although but a stripling, one to whom I've often thought it well and expedient to lay bare my life, you who have oft—"

Daniel broke off in another attack of laboured breathing, but again he fought it through, braced himself, and continued in a voice which was now become high-pitched and crouped,

"You turned witness for the prosecution. You came with him, to bring me here... hunted me down... took away the only thing I had left in the world... and cherished most... my freedom to live and die as I chose. You took it away... held me down like some animal and once my physical strength was taken from me... he could take away everything else as well... as he has done... as he has do—"

Daniel then broke off physically and emotionally exhausted, and lapsed distraught into quiet bitter sobbing. A young doctor came into the room, and without a word, administered an injection.

Within three weeks, Daniel Quinton died. From *natural causes* they wrote. We buried him quietly in the little churchyard, just adjacent to the garden wall of the little cottage where he had lived out the longer portion of his tragic life. And all the mystery, and all the misery of that lonely life was interred with him. I said my little piece at last; that charming selection of scriptural quotes which I had never succeeded in delivering to him in life. We prayed, and I dropped a handful of fresh Northern soil onto the lid of his simple coffin, committing his body to the earth and his soul to the everlasting mercy of God.

Most of the village folk had gathered at the graveyard for the modest funeral, stood around reverently, and quietly walked away when it was all over. They may not have realised it at the time, but this was not merely another funeral for the little village of Swarsgill; it was the end of an era.

Doctors have their dilemmas, and Ministers of the church reap the bitter fruits of good purposes gone wrong, stumble over their mistaken judgements, or lose their way amidst the complexities of human living and dying.

And each error, each rebuke, each hurt, leaves a lifelong scar. As I strolled slowly back to my little car, I knew that the deep regrets of this day would follow me all the days of my life.

Chapter 9

IF YOU KNOW A BETTER HOLE

"We'll hev tae gaw down about fower foot or mare. That's what Jack says, or t'new boiler'll not work proper," announced the rather senior Jos Thacket to a well attended meeting of the Board of Trustees of the Lyndassby Chapel.

Although it was only September, these Northern country folk were already, by instinct, casting their minds forward towards the rigours of their native Winter. The said august body had been duly convened for the specific purpose of administering the proposed improvements to the ancient and highly inefficient heating apparatus. A small external boiler house was required to be built at one end of the main building, and as aforementioned, it was essential for its floor to be well below ground level. That unfortunately was precisely the level at which the church finances currently stood. Some of the more adventurous men of the place had therefore volunteered to carry out the necessary spadework themselves. The plan entailed the clearing of a portion of virgin ground by the North gable, and to the surprise of some, and the consternation of others, the digging out of about four hundred cubic feet of hallowed earth.

"Reyght then," went on Jos, "As ye've all agreed, we'll seyen get it dug out if there's plenty on ye turns up. So fetch your picks and spades, and owt else tha can meyeke holes wi' next Saturder morn. If we gets a good sharp stairt afore fotherin' and the leykes, we'll git it all dug out be dinner teyme."

"What abowt if it's rainin' or owt on Saturder morn?" chirped up a hesitant voice from a diminutive occupant of a back seat.

"Meyeke grownd all t'softer tae dig wiln't it. Onyweys, it's t'Lord's work so it'll not meyeke ony difference either way," boomed Jos, with a triumphant air accompanied by one of his habitual displays of stroking out his dark Stalinite moustache. Jos was big and brawny, and was remarkably agile for his seventy-six years. He had been a quarryman at the nearby granite works for most of his working life. It was rumoured in the village that he had been made redundant when the firm purchased a bulldozer. The digging out of a ten-by-ten-by-four feet hole from the lush chapel green was but a paltry prospect in Jos's reckoning.

"If I meyght be permitted tae say summat," the back seat voice a little bolder now, "but if it's alreyght wi—"

"There's fust volunteer - good owld Sidney, tha's a la'al brick," snapped up Jos, treating his moustache to an enthusiastic twist.

"If I might be permitted tae say summat," persisted the little man, now risen to his feet, "I think we should gaw about this here job in t'proper manner, wi' some soort o' formality or summat leyke."

"Hear - hear- hear-hear," came resounding agreement ubiquitously.

"And if I might be permitted tae say summat else," waxed the now irrepressible small Sidney, "I think it's only reyght an' proper for t'Minister here tae be asked—"

"Tae dig th'ole - hear-hear-hear," sounded an extremely boisterous chorus, and suddenly in my mind's eye that ten-by-ten-by-four trench assumed the proportions of a dry dock.

"Gross impropriety - couldn't countenance it," protested Miss Cecily Simms, the disgustingly robust headmistress of the local infant school, completely obliterating the sight and sound of poor Sidney as she rose to her feet. "Not at all decent I say, not at all decent. The Minister is here among us as a gentleman and pastor, and should be respected as such. What's come over us all? It's... unthinkable."

"Tha's reyght Miss Simms... Minister diggin' th'ole? Nay, it is unthinkable - it is that." The chorus of feigned disgust got a fairly long run before being blasted out by the booming voice of big Will Mattinson, his massive face suffused in deep red-hot emotion and his jugulars raising up tracks in his thick neck, "Just what I say... not deycent at all... not deycent... that's what it's not... it's not... n—" and he sank back into his seat choking with indignation.

One factor had by now firmly established itself in the meeting, and it was that the Chair had little relevance - meaning that I didn't count for very much, at this particular stage of the proceedings at any rate. I therefore resolved to restore the authority vested in me as the rightful occupier of the said Chair. Beating the table hard with my right fist, I firmly pronounced,

"Let's have some order please. After all our friends were only jesting were they not. There's no need for anybody to get all het up is there? Besides, I'm a very energetic and proficient digger actually. Anyone noticed the Manse front garden lately?"

This restored some measure of calm, giving the indomitable Sidney the opportunity to take the floor again,

"And if I might be permitted tae say summat else - that is continue leyke wi' what I was sayin' afore - Minister 'ere could be officially invited tae cut t'fust sod, or summat special leyke."

"Sidney's reyght," shouted old Ella Carrick, "This is a big occasion in t'life o' this chapel, and it wants a bit o' proper formality wi' it." This triggered off the resumption of the rowdy hubbub, and I resorted to another hefty thump on the tabletop and a near scream of, "ORDER PLEASE"

"Got a good strang arm," came the first voice to venture into the ensuing vacuum, "Reckon minister'd dig th'ole a lot sharper'n some on us awld yans. Propose we asks minister tae—"

At this point Mollie Baxter deemed that this meeting required a change of mood, and so she broke in with a clarion call for the ladies,

"We'll arrange a tea - that is, if tha puts thingabejig back a bit int'th'efternoon stead o' morning sharp on." By this splendid suggestion Mollie achieved the desired change of direction, but as to what that direction might be, was more than one dared to speculate upon.

"Of course. A tea! Let's have a tea!" arose the spontaneous rush of many voices in soprano and contralto pitch. For the next ten minutes, at least until my next impatient thump on the tabletop, the meeting belonged exclusively to the women.

From then on however, the said meeting disorganised itself into several *ad hoc* sub-committees, none of which had any use for such trivialities as the official Agenda, and all of which were totally impervious to the Chairman's thump. Neither did the men show any respect for formal administrative discipline, the snippets of conversation I was able to extricate from the general babble indicating that subjects under discussion varied from front gardens to farms, the present state of the weather (unsatisfactory of course) to current stock prices (also unsatisfactory). When this latest session had worked itself out, the timorous little man in the back row managed to squeeze in his next squeak,

"If I meyght be permitted tae say summat - leyke I was saying at t'stairt o' t'meeting, cos we didn't cum tae any proper conclusions. What about if it rains?"

"Meyght git th'ole wet," heckled one of the younger set.

"Hev tae join t'Baptists 'appen." chimed another.

"Be gittin' our owen swimmin' pool wiln't we," enthused a third.

"Nay - sheeyep dip mare leyke - mare useful onywey," concluded a big bucolic type.

As I have previously stated, my official thumps had lost all their relevance by now, and in desperation I was pondering as to how to restore some modicum of order, when above the din old Jos's voice boomed out,

"We leykes our bit o' fun, but it's gittin' layete ye knaw and we've not gittin' owt proper done yet. So let's hev a proper proposition fra sumbody."

After quick glances all round at the huge brazen-faced clock on the sidewall (the kind of unwelcome gift bequeathed by well-wishers) the meeting became a model of swift and decisive efficiency. In the space of minutes it had been firmly resolved that:

(1) Jos would organise the big dig,
(2) Bessie Marchant would be asked (as usual) to arrange a tea - price one shilling, children half-price,
(3) the minister here would be asked to start things off proper with a short service (no sermon though), and then officially start off the hole,
(4) all friends (including the vicar, if he would come) to be heartily invited, and
(5) donations would be gratefully received.

Highly satisfied, the entire Board of Trustees began to exhibit those impatient shuffling motions which signal a unanimous desire for the meeting to conclude instantly. This however, was the precise moment when the persistent little Sidney elected to have his final postponing word,

"If I meyght be permitted tae say summat. There's a gay lot tae git through there... we'll nivver git all that laid on be Saturder."

"Aye that's reyght," came the loud unchallenged approval, "Jos'll put it all back a bit... fortnight's teyme - alreyght Mr.Chairman."

"Any other business?" I intoned with an authoritative flourish, only to be met with an incredulous, if not threatening, stare from the composite face of the Board of Trustees of Lyndassby Chapel.

The Meeting closed with due correctness, at the pronouncement of the Benediction - by the Minister of course.

******

The sun came up over the hills that Saturday morning as though he was going somewhere special today. The sultriness of the late Summer months was giving way to a slight Autumnal chilling of the morning air. This was going to be the perfect day for the digging of a very special hole, ten-by-ten-by-four. The Committee responsible for the self-help project to sink this minor shaft for the foundations of the new heating chamber had already been hard at work. They had made preparations befitting an event of no less magnitude than a coronation, or a public hanging. It was obviously the intention that this excavation should be regarded in a large perspective, and must therefore be executed with due reverence and formal correctness; after all, that is what committees are for. Hard forms had been brought outside to accommodate the ladies. A harmonium was there, and a table bedecked with a deep red cloth, bearing a bible, hymnbook, and the inevitable collection plates. The vital patch of ground had been meticulously marked out with white wooden pegs and thick string, and the entire business area cordoned off with a makeshift fence of rough posts and hairy binder twine. The lush green grass had been mowed to within an inch of its life, and the oblong plot soon to be transformed into a gaping hole was immaculately trimmed, like a victim prepared for sacrifice. The publicity had doubtless been thorough, for when the afternoon came, it seemed the entire population of the valley had turned out for the great spectacular.

You won't get your suit all muckied up darling, will you?" Gina whispered plaintively into my left ear. "Only one you've got, and for the time being, quite irreplaceable you know."

"I'm only starting the job off dear... one teeny-weeny little first clod... won't even dirty my hands."

The bird-like Dora Perkins moved jerkily across the scene, took up her official position on the organ stool, and began to pedal with frantic enthusiasm in order to raise the required head of steam, or whatever propellant it was that worked these musical monsters. Next in line was her husband Matt, a big red-faced ponderous man, who had presumably been drawn in as appointed page-turner-overer. The great hulk of a man got proceedings off to an interesting start when he drew up a chair alongside the organ stool, and plonking himself indelicately upon it, drove one of the chair-legs six inches down into the soft earth. Order was eventually restored, and now enter the special guest, none less than the pompous Desmond Charles Harrington. Moving sedately into the commanding position at the table, he proceeded to render a superb performance of the hymnbook fingering routine which all habitual churchgoers recognise as the signal for "Shut up you lot, it's time we got started". This gesture brought the crowd shuffling in towards the perimeter string, and instituted the appropriate solemn hush.

It should be pointed out that Desmond had been singled out for this singular honour, not because of his reputation as a fine orator or leader of crowds, but ostensibly by reason of his 'connections'. Had not his venerated grandfather donated this very patch of fell-side land upon which the chapel was built, away back in 1873? It was maybe purely co-incidental, or of no immediate or conscious consideration, but Desmond and his family were extremely well-heeled, tradition minded, and reputedly generous when on public display; indeed a most worthy combination of admirable qualities on such an occasion as this.

"Pssaaaaaalmmmmm... a-one... a-two... a-seven... the one-'undred-and a'twenty-seventh-a-pssaaaaaalmmm... Except the Lord a-build the 'ouse, Their labour is in a-vain that a-build it." Desmond's annunciation seemed to emanate from a bottomless pit. Nevertheless the remainder of the reading was lost on me, for I irreverently mused on the idea of the good Lord getting on with the digging of this here hole for us, if only to be true to His word, and save us from labouring in vain.

"Now we'll sing an hymn second yan on them sheets tha's got in tha hands - The Church's One Foundation", Desmond hollered, for me inducing a further excursion into impious fancies. Not for very long however, for the sudden blast on the word 'Church' from the four bassoonitudinous basses positioned immediately behind me brought me painfully back to reality. The high honour of leading the prayers fell to one George Jenner, a lay preacher of many grey hairs and ancient standing. I was never completely aware of what George was fervently explaining to the Lord, or what signs and wonders he was requesting of Him, for my mind persisted in drifting away towards more mundane matters. I did know however, that the old patriarch was taking a long time over it; so much that I began to wonder whether his ramblings, as well as being out of this world, had also moved us out of the time scale. By the time we had got to the singing of 'Christ Is Our Corner Stone' I had overrun the limits of my small capacity for concentration and had lapsed into another unholy dream state.

We were now treated to an ostentatious bout of oratorial throat clearing by Desmond, the guttural ritual being intended as a necessary preliminary to what held early promise of being a word of considerable moment. The first ten minutes were occupied in informing us that he was right glad to be here in our midst, two more to say how privileged he felt, and a couple of seconds to assure us that God was here also. Our noble forefathers, and especially his own grandfather, would look down with justifiable pride on what we were about to accomplish on this grand occasion, and you cannot expect folks to have warm hearts unless you do summat to keep their feet warm, and that is why it is so important for all us churches to make sure we have 'hefficient eating happaratus'. This bolt of unexpected inspiration necessitated a brief pause for recuperation, and then he was off again. Now it was to inform us at great length, that his few words were really only the Chairman's Remarks, so he mustn't steal any more of our valuable time, he himself would be putting a pound note into the collection, he hoped we likewise would dig deep into our pockets because this cause was worth sacrificing for, the proper speaker would be on in a minute or two, and so without further ado it gave him great pleasure to introduce Mr. Wilson Kellett, whom of course "tha all knaws better than me."

"When are they going to get down to the digging darling?" murmured a weary voice into my ear.

"Not until I've broken the first sod love."

"I do wish they'd get a move on - if they talk for much longer we'll need to cut the grass again."

"Tut tut Gina dear, don't you know, *The grass withereth, and the flower fadeth, but the words of that lot up there endures for ever* - Isaiah chapter forty. Aren't I clever?"

"Enough unconscious irreverence going on already without you starting... Not so loud darling, somebody might wake up and hear it..."

"Sorry, won't do it again Ma'am. Anyway perhaps it won't be long now before we can make a start on that holy hole eh."

By this time Wilson was in full cry, waxing strong and eruditely upon the story of Noah and the building of the ark. Citing columns of complicated technical data which he had allegedly culled from the Old Testament, amply spiced with various irrelevant details from some commentary of dubious merit, and appended much of his own thereto, he proceeded to lose his bearings. He then got himself carried away in drawing erroneous parallels between the Biblical account of Nathan sinking his wine press, and his own recent digging out of a bankside silage pit at his farm up in Slidale. Occasionally we caught hints as to our main purpose in being here today among his pious references to this here holy ground upon which we're all standing. But it was only when Wilson had exhausted his considerable lung capacity, and his vast store of earthly wisdom on twenty-eight minutes of five guineas per yard oratory, that there was any positive sign that the great moment was imminent.

At long last, as though at some private signal from the Great Beyond, ex-quarryman Jos stepped forward into the arena, followed closely by a group of assorted burleys. All were wearing working clothes and bearing a variety of fearsome excavating tools - this explaining why they had concealed themselves in the shadows until this late moment. Disporting themselves inside the area within the white pegs and tatty binder twine, they awkwardly assumed pious postures as though the place whereon they now stood was holy, and for the moment, untouchable.

"I will now call upon our young sod—" Jos had to cut himself short at the shock of this gaff, and devote his full attention to a spasm of laryngeal quarrying. "Our young minister standin' here has tae pi—" he resumed, "I mean I must ask 'im... that is... I mean... onyweys, I mean this here sod's gawn tae b—" The little speech which poor Jos had so painstakingly prepared, and had stood silently rehearsing for the whole of the past hour, was totally in shreds, and so was Jos's nerve. I hurried forward to try and rescue him from his predicament, but there was no need, for mustering his considerable range of personal charm, going through his moustache stroking routine, he braced himself, and let blast,

"Aye... here's t'fella tha's all been waitin' for... Minister 'ere will 'appen stairt us off - meyeke it a big 'un Mister!"

I tried hard to match this hour, but it was not in my nature, which by now was fighting hard to ward off the uncomfortable conviction that my friends were getting this bizarre event somewhat out of proportion. I began to feel very foolish. Nevertheless, I reasoned, standing here before this expectant crowd, I must at least conduct myself with some decent semblance of propriety. I was musing thus when Jos strode up towards me and with great aplomb, thrust into my lily-white hands the biggest, brightest, sharpest pickaxe I had ever beheld. Surely this was no common or garden pickaxe, but a ceremonial implement, reserved exclusively for the cutting of sacred sods or breaking up of holy ground.

"New un this...fetched it specially fra t'quarry," Jos whispered.

There then followed a few mumbled instructions, a mock run of the correct swinging and striking postures, and I was ready for action. A deathly silence fell over the crowd, now tense with expectancy. I began to feel something like a soccer star when about to take a vital penalty kick upon which the final outcome of the match depends. Yet I swear, they were leering cynically, and that got my hackles up. Gina was the one exception, and she was bobbing up and down on her chair in excited anticipation, even though her hands were held partially over her eyes. Alright, I'd show them. Why do people generally regard parsons as a specially refined breed who although sometimes strong in the head, are invariably weak in limb, delicate in demeanour, and thoroughly ham-handed? Did this lot not know that until recently I had been an experienced tough fighting soldier, and more recently a keen University sportsman? And what about that half-acre of walled wilderness which had now become the neat, tidy, and productive Manse garden?

I therefore resolved to smite this meagre portion of God's earth with such a mighty smite as had never before been witnessed by mortal man, nor placed on record even within the annals of the Old Testament. I removed my jacket and rolled up my shirt sleeves to demonstrate to these folk that I indeed had muscles like other men, and better than most at that. Holding the fearsome pickaxe out at full stretch, I affected a measured sequence of limbering up motions, trial stances and experimental swings, then confidently braced myself for the mighty onslaught. With every available ounce of physical strength, every drop of adrenaline and incredible force of will all concentrated on those rippling muscles of shoulders, fore-arms, back and thighs.

The crowd held its breath as I brought down that flashing pick-axe with mighty momentum, then gasped as one great body,

"Aaaaaaaaaaaggggghhhhhhhh!"

To say that for the next few seconds my feet defied the laws of gravity would be the quintessence of understatement. The harsh metallic 'CLANG' reverberated throughout every fibre of my body, dislocated my brain, and set up a violent vibration which threatened to tear all my limbs and joints apart. For a timeless period I stood transfixed and detached, clutching frantically at the only object of tangible reality left to me, that shining implement of destruction. My tough accomplices had gathered about the spot, and were gazing with dismay at the minor graze which my colossal stroke had inflicted upon the soft green turf; small, but sufficient to expose a portion of solid, reddish rock underneath. I had in fact struck the summit of a submerged granite mountain.

The great occasion thus ended in farce, but not without a final hymn. I cannot comment upon the appropriateness of that hymn, for I didn't hear it. Then came the collection, gratefully received. Finally, I think, there was the Benediction, but on this occasion not according to the unbending custom, pronounced by our young minister here. He was temporarily unavailable, having been transformed into a pillar of abject misery, a shattered wreck, totally disorientated, standing rigid, gaping vacantly into space. Next to his left foot was a raised sliver of turf with a small exposed portion of clean rock showing through a shallow depth of soil. Gina had come close to me and was frantically endeavouring to help me find where my soul had flown off to on the dreadful impact.

Incidentally, the hole, ten-by-ten-by-four, which was to have been dug on that fateful afternoon, was finally completed after three weeks of hard rock hand quarrying (couldn't use dynamite - ower close tae t'chapel wall), by Jos and his brawny stalwarts. But one thing cannot be denied - I started off the process, didn't I.

I seem to remember that somewhere in the Good Book, there is a story about a man who chose to dig the foundation of his new house in the sand. And it is written that he was a very foolish man.

Chapter 10

LET EVERYTHING THAT HATH BREATH

Claversford was a small market town, strategically situated at a point where three valleys converged and the River Lyndass was met by two young tributaries. It was the focal point of all life for miles around, and the single reference mark for everything of consequence. Although its population numbered no more than about three thousand souls, the little town was endowed with all the services and facilities concomitant with its status. There was the weekly market day, stock mart, a variety of shops, including the Co-op, a garage and engineering works, a county grammar school, a cottage hospital, a medieval parish church, a magistrates court, and the area police headquarters. There was also a large chapel, prominently poised in the main square.

"Tha'll hev a grand teyme at t'big chapel 'appen." This assurance had been reiterated to me by several of my humbler village church officials, commenting upon the fact that on the next Sunday in line I was scheduled to make the first of my three-monthly appearances at the mighty basilica.

The journey to Claversford on that day was markedly unpleasant. A combination of overcast sky, cold wind, erratic ignition, indigestion, and an overall feeling of apprehension produced the kind of headache which would adversely temper my reactions to all that befell me during the next twelve hours. The big chapel was a monumental monstrosity, fronted by a bold facade of red brick and terracotta which inflicted a rude shock on the aesthetic senses. Similarly the interior, an over-ornate, over-indulgent, over-bearing Victorian temple to the gods of cast iron, pitch pine, and heavy varnish. The massive arena was laid out in wide sweeps, curves and angles, with an oppressive symmetry which created the illusion of length, breadth, and height being equal, reminiscent of the dimensions of the New Jerusalem of the Apocalypse. Each of the four walls bore a spacious slanting gallery, supported upon florid iron pillars in the aisles. The largest of the galleries was at the business end, the front. This was occupied in obtrusive descending layers by the great organ (a grandiose array of monolithic plumbing), the choir stalls in curved stepped rows reminding one of firing butts, and two out-size hymn number boards which would have done good service at Lords. Prominently positioned up at centre front, slightly below the level of the gallery rail, was the almighty pulpit, a grotesque mass of cunningly crafted timber, tassels, and red velvet, which seemed to have been originally designed with heavyweight corybantics in mind. This lofty edifice was elevated on six short pillars which from certain aspects gave it an appearance like an oil rig or an unassailable estuary fort. The mere sight of the thing evoked a strong feeling that whatever issued from there, it would come forth with fearsome heat or considerable velocity. The building was so appointed, that none of the large congregation which gathered together in questionable comfort within its portals, could ever be beyond the range of that frontal sound source. The emphasis was ostensibly upon audio excess rather than visual splendour, for although the place was an offence to all aesthetic sensitivity the acoustics were superb.

Which brings us up to the start of the morning service in question, or more precisely the local *modus voce*. The primary premise seemed to be that volume was the true measure of sincerity, and that in the pursuit of worship ardour had something to do with vibration. Such fine virtues as tonal quality had, like other familiar axioms of formal devotion, gone by the board, the criterion for a successful service being 'a good sing'.

In all of this the congregation was amply aided and abetted by a large choir stacked immediately behind me at ear level. This was indeed a Jubilate Deo choir. Whatever may have been lacking in musical exactness was well compensated for in the fervour of its jubilate-ing. It seemed to be generally assumed that the divine object of their adulation dwelt in a 'happy land far far away', or else was handicapped by some severe aural deficiency. The enthusiasm for song was boundless, each rank of singers earnestly holding its line as if in combat to the death against the other three, and gobbling up the staff notation as though it was a machine-gun ammunition belt. Although void of any of the finer nuances, expression did vary somewhat at times, but only as affecting the extreme ends of the sound spectrum, so that *ff*s and *pp*s jolted your tympanums with painful alternation. This was a choir of very earnest soloists, with forty or fifty voices each determined to do its individual utmost. This phenomenon became fearfully apparent during the great highlight of the service, the rendering of the Anthem.

A combination of fate and my holy calling decreed that I would be seated in the direct line of fire and was thus compelled to endure at close range a performance of 'O Lord How Manifold Are Thy Works' which the choir, with its own idiosyncratic harmonic progressions (and digressions) and clashing dissonances, took seventeen-and-a-half minutes of sheer torture to demolish. The dominants were laid down by a battery of strident sopranos shrieking in joyous abandon. In closest proximity with my ears was the *solo voce* of three elderly maidens, the Docherty sisters, who screamed intermittent cadences at me without mercy. They produced a weird triple tone from their combined larynxes which penetrated where no other sound could reach. The high pitched whine, I think, was contributed by the thin one to my left and was mildly tolerable until she approached her peak register which was an F Sharp that sounded like a nasty compromise with E Flat. The middle sister enriched the tone with a shrill metallic timbre, punctuated on consonants with clearly audible 'clacks' from the epiglottis. Then the total tonal value was richly enhanced by the warbling *vibrato* of the long lean sister to my right, as the rhythmic quivering of her sinewy neck muscles testified. The Contraltos, all generously proportioned matrons, bellowed and bayed their line, their frequent inaccuracies lost in a long-range *tremolo*. Mercifully for me, the Basses, ten good men and true, were strategically positioned up on the back row to my right. Most notable among them was a ballistic baritone with a rifle-barrelled thorax, who habitually varied the fuchsia pink hue of his face in accordance with the value of a sustain in the lower base clef. Six perpetually breathless brethren occupied the upper echelons of the Tenor rank, executing incredible facial contortions whenever their allotted score ventured above the level of Middle C, and gargling in tortuously gasped cadences each time the sounds of 'Ay', 'Arr', 'Ee', or 'Oo' were called for. For musical genius however, none could match the plump, bald-headed, short-legged organist up there on his mighty throne. This agile performer obviously had no intention of having himself upstaged, nor of allowing the grand sound which poured forth from his assortment of multi-barrelled ordnance to be swamped by the *multi-vox humana* to his rear. In the rendering of the Anthem he displayed an astonishing technique, by playing the accompaniment with his right hand and his feet whilst simultaneously conducting the choir with his raised left hand. The resulting jerky sweeps of the arm in sequence with some acrobatic gluteal convolutions gave an appearance of the Highland Fling viewed from behind. Bad planning here, for such was the geography of the place that the organist and choir were permanently juxtapositioned back-to-back.

True to promise, that morning service was an unforgettable affair, with the choir in full cry, the great organ up to full pressure, the congregation eager and expectant, and deafening decibels rampaging all over the place. I had nevertheless begun to feel small and irrelevant, and oppressed by a feeling of the utter passivity of my role. But now, at last, it came up to time for the Sermon; the show was all mine! Unfortunately the Anthem, coming immediately before, had not only tangled up my aural mechanism, but also left me befuddled, and drained of any capacity for coherent thought. To make matters worse, in my confusion I had closed one of the large books on the desk upon my sermon notes, but which book I could not tell. The place grew silent, with an eerie silence like that which falls at the abrupt ending of a storm; the congregation was waiting. This would have to be a time for freewheeling. That sermon had been meticulously prepared, over many hard hours of painful sweat. It was intended to be an epic, appropriate to so august an occasion.

It fell flat at the utterance of the first few syllables, chiefly I supposed because the faces of the congregation had fixed on me with cold, stark, unsmiling stares. But heroic to the last I blundered on regardless of response, or lack of it, also of either my wristwatch, or the big barefaced wooden clock with the frantic tick, which was also staring straight at me from the rear balcony. By some lucky chance rather than conscious design, and incidentally in accordance with instruction emphatically given to me beforehand, I got to the Benediction on the stroke of twelve, ostensibly heard by all, from the distant Parish Church chimes.

I had hardly completed the last syllable of the final 'Amen' when the great organ erupted into a shattering Toccata which, I had no doubt, was the chief cause of the congregation's precipitous exit. I was unable to complete my obligatory solo procession down the aisle towards the main door, the said aisle being crammed with the departing faithful, and I was thus obliged to linger at the bottom and endure the organist's *multi-fortissimo* alone. Presently I was apprehended by a 'tweedy' gentleman of great bulk, carrying a very large hymnbook under one arm and having a minuscule wife clinging dutifully to the other.

"Alstonbeck's t'name, John Henry Alstonbeck. Tha's feedin' with us today if ye please. And this is t'wife, Mrs. Alstonbeck."

"Aye - hev a grand dinner ready for tha soon as we gets up to th'ouse," piped the small woman, the disproportionate resonance of her voice revealing beyond all doubt her membership of the choir, as did the big red book protruding from her handbag. Yet somehow that voice did not seem to belong, for the general demeanour betokened a rare blend of rectitude, fortitude and servitude.

"Prompt half-past we feeds, so we'll hev tae put a move on," the big man heartily enjoined, his raucous manner betraying the fact that to him at any rate, Sunday dinner was an institution to be pursued with the same enthusiasm as the recent morning service. Now among the intelligence with which some of my rural church officials had primed me in anticipation of this first 'big chapel' ordeal, was a reference to a feature explicitly described as 'good fothering'. In more refined terms this indicated that the good folk of Claversford had earned a wide reputation for their excellent cuisine. I consequently pondered over several misgivings as we walked briskly towards the Alstonbeck residence, not least as to what kind of 'grand dinner' or 'good fothering' could be prepared within the fifteen minutes yet left to us before the statutory 'prompt half-past'. I knew that my hosts did not have a cook, housemaid, or any other form of domestic assistance. I had also been emphatically informed as to their strict rule of Sabbath observance, and especially their ban upon any unnecessary work on that holy day. And this was many years before the invention of such instant culinary gadgetry as the microwave oven. I was soon to learn however that the Lord alone was their Helper, to Whom they faithfully entrusted all things great and small. The only culinary assistance which the good Lord seemed to warrant was that of the shaggy old mongrel dog that was sitting close-up facing an enormous open fire. As we entered the room, this sombre creature remained indifferent and transfixed, neither turning to greet its master nor rushing out to threaten me. And there it remained totally immobile, like the work of a taxidermist, until Mrs. Alstonbeck had stooped down to its level and cut a generous slice from the luxurious joint of roast beef which was precariously poised on the brass fender before the fire, not six inches from the animal's nose end.

"Owld Gyp alweys bides there and waits for 'is reward for watchin' ower t'meat whilst we're at Chapel... there's a good boy... good boy... who's mother's good boy then... there you are."

As for the much anticipated feast, the array of simmering cooking vessels visible through the open kitchen door indicated that all was well, having been safely kept under divine/canine supervision during the family's devout absence.

"T'good Lord nivver lets us down with t'dinner, does He missus," enthused the master of ceremonies, his eyes turned heavenward, and a pious tremor in his voice.

There was soon laid before us a sumptuous spread of such luxury and proportions that the very sight of it caused my gastrochemistry to suddenly switch on to 'supercharge' and treated my abdominal machinery to a severe jolt. But first, "Grace", called my host, rising with ponderous formality to his feet from his highly polished, leather clad carver chair at the head of the long table. Most 'graces' are brief, to the point, familiar, and even perfunctory. Mr. Alstonbeck's was none of these things. He was carried away in an ecstasy of solemn gratitude to the good Lord who had so graciously, generously, wondrously, and undeservedly provided this great abundance - and his great appetite, which he referred to as 'humble appreciation'. The rambling prayer took us on excursions to many interesting places, eschewed many noble causes, and occasionally made mention of food in general, but often more specifically to this here repast now spread before us. There was a fleeting mention of the labours of his good and faithful wife, thy loyal servant here with us today to share in thy generosity, that unknown quantity the hungry, our sins and short comings, some ardent thanksgiving for the grand service we had this morning, and again for this splendid repast. Eventually the great peroration came to an end - hunger or exhaustion I think. Meanwhile I still found myself doing battle with impious thoughts, and a rumbling tummy, and the unholy notion that whilst Alstonbeck's spiritual temperature had been gradually rising, the food was getting cold. With much encouragement from my hosts I ate far too much, purely to show my appreciation of course, and laid the formidable foundations for an uncomfortable afternoon.

After the meal, and the customary coffee, I rose from the table with necessary caution, for fear of precipitating a less than silent ballast shift in my overloaded stomach. I was instantly invited to a large plush chair on one side of the fireplace where I immediately sought to condition myself for the afternoon of small talk which traditionally attends the entertainment of the visiting Minister. When Mr. Alstonbeck crunched himself down into the opposite large chair, and painstakingly ignited a flamboyant pipe, I suspected that my vociferous friend was bracing himself for the task. Meanwhile the good wife had made a rapid clearance of the table, and merged into a mountain of dirty dishes in the kitchen, quietly closing the door behind her. Expanding to his full latitude and longitude, and sending up a dense blue cloud of spent St. Bruno, the man made a surprising pronouncement.

"Now we all knaws that you gentlemen likes some quiet on a Suntha afternoon, tae collect your thoughts and inspirations and the like together afore th'evening service. So, as not tae disturb or hinterrupt ye or owt, t'wife and me'll gaw and keep nice an' quiet. Onyweys, we's gawn' tae be a bit busy oursel's for an hour or so, if tha doesn't mind or owt. So, if ye'll just excuse us, we'll just leave ye on your own for a la'al while... we've got just the place for tha."

Before I could fashion a suitable response I was ushered into the lush parlour, where I was set down in a cosy arm-chair before a homely fire, and left to my own devices. Not being very adept in the management of solitude, and notwithstanding my abdominal embarrassments, I would have much preferred some genial company, or even a long walk.

I had spent some time perusing the bulging bookshelves, examining pictures and wall-hangings, boring myself stiff with the contents of yesterday's local newspaper, gazing into the fire, out of the window, or into empty space, repudiating the entire content of the Christian Herald and pacing the floor aimlessly, when I perceived that the house had become strangely quiet. Not entirely however, for filtering through the portals there came to my ear the sound of distant snoring - in three distinct and inharmonious tones. I traced it to the two plush chairs before the dining-room fire.

I slipped silently out of the house, and took that long walk.

Chapter 11

THOSE ENDEARING YOUNG CHARMS

I had no difficulty in persuading myself that there was legitimate cause for my having made the unnecessary detour on my journey to Gilton. Call it a fortuitous accident. I would just happen to be passing by Brent Lea Farm. And after all, was not practical pastoral concern the raison d'être for every journey I undertook, every call I made, and every encounter, even when simply chanced upon - or contrived? Nat Browell lived at Brent Lea, and he was neither amenable to, nor consciously in need of any of my sacred solicitations. But his daughter Mabel, the charming sugarplum organist of my Fellsyke chapel, was invariably welcoming, hospitable, and warmly responsive. The said Nat paused briefly to regard me as I let myself through the iron gate into the spacious cobbled farmyard. Without so much as setting down the bucket which he was carrying, or making the slightest hint of a smile, he motioned vaguely with his free hand in the direction of the house,

"T'lass's in t'kitchen yonder if tha's wantin' her".

Now why ever did Nat presume it was the lass I had called to see? Heaven knows, he probably had sufficient spiritual need of his own to warrant the attention of a pastor. The lass soon appeared in the open doorway, radiant, and beckoning enthusiastically. As I approached, she smiled a pair of dimples into her cheeks, her face as inviting as a sun-kissed apple still on the tree.

"Gay nice to see tha... now just cum theesel' inside... reyght time an' all... just this minute put kettle on... musta knawn you were cumin' by this way somehow."

The room reflected the character of its keeper, neat, immaculate, proportionate to the finest detail. Every item of furniture, every picture on the wall, and each ornament and nick-nack, seemed to occupy a position which had been specifically created for it. This was especially true of the American reed organ, a monolithic specimen in mahogany, to which pride of place had been given at the centre of the best wall. On the music desk there was a well-worn hymnbook with tunes, and another volume bearing an ornate title, 'Six Short and Easy Pieces For The Harmonium'.

Either Nat's ears were finely tuned to the sound of rattling teacups or, true to universal clerical tradition, my chance visit had coincided with the regular afternoon tea break, for it was not long before he came in and joined us. Nat was a scrawny little man who seemed to be sheltering underneath his outsize cloth cap, which he was very loath to remove. He was disorganised down to the last detail, and his work clothes hung about him so loosely as to cause one to wonder whether there was anybody inside them. As he stood there alongside his elegant daughter, I strove hard to perish the mischievous notion which Charlie Crispen, Nat's gloomy cowman, not being well-versed in the subtleties of our language, put to me rather succinctly as,

"Naebody knaws hoo that yan faathered that yan."

Whether of animals or men, breeding and bloodstock were always matters for conjecture in these fair parts. Ah well, mother must have been a noble woman! Nat was a taciturn man, using his voice so sparingly that it sounded like the rustle among dry leaves in a mild breeze. He mainly conversed by means of a system of exaggerated nods and wags of the head, punctuated by drawn-out gasps of "Airrrrgh" or "Appen." His most audible sound was generated in the act of drawing long draughts of hot tea from his enormous mug, pausing at intervals to utter ostentatious sighs of concurrence with whatever conversation was taking place at the time. Each colossal intake of an equal mix of fluid and air-bubbles produced a sound like a minor volcanic eruption in reverse, and each was followed in turn by a great exhalation of excruciating satisfaction. Meanwhile I was doing my dainty best with the super-fine bone china piece poised perilously between the forefinger and thumb of my right hand.

"Keyak?" came Nat's voice from out of nowhere, as he indelicately thrust a plate of dainties in my direction, "My Mabel meyakes'm hersel' ye knaw... dab hand at keyakes my Mabel."

"Your daughter is obviously a first-class cook Mr. Browell."

"Aye - airrgh - aye. Gat it fra t'mother."

"Feeds you up well I bet. You're a very lucky man."

"Aye - nap hand at t'fotherin-up... aye... aye... aye." Now a long bubbly pull at his tea, which was obviously reaching near bottom.

Mabel was peeping coyly over the brim of her teacup, blushing a little and seemingly embarrassed at her father's inability to sustain conversation - among other things. Now and again she would flex her shapely eyebrows, or nervously twitch the corner of her mouth. The pause for refreshment ended as abruptly as it had begun, as Nat, pushing a large and final morsel of fruit cake into his already full mouth, and swilling it with a noisy quaff of hot tea from his recently re-charged mug, prepared to take his leave and continue with whatever urgent task had been interrupted by this hurried tea break. As he reached the door, still clutching his mug of tea, he noticed that I was looking out of the window close beside me.

"That's t'Smailes place tha can see ower t'fields yonder. Nae doubt tha'll be wantin' tae call up there when tha's this far?"

"I did have it in mind - yes."

"Lang way round be t'road mind ye... nae proper brig nor nowt... but tha can walk ower t'fields if tha leykes, and 'appen lowp ower t'beck in t'bottom."

"Might get lost. Is there a path or anything, and well marked?" said I, confirming Nat's distrust of the clergy's sense of direction.

"Lass'll gaw part o' t'way witha if tha leykes, maybees keep tha on t'streight an' narra. She can shut up t'stock in t'bottom pasture whilst she's abowt it - save me a lang walk later."

That seemed like a very pleasant prospect, and I readily agreed. The afternoon air was still and whispered a solemn symphony of silence, only broken at rare intervals by a few bars of a blackbird solo, or the melodic call of a passing curlew. Speech deserted my companion and me as together we trod the soft grassy footpath. The very air we breathed was richly spiced with the heady scents of early Autumn. Then, with no warning other than a brief nervous cough, Mabel broke into a spate of compulsive chatter. Yes, she missed her mother, and her acute sense of loss had never abated throughout the twelve years since her tragic and untimely death. No, she didn't have any boy friends, of course. She had to look after her father, and help with the farm, had she not.

"Onyweys, who'd want owt tae do wi' a big soft lump leykes o' me? Hev tae be blind or stupid or summat wouldn't he."

My eagerness to kindly remonstrate brought forth an ill-conceived suggestion to the effect that, if one is really nice, as she undoubtedly was, then the more there is of one the better. A foolish and misplaced compliment admittedly, but it nevertheless drew from Mabel a delightful response. She tilted her head to the side and thought for a while, then pouted her lips into a rich red rose bud, before breaking into an alluring wide-angled smile. This fascinating sequence of expressions was one of Mabel's typical feints, but came over without any hint of mischief in it. There had of course been a boy once, she confessed ruefully.

"Cedric tha called him...Cedric," and as she softly uttered his name a gentle quiver came into her breathing.

Cedric was only a farm lad, unaccustomed to anything beyond the hard working life of the fields and fells. But he had had a mind for adventure, always longing to do things and go places. The war brought him his one chance to make a break. He did not need to join the Forces of course, for as a farmer his was a reserved occupation. With all his heart Cedric had wanted to fly, and he constantly imagined himself tearing apart the sky with his Spitfire.

"Joined t'Royal Air Force he did, and he looked reyght smart in his eweniform, that he did. He was airscrew or summat o' the sort. Said his job was a tail-end-

Charlie or summat daft like that. Nivver bothered tae ask him what that was... onyweys I think he was just havin' me on a bit. Used tae tell me alsoorts o' daft things."

Cedric had never made the suggestion outright, nor in so many words, but Mabel had suspected that if he'd had the nerve to say so, or if she had been able to muster the courage to ask, he wanted to marry her. There was just something which seemed to hold them back from so much as a mention of the matter. People who lived deep in the country were sometimes not very articulate in the actual words of love, and would seem loath to own the emotion. In the case of Cedric and Mabel, there were also other impediments. Mabel's mother had died when the girl was but twelve years old, since when, like so many country girls in similar circumstances, she had been her father's sole companion, housekeeper, cook, and spare farm labourer. A more serious obstacle was Cedric's parents. His mother was not only extremely possessive, but overtly jealous of the Browel girl's affections. The father was arrogant and self-willed, especially in his dealings with his son and heir. He had a reputation for reacting violently towards any questioning of his prejudices. Furthermore, it would seem that there was, in the annals of the Browels and the Keltons, a history of an ancient feud concerning a boundary fence. An irrational tradition of mutual antagonism had persisted in the bloodstream of all succeeding generations to this day, as though it had been passed down the genetic chain.

"It wasn't really all that serious you knaw... Cedric and me I mean... just - well - we nivver got round to talking abowt things like gettin' married or owt leyke that." Mabel's voice atrophied as she uttered these words.

We strolled almost reverently, without speech, for the entire length of the meadow which sloped downward towards the copse of trees at the bottom. Simultaneously a glistening bend in the stream broke into view, there came the merry sound of running water, and the gentle rustle of leaves on an over-hanging elm. Mabel sighed.

"Lost him," the girl tried to slip that one in unnoticed, and glancing momentarily at her clear sensitive face I could see that the effort had affected her deeply. A further spell of awkward speechlessness, which I tried to dispel, rather brashly I'm afraid.

"Nearly got knocked off myself a time or two you know. Was a bit luckier than some I suppose - at least - I mean - I'm still around aren't I - what I mean is - well don't misunderstand - I mean - well you know how it goes - it's sort of fa... "

I ought not to have said that, and it's no wonder that it nearly choked me. Indeed I was not fully aware of saying it at all, not those actual words anyway, but I had been caught on the wrong foot and simply panicked. I saw my companion wince with pain, and for some tense moments she regarded me with a waxen gaze. The crisis soon passed over however, and a controlled smile on Mabel's face told me that all was well. Yet there was mystery in that smile, something which held me in a reciprocal eye-to-eye encounter until a mutual throat-clearing broke the spell. We moved on slowly, and eventually reached the sturdy wooden gate at the field bottom. For some inexplicable reason our two hands arrived co-incidentally upon the demonic device which substituted for a latch. It was in fact but a strong wire loop between gate and post, uncomplicated except that it was designed to resist any effort to undo it. The normal and accepted procedure in such a predicament was to lift up the heavy gate a few inches. This would of necessity have to be a joint effort. For some further inexplicable reason, this got us no further than leaning over the top bar of the gate, ostensibly pondering over the crystal clear water of the passing stream. Mabel's large brown eyes had acquired that dreamy expression again, and they fixed on me like liquid passion. I suspected that there were tears in them.

"I always feels a bit queer when I cum down to this here gate, don't know why, just—" and there was now croupiness in her voice.

"Why Mabel? You can tell me. In fact you can tell me anything."

"Don't knaw really... doesn't matter... daft a bit I suppose... plain daft... soft a bit... silly owld me. What do you think abowt me? How do you feel about this silly lass? Honestly."

My initial response to this was to feel a great deal confused. Then there came an upsurge of profound pity, and my very soul began to tug at its moorings. There was worse to come, for I drifted away into one of those terrible lapses which occur when my emotions become over-loaded. By a curious trick of the subconscious mind, certain circumstances are apt to induce painful memories of filed away wartime experiences. They can be so vivid that I feel myself losing touch with present reality. All the creeping fear, cold sweat, tortured faces, agonised screams come up to torment me in one horrible timeless moment; only a flash, a fleeting second, a hellish dream. But the seconds of a dream can present as a lifetime.

"Are you alreyght mister? You were starin' summat awful - leyke at nowt - blank leyke - and I think your face is all pale."

"I'm alright... OK... nothing wrong... just thinking I suppose."

"Not embarrassed or nowt are ye, or cross or owt?"

The dear girl was still there, leaning as I was over the top of the gate. Her eyes were moist and searching, and her voice now turned husky, methought pleading. I made no reply, for it was becoming patently obvious to me that my emotions were capable of out-running my words. The only external sound now was the persistent bird song, and the beguiling undertone of water tumbling over stones. The loss of the urge to talk was painful to endure. In a bid to break the lull I lunged forward slightly as if to push open the gate. It did not yield, and neither did Mabel's cool hand still resting gently atop of mine, on the upper rail.

"Used to cum down here with Cedric quite a lot, to this very spot. Lived up yonder at what's now Smails's place," said Mabel, her voice now diminished to a low whisper.

"Neighbours?"

"In a way, yes, that's all really. Used tae cum this far ower fields with 'im, or see 'im when I came down tae fasten stock up. We used tae stop here for a la'al while aside this here gate afore he went up home leyke. We used tae sumtimes lean on here just leyke this and - you know - just talk - and things."

This intimate recollection brought a small blush into her pretty cheeks. Then after a little trouble with a surfeit of saliva, she swallowed hard, forced a flashing smile, and continued. breathlessly,

"Used to alweys gi' me a kiss here."

"That must have been very nice I'm sure," I said, albeit blandly.

"Really think so?" she tittered girlishly, and went on at length, "Last time he came hoame, special leave of sum soort he said, just same as usual, we cums down here and walked around a la'al bit, slow like, and talked and that - ye knaw - then after a bit he looked at his watch and said it was time he gat away up hoame. Afore that we stood leaning ower t'gate for a bit, just like you an me's doing now, and just soort o' starin' at yan another, like this. Then he gives me kiss as usual, looks at me hard for a bit, then pushes gate oppen, gaws through, teks yan lowp ower t'beck there, and runs all the way up t'field ont'other side. When he gets to top he turns round, stood there for a bit, and waves... That was t'last ti—"

The pain of sweet remembrance cut her short, and try as she would, no more words would come. She stood there motionless, majestic in her grief. Concentrating all the power of those tender eyes upon mine she extracted from me a greater wealth of sympathy than I realised I possessed. There followed inevitably another interlude of silence. For my own part I felt it expedient that this delicate moment should be allowed to pass without any promptings from without. A little breeze had stirred, which brought down a few locks of her rich brown hair over her forehead. Deftly brushing them aside with her forefinger, almost provocatively, she smiled nervously, and although having some apparent difficulty with her breathing, she tried to reinstate conversation.

"You telt me I could tell you owt I liked, or summat leyke that didn't ye."

"Yes that's right, I believe I did Mabel, and of course I meant it, quite seriously."

"Well you see... what I was wonderin'... stupid I knaw... but sumhow I think ye'll understand... hope so onywey." Mabel's voice had become soft and languid, her eyes sultry as a late Summer sunset, and her rose red lips were trembling slightly. "Well... what I mean... well you see... I can only have memories and pretends now can't I... and that's about all... if ye understand... what I really mean... if say—"

I confess I was not accustomed to dizzy moments such as this and as yet not quite sure how to handle them without hurt. Mind you I already knew about the vulnerability of young parsons to scheming or pathetic young maidens, and *vice versa*, but I admit this situation was getting me somewhat befuddled. Then Mabel suddenly blurted out,

"O dear, O dear, whatever's gittin' into me? What am I feelin'? What am I saying? I want you tae gi' me a kiss - just for me feelings and old times sake or summat. O dear, O dear - you must be thinkin' that I've gone potty or summat - or I'm just a wicked cow mare leykely. Honestly I just din't knaw what's cum ower me - please please understand - and forget all abowt it will tha?"

When I looked across at her, I saw that she was trembling - and very beautiful. 'Take yourself in hand brother,' I said deep down within myself, 'Pity can beguile.

Sympathy at this level can beget indiscretion. You are yet young. So is she, and lovely. Her problems cannot be solved by creating problems of your own. For many years to come brother, you will be called upon to assist sad and vulnerable people and to help them sort out their run-away fancies. So don't get carried away by your own.' All of this flashed through my mind in a panic split second, silently, yet with such powerful potency that the monition must have communicated itself to Mabel. She blushed the most glorious twilight I have ever beheld. There ensued yet another of those stark staring silences; very hard on a young parson not yet inured to exposure to such a heady mixture of volatile emotions. Bracing myself and resuming control of my air intake, I said quietly,

"Guess I've got to be getting along now Mabel, got to see my flock you know. And you've still got some stock to fasten up in the bottom pasture - remember?"

With calm and gentle deliberation I moved her cool hand from off the top of mine which rested on the rail. I opened the gate a fraction, squeezed through, and walked with a feigned air of cool composure down to the edge of the stream. I surprised myself by clearing the eight feet width in one clean bound, and then I sprinted all the way up the hill on the other side. On reaching the top I turned about and looked back. Mabel was still down there, standing motionless by the gate, holding it ajar, just as she was when I came through. I waved, turned away, and left her to mourn her Cedric - alone.

Mrs. Smailes and two amorous cats were the only members of the hill top family at home when I called. The lady was plump, jolly, and frank to within a hair's-breadth of indiscretion.

"Me men's all out at sheep just now, so if tha's wantin' tae see ony o' them tha'll hev tae gaw out and find them - 'appen tha might gi' them a hand."

'That would be fine," I replied with certain unrevealed reservations, "Which way do I go?"

"Tha'd nivver catch up on them... be right ower t'fell be now. Onyweys, that's not what tha's cummed for is it? You ministers... all alike...Tha'll be wantin' tha cup o' tea willn't tha?"

"No thanks - not at all - just recently had a cuppa and some cake down at Brent Lea. Came over here on foot you know... left the car, walked over the fields and jumped over the beck."

"Hope tha kept be th'edge o' Nat's bottom meadda yonder - grass's ready for t'second cut - gittin' a bit ower lang. A bit touchy ower that meadda is Nat. Touchy abowt meyest things if tha asks me."

"He never mentioned actually, although it was his suggestion that I leave the car at his place and walk over to your place."

"Really! Well tha' wouldn't make much o' Nat I suppose. Nice bit lass he's got. Poor thing - not much of a life for her, is it?"

"Young Mabel, yes she is, isn't she - lovely girl."

"Teks after t'mother. Poor Annie... that young she was, and that lass just a bit bairn at time."

"You knew Mrs. Browell then?"

"All me life. Went to scheyel together. Grand lass - iverybody's favorite, and sae kind and lovable. Good singer an' all and played piano well. Used to sing a bit in t'pubs afore she gat on wi' Nat, then she went ower to t'chapel. Bonnie lass an' all and always well turned-out. Died quite suddenly she did. Nat's not got much abowt 'im, but he took it hard - nivver really gat ower it. But all this was afore we moved back into these parts."

"You haven't been here long?"

"Nay, only a couple o' years. Came in after Mr. Kelton died with a heart attack. T'wife seyen sold up and moved in with sister up North. They reckon she nivver gat ower that lad o' theirs - Cecil or summat they called him."

"Cedric you mean?"

"Aha! tha's heard abowt him then?"

"Vaguely. So sad and tragic for him poor chap, and thousands like him."

"We can well dae without ony o' his soort around here I'm telling tha. Dark horse that yan - should be drowned at birth that soort."

"Mrs. Smailes. I'm afraid I don't quite understand - you're surely being a little unkind - outrageous actually - and well, it's just not on is it - not like you at all."

"Well if tha thinks that, then all I can say is that tha obviously doesn't knaw much about that youth. Bad lot reight fra t'stairt that yan I tells tha streight."

"I'm so sorry you think that, and sorry you've said it. But now he's gone - tragically - and in a great and noble cause at that don't you thi—"

"Tragic is it? Plenty tragic for other foalkes I'd say. Alweys looked after number one that yan. Like that fra being a kid he was - number one every time. But hey Mister, I think tha's pickin' me up wrang, tha musta gittin howld o' t'wrang end o' t'stick as far as this Cedric youth's concerned."

"I'm afraid I don't understand, Mrs Smailes."

"I thowt not. Naebody must hev mentioned it to ye, mebees not to your wife neither. So listen - in strict confidence mind ye," and here the mouth was screwed up to within half an inch of one corner, and she went over onto *sotto voce*, "You see meyest folks say he was t'father o' that babby o' hers."

"Baby? Of whose?"

"Well Nat's lass yonder - didn't tha knaw? All cleared up be now, went hush very sharp - a lot sharper than most things in these parts. But it was a reight mess at the time. They say Nat was goin' rownd at nights wi' a shotgun looking for sum youth tae blame, and he gat in a reight stew wi' hissel', and ivrybody else as well. In a way it's a blessing poor Annie nivver lived tae see the day, bless her... it would'ave killed her it would."

"I see, I see. Well I assure you Mrs. Smailes it's the first I've heard, and I hope the last. Thanks a lot for telling me, and perhaps we can now leave the matter as a confidence just between you and me. Mind you, I still say it's tragic - about young Cedric as well, with all his alleged faults. Perhaps if he'd lived he might have done the honourable thing an—"

"Now I do knaw you haven't heard the whole story young man. You see this Cedric youth nivver came back here fra the RAF after t'war was ower. Deserted t'lass he did. They say he gat another yan into trouble down in t'South sumwhere - wouldn't surprise me mind ye. Last onybody heard on him he was living wi' an uncle in New Zealand or summat. Tha can't git much farther away fra trouble than that, can tha?"

"The baby - Nat's girl - Mabel I mean?"

"O aye, t'babby. Went away sumwhere tae have it - yan o' your predecessors gat her in sumwhere quiet - naebody knaws where. She didn't fetch babby back wi' her - Nat wouldn't hev it in th'ouse. Gat it adopted sumwhere I suppose. Onyweys, it's all ower and done wi' by now - just as though nowt had iver happened... best forgetten... things like that are 'appen best put out o' mind aren't they. Although as I always says, 'Being cruel tae be kind's alweys a mixed blessing for sumbody'. Now what abowt that cuppa tea tha cummed for?"

Walking slowly back towards Brent Lea Farm an hour later, I came with some trepidation to the edge of the stream. My leap was not quite so certain as the previous one and I landed clumsily on the other side. The big wooden gate was closed, so I climbed over it. Still assailed by many conflicts I lingered awhile, leaning heavily over the top rail, remembering, and pondering. Music was still in the clean cool air, birdsong, whispering leaves, and running water. But now it was sad music, murmuring many sorrows and weeping over wounds which time had not healed. I was aware of treading softly and reverently as I moved away from the place, and likewise as I walked up the hill and through the lush meadow. I had been deeply affected by the events of that afternoon. For one thing, they seemed to have pushed my credibility to the very limit. Above all they revealed that at this early stage of ministry I was yet too easily deluded by my own sensitivities. I began to realise with some degree of shock that the good pastor's relationship with his people is fraught with many unique, delicate, intimate, and sometimes perilous factors. The people who seek our ministrations are not customers, clients, patients, admirers, fans nor followers. Even the term 'parishioners' does not suffice, for it is inevitably limited by certain geographical connotations. Neither was I happy with the shepherd and flock analogy, for often that in modern terms is no more than a distortion of the New Testament ideal. Whilst it may in some cases exalt the prestige, and even the ego of the pastor, it does less than justice to the intelligence and integrity of his people. Every day, in a multitude of varying circumstances, I was discovering that there is a stronger bond than all of these. It is a brotherhood, a family concern, a kindred spirit, a vital interaction at the level of the soul wherein the minister finds himself, for better or for worse, inexorably drawn into an empathy with the joys, sorrows, and baffling complexities of the lives of others who trust him. But I was young yet, and was still having my own youth to contend with. Perhaps therefore, in situations such as the present one, there were 'affinities' which needed to be curbed. It became abundantly clear to me that I had to continue to work hard on the matter of balance within the varied implications of this hallowed state of ordained ministry. The distressing experience of the past two hours was a timely reminder that of all the hazards which the young pastor may encounter, none is more fraught with risk, or prone to misunderstanding than that which arises out of his susceptibility to the pulchritude of certain earnest suppliants after his good offices. The alluring combination of feminine charm and genuine pathos constitute a force to be reckoned with and compassion can beguile.

I took a long time, with many pauses, over that walk back to Brent Lea Farm. By an odd quirk of circumstance Nat was again crossing over the cobbled yard as I arrived outside the gate. Pausing briefly to regard me, without so much as setting down the bucket which he was carrying, nor making the slightest hint of a smile, he motioned vaguely with his free hand in the direction of the house,

"T'lass is in t'kitchen if tha's wantin' her."

This time that gorgeous creature was not beckoning in the doorway, nor standing smiling at the window. For a thousand indefinable reasons I did not open the iron gate which led into the yard, but made directly to where my little yellow MG Sport was waiting to greet me. On the driver's seat lay a coloured box of neatly assorted cakes and dainties labelled 'Minister', and on the other a large bunch of freshly cut garden flowers,

'To dear Gina, with all my love. M."

******

And Gina's greeting on my arrival home said it all,

"Nice to have you home - soldier!"

Chapter 12

TRAVELLERS' TALES

On each Sunday, the little wayside chapels in the dale were mainly served by lay preachers. Only a very small minority of these owned cars, and those fortunate brethren operated a system of sharing and ferrying which sometioes entailed long circuitous journeys. Others who on some particular occasion would fall outside the purview of this service undertook considerable mileages by bicycle, whilst there were those who trudged on foot along ancient footpaths over the wild moors and rugged valleys. Many were the tales which grew up around the exploits of these humble men of God. Some had expanded dramatically in the oft re-telling, accumulating their full quota of variation and colour. Others, especially after the demise of their subjects, had been translated into the realm of the apocryphal or been elevated to the status of local tradition and folklore. The best safeguard against the scepticism with which one was wont to treat such tales, was to pay heed only to those of the autobiographical kind, most of which were sufficiently in character to be credible.

In my estimation, there was nothing to match the account of big Hector Bolam's fateful ride to Stirkbeck one hot Sunday afternoon. Hector began with a spectacular disadvantage, his weighing in at twenty-one stones. His bike was (of necessity) rather special also; a massive dull black no nonsense roadster with double reinforced crossbar, and an expansive leather saddle resembling an outsize bosun's chair. The great machine groaned ominously when put into motion, giving the impression that it was never more than a few squeals away from total seize-up. On the day at issue, Hector's trouble began just as he was steaming out of Fennelmere village, past Henry Hogarth's road-side cow byre. There was only one solitary bolt-hole throughout the entire length of the dense hedgerow, and by some peculiar improvidence Hector just had to be passing it when a full grown rabbit, hotly pursued by a local cur suddenly shot out of it. By a masterly manoeuvre, utterly incredible given Hector's bulk, he swung his front wheel clear. He missed the rabbit, but miscalculated for the unfortunate dog. The poor creature's head crashed through the front wheel, dislodged a few spokes, and jammed firmly in the forks. The canine was dead of course. Although the impact had unseated Hector and launched him on an unscheduled flight into the hedge, he was nothing the worse, nature having generously equipped his anatomy with efficient shock-absorbing features. Picking himself up, dusting himself down, extricating and furtively disposing of the casualty, regaining his breath, then offering a hasty thanksgiving for safe deliverance, he continued on the Lord's errand. The front wheel of the bicycle had acquired a distinct buckle, and now that big black monster hobbled along with a rhythmic up-and-down motion which lulled Hector into a blissful state of inattention. So it was that some rapid acceleration in the rocking rhythm of the saddle caught him unawares. Before he had re-assembled all his senses he was hurtling down the steep slope of Kirklees Bank - three quarters of a mile of Tarmacadam Hell. The eccentric trim of that stricken front wheel left him with only the rear brake effective - sufficient maybe, except when your gross weight is twenty-one stones. There may have to be certain reservations about accepting the precise factuality of the remainder of the story. On second thoughts however, it may be considered that these are not the sort of details which the teller would wish to include at the expense of his own reputation. And besides, you see, there was from this point onwards, and totally unobserved by the otherwise pre-occupied Hector, a thoroughly reliable eyewitness.

Faster and faster spun the rear wheel, occasionally affecting a perilous forward skid or sideways lurch. Hoppity-hop rattled the warped front wheel, shaking Hector's huge hulk up and down until it got his diaphragm confused and seriously inhibited his breathing. The painful squeal of that lone rear brake intensified into a harsh metallic vibration which, transmitting through the entire frame of the machine was amplified to rack Hector's body with a searing torment from his toe-nails to his teeth. In spite of the many speculations upon the matter, it is not known up to this very day how big Hector remained in the saddle; that is unless it had something to do with his particular rapport with the force of gravity. Nor is it known how it was that he kept his hold upon those handle-bars which shook with such terrible violence, nor how he kept those two wheels on the road, albeit rarely both at the same time. Neither is it known how he performed the impossible and negotiated the sharp bends, evil cambers and frequent pot-holes for which that dread hill is notorious. Hector had no doubts, although he would never discuss it, beyond a confident "I knaws, I knaws."

There are various theories as to how Hector finally came to a halt. The startled eyewitness offered a vaguely plausible explanation,

"I thowt t'bike had an ingine or summit leyke, or a moater o' sum soort. Greet thick clouds o' smoake was fleein' off t'back wheel ahintonim, all blue leyke, and an awful smell it had."

From which we are to logically conclude that so great was the friction, the rubber brake blocks began to melt against the rim of the rear wheel, or even burn-up and perhaps adhere somewhat, finally bringing the great machine to a squelching halt right by the gate of Stirbeck chapel. A clear case of divine deliverance right down to the last inch of the way. That, one suspects, was not the whole story, or how else do we explain the rusted remains of an exceptionally large bicycle among the heap of farm scrap iron in Tom Skelton's stack yard? Nevertheless in fairness, we should have concluded the story before arriving at this point, and cut it short with a flourish, just as Hector himself would do,

"Praise the Lord, I kept me appointment didn't I."

******

There were many tales, still extant, of the long arduous foot- slogging journeys undertaken by a former generation of hard men who would flinch at nothing in faithful pursuit of their weekly calling. Undeterred by weather, distance or terrain, they would shake off the weariness of six days of toil and willingly expend their day of rest on some incredible feat of physical endurance on behalf of the furtherance of the Gospel. Aye, we don't breed 'em like that any more. And yet, be it noted, even in these present more comfortable days there were men who stubbornly, or stupidly, clung to the tradition of their fathers. They were on the whole quite reasonable men, and yet for some inexplicable reason they spurned the wheel or any mode of mechanical conveyance as Sunday by Sunday they plied the long roads, winding lanes, and rough byways to fulfil their sacred duty. The only equipment these hardy stalwarts required was a rock-like constitution, a good pair of feet, some generous measure of divine grace, and a degree in madness. These were tough men who seemed to obtain pious satisfaction from following in the footsteps of the Man of Galilee with crude literalness and fanatical zeal. Or was it that by some quirk in their nature they chose to tread where the saints (their immediate ancestors) had trod? Certain of them were reputed to prepare their sermons from scratch as they walked - a factor which was often patently obvious in their subsequent pulpit performance.

Take the case of Charlie Brampton who, on a certain Sunday in late November, was due to conduct evening service at Torrysmoor, a paltry nine miles distant from his home village of Nether Beck. He would not go by the hard tarmac road (bad on the feet) but, even as he had done on countless previous occasions over many years, he would trudge his way along the less circuitous track across the fellside and up and over the high moor. This was in fact an ancient packhorse trail, seldom used by this time except by vagrants or the odd shepherd seeking for some very lost sheep. Consequently there were patches where the rough track was scarcely discernible, but what matter, for long association had etched its curves and contours indelibly upon Charlie's mind. All was well with his world as he plodded on, singing softly to himself hymns and psalms and spiritual songs in full compliance with the injunction of Saint Paul. As I have said, he was one of the tough ones, and therefore totally impervious to the effects of the chill damp air upon his lungs, or the biting winds which buffeted him as he reached the higher ground. Incredibly, he arrived at Torrysmoor chapel dead on time, launching himself immediately into the leading of a lively service of worship, which included the preaching of an even more lively double-length sermon. He finished half-an-hour behind schedule. It is written that the preacher is worthy of his hire, and so in accordance with the undying custom in these remote parts, Charlie was treated to a handsome repast at the home of Bill and Dora Fletts. He ate too much, talked too much, and stayed too long. And so it had grown late and very dark ere he took leave of his patient hosts.

"Tha'll be gawin' back be t'roaad then Charlie ist tha not?" said Bill, "Might git theesel' lost or summat ower t'moor if tha gaws the way tha cummed. Hest got torch or owt?"

"Nay, nay Bill lad - torch? Man I knaws that owld path leyke t'back of me hand... could walk it wi' beyth me eyes shut 'appen... ony time."

And so, quoting something about the Lord being his light and salvation, the indomitable Charlie sallied forth, soon disappearing into the black darkness and the bitter cold, again singing softly to himself hymns and psalms and spiritual songs in full compliance with the injunction of Saint Paul, and praising God for an uplifting evening and a good supper. Arriving onto higher ground Charlie walked smack into the dense cloud bank which had settled over the moor. He blundered on however, assuming that as was usually the case, he would soon come out into the clear. A vain hope, for the thick mist became thicker at every step, the cold air grew colder, more clinging, and there was a touch of frost in it. There was, of course, no point in turning back for Charlie could not tolerate failure, and besides, he had calculated that by now he had passed the halfway mark and would soon be making his gradual descent. His memory continued to serve him well as familiar landmarks appeared before him, or their smudged outlines grew out of the mist to his sides. Every change of direction was made at precisely the right moment in accordance with long association and inscrutable instinct. And yet he was not singing now - the hymns and psalms and spiritual songs had, although he didn't realize it, faded out. An unfamiliar sensation, a feeling of creeping, penetrating cold, weakening the limbs and destabilizing the joints, torturing his chest with the pain of laboured breath and turning his stomach into a bottomless pit of crippling nausea. No, it wasn't really that kind of chill, not a distinct pain either, for somehow it seemed to reach beyond the range of bodily sensations. The onset of deadly, creeping fear? He was lost in the deep murky dark, impenetrable cloud, a strange country, with no footpath to follow for it had long since petered out, no landmark to guide, except the unfamiliar forms which loomed up out of the mist, ugly and sinister. Charlie was on a journey from nowhere to nowhere, that had never begun, and would never have an ending, which had no reason, no purpose. Panic began to insinuate itself into his numbed reasoning, got through to his very soul, devastated his resolve, and turned his legs into palpable rubber. Hypothermia was tightening its deadly grip on Charlie, and yet he staggered on, his sense of direction turned to vapour. A jagged outcrop of rock, an impoverished tree, warped and stunted, striking a threatening pose, or a clump of withered bracken like a crouching pack of hungry wolves, filled Charlie with awesome fear. Ordinary and otherwise familiar objects began to assume the shape of devils and the proportion of giants. Finally, slumping down heavily upon a rounded boulder, and completely exhausted in body, mind and spirit, Charlie fell into a trembling confusion of fear, self-pity, rage, and something less defined which might have passed for praying. And yet even when the instinctive urge to pray was chilled out of him there persisted somewhere just above the level of the subconscious, a distant ditty, a fleeting echo - or was it a 'still small voice'? There it was again - 'Lead Kindly Light amidst the encircling gloom, Lead thou me on... The night is dark...and I am far from home... lead thou me on...' He tried desperately to hold on to the elusive fantasy, but it dissolved into the swirling mist. 'O'er moor and fen, o'er crag and torrent...' the nebulous notion resurfaced briefly, and what was that... the distant sound of rushing water? Charlie now clutched his frozen hands more closely about his face, muttered uncontrollably, shook violently, and wept bitterly. He was irretrievably lost, abandoned, forsaken, albeit it in a very worthy cause.

Alastair Murray was just finishing off his usual gargantuan supper when he stopped suddenly half way through a noisy slurp of hot coffee.

"Th'ens... th'ens... that's what... sudden thowt... aye."

"What's up wi th'ens? I din't hear nowt... finish tha coffee," croaked his good wife Annie May.

"Canna mind o' shuttinem up, that's what. Syne tha went off colour I've gat ower mony o' your jobs on me hands as well as me own, and you fratchin' on abowt nowt all day."

"Well ony road, tha'd better git tha boots on and hev a leyke, or there'll be nae sleep witha this neyght will there... tossin' and turnin' and lowpin' about... tha knaws what tha's leyke when tha gits summat on tha mind."

There was but a thin spread of mist outside, but nevertheless Alastair deemed it necessary to collect the battered old hurricane lamp which hung on a large nail by the kitchen door. Except for the low murmuring of drowsy animals, and the sound of chickens exchanging bedtime stories, all was quiet about the stack-yard. Alastair was not the tidiest of farmers in the best of circumstances, and now for the reason aforestated even what small power of organisation was his normal wont was somewhat confounded... 'that woman o' mine... what for she doesn't try an' pull hersel' togither a bit mare?' It was bitterly cold, and even for one so hardened against the elements as Alastair, shirt sleeve order proved inadequate a protection from the damp chill air. He scurried through the yard, past the small round stack of straw, and was making directly for the hen-house when - "Who the H— musta left that bl— bucket lying there?" Half-a-dozen yards of high-speed hop scotch acrobatics sent Alastair sprawling and cursing face down on the wet cobbles, with near perfect timing and precision. Involuntarily releasing his hold on the battered old oil lamp he catapulted it backwards over his head to shatter, spill, and explode right at the foot of the precious stack. A more deftly executed torching job could not have been achieved deliberately. The bruised and battered farmer sprung to his feet with elastic agility and amid a disgusting cascade of screamed oaths and blasphemies, grabbed the offending bucket and frantically set about the futile task of transporting water from the trough at the opposite end of the stack yard. But he fought alone, and his vain shouting alerted no one, for his little farmstead was situated in lonely isolation near the edge of the vast moor. The only witness of the calamity was Annie May who stood in the doorway of the house, writhing her whole body, ringing her hands and gathering her skirts tightly about her legs, and screaming impracticable advice across the yard. The fire gained a stranglehold in a surprisingly short time, forcing Alastair back from the scene to concentrate his effort on safeguarding other highly combustibles about the yard.

Meanwhile back on the high moor, swathed in impenetrable mist, benumbed by panic and confusion, terrified by the eerie silence, Charlie sat tight on his damp cold rock. Totally distraught he muttered one string of nonsense after another, whimpered childishly, and shuddered violently. Praying normally came easily to Charlie - too easily in fact, and consequently it had never contained a great deal of substance or specific purpose. It was usually but the pseudo-pious fondling of sporadic thoughts. There was little difference when it was vocalised, as in the leading of public worship, except of course, for the addition of sound. Indeed it could be said that the habit was so spontaneous that the idea of direct results never crossed Charlie's mind. But now a new dimension; his praying was coming from a different area of his being. It is easy to pray at depth when you are alone and scared to death, or totally lost in darkness. Although unuttered this praying seemed to hold some kind of promise; it felt like a living thing, almost like a voice from out of a cloud. The sudden shock caused Charlie to uncover his face and raise up his head, and - Holy Moses - there ahead, distant, the very mist was aglow, red, bright, shimmering. This was surely that very pillar of fire which in ancient times had guided the Israelites through their wilderness ordeal, and directed them to the Promised Land. Surely it had been sent back to bring him home. The bones came back into his limbs, his veins and arteries filled with warm pulsating blood, and his nervous system had the current switched back on. Half running, half walking, and loudly praising the Lord as he went, he stumbled and staggered with frantic urgency in the direction of that mystic ethereal luminescence. He never noticed that his wild traverse was taking him steeply downhill, nor did it ever strike him that he was maybe being lured towards the gates of Hell itself. Then with a suddenness which produced a shock to the whole system, he was out, in the clear, and beneath his feet was a well-defined track, with dry-stone walls on either side. And there but a few hundred yards ahead lighting up the night sky, was the very torch of his salvation. Surely this was the burning bush itself, straight out of the Old Testament, for it was undiminishing, and beckoning him onwards towards its bright and marvellous light. Almost hypnotised by the wonder of the situation, he hadn't noticed the open gate, nor been aware of the fact that he had stumbled right into the stack yard of Brackenburrow Farm. Exhausted physically, and emotionally drained, he sank down to rest on the edge of a near empty horse-trough.

"What's tha doin' ower here?" mumbled Charlie on recognising the gaunt figure of Alastair Murray standing before him black and dishevelled.

"What's tha doin' reyght ower here mare leyke? Dost not knaw where tha's gittin theesell to or summat, and at this teyme o' neyght?"

"Just on me way hoame fra Torriesmoor," burbled Charlie, "Thowt I'd gittin' meesell lost or summat when I see-ed thee standin' there."

"Tha IS lost tha silly god-smacked b— This is me own place I'm standin' at... me own stack yard... and that's me own stack that's smowldrin' all brunt up ower there. And I'll tell tha what... if tha's on tha way fra Torriesmoor to your place then tha musta been wanderin' in th'opposite direction for a gay lang time."

"Been worried tae death about my Alastair," whined Annie May who had suddenly materialised, "That I have... knock 'im up bad it will, all that smoake and fire an' stuff... didn't finish 'is supper neither."

Alas there was no loving wife, nor anyone else similarly devoted, to worry about the long overdue Charlie. He was an inevitable bachelor, and lived alone. Thus he was offered the hospitality of a hot supper, some dry clothes, and a bed for the night - not fit for even an animal to be out on a night like this! Charlie accepted the supper, for the stomach which had suffered so much during his recent ordeal had by now unravelled itself and of course the warm, cosy bed would be welcome.

Did Charlie and Alastair console each other on their mutual misadventures? Rumour has it that in fact things turned out very much to the contrary. For Alastair's part, he was not at all amenable towards accepting Charlie's 'Providential' interpretation of the stockyard accident. There was further friction over Charlie's indignant refusal of the large mug of hot beverage with a 'drop of something' added to stop his shivering. This ingratitude might have been excusable had not Charlie accompanied it with a crude diatribe on the evils of alcoholic drink. The disagreements continued right into the small hours, Annie May having departed to bed and left the conflagration at the supper table to exhaust itself. It was said however that it went on until long after the dying embers of the ill-fated stack had fizzled out. It is also said that Charlie was found next morning deeply asleep on one of the hard wooden chairs in Annie May's simple kitchen, still fully clad in his sodden clothes.

Aye, 'God moves in a mysterious way, His wonders to perform!'

******

Edgar Foulds was obviously a well-read man who kept up-to-date on current affairs, pursued a wide range of interests, and possessed a philosophical turn of mind. He was also a good progressive farmer. But that same Edgar was nevertheless a daunting travelling companion, for he did not readily indulge in conversation, and was adept at making you feel that you were talking too much. He would punctuate the consequent long drawn out silences with the odd unsolicited 'Aha', or mumble droll responses of 'Appen' (which expression would double for either concurrence or scepticism) to my laboured attempts at initiating some form of vocal exchange.

The sun was well into its closing down routine when I picked up Edgar at the village of Knowlesby, and proceeded on the wide detour which would enable me to put him down by his farm house alongside the road to Cleaton. This would take us across Styrralpike Moor, as desolate a stretch of heather clad plateau as any in the land. It was dissected by this one narrow white road, unfenced and undulating, but never bending. The combination of mechanical sounds from the innards of my small open car with the strong slipstream of cool evening air gushing about her was not conducive to conversation anyway. For my own part this made the lack of it more tolerable. There came an untypical moment however when, glancing sideways, I fancied I detected some sign of uneasiness in my passenger. He was shuffling a little, and seemed to be having some trouble with his larynx. We had just rounded over the crest of a ridge of high ground, and were facing down a gentle descent of about three-quarters of a mile dead straight, when Edgar surprisingly entered into the motions of speech. His first attempt foundered before the windy blast over the top of the windscreen. It then took several minutes for him to regain the impetus to speak, and closing in on my left ear he began to articulate, with some urgency,

"Used tae alweys meyeke this trip on th'bike ye knaw. O aye, alweys on th'owld bike... aye... that is... well... until about this time last year... aye... just about this time it was."

"Getting a bit too old now eh?" I jested.

"Nay nowt like that... nay," and then he relapsed into silence.

It was not for long however, and he came back in more urgent tone, "Gat t'biggest freyght I ivver had in me whole life I did... aye... aye... just cumin' down this bank leyke you an' me's doin' now. If tha gaws just a bit mare slaw... just a la'al bit... I'll tell tha."

I throttled back obediently, the little car protesting with the usual display of snarls and plops.

"Aye... just cumin' hoame efter tekin' th'evening service at Knowlesby back yonder... just leyke toneyght... aye. On th'bike of coourse... nay minister wi' fancy car then... aye... just nice and steady leyke down this incline... can dae a lot o' thinkin' on th'bike ye knaw. Aye, neyght just leyke this yan... about seyame teyme o' neyght as well... ivrything was sae quiet and still... just soort o' enjoying dawdlin' down this lang bank here... aye... nice and steady leyke..."

"Not so noisy and windy as this lot eh?" I broke in.

"Aha... aye now slaw down a bit mare will tha, till I tells tha. See yon la'al brig yonder, ower th'beck, just cumin' into view at th'bottom?"

I observed a small stone hump-backed bridge ahead, carrying the narrow white road over a moorland stream, less than half a mile away.

"Well now, as I was tellin' tha, I was just cumin' down on th'bike as I said afore." Here Edgar paused unnecessarily for breath, "And as I was sayin', just nice and steady... aye... and when I gat close up to th'brig... I sees owld Charlie Carruthers cumin' down th'roaad on t'other side. He gets on th'middle o' th'brig afore me... and just stands there a-starin' ower th'wall... into th'watter... aye... just stood there nivver movin' or owt... starin' at summat in there."

Another pause for laboured breathing gave me the chance to butt in with,

"Spotted something interesting or rather odd had he?"

"Nay nay, nowt leyke that... it was just—" and here Edgar's voice faltered, "Gay funny I thowt... gay funny... aye, gay funny."

"What's so funny about an old man pausing on a bridge to look down into the water?" I mused.

"Aye... gay funny I thowt... because ye see... owld Charlie died in his sleep six months afore. Buried him in Knowlesby Churchyard we did... wife and me went tae t'funeral... see-ed him in t'coffin afore they screwed him down I did."

I heard myself gasp a sound with no words in it. The involuntary gesture however gave Edgar sufficient re-assurance to continue with his tale.

"I went all stiff an' cawld, I gat sic a freyght. I tried tae speak tae 'im as I went past... gay slow... me legs had gawn all weak, shakky voice an' all, just leyke a Nanny goat. 'Hey there Charlie, I says, How ist tha lad - gayly nice neyght isn't it'. Then I tries tae pedal a bit faster, but I gat me front wheel twisted round a bit, and I falls off. I gat sic an awful freyght I tells tha. Onywey, Charlie was still standin' there on th'brig. Then he turns round, all slow, looks at me streight in t'face... it was an awful look was that, an awful look... Then he puts his hand on th'wall, and lowps clean ower into t'beck. I picks meesel' up gayly sharp, and runs back onto th'brig, and looks ower th'side. There was nowt tae see... nowt at all... neither side. Then I gaws down and looks under it, and all around it, but there was nay sign o' Charlie, nor onybody else for that matter. Nay, now I knaws just what tha's gawin' tae say, but tha's wrang onywey - because he couldn't have sunk or drooned or onything leyke that. Ye see watter's nivver mare than about three inches dee-yp under there."

"Shall we stop now, and have a look round?"

"Nay lad, I wouldn't bother - not this time - let's away hoame, sharp. Can dae wit a bite o' supper onywey. But a tells tha what... dae ye knaw, I've nivver telt ony yan else about this - not a soul not me missus even. They'd all want me put away or summat if I did. But I tell tha - it was Charlie all reyght, O aye, it was Charlie."

"You seem to be quite certain of that, I'm sure."

"Aye, and I'll tell tha summat else if tha's still listening. I've nivver been back ower this brig ony mare neither - not be mesel' that is, and I'll not be in ony hurry tae cum back neither - not be mesel'. And another thing - if ony o' my stock gets a-wanderin' ower here, or kessened in t'ling, or fallen in th'beck or owt leyke, it'll just hev tae bide there, cos I'll not be cumin' back ower here tae fetch it - not be mesel' ony roaad - nivver."

I managed to squeeze out a semi-mocking 'Appen', but the effect was lost, for by now we were actually astride that terrible bridge and were crossing it at dead slow, much to Edgar's obvious discomfort. Then a strange and inexplicable thing happened. Without any conscious prompting from me, the car suddenly let out a tremendous roar, split the air with a scream of tyres, discharged a cloud of blue smoke from the exhaust, took to its heels and shot up the hill on the other side with incredible velocity. Once we had cleared the crest of the hill,

Edgar became relaxed once more, although still remaining uncharacteristically talkative. He was obviously intent upon securing a necessary change of subject. After some stilted discussion on a wide variety of unrelated subjects, ranging from current live-stock prices to the state of the Church Militant Here Upon Earth (carefully avoiding any mention of the Church Triumphant in Heaven, be it noted), Edgar finally got round to inviting me to stop off at his place for a 'la'al bite of supper - th'missus will be very pleased, and is sure to have it already laid out on th'table waitin' for tha'. A great and wondrous institution was this, with which the wise readily complied.

When we arrived at the farm the departing sun was leaving behind a pinkish sky to the West, and sporadic clouds were turning out in evening dress. As I left the farm, two hours later, a rising full moon was saturating the landscape in an eerie yellow light. I had travelled but a few dozen yards, when a sinister urge took possession of me. Without premeditation or any recourse to reason, I obeyed a powerful compunction to turn the car about, and return home by the way I had lately come. There was no thought in my mind of the little bridge over the beck, nor any awareness of doing this only to prove to myself that I was not to be taken in by the crazy delusions of superstitious farmers; nor in fact merely to endorse my disbelief. Figment of Edgar's over-sensitive imagination - purely subjective - trick of the subconscious mind - his experience was neither singular nor unique - nor was it proof of the possession of extrasensory perception, nor the existence of ghosts - pure hallucination, that's what - visual conditioned reflex of course - Edgar's doppelganger, for that's obviously what it was - all so easily explained in the clear light of elementary psychology. Pleasingly fascinated by this one-man debate, I reached the descent to the bridge rather unexpectedly. I would make my approach slowly, although not of necessity furtively. I would cross over with calm and cool deliberation, and enjoy a good laugh to myself as I went. There was no other living creature in sight, neither the night call of animal or bird. There was only the rippling sound of shallow water passing over the stones under the bridge, and the slow rhythmic tick- over of the throttled back car engine. The air in the immediate vicinity of the bridge was noticeably colder by several degrees, and I drew my thick woollen scarf more closely about my neck. Crossing the bridge at less than dead slow, I looked neither to the left nor the right, for to do so would have been an admission of fear, foreboding, or even credulity; none of which applied of course. At the same time I was assured that there was certainly no danger of my entertaining a sense experience for which there was no corresponding reality. Needless to say, the apparition, or whatever, did not oblige. But then, just at the very moment I reached the crest of the little hump-backed bridge, indifferently, with not even the vaguest flutter of a butterfly in my stomach, the weirdest thing happened. The butterfly valve in the car's high-performance SU carburettor quite suddenly and without cause, flicked and jammed wide open. The engine raced madly beyond control, and we had careered furiously for nearly a mile before I had collected sufficient composure to even think of switching off the engine or applying the brakes. For the next half-hour, it was bonnet up, and a dirty session working on the carburettor seize-up.

All perfectly simple to explain of course, in purely mechanical categories!

******

There was the day of the horse, long since, when parsons, preachers and the like travelled in traps, gigs, and a multiple variety of animal-drawn conveyances. Or, as in the case of the venerable Rufus Thringby, they traversed their wide itinerary in the saddle. This hardy ancient, now eighty-seven years of age, if given the slightest opportunity, would regale his audience long and eloquently with tales of his equine escapades of many years since. The stories were oft repeated, and on each re-telling, one was obliged to re-act as though listening to it for the very first time. Rufus had outlived, or worn out, many fine horses in his time, but none was remembered so vividly and with such tender affection as 'Owld Nel'. And no other featured so frequently as Nel in Rufus's nostalgic ramblings.

Nel was as fine a creature as any man had ever sat astride. Fifteen hands she stood, and she was the colour of a peat bog. She had an eye (two actually) as sharp as an eagle's, and an ear (two actually) that could hear a man thinking. Nay, she wasn't a fell pony, or ony o' them fancy breeds with a fine pedigree. She was what was called 'local', but she was a gayly good-un for all that. In fact, Nel had mare sense atwixt her ears than many a man, or woman an' all for that matter. Good solid horse sense it was. Many and varied were the exploits of Rufus and Nel, all classics in their own right. Surprisingly I never tired of listening to them, although I do admit that I found the soft sobbing with which Rufus concluded each well-told tale somewhat embarrassing. The faithful horse would carry Rufus, both already weary from a hard day's work on the small hill farm, along narrow fell road, rough mountain track, or miles of open moor to his appointment at some remote and distant country chapel. Tethered to the cast-iron railings outside, she would stand and wait patiently, one hour, and sometimes two, while her master led the faithful in worship, and in prayers that they might be endued with such virtues and graces that were hers by nature. Occasionally she would snort, sigh, shuffle, redistribute the weight on her feet, or shake the brasses of her harness, only to indicate to Rufus that all was well with her outside.

Then, the Lord's work completed, and with the long lean Rufus mounted, she would plod steadily home, often without the guidance of bridle, for her exhausted master would invariably fall asleep in the saddle. Nel possessed a unique homing instinct, and would always deliver her charge safely home, although often near to midnight. Sarah Thringby, elderly sister to Rufus, would be up and waiting for the sharp metallic rap of Nel's hooves on the cobbles of the farmyard. As soon as they paused, directly opposite the back door, Sarah would go out and gently ease her weary brother down to ground, into the house, and onto his big easy chair. Then he would draw up to the table, and in spite of his drowsiness, he would devour an enormous supper. Then he would retire to bed, satisfied that his duties unto the Lord had been faithfully discharged, and the day's journeys were done. Meanwhile, the loyal steed would have wandered slowly to her stall, and laid her down in deep straw, still geared up and in harness.

Sometimes Sunday would find Rufus unwell, for he had a chronic digestive disorder, a chronic 'water' problem, a chronic heart, chronic headaches, a chronic chest, and some chronic pains in his joints. All of these he had suffered from his youth up. There were times when one or more of these sore afflictions would assail him in the saddle. No matter however, for so sensitive and knowing was Owld Nel, that at such times she would tread softly, lest by one indiscreet step she should bring pain to some defective area of her master's frail physique. On reaching home on such occasions, she would pause as usual by the back door, and utter a gentle 'Ninny' to prepare Sarah for coming to take over her fragile burden.

"Aye... she was a gayly fine owld horse was my Nel... and there'll nivver be another yan the leykes on her... in this world or the next."

And then, poor old Rufus would enjoy a little weep.

Chapter 13

OUT OF THE MOUTHS OF BABES

No one realized at the time what caused the old canon to collapse at the end of his soporific sermon on Sunday morning. And no-one seemed surprised, most of the congregation simply dismissing the subject with such carefree sentiments as 'Gittin' ower owld that yan... should've geyen up lang seyne.' By the end of the following week however, the news was generally disseminated that the canon was slowly sinking, gradually growing weaker, gently fading away, or by whatever unclinical metaphor people chose to describe the process of dying.

Canon Emrys Rhos was, as his name strongly indicated, a Welshman. It was so long ago that he had left his native valleys to minister here that he had become totally integrated into the life of this Pennine country. More precisely, he had been incumbent in his present parish for at least forty of his seventy-nine years and in that time the impression had grown that there had never been a time when the place was without him. In some of his ways he was unique, in others quite eccentric, but in all thoroughly good. The pious loved him, the nominally religious respected him, and the retrogrades tolerated him. Even the most crusty old Nonconformist would acknowledge that this man possessed some indefinable quality of saintliness. He had never married. And yet he was greatly perturbed on one occasion when Gina kindly and innocently referred to him as a bachelor. He certainly was not a bachelor, and upon this he was most emphatic. He was celibate. Whatever subtle distinction was here implied, Emrys Rhos had worked it out with pious lucidity. At times I would teasingly allude to the subject, hoping to wring from him some precious gem of his eruditious reasoning, or perhaps, if I could catch him off his guard, some confession of a former romance, or a sad remembrance of a girl who got away. But he would steadfastly assert, with pragmatic precision, that whilst a bachelor may acquire and retain his state by dint of accident or circumstance, a celibate is single out of studied and deliberate choice. Knowing this fine man as well as I did, I had no difficulty in settling for the premise that he was, by choice, thoroughly espoused to his holy calling and totally dedicated for as long as he should live to tending his scattered flock. From the earliest days of his incumbency he had cherished the desire to remain among these lovely people, minister to their souls, baptise their babies, marry their sons and daughters, bury their dead, and then at the end to lay down to rest among them in their quiet little churchyard by the river. In his own lifetime this cycle of vital human statistics had turned full circle many times over. He did not like the title 'canon', for as he stated, it had explosive overtones to it. He preferred to think of himself, and be regarded by others, as a gentle country priest. To the chagrin of many of the local low churchmen, he chose to be addressed as 'Father'. Local youths however would persistently refer to him as 'Owld Banger'.

"Shot off his last yan then," one commented to me, this not being the crude play upon words that it might seem. It could have been, in fact, a terse reference to the canon's peculiar style of delivering sermons.

"Owld father's nivver been owt of a preacher hes he," pleaded one of his younger church wardens, "He just gaws a-ramblin' on an on fra' stairt to near t'finish, and that's a gayly lang time an' all."

By any standard, dear old Rhos was not singularly blessed with oratorial skills. His slow, ponderous, undramatic, unvarying mode of speech induced drowsiness. It acted as a kind of vocal anaesthetic. One by one the listeners' senses decayed until consciousness was suspended at a point near to oblivion. A sudden shuffle or spasmodic jerk here and there among the congregation would indicate that some members had left one faculty, perhaps distantly associated with hearing, standing sentinel, to warn of any emergency which might arise - such as the end of the sermon. Now and again, but only for the duration of a few words or brief phrases, the canon would raise his voice to a pitch slightly above the level of his liturgical drone. These junctures were also the only occasions when he would lift up his eyes from his copious manuscript and peer straight out at his dazed 'listeners'. There invariably followed an inevitable long pause, and a low key, stammering, tautological sequence to enable him to get his eyes back into mesh with the script. One would no doubt wish to observe, 'How untypically Welsh'. This was by no means the case, for no more had Canon Emrys Rhos's Welshness deserted him than had the distinctive accent of his native valleys to which his speech involuntarily reverted during the preaching of the sermon. Furthermore, there was one substantial piece of Welsh ordnance which was yet to be brought up, and this usually happened about five minutes before the end. In Wales it is called the 'Hwyl'. The preacher would affect a few seconds of ominous silence, as though he was setting his sights on a new range. Then he would all of a sudden let loose a loud barrage of fiery eloquence which blasted to shreds the mental defences of the hitherto somnolent worshippers. The echo of the mighty voice filled the place where they were sitting, bounced back and forth about those ancient walls, rattled among the rafters, set up irritating vibrations in a loose panel in the organ casing, and twirled in gathering confusion around the pillars. This fusillade would be followed by another, and another, after very brief pauses for reloading, or breathing, the canon booming and spuming, hurling charges of mighty invective at the evils of the world, the flesh, and the devil. A few salvos directed at mankind's indifference to God and inhumanity to man would resolve into a thunderous exhortation to this congregation here present to patiently lay hold on that peace which passeth understanding, and that serenity of spirit known only to those who walk blissfully with God. The harangue would terminate abruptly. The effect was like that of the too sudden application of brakes, a feeling of deafness or having all the sensibilities jammed. Then in an astonishing flash of mood change, the preacher would revert to his normally serene composure, render a small correcting cough, and pronounce in deep ecclesiastical tones the age-old formula,

"And now to God the Father, God the Son, and God the Holy Ghost Be ascribed all honour, and might, and majesty, and dominion, World without end. Amen."

Thus for more than forty years dear old Canon Rhos had faithfully proclaimed the Word of God to his loyal congregation. Only the good Lord knows what subliminal patterns of truth his wearisome wanderings and occasional explosive outbursts may have etched upon the minds of his comatose hearers. Mind you, even I can testify to the effectiveness of that classical *Coup de Grace*, that mighty verbal orgasm with which his finest sermons concluded. They simply loved him for it.

That last Sunday service was, in every respect, no different from any which had preceded it. And the sermon was characterised by the usual twenty minutes of painful preliminaries. Then came the affected brief sequence of dramatic quiet before the storm. BOOM...loud and clear the words sounded forth,

"We cannot remain indifferent to the indifference of this wicked, wicked, wicked world, the dreadful s-sins, the s-suffering... the insin.. indifs... ins-sinuance... the... no, non, n-no... th-that we can... ca... cannot d-d-do... can-n-n..."

The echo of the unfinished sentence was still rampant when he continued,

"I w-want t-to t-tell you, t-to t-te...O my Go-god, g-g-g..."

Reeling backwards and sideways, the preacher slithered halfway down the iron spiral stairs which led up to the pulpit. And thus ended Matins on that memorable Sunday morning.

"Doctor says its sum soort o' aplopsy or summat, but it's mare leyke a stroke I reckons," confided Mrs. Shanks to all enquirers during the following few weeks.

Mrs. Shanks, a widow of very long standing, was the canon's loyal, efficient, and homely housekeeper. Age-wise she was certainly his contemporary, and always seemed to be close at hand. Needless to add, she was first to those pulpit stairs when the canon collapsed. Under normal circumstances, whenever she ushered a visitor into the rectory, she would leave the study door slightly ajar and, if called, or her name was mentioned in the conversation which issued from within, she would appear in a surprisingly short time. Now alas, there was little that could be done for the dear old man except to wait, and watch, and pray. Thus they had sent him home from hospital, to the disordered tranquillity of the old rectory, committing him to the tender loving care of the dear, devoted Mrs. Shanks. I made it a bounden duty to call each time I passed by that way, and noted with sadness that his condition was deteriorating rapidly. His speech became increasingly blurred, his breathing almost imperceptible, and the strained contortions of his facial muscles would produce no legible words. We tried to converse silently with our eyes, for his remained bright. If there was any form of communication left between us, it must surely have been at the level of spirit to spirit.

On one such quiet afternoon, when I had felt strongly constrained to call on my old friend, I sat by his bedside, sad and frustrated, unable to achieve anything except to watch prayerfully - a particularly agonising business I tell you. Suddenly the peace of the place was rudely shattered by the loud rustling of taut wires being drawn along some distant wall cavity, followed by the harsh clanging of a spring bell somewhere down in the bowels of the house. Again it rang, and again, persistent, urgent. Obviously children. Mrs. Shanks abruptly deserted her post by the bedroom door, and with agility quite remarkable in one of her years, she scurried down the stairs to quell the menace. Tenderly she ushered in through the front door three little children, who although feigning infantile shyness, were simply bursting at the seams with sweet audacity. One of them, the elder of the two girls, was holding up high a dishevelled bunch of garden flowers.

"Dickie says he pinched them fra t'chapel garden, but he says if they growed in there they must be God's flowers onyweys, mustn't they, and he says that when he said his prayers this mornin' God telt him he could hev summonem... didn't he Dickie."

The children ascended the stairs with as much stealth as a gaggle of geese, and the efforts of Mrs. Shanks to shush them, only exacerbated the problem, for children have noisy working parts throughout. Just as they reached the bedroom door there came a strident whisper,

"Is th'owd faather really gawn' tae dee?"

Before we could organise our reaction, the children were right inside the room, and gathered round staring bashfully upon the still, pallid figure in the bed. Childish innocence, although perhaps naïve, is no less beautiful, and their candour though sweet, is no less devastating. In the situation I elected to remain outside the open door, on the wide landing, ostensibly to be at hand should Mrs. Shanks require any assistance. I am glad that I stayed, for otherwise this episode would have had to end here. There would have been no worthy purpose in writing this chapter. Likewise a vital element would have been missing from the whole of my subsequent life. The arrival of the children seemed to release some secret reserve of energy, and to deliver a surge of cognizance into the thin drawn face. Vague, and a little tortuously, the canon's features waxed into an expression of gentle serenity, and a precarious smile wavered across those parched lips. His breath came stertorously, yet there were words in it,

"So kind... so kind... you lovely little children... so kind..."

The effort of speaking exhausted him, and there followed a long and painful silence. All silences are arduous to children, and these three were about to venture upon their version of a tactful withdrawal, when the faint smile re-appeared on the old man's face.

"These beaut... iffffful... ffflower... sss... are they for... can I take... ?"

"Oo aye," rasped the little boy, "Oo aye, that's what we browt them for, isn't it Val, isn't it Sadie?"

"Thank you sweet little children... thank ..."

"Mrs. Shanks says tha's not gonna dee, doesn't she Dickie, doesn't she Sadie," declared little Val in a voice which would have shattered plate glass.

The canon made no attempt to comment on that one, and mercifully neither did anyone else. He was trying to reach out a wilted hand towards the elder of the two girls, who was still holding the flowers. Sadie was about eight years of age, and very beautiful. Her rich tresses of dark brown hair coiled softly about her shoulders, framing a rose pink face moulded to as near perfection as had ever been beheld. With an inspired flush of nobility sometimes seen in children, Sadie set out to rescue the awkward moment. Her lovely features broke out into bloom like some exquisite blossom on a warm June day, and her large brown eyes shone out brightly with mirth and laughter. Her little rosebud lips quivered gently as she shaped them to say something lovely and soothing, but the sweet words would not pass through. She only breathed, and even that soft breath was life and peace. The old man tried to speak but the effort was too costly, and in the event the little girl got there first.

"Are you really goin' away Faather?" she said in a voice as crisp and clear as her crystal smile. "Are you goin' off tae 'eaven or sum place like? All the good yans gaw tae 'eaven ye knaw - din't they Val - din't they Dickie. And you're t'best yan o' t'lot - isn't he Val - isn't he Dickie."

"Wilt tek flowers with tha then, when tha gaws?" queried young Dickie.

"Better put them in sum watter, stop 'em witherin' or summat," advised Val. "Might be a lang way tae 'eaven fra here 'appen. Dost tha knaw t'way there Faather? We din't want tha gettin' lost or owt leyke."

Mrs. Shanks and I stood dumfounded, for here we were witnessing a rare compound of the ludicrous and the sublime which can only be successfully stage-managed by little children. The canon seemed to smile, and this encouraged Sadie to resume her enquiries,

"Val wants to knaw if it's very far to 'eaven."

Old Emrys had, by now, regained sufficient strength to enable him to raise albeit a weak hand to gently fondle the nearest tress of Sadie's rich brown hair,

"Not very far away my dears... never very far away... never..."

Mrs. Shanks made a move as though to lead the children out of the room, but the canon checked the action with a long deep sigh.

"Whenever little children are near you... you're near to Heaven too... never very far... nev..." And Canon Rhos paused, slowly sank back, and continued his sleep. The final sleep.

A few months later, the sad parishioners erected over his grave a handsome memorial stone in the local pink granite. I was disappointed, indeed a little angered, that none would heed my suggestion that an appropriate epitaph to inscribe upon that stone would be,

Not very far away, never very far away;
Whenever little children are near you,
You're near to Heaven too.

But those stolid countrymen would have nothing of it. In pious accord with local custom it had to be a verse of Scripture, and a pretty trite affair at that. So it is therefore, that in plain bold letters cut deep into that thick slab of cold granite, succeeding generations will be bidden to remember:

THE REVEREND CANON EMRYS G. RHOS, M.A.
BORN 1871 - DIED 1950
WELL DONE THOU GOOD AND FAITHFUL SERVANT
ENTER THOU INTO THE JOY OF THY LORD

Of course those well-meaning parishioners could in no wise have been expected to appreciate the fine implications of my splendid suggestion, could they? After all, none of them was so fortunate as Mrs. Shanks and me in being on hand at that glorious moment and getting that little peep into Heaven as the door opened to let the old saint in.

Chapter 14

SLITHERING HEIGHTS

Winter had hung over the dale like a veiled threat for the past few days. For the most part, there had been nothing more ominous than some occasional flurries of powdery snow making rapid reconnaissance forays across the landscape. On this second Sunday in December the air had become colder, and icy fingers snaking over the dry road surface gave warning that Winter was groping for a hold.

"Could 'appen be gittin' an 'appin-up", croaked my elderly neighbour as he observed me preparing the car for the day's travels.

Neither this intelligence (which being translated reads 'The signs are that it's probably going to snow rather heavily') nor the accompanying meteorological indications aroused any foreboding in me as I started off on one of my typical Sunday tours of duty o'er hill and dale and far away. On this particular afternoon I would be accompanied by a lay preacher, whom I would set down at a village chapel en route for my own destination, and collect on my return journey about five hours later. The arrangement was a regular feature of church life in the dale but on this day, however, there was to be a quite unique variation.

"Aren't you a lucky boy," teased Gina, "Miss Victoria– Wow. Don't know what you've got that no other man in the world's got? I know– you're an irresistible attraction to plain Janes– that's it."

"That explain why YOU went crazy over me?"

"Alright– I suppose I asked for that one. But seriously darling, Miss Victoria's so primly poised, so formal, composed, and without being catty or anything I'd say, staid a wee bit. Very sweet mind you, although distant it seems. Or is she simply shy... or proud maybe?"

"I don't get your point."

"Just that it makes the mind boggle... I mean you... well you know what I mean... you're so terribly...terribly... so–"

"Brash?"

"O no darling, nothing like that at all. Just sort of... how shall I put it... er... outgoing...that's what. All the same, a perfect gentleman, courteous, kind and... Oo I do love you... "

"Stop it dear before my head explodes," I checked the drift.

"It's just that I can't get over this one. Miss Victoria actually consenting to go off with a man in a car– even you– and OUR car at that... funny little open-topped banger. Mind you, on second thoughts, it's maybe just as well it isn't a closed in model. Whatever's come over the lady? Just not in character is it?"

"Nor is her mother's consenting to allow her. Victoria's still quite a youngster you know– in her mere thirties I'd say. Mind you, today the poor girl has little choice. Her own car went into dock yesterday, and she has an appointment at Rewbeck this afternoon, in my direction that is. So it seems she has to accept any old thing going her way."

"Is that a reference to our car, or to you? In either case I think the poor lady needs a good chaperone. Better come along with you." Gina's merry jest I suspected was an oblique reference to the cramped accommodation afforded by our two's company-three's-a -crowd MG Midget.

My prospective passenger lived with her parents in a large Georgian house, situated about two miles up the valley road North of Lyndassby. On arrival I did not take the car right up the drive to the door, electing to sacrifice propriety for other considerations, not least the fear that she, on beholding the nature of her conveyance should hastily flee indoors. I waited, as pre-arranged, at the gate. The timing was perfect, which was fortunate, for there was no question of my sounding the horn– a vulgar klaxonic growl and quite inappropriate. The lady soon presented herself, and after a notably polite exchange of greetings, stepped down cautiously into my little roadster in the manner of one boarding a wobbly narrow-boat, or (more in line with my own banal observations) as demurely as she would enter her bath.

"And a very good afternoon to you Mr. Teviot. It's so extraordinarily kind of you to help me in this way," she charmed over the tops of her gold-rimmed spectacles, with flawless decorum.

Miss Victoria Athersedge appeared to most people as one from another age of courtesy, conventionalism, and genteel ways, or as belonging to another world where all was sweetness and light. Elegant from every angle, with exquisite facial geometry, she had a singular beauty which required no enhancing. She dressed immaculately, expensively, yet soberly and in excellent taste. She conducted herself with cultured reserve and communicated in carefully manipulated speech. She dispensed a smile which, although spilling over with winning charm, was sufficiently restrained to suggest that she feared lest by it she might inadvertently exceed the measured bounds of propriety. She was firmly established in the school of classical spinsterhood, and was indigenous to that order of femineity where the male is totally irrelevant and absolute anathema. And yet, in spite of the independent airs and manifest self-control, one fancied that it was easy to detect in this prim little protegé of over-protectedness an element of pathos. It was as though the shadow before which she walked was not her own, but that of her proud and snobbish mother, and/or that of her pompous, prosperous and possessive father, both of whom be it noted, invariably rendered her name complete with prefix. Miss Victoria's general demeanour marked her out as the product (some would have said 'victim') of a well-ordered preserve of obsolescent social patterns where precise rectitude was the hallowed norm. She conformed to the model with uncompromising rigidity, and was devastating in her hands-off appeal. But she adored little children, and they responded with simple love. Although she served on a voluntary basis, she had become an institution in assisting the legendary Miss Fotherthwaite at the little primary school at Brockleborough crossroads. The said Miss Victoria however was perhaps more widely known in church circles, both by reason of her father's prestigious and influential involvement at a generous financial level, and by herself being a highly respected, and much sought after, lay preacher.

The car started with the usual undignified display of throaty roar, splutters, coughs and pops, and the usual trail of disgusting blue-black tail-pipe emission. As was her wont, my distinguished passenger sat up as erectly as was physically possible in the low spartan seat of the little sports car; but not for long. As we gathered speed, and noise, and the biting wind began to screech over and around the screen, the lady was compelled to abandon her formal posture and adopt an untypically inelegant crouch. Next she proceeded to anchor her black wide-brimmed hat to her chin with a fine silk scarf, and to gather her stylish coat and tweed suit tightly about her. Hardly a word escaped her lips as we sped along nine miles of the rough winding road, up and over the notorious Blackrock Fell, and down the long steady descent towards the village of Rewbeck. As we neared the village Miss Victoria straightened herself up as best she could, removed the headscarf, and busied herself in a frantic effort to make herself presentable. Arriving at the village I set my passenger down at the door of the roadside chapel, before going on for another four miles to my own destination. Alighting discreetly from her conveyance, she greeted the waiting church officials with a splendid display of formal charm. Then to the obvious astonishment of all she relaxed momentarily and broke protocol with,

"Phew. That was indeed a thrilling trip... great fun... I could really go some more of that."

"Tha'll 'appen git plenty mare when t'minister cums back for tha... leyke a wild horse that yan when he gits g ..."

I lost the rest of this comment as the car shot off towards my next port of call, but it must have been interesting.

Right on schedule, five hours later, I returned to Rewbeck, but only to discover that the scene at the fell bottom had altered dramatically. The snow had arrived in force, and was already blanketing the ground with a significant first coat.

"Better be gittin' this la'al lass– I mean Miss Victoria here back heyeme afore t'sney gits ony wuss," administered George Varn, the elderly church steward.

"Ney, tha should beyth cum in and bide t'neyght wi' us I reckon. It's gayly dark, and blowin' up bad. Not fit for onybody tae be out on t'roads I say," tendered his gentle wife Moira.

"That is most awfully kind of you I'm sure," burst in Miss Victoria with some urgency, "But I really must get home right away. Poor mother would surely begin to fret if I wasn't home by about nine-thirty. And father, well he becomes agitated if supper is delayed beyond that hour."

"And of course we don't know what things might be like by morning do we," I appended. "Might be stranded here for days... eat you out of house and home we would. Besides, I haven't brought my pyjamas with me." (Ghastly looks all round– and an inner blush on my part).

"Ah, but this little yellow bus here... it can tackle anything I'm sure. It's absolutely unstoppable, isn't it Mr. Teviot. And come to think of it, so is th... what I mean is we have an excellent driver to boot." Miss Victoria firmly assured us.

"Well tha's been preachin' tae us all about faith and that, hest tha not Miss, and as tha said mony times ower, we all want mare o' that stuff din't we?" solemnly pronounced the melancholy Martha, the Varns' daughter-in-law. Then piously lifting her eyes heavenward, or maybe upwards onto the hills (towards Blackrock Fell?) she added, "And as tha telt us Miss Victoria, faith alweys gits us through, ney matter what cums in t'way, or troubles afflict us. Faith can 'appen move mountains."

"If tha gits tae t'top o' t'fell, tha'll not need ony faith or owt leyke that will tha. If sney gits ower deyep, that la'al buggy'll slide reyght back down t'bank, and tha'll hev tae bide here for t'neyght t'pair on ye," droled her lugubrious husband Cyril with a dubious glint in his eyes, and typical unapt bad taste, "Faith'll not shift Blackrock for tha."

It was all very good fun, yet it did little to conceal the unease of the chapel folk, nor staunch the vague fluttering sensation which was developing in the pit of my stomach. Miss Victoria had pre-empted any unfavourable decision, and already climbed down into the car (like boarding an unsteady boat or entering her bath). I therefore elected to share her naive optimism or astounding faith in the car, the driver, and whatever.

"Better be gittin' tha tent up," came a split voice from among a coterie of pubescent males drooling and tittering in the chapel doorway, "Keyep sney off t'lass, and 'appen keyep her warrm an' all."

Half-a-dozen swarthy volunteers immediately set about the folded canopy, tugging, wrenching, and crushing with powerful agricultural hands, in an effort to cajole the seldom used, shrunken canvas to come over and latch onto the windscreen. The rigging made secure, this posse, with the same brute force got to grips with the body of the car, and to the accompaniment of much bawling, cheering and whistling, they shot her off on an undignified although fully authentic racing start. Once away from the lighted windows of the village, the night was dark, and the snow was falling gently in feather sized flakes. My passenger had soon forgotten all that she had ever been taught about posture, and was huddled down in her seat, leaving me to peer anxiously along the deckled beams of the little MG's outsized headlamps towards the daunting prospect of the Eastern approaches of Blackrock Fell. We had not proceeded far when the lady abruptly stirred and sat bolt upright,

"O dear, I'm so sorry to be a nuisance... but can you please stop... emergency I'm afraid... rather urgent you see."

"O dear must we? Can't you hang on a bit? O alright, but it'll not be very pleasant out there you know. And of course I'll have to turn the car lights off won't I?" *O dear my bad mind getting to work.*

"Please Mr. Teviot, you see I would like you to turn back... I've just noticed that I'm still wearing Mrs. Martha's wellingtons. She kindly loaned them to me to cross over from the chapel door to the car, and we shot off before—"

"Frankly Miss Victoria, I don't think Martha will mind a bit. She probably intended you to hang on to the things anyway, and for a very good reason at that."

"O thank you Mr. Teviot, I am much relieved I assure you."

"Relieved eh. I'm so glad, so you can now sit back and make yourself comfortable. Mind you that mightn't be so easy when I tell you that there's no possible chance of turning this thing about anyway. Road's too narrow, snow's getting deeper, slippery, on steep incline, car's starting to lose its grip."

Far from being shocked at this information, from then on the lady began to engage in an uncharacteristic spate of carefree conversation, as though self-consciously striving to keep any dire forebodings in abeyance. The ascent towards the high moor consisted of a tantalising succession of bends, crests, and troughs, causing the car to frequently slew and lose precious momentum. As we climbed higher the wind became correspondingly more aggressive and chilling. In places the snow had reached depths of over five inches and was drifting ominously. And still the brave little jalopy slithered and rammed her way through, whilst my dutiful companion kept up her recital of irrelevant chatter - pleasant, but somewhat hard on necessary concentration.

"Miss Victoria," I interjected, " I think it would be a splendid idea for you to put your scarf over your face."

"O dear, am I talking too much? I'm frightfully sorry... I'm an absolute chatterbox you know... that is under certain circumstances."

"No, no, no, it's not that at all. What I mean is cover your face and button up your coat collar. This bitter wind is not good for a lady's complexion you know... and it's going to become colder and colder. Mind you by my reckoning, for what it's worth, we should soon be at the summit, and once over there the going should become a bit easier."

This was a very wild guess on my part, for by this stage I had not even a vague clue as to where we were. All the familiar landmarks had merged into the bleak, blank snowscape, and what I assumed was the road was without continuous demarcation or even the guiding wheel marks from some recently previous passer by. Soon my worst fears began to assume sinister shape. Firm soft snow was leaning ponderously over roadside walls and eminences in massive folds, and high ridges were blowing up between opposing gateways. The car took to proceeding precariously in jerky waltzing movements, reminiscent of my days with tanks. Overall we were faced with the frightening prospect of worse to come when we broke out beyond the final extent of the roadside walls– such as were still visible– and out onto the wide sweep of the high open moor. I feared that this peril would spring upon us at any moment. I also fancied that Miss Victoria, now grown silent, was unwittingly displaying signs of becoming more tense.

"O Mr. Teviot it seems to be getting bad... I think I've changed my mind again... difficult I know but I think we should try and go back, don't you," Was she losing her former faith in the car, the driver, and whatever?

"A splendid suggestion dear lady, and I'm all for it. Except... except that it's not a very practical one. You see, at this rate of fall, and with this wind, the road will most certainly have completely closed behind us. And O, another small matter– we daren't stop. If we do we'll never get this car back into motion. Once she's lost her swing, we're stuck good and proper. Only one thing left for us– it's onward– or bust."

"And so... we soldier on?"

"Very well put Miss Victoria. There's no alternative and no choice for we've past the point of no return have you and I. Alright?"

"In which case I'm game if you are. We'll soldier on... and we'll win through will you and I... won't we Mr. Teviot."

The wind grew more vicious with every painful yard we pressed towards that elusive summit. Reaching a savage gale force, it excited the falling snow into wild menacing spirals, and carved knife-edged drifts in a confusion of irregular patterns on all sides. By now there was neither verge nor any other indication as to where the road lay buried, nor at what places deep drainage ditches, now levelled out by the snow, threatened us at the sides. Still the little car battled on, yawing this way and that, sliding, skidding, pitching, yet still managing to keep her nose head on. The wind turned more hostile and spitefully picked on our flimsy canopy for punishment, buffeting it mercilessly until it could endure no longer. With an ear-splitting slam, it snapped away from the turn-buttons securing it to the windscreen, and the entire contraption heeled upwards and backwards over our heads. It would have been unwise, indeed impossible, to stop to try and attempt a rescue or repair, or even jettison the canvas dragging in writhing contortions behind us, like a broken bird's wing.

"Back to open-air motoring Miss Victoria," I called out with feigned nonchalance, "Very sporting what? Don't you think?"

"Slightly cooler." was the lady's equally nonchalant reply.

The solitary windscreen wiper, a puny thing at the best of times, was by now set solid against the glass, and I thus had to sacrifice the only windbreak I'd had, and peer over the top rim– a most refreshing exercise.

"Soon be at that blessed summit," I muttered wishfully, "Start descent... much easier other side...wind behind... better grip..."

The velocity of the wind continued to increase with every miserable minute, and the falling snow harried us in blinding clouds and lashing swipes before gathering in deep undulating drifts before us, behind, and on every side. Miss Victoria's black broad-brimmed hat deserted us without warning and fled for ignominious oblivion. Fortunately the headscarf knotted under her chin had remained, and this she endeavoured to extend to cover her light auburn hair. The car now added heaving and tossing to its catalogue of crazy convulantics and was also showing warning signs of wanting to give up the fight. Snow was becoming tightly compacted within the wire-spoked wheels, making them more akin to road rollers than the fine instruments of traction they were meant to be. The same snow was jamming the steering mechanism, rendering the car about as manoeuvrable as a runaway dog sleigh. Whenever the car faltered completely, which by now was quite frequently, my brave companion would leap overboard to rock and push the thing with all her might until some forward movement was restored. Was this sedate and highly refined young woman secretly familiar with the crazy sport of motor scramble, now greatly in vogue amongst the newly emerging smart set?

The big one came abruptly, although by no means as a surprise. It totally obliterated the entire scene ahead, behind, and beside. We had struck the massive drift head-on, engulfing the forward half of the car with huge daubs of packed snow spilling over into the cockpit. No amount of grinding and churning would dislodge us, and even my mate saw the futility of a resumption of her rocking routine. Not a word took form for several minutes, as gasping and panting we tried to take in the shock, and the belief that our predicament was terribly real. Twelve hundred feet is not a good altitude at which to be stranded on such a night as this.

"O Mr. Teviot, whatever shall we do now?"

"We try and wriggle out and start digging Miss Victoria... digging like He— anything. You take the little trenching spade from behind your seat, and I'll go at it with my paws... not get us far but..."

"An admirable sugges...O dear... I can't budge this door..."

My big leather gloves were soon reduced to the consistency of raw liver and had to be jettisoned, and my hands were beyond feeling. The poor lady dug furiously, occasionally sinking back in near exhaustion and sometimes uttering faint whimpering sounds. We quarried for almost an hour, inching the car forward now and again, but only to slip, slide, or lunge into further trouble with every hard won advance.

"O dear... O dear...'fraid I'll have to rest a while... just a little while... Phew!" gasped Miss Victoria as she flopped over the offside wing which she had recently extricated from the grip of a multi-ton snowdrift.

"No need for you to apologise dear friend. This is totally hopeless and all our effort is for nothing... wasted... futile. You know what... I reckon we'll need to conserve what physical energy we have left and put it into something more worthwhile. Would you agree?"

"Energy! Why now that reminds me. I have a bar of milk chocolate in my shoulder bag. Should be lying on the floor somewhere... buried."

"Whoopee! Come on, swish the snow off the seats... in we get... time for break. Have to watch out we don't get buried alive mind you, if one of those big uns topples over in our direction eh."

Strange but true, but the car engine was still idling in perfectly synchronised four stroke rhythm, for I hadn't dared to risk switching it off– ah sweet music, the sound of pulsating life. Small comfort however with the wheels jammed solid, with the way ahead blockaded as far as the eye could see and our troubled minds could conceive.

"Miss Victoria, far be it from me to cause you any unnecessary anxiety," I ventured with some trepidation, "But before we spring back into the fray, amply refreshed and invigorated by this simply heavenly chocolate, we must together make a full and open assessment of our position here."

"On the face of it not a very complicated process I suspect. Am I correct Mr. Teviot?"

"You are always correct Miss Victoria, in which case you'll fully understand when I say we've now got to have a definite plan."

"Such as...for digging ourselves out of this mess?"

"No dear girl– for digging ourselves in. The car will soon be a dead duck– fuel's getting low for one thing– and we'll be dead ducks as well, if we don't do something– maybe quite drastic."

"Then if as you say I'm always correct... might I suggest we set off spade in hand, and try and make it down to Ackersgill. Surely it must be nearer than where we've come from."

"Sorry– can't agree. Indeed from now on I'm afraid everything we try to do has to be not spade in hand, but very much hand in hand."

"Of course, silly me. Anyway my suggestion would mean deserting this little car, and I'm not sure I'd be in favour of that."

"My dear friend I suspect you don't as yet perceive the seriousness of our mutual plight. For either or even both of us to try to get down to what I think might be the nearest place, that is Duncragg Farm, assuming we are where I think we are, could be suicidal. You, me, or both of us, wouldn't make a hundred yards. Miss Victoria, we are stuck fast in a blizzard with shifting snow drifts at an altitude of some twelve hundred feet. Lost in a fearsome storm near Blackrock Crag."

"Someone may miss us and come out and seek us– big horse or something." the lady pathetically beseeched. "Mother and father? O dear."

"Sweet thought, but no chance at all Miss V. You see surely the folk at the bottom, in either direction, can no more get to us than we to them."

"You just called me Miss V. I liked it... I did... you know that... I liked it... feel better already... please say it again."

"I apologise and I'm really sorry, but it just slipped out I'm afraid... accident. Reckon this lot's making us more like close friends."

"They always called me Vicky at boarding school you know. My parents put a stop to it– said it sounded too common."

"May I call you Vicky then? I'm pretty common myself. O and please, Vicky, do deign to call me Don. Short for either MacDonald or Gordon."

"Well now... that we've broken the ice... what a badly worded remark in the present circumstances... what I mean is now that communication is less formal and restrained, perhaps we can make some useful progress. Agree Mr. Tev– er– D-ddon?"

"The appropriate moment I think to establish the grim fact that we are partners in peril, you, me, and the car, inseparable, and must remain together at all costs."

"But Don, O Don, we might be buried alive."

"In which case, first priority is to try and do something about that canopy, and the side screens. Got to make this thing as secure as possible. Because Vicky, our only chance is to hole up in that small cockpit you and I, and stay fast."

"Hole up? I don't think I understand," quizzed Vicky nervously.

"Hole up– bed down. O dear me that was badly put. What I'm trying to say Vicky, albeit not without a measure of reticence because of my overpowering fear of being misunderstood, is that from this moment this little capsule has to be our shield and fortress."

The struggle with the ill-fated canopy left both of us well nigh exhausted, our limbs trembling uncontrollably in excruciating pain, our lungs threatening to explode, and our faces frozen into blank stares. We sank back into our low seats panting and gasping, whilst the frenzied wind immediately got to work on its revenge, and Vicky's digestion strove to cope with this strange notion of 'holing up'.

"This just won't do Vicky," I managed to squeeze from behind chattering teeth. "Musn't sit still too long...come on... out we get... we need some exercise."

For what I estimated to be about ten minutes we stamped our feet, ran on the spot, hopped, skipped and jumped, danced, and even sparred, until we had restored a modicum of circulation into our aching limbs, and totally spent up what reserves of physical energy left to us. Our spirits were a little revived however and so it was back to the cold, cramped confines of the cockpit to crouch, shuffle, bounce up and down in our seats, struggle to keep up conversation (futile), and generate silly forced laughter. Inevitably we soon ran out of words, ideas, and pretensions, and sank into an agonising impasse. And then, quite suddenly and unexpectedly, Vicky burst forth into song. Her voice, no longer strained, husky, or breathless, came over with astonishing zest and rich resonance, echoing over the turmoil about us.

"Hark the Herald Angels sing, Glory to the New-born King..." she rang out into the darkness, challenging the eerie moaning of the bitter wind, and the swish of driven snow. "Come on Don my boy, sing up, sing along with me, and don't let us drift into drowsiness... dangerous that... come on... together... 'It came upon a Midnight clear' ...O dear, what comes next? O I don't know Don, I don't know...

in any case come on Don... keep it up... let's sing our hearts out... help us keep our heads eh..." and her voice faded away in weak hysterical laughter.

But that voice– a wee bit unnatural surely– a shade uncanny– heavenly– O God one of us, or both of us– becoming detached? Try as I may, my own voice, awe-stricken, or lost in grim fatigue, offered but puny assistance. Vicky revived and resumed her singing, but finally her voice weakened beyond recall and dissolved into the storm. Surely it was time for me to take over the vocals, but only a low, warbling, crooning sound would come. I swear I had no conscious control over what came out. Some maverick emotion must have arisen from the subconscious and betrayed my secret pre-occupations. I was mouthing an old wartime ditty, not sure of the genuineness of the words or the order of the lines, but only that they were slipping out of their own accord,

"I'll get by, as long as I have you... Though there be rain and darkness too... I'll not complain... I'll see it through... Though the way be dark it's true, I'll stay with you... I'll cling to you..." and here both voice and memory fizzled out, and the cruel night continued to mock at us.

Vicky's brave endeavour had obviously taken a heavy toll of her strength and her emotions, for she sat slumped down in her seat for quite some time, breathing noisily. Then quite abruptly, as though summoning another surge of high spirits from some secret store, she straightened up and broke into a jerky, crazy discourse on hot coffee, sizzling toast with rich melted butter oozing from between the golden slices, big log fires singeing the skin of the shins and making the toes tingle, fluffy slippers, hot water bottles– O and thick, warm, woolly rugs wrapped snugly around. The she laughed and laughed as though beside herself.

"Hey." I exploded, "Vicky girl... bless you Vicky... in the locker behind us. Big rug in there... Otterburn... forgot about it... Gina's... for emergencies she always says... like keeping her legs warm. Vicky the rug, let's have it out."

In a painful display of rare acrobatics which nearly tore apart my frozen ligaments I dug out the precious Otterburn. My spate of fresh enthusiasm soon evaporated however, and I knew not why. I seemed to run up against another massive, impenetrable snowdrift. But this one was right inside me, a feeling of foreboding, unforeseen difficulties ahead, mystified by the onset of unfamiliar emotions. I very abruptly rid myself of the neatly folded rug, and dumped it onto the lady's knees. Fastidious to the last, Vicky unravelled it with patient feminine dexterity, gently stroked her hand over its rich comforting surface, and held it up before her, and contemplated it. "What now?" she said.

"Well, I suppose, er, I mean–" I mumbled, for some reason taken aback, "Well, shouldn't you wrap it round you... I believe that's what rugs are for isn't it... I mean, warming up frigid ladies." *O gosh, wherever did that one come from?* "Go on, and don't forget your legs... I mean your extremities and all that... you look so..." *O gosh again*, "cold and wet down there– Martha's wellies are over the tops with snow."

"No Don, please no," she protested, pushing the precious rug in my direction. "Can't sit here and watch you freeze while I'm snuggled up in your rug. It's your rug you know, all yours."

“Not mine Vicky, Gina’s, to keep her warm on cold trips. All of which reminds me, Gina’s. Good gracious Vicky, looking across at you now.– could just as well have been Gina sitting there all tired and cold and frightened. So Vicky, just as she would wish me to, I’m going to take good care of you, whatever the odds. Just as though you were Gina, that I am.”

“But surely Don, you also are cold and tired and... er... anxious.”

“Maybe so, but– and please don’t misunderstand me. Being a male, I am better endowed by nature than you are for this sort of endurance. And of course, being a male, I just don’t know what you may be wearing and all that, but I sh—”

“Really Mr. Teviot. Surely as a minister and a gentleman you just do no—”

“Vicky please, please, don’t pick me up wrong. Surely you agree that under normal circumstances the chances are that I would be more suitably clad for this sort of exposure to the elements than you are. I am a man, and you are a woman– *vive la différence”– O gosh here we go again*. “And another thing, you must surely realise that nature has also splendidly organised things so that as a male it’s my instinct and prerogative to take care of you.” I protested with a touch of male chauvinism trying to masquerade as chivalry. I also began to fear that I was maybe unwittingly beginning to venture into dangerous territory where I would have to tread with care and the utmost delicacy, without unseemly hurry, and carefully weighing every word before utterance.

“Most noble of you Mr. Tev… Don I mean, and be assured I really do appreciate your concern even though the credit has to go to Mother Nature and all that but O Don what are we going to do?”

“Share everything Vicky... everything... starting with the rug... half each. We’re in this thing together. Now both of us, together with the rug—” I bolted.

“Are you suggesting we split this precious rug down the middle so that we have half each? Not much benefit I reckon. Wouldn’t do the rug a lot of good neither I warrant.”

This idiotic turn in the conversation provided some welcome light relief and prompted us to giggle uncontrollably through chattering teeth and quivering lips, and to indulge ourselves in the fatuous talk which issues from shivering flesh and chilled brains. How long this mood endured I could not tell, for we were losing the acuteness from some of our senses, chiefly that one which marks the passage of time. Feeling the encroachment of seize-up I prescribed more physical jerks, but by now we were too distressed to try.

“No use Don... no use... exhausted I am. But I suppose you’re taking it all in your stride... being a man I mean. O Don I’m sorry, I didn’t mean to be rude... just my idea of a wisecrack. Don, you and I together have got to find some other way to... to... to–”

“Survive.” The word fell like shattering glass on the turbulent air, and brought frightening misgivings in its wake. “So sorry Vicky, but ‘survive’ is the operative word, as well as the stark fact, and Vicky, whatever the cost to feelings, I fear we must from this moment conduct ourselves accordingly.” *O dear, now I’ve jumped into it, right up to the neck.*

“Right Don, survive it is. O Don what are we to do? I feel so scared.”

“Well in the first place, we cannot just sit here and freeze to death, so, we’ve got to work something out.” I was stalling already.

“Got any great ideas Don? Mine seem to have gone all haywire or proved impracticable or even just plain stupid– like setting off to dig our way down to the village.”

“Vicky bless you. You’ve just given me an idea. We maybe couldn’t survive hoofing it right down to the village, but it is just possible we might be able to make it part way. If this is indeed the summit, and we have every reason to believe it is, in fact we might be slightly over onto the West side, then Jesse Traver’s field barn can’t be far down from here. Come on Vicky, some shelter, smelly perhaps, but sure to be plenty of dry, warm straw in there, stocked up for winter. Why, we could bed down comfortably and safely in there– not forgetting the blanket of course.” *O no, now my tact has surrendered to the elements.*

Something in the atmosphere indicated that Vicky had suddenly stiffened out, as though in some sort of recoil. It was maybe purely subjective on my part, but it nevertheless cut me dead. Ten minutes or more passed by without a word from either of us, nor even a glance. And the wind continued to jeer at us and wrestle mockingly with the canvas. Feeling the onset of drowsiness, and my mind going adrift, I blurted out on sudden impulse,

“Vicky– Vicky– come on lass– if we’ve to lounge about in here, surely we can find something more pleasurable...er... I mean pleasant to do than just doze. Are you game?” I swear I did not intend the words to come out in that form– they just happened. Imagining, that Vicky’s emotional temperature would have plummeted a few more degrees toward zero, I pondered long to try and resolve my thinking into some rational perspective. I became terrified at the waywardness of my impromptu words. There seemed to be innuendo traps all over the place, and I was slipping blindly into them. It was Vicky, bless her, who broke the tension which I had suspected was building up between us, to our mutual peril.

“Don– Don– still with us are you? Yes I’ve been sitting here thinking also, and I thoroughly agree with your... er... proposition. At least something more profitable than dozing ourselves into a fatal stupor. Come on, let’s get talking, and keep on talking, about any old stupid thing– ourselves or something.”

“Alright Vicky, let’s try. But I have to warn you, I think my brain’s got into a twist of some sort, or got ice crystals into it. Nothing seems to come out as intended. Sounds crude and improper. So Vicky please, it’s for you to start us off, I just can’t trust me. Induce the necessary stimulus, initiate the action, get me going– ball’s in your court.” *O God there I go again.*

After that one I fell into shock, dismayed to discover that I had no more control over the drift of my words than I had over the sinister shifts and shapes of the masses of snow all around us... threatening to engulf us. Good Lord, how would they be construed by my genteel and over-sensitive companion?

“Don– Don– alright are you? You look like you’re in a trance. Come on snap out of it– on with the talking.” At which point Vicky proceeded to regale me with a rapid resume of the important events and influences in her life past and present. Most revealing and not without surprises. Sometimes a little disturbing. There were frequent digressions of course, and lapses into the irrelevant, facetious, and sometimes even nonsense talk. Yet over-all she laid bare her very soul, with ruthless and uncharacteristic abandon. The sheer inspiration of being taken into the trust and confidence of this wonderful young woman was humbling, and touching in the extreme.

"Don– O Don– Phew! Whatever's got into me– never talked so much in all my life nor to anybody– and enjoyed it– for the sheer joy of it– talking to you I mean. Must be intoxicated I think– whatever was in that chocolate Don?"

"Nothing at all Vicky. I honour your trust, and share mine equally. Maybe pathological fear, apprehensive, each need the other to lean heavily upon. Seems the right time to pull ourselves together– that is, quite literally."

"I'm afraid I don't quite understand," the lady declared, "The meaning of 'literally', here I mean."

This unexpected response caused me to abort what I had carefully prepared to say next, for I was not certain that I had shaken off the effects of the recent fear syndrome wherein all my splendid ideas fell foul (quite literally) on conversion to speech. Even though these were the days before the pseudo-Freudian ethic had saturated all grades of human society, and respectable people were not generally prone to imbuing with lewd or mischievous connotations any verbal exchange between the sexes, in my present situation, and condition, I recognised the need for extreme caution. My elegant and modest companion and trusting friend was none other than Miss Victoria Athersage, delightfully awesome, and no ordinary Miss at that. She must be handled with great care, even though it was unthinkable that this courtly personage would ever invest any innocent remark or suggestion falling upon her ears, with carnal overtones. And this especially having due regard to our respective stations– hers by nature, mine by calling. How could I safely impress upon the politely reticent Vicky the vital premise that precedence must be given to our survival, even if at the cost of some elements of natural reserve and self-respect? And especially considering my bent for being accident prone in terms of faux pas when under duress, or simply, being especially cautious.

"Please Don don't just sit there– it's frightening and I don't know why. I know some sort of drastic action is now urgent, and Don, I'm game for anything."

"Right, let me first of all assure you that together with you, I also am game for anything - no holds barred," I found that one a bit dicey, but couldn't prevent myself continuing, "What I propose Vicky– not easy I know– but delicate a bit– rather personal maybe– intimate." *O damn, here we-go again.*

"Yes Don... but... delicate, personal, intimate? Not a potion I relish, and a rather scary proposition too." Was there a new note of indignation in her voice?

This shot completely demolished my carefully prepared stratagem, and my breathing became laboured.

"Let me assure you dear Vicky, my motives are good and for our mutual benefit. Let's keep our composure... get cracking before the mood wears off... I mean fades away..."

"Don, Don, dearest friend, sorry to appear to be stalling at every suggestion you make...Don... Don. I'm getting scared."

"Surely then it's time for action Vicky... to divest ourselves of all encumbrances... I mean remove all barriers... lay bare– that is strip oursel... show complete disregard for precedent...our crazy complexes... crippling inhibi—" *Why doesn't this thing go away? Every time I open my mouth, I slip further into trouble.*

Now in my young life as a soldier I had been embroiled in enough deadly battles to know that once you have strayed deeply into a minefield it is as risky to retract as to proceed. Verbal minefields also; so I blundered on.

"Vicky– to be frank about it– each of us badly needs what the other has got... the one vital thing each can contribute to our wellbeing...the only resource we have left... what I'm struggling to say is..." Another slip halfway across the high wire stopped me dead, giving Vicky a chance to interject with,

"O really. I don't think I follow."

"Warmth Vicky, is our only hope– warmth. Neither of us is any longer able to generate sufficient on our own... O Vicky this is all fraught with so many difficulties– that is, trying to avoid any rude trespass on your sensitivities."

"Would it help if I were to tell you that I am indeed aware of that. And yet, I feel so powerless to do anything about it. I also fully realise that if help is to come, it will have to wait until daylight, and that must be about eight or nine hours away. O Don you think we can't hang out that long?"

"Correct– yes– tough as we are we can't– unless– mutual warmth is the vital factor. I fear the implications of that suggestion may shock you somewhat... if so you'll just have to run away screaming."

"Wouldn't get very far would I? I know you'd just come after me and catch me and bring me back, still screaming. But no-one would hear."

"Of course I would chase you Vicky. I'm resolved not to let you out of my sight, or care, whatever the cost to me, either my person or my reputation." I declared heroically, "I'm going to see you safely through this lot even if it means going through Hell and back."

"Greater love hath no man than this, than a man lay down his life for his friends," Vicky declared in her preaching voice.

"I hope you're not making that famous quotation as a kind of joke Vicky, for it represents precisely how it is with me. Dear me I've had to risk my young life in much less worthy causes than this. Blimey Vicky, do you think the cold's turning me delirious?"

"No Don, just desperate to help me– to look after me."

"Yes Vicky, perfectly true. Indeed I'd go further and tell you that we've reached the stage where safeguarding your precious life must take precedence over preserving your privacy. I've tried hard, honestly I have, to break this to you as tactfully and gently I was able, for you see my dear friend I am fully cognizant of your slight excess of prudery– for which, by the way, I respect you most highly. But as is often the case, deliberate caution can be counter productive, and more so when like mine, the brain's gone into cold storage. So please Vicky, please, be assured that any appearance of vulgarity or presumption on my part is purely circumstantial, and indeed– accidental."

"I hadn't noticed anything untoward Don. I'm getting a bit thick... cold's making me light-headed. And besides, I am by nature a bit– er– naive I think it's called." Which confession made me fly for the crude consolation that any sensual overtones of mine were purely subjective. And this had the effect of making me bolder. "Vicky it's urgent... so much that notwithstanding the high risk factor we've got to go all out for desperate measures, and brutal frankness, even sending our natural reticence to the wind. Got to get our warm bodies rather than our dulled wits into closer contact." That Freudian slip must have added substantially to the girl's difficulties. It momentarily shattered me.

"O Don, I do understand, I really do, but– so difficult for me you know. What I think you're suggesting is sensible... right for us in the present circumstances... but... well I mean... you being the Minister... makes it a bit different... doesn't it."

"And you being no less a personage than Miss Victoria Athersage of course– that's got to be considered. O Vicky I'm so sorry I said that. I meant no offence. One fully appreciates the fact that our respective stations require a certain mode of propriety between us. That is, under normal circumstances. But Vicky, these are not normal circumstances at all, that they're not. Therefore surely we should perhaps not be concerning ourselves over much with conducting ourselves strictly within the letter of 'regular' norms."

"But the MINISTER. That IS kind of special... isn't it? O Don..."

"Vicky, Vicky, what am I to do with you? The collar, the sombre grey clerical garb, the title, the pious inflexions of voice, the whole gamut of prestige and privilege. So please Vicky, let's away with this priestly prerogative nonsense eh."

"Could try... if you say," she said, impervious to rebuke.

"Let's strip ourselves of all impediments you and I... er... what I mean is... the plain adulter– undul– the simple fact is that beneath them, the naked truth is... the bare fact is... I mean that inside is an ordinary, perfectly normal man... same thoughts... feelings... appetites... impulses... instincts as any other hum—" I recoiled at this one, wishing I could recoup it. *O dear me, does it mean the devil's come back into my mouth?*

"And of course my being none other than Miss Victoria Athersage, as you just remarked. Don that hurt me deeply because– well– it's absolutely true you see. I am no more than a disgusting, pompous little snob, and, despite appearances, with more inhibitions and hang-ups than most. That's what I am Don, and you know it."

"Wrong, wrong, wrong Miss Athersage. You see, and I know this too, behind the façade we respect, is the person we love. And not only a lovely lady of elegance and exquisite charm, but a delightful girl. And as I am finding out, gracious, brave, and true. Vicky I want to tell you, sincerely, and in plain English– you are a real smasher."

"I'm certainly vain enough to like the last bit. But Don, nobody has ever said such a nice thing to me before. Please stop flattering."

"Maybe no-one has ever got near enough to you. I'm so sorry Vicky, that was a slip, I didn't mean to be unkind. Just having trouble in making my thoughts and words correspond. Must be the cold or something."

"Don, and this is not intended as escapism, but, don't you think we should pray?" Vicky made her switch with unforced solemnity.

"Vicky, Vicky, what do you think I've been doing secretly inside me all along, without making a song and dance of it. Is the good Lord only responsive to ostentatious acts of piety, only hearing prayer that is performed before witnesses?" I burst in impatiently, for I confess that at that moment my pre-occupations were more practical than pious, and of dire necessity my aspirations more earthly than heavenly.

"So sorry Don... silly question... just another straw for me to clutch on to... futile I know but... poor excuse... poor... old... me."

"All of which reminds me that we'll need a good deal more than a straw to cling on to ere this grim night's through. This is turning into a very nasty emergency... in more ways than one. So Vicky... whatever our predicament compels us to do... we must get down to it pretty fast. Vicky my girl you're shaking... shaking... got to do something... right away... now... no…"

In spite of this bold assertion the logjam persisted and I was at a loss to know what to say or do that would budge it. Perhaps I was becoming scared of my traumatic lack of tact, which failure had probably precipitated the jam anyway. An insidious voice inside me began to demand something more drastic... cunning perhaps. No, that wouldn't do... try shock tactics... daring... sudden... an explosion... purely verbal of course... might get things moving… a bit... hurry boy before the mood goes off... or you lose your nerve again.

"Right, Vicky my friend," I bolted stumbling over a weak cough, "what I now try to say, and any subsequent action I propose, perhaps requires a certain... degree of... what a modest girl like you may regard as unwarranted familiar... some er... er... permissiveness which to you would be... infra dig. what I mean is... er... we may have to delve into those areas of privacy we don't usua—" *O damn here we go again– good Lord help*. "Vicky please understand, try hard... my inappropriate, and alas oftimes crass turn of phrase... neither implies nor indicates anything improper. It's just that... well. I'm having trouble with my choice of words... they just sort of... slip out."

"No harm done at all I assure you. Bit woozy and irresponsible myself actually. Cold's frozen everything up... resolve... reason... perception of things around... the lot. Please Don, I implore you, I'm neither shocked nor embarrassed. I'm a real smasher aren't I. You said it... so it must be true."

"OK then, so it's bold, brazen, reckless eh. First essential is heat. Got to hot things up a bit you and I." *Gosh how will she react to that one?* "What I'm trying to say is, that the only way available to us to generate and preserve our bodily heat is to get our bodies together... share it... that is, get into a tighter... clinch... a close...

er... well... is to embrace." *Phew that's torn it I bet. Pity I had to let the old vulgarism slip into that one. O just give up brother– just sit back– and freeze to death.*

"Dddo you mmean ssame as 'cuddle'? But Don... really... well you see. believe it or not... you see, I've never—" she blurted out as though some clumsy fool had slammed a heavy foot down on her stomach.

"Yes I know, Vicky. Nice ladies like you are not in the habit of snuggling under rugs in cars with young parsons," I pontificated, "Even at over a thousand feet. But Vicky it's elementary, why even animals..." *O dear!*

"Indeed– indeed! I'd have you know my man, I don't go snuggling under rugs with young anythings– at any elevation." said Vicky with some mock indignation in her voice. This tension breaker let loose spasms of hilarious laughter from us both. Not for long however. The laughter ceased as abruptly as it had begun, and we resumed our involuntary shaking, not sure as to whether this was caused by the bitter cold, or the release of hitherto pent-up emotions, "Well," she continued jerkily, "suppose what we have to do can be quite ...er... harmless in itself can't it, fundamentally that is, and of course considering the cause for which we have to do it. That's the ultimate judgement isn't it... I mean the merits of any act... no matter ho—"

"Then come along Vicky, don't let the vital moment freeze up. Let's contrive some way of getting ourselves up closer, for if we get any colder we'll be incapable of moving at all– in any direction."

"O Don, I've still got this awful funny feeling deep down inside me. You see... very unlikely I know... but what if we were to be seen?"

"And so what? Surely Vicky 'twould be a far far better thing to be discovered clinging to each other still warm and alive, than all cold, and stiff, and dead, in our respective, respectable seats. As for me, I would much rather live in dire disgrace than die of folly, or whatever it is that's holding us back from the only practical solution to our problem."

Vicky shook the more, and began to have difficulty with articulation, "D-don't missss-understand me D-don plllease," she spluttered, "You s-see I jusht w-want to lllook after you... I d-do rrreally... f-for d-dear Gina you ssee... Gina... Gi... and because I f-feel I'm sssort of in hher p-place here... and because yyou're looking after me jusht l-like you'd be c-caring for her. Wouldn't be in this m-mess if... O D-don... s-so s-sorry. P-pulll yourself tog-gether V-victoria Ather-sssage... must k-keep wwwwarm... fair bmeans or f-foul... mmusn't we. Pllllease D-don... help me... in your hands I am... just d-don't know... pleasse D-don... do the honours or whatever... before I'm completely addled... please Don—"

I moved up closer. It was like touching an electric fence. With my frozen hands, insensitive to the bone, and trembling limbs, getting the blanket enshrouded about us became a complicated procedure, and there were some awkward moments. Vicky simpered a little, shuddered, and actually seemed to shrink. Then quite suddenly she relaxed, as though shock had exhausted her. Or had she collapsed? Eventually she shuffled and edged more closely up to me, clinging like a distressed child, and quietly weeping. Good Lord, had this poor creature never known tenderness? The effort to organise a compact bundle of ourselves was fraught with more problems, emotional as well as practical. The low-level canopy, spartan bucket seats with gear shift interposed between, and the marine size steering wheel precipitated certain unseemly convolutions which tempered the sense of expediency with, for me at any rate, a disturbance of some residual guilt feelings. If any instinctive, or irregular emotions plied between us, they operated without the exchange of so much as a single word. To my grave disappointment, I experienced neither consolation, relief, nor sense of security in the exercise. Much to the contrary, for if any morsel of bodily warmth ensued it was rudely countered by a cold morbidity at the very depths of my soul. A tumult of shame and disgust came over me and vexed my mind with unrelenting remorse, and painful spasms of neat shame– dubious devices which my brain devises to ward off acute temptation, or panic. Had my designs been truly wholesome, totally free from selfish intent, or– devious? Yes, of course, I had used this perilous situation as a means to cajole this fine, attractive young woman into what was, for her, some quite unacceptable conduct. Surely I was, for subtly selfish reasons at that, attempting to shift the parameters of common decency. It was then that an earlier remark of Vicky's came and taunted me 'You being the Minister'– those were her very words. Surely here was a timely reminder that a particular mode of behaviour is demanded by the mores of my profession. It must not be sidestepped, not even in the name of or for the sake of survival. Maybe an irrational thought, self defence again, but it haunted and irritated me intolerably. A chance glance upward through a rough rent in the fabric of the trembling remains of the car canopy produced a devastating effect. I suffered two kinds of withering claustrophobia at once. An acute fear of our being gradually or suddenly overwhelmed by the encroaching snowdrifts was compounded by a suffocating dread of inescapable moral retribution. How long I wrangled with such torment, or strove to break out of this throbbing, pulsating brain storm I could not tell, for I had lost my mental bearings, and even time had paused in its own tracks,

Another defensive fluctuation switched me over into a mood of calm relief and sweet reasoning. My befuddled mind calculated that in such circumstances as we were in there was surely no grave sin in allowing one's moral sense to yield to expediency– the 'end justifies the means' chestnut. And so, encapsulated within the lush folds of the big Otterburn rug we clung nervously to each other ever sinking more deeply into a daze of stupefied tranquillity.

With searing suddenness it came, out of the black darkness and the swirling snow. A shaft of piercing white light, unnaturally white, eerie, sinister, so intense that it penetrated through closely clenched eyelids. Searching out– burning down to the depths of the soul. Rending the heavens like all the thunders of creation there came forth out of the light a great voice, resounding, echoing, shattering, terrible, as though it issued from the courts of the great Beyond,

"AND WHAT IS GOING ON DOWN IN THERE?"

"S'nothing... s'alright... really... really... harmless... really nothing... nothing... amiss... only trying to get ourselves warmed up...frozen see... what I mean is...

keep alive that is," came an involuntary squeak from my larynx.

"O I say, I'm sorry mate. Didn't think there'd be any bodies in there– certainly not two anyway. Never mind though, just carry on the pair of you and enjoy yourselves. It's gonna be a long night I reckon– do have fun." The 'voice' then doffed the great light before adding with what sounded like a mischievous chuckle, "Say, what a pleasant way to die."

That last remark however elicited a shocked reaction from us so swift that with astonishing agility we painfully extracted ourselves out of our tortuous embrace and re-established our innocently independent postures in our separate seats.

"Just dropped in while passing," called the spectre of the snow, "Be on my way now– and do take care you two."

"Not the time to be flitting around alone surely," chided the subdued voice from the seat beside me, "whoever, or whatever you are."

"Not just flitting about lady, nor out for a walk. Not joking either. I am alone though– no nice bird to snuggle up to for warmth and you know what. Otherwise in pretty much the same mess as yourselves. Got stuck farther back down the hill– was following what I thought were your tracks I think. Ran off road, wherever that damn well is. Right over on her side she is, in deep snow– never shift the blasted thing. Morris Ten/Four it is... heavy a bit... no use for this lark."

"What about yourself, alright are you, not hurt or anything? You're shaking a lot you know." I said.

"Alright? Well, yes and no. Tried to hole up for the night– wisest thing to do isn't it– nobody could survive for long outside in this lot. Thought I could maybe sit it out for the night, but the old bus is lying a bit lop-sided. Tried sprawling, and this was OK until I felt myself turning a bit queazy, and I got real scared, and something worse than that. Thought I could hear a voice... singing it was... way up aloft... in the sky actually... female I think... or maybe kids. But women or kids... what... up here... on a night like this? Hell... must be angels or something queer like that. Decided I must be going bonkers– you know, happens with hypothermia they say– hallucinations and the lot. Thought I'd better climb out and get on the move before my brain completely froze up. I'd risk trying to make it to the village. Not far from the top here I thought... soon be over... better on West side surely... wind behind and all that trash... really I'm going dippy I am... I'm going compl--"

"Hold on pal, take it easy. The cold's really getting in to you isn't it. We've been having the same problem, and that's why we're crushed together in here... sharing our body heat and the like."

"O yes... and the like... I'll believe you this time... in the circumstances. But hey, you never said, you must have been up here longer than me. Haven't you heard anything strange? But then of course you've perhaps been too busy to hear any heavenly voices eh? Never mind, just forget it– ask a silly question et cetera."

The stranger was leaning over the only portion of free-board left to the little car, which was up to the elbows in deep drifted snow. He set to work in trying to free the side gate to enable me to clamber out. "I was saying," the man insisted with pressing urgency, "Did you hear anything odd out there, about half to three-quarters of an hour ago– like singing? Or was it my flaming head?"

Suddenly a voice broke forth from the silent bundle crouched on the passenger seat of the car, ringing out with loud crystal clarity into the turbulent night air.

"Hark The Herald Angels Sing, Glory To The New-born King... "

Something had to give way, and it did. For at least ten minutes we shook with near hysterical laughter, like three drunks. The outburst cheered our spirits and served as a foil to the lethargy which we feared we were sinking into. Suddenly the stranger paused,

"Quite a lass you've got there eh. But look, it'll take more than standing here laughing our bloomin' heads off to get us out of this lot. I say we've got to pull ourselves together, and get cracking on some sort of plan of action. I say, that engine's ticking over nicely, keeping it warm, and battery charged eh? Why not switch your headlights on– you've no need to be in the dark now– let's see what we're about."

The man was young, tall, very handsome, and in the weird luminance from the submerged headlamps he looked eerie—rather than earthly.

"Your chario—I mean your car's a saloon you said?" I ventured. "What we need most is shelter, and there's the answer. Why not all of us try and trudge back to her and hole up until daylight? We've got a large warm Otterburn rug here."

"Never do. For one thing, you two wouldn't want me hanging around, would you? Anyway, damned thing's almost on its side, probably still sliding, petrol's pouring out of tank... that could be nasty... I smoke in my sleep you know. Three of us in one bed– not very convenient I'd say– er– that is– er– under the present circumstances eh."

"If only we had a bit of rope," put in the voice of womanly genius, "then we could go back and pull your car back onto its wheels, couldn't we." Vicky cut herself short with a retractive cough, realising that her suggestion was not very practicable.

"Hey! Not as stupid as you think Missus. Rope. Of course man, rope. Got a hank of it back down there in the car– whopping big shovel as well. I'll get me back there and fetch the b—"

"But what's the use of rope?" I muttered dejectedly, "with both vehicles held fast, and being buried before our very eyes. In which case how do we get this one close enough? Unless of course you've got about half a mile of rope down there."

He did not linger to argue, but even before I had finished speaking was already thrashing his way back downhill to wherever it was his saloon had foundered. Vicky and I peered anxiously after him as his flickering light gradually dissolved into the sinister snow-flecked darkness. We leaned upon each other with surprising spontaneity, breathing noisily, secretly wondering whether or not we would ever see him again, there being no small chance that this welcome visitation had been no more than a mutual hallucination, induced by cold or shock. For an agonisingly long time we stood still and stared silently into the snowy gloom. Vicky slowly slipped her arm through mine and inclined her head languidly upon my shoulder. Then out of the darkness, a voice, less than ethereal,

"Where the hell are you? Clear the snow away from your tail lamps man– blasted torch's snuffed it."

The sad fact was, that the said tail lamps had also snuffed it, having been 'shorted' by the encroaching snow pile. I tried to assemble my vocals to hail the man, but in vain. It was then that the resourceful Vicky burst into song once more, 'In the Bleak Mid-winter...' Soon our friend re-appeared, and although well nigh exhausted, triumphantly brandishing his precious rope and shovel.

"Bloomin' marvellous what angels can do for a fella that's lost and scared to hell isn't it. By the way, suddenly struck me as I came back, who are you two? Haven't been introduced have we. Might just be imagining one another– you know. Head's feeling queer again."

"Might even be a bunch of angels out for the evening," chirruped Vicky. "Well I assure you lady, this one ain't no angel. Name's Harold Bates. Been staying few weeks with aunt and uncle at Ackersgill. Never bargained for this lot though when I went off over across to York this morning. Everything happens so suddenly and unexpectedly around here doesn't it."

"You can say that again," I replied reflectively. "And O... me... I'm Don Teviot... local mi– er– local man... Lyndassby." I checked midway on realising that the term 'minister' could add an element of extra spice should the story of this episode ever be circulated.

"And the lady here? The Missus of course."

"O yes, the lady... er... Sister Victoria." I chimed in with some deliberate discretion, conveniently resorting to the custom within our denomination of addressing our lady lay preachers thus.

"Sister eh? Ahem... O yes I see. Well Don and er... Victoria, this little beggar here's got wire-spoked wheels I see. Now that's what I call just the job. And she's our best bet... lighter... smaller... tough power pack under the bonnet... cor still running as well. And she's standing on all fours. Further up the hill too I reckon."

"Lot of good that'll all do us," I moaned despondently.

"Come on mate, don't just stand there propping the girl up and wailing. Now listen. We lace this rope round and round through the spokes and over the tyres, and we'll turn this here little yellow jalopy into a Tiger tank. Alright?"

"Magnificent thinking," cheered Vicky, "Simply ingenious. Come on men, let's get cracking."

"By the way... fetched a full bottle of Newcastle Brown back from the car. Be nice and cool. Each a swig before we start eh."

"No thanks," said Vicky very politely, "Don't like the colour."

"Sister's very fussy about her beverages, aren't you dear?" I contributed with incredible composure.

"Come on then, forget it, probably frozen in bottle anyway. Better start putting a move on, things are getting worse around here, and so are we. Let's get them two headlamps dug out first and get a spot of light back on the subject.' And try and kick up a racket with the horn."

Our frantic concerted effort had no sooner got under way than we created another short circuit somewhere and blew a fuse. The next ten minutes was spent in digging out and releasing the bonnet, sending up a welcome waft of hot air from the engine, nonchalantly ticking over. We were still luxuriating over the open engine compartment when the horrendous thought struck me like a stab with an icicle. "No fuses... got no spare fuses... never thought of them before."

"While we ponder over whatever the implications of that are, and by the silence of you two I gather that might be pretty serious– I have three squares of chocolate left here. That is if my frozen fingers can peel off the silver paper."

"Bless you Vicky... never mind the chocolate... you eat it... just give me the wrapping... dear girl you have such a genius for being in the right place at the right time," I enthused chokingly.

A tight twist of the foil made an adequate substitute for a fuse, and both light and enthusiasm were quickly restored.

"Right, you two get digging, get her nose completely free, and her tail, try and make some tracks ahead of her when you've cut through that ten ton drift there. I'll attend to the rear wheels, try and get some grip into them– where's my bleedin' knife? Chuck that rope over will you. I say when you have a moment, you better try and get that shaggy old hood open... if you've got any punch left by now, that is," called out Harold vigorously, seeming to transform into a whirlwind.

The next hour well-nigh exhausted us, and at the end Vicky involuntarily dropped her shovel– I was digging with my bare hands -and we all sprawled about over the car body, panting, wheezing, and vainly trying to force our mouths to articulate words. It was the indefatigable Harold who succeeded in breaking through first.

"Alright, all set, let battle re-commence," he ordered before total torpidity took over. "Come on Don me lad, get them wheels a-turning."

With a fearsome roar the little 'tiger tank' took a determined bite at the snow beneath her, slithering and churning violently. I pushed hard on the throttle pedal, clung tightly to the steering wheel, and bounced up and down on the driving seat, as do professional scramblers to gain extra traction. Eventually we got a wheel hold, then inch by inch at first, foot by foot, to yard by yard, we were on the move, battering, slamming, and screwing our tortuous way through the deep, drifted snow. After the first enforced halt, Vicky took over the wheel, adopting the same bouncing procedure, rigorously cheering the car forward, and the rope-clad wheels spinning thunderously. The two gallants had now moved to a position ahead of her and were slashing and chopping at the drifts ahead like mediaeval infantry gone berserk. So immersed in the fray did we become, that none noticed that we had indeed crossed over the summit, the drifts were more widely spaced, and the wind blew with less menace in its voice. The car began to make better headway, with Vicky still performing enthusiastically at the wheel, and the two males now pushing from behind. So determined was our driver that giving the car an extra surge of power in order to attack a drift directly in her path, she did not notice the slight depression to the side. The car shot forward, slewed at the rear, and plunged– bonnet deep into a snow filled ravine, with the back wheels in the air, and the engine stalled. The unfortunate Vicky having been violently hurled upwards and over the front, was sprawled out in the deep snow. Like a shot I was by her side, holding her head in the crook of my arm, and tenderly stroking her face.

"Alright my love. you're going to be alright... don't worry... we'll look after you... where are you hurting? Steady now... don't tr—"

"Stop it, silly Don. I'm still in the fight... soft landing... not a scratch... no bones broken... even if there were I'm too cold to feel it... not even shaken... not even sha... O Don... Don... I'm so terribly sorry... so terribly so—" and she wept like a child. By now Harold had joined me by her side, and we slowly and gently sat her upright.

"Now lady don't you upset yourself... not your fault at all... done well to get us this far at all I'd say. We are in a bit of a mess I suppose... aren't we. Need nothing less than a tractor to bail us out of this lot I reckon. Otherwise I'm afraid it's—"

"Tractor!" exclaimed Vicky quizzically, struggling to her feet, with some obvious pain. "Tractor– shut up you two please, and listen. O dear, O dear me... must have bumped my head... going bonkers I think... hearing noises... seeing lights... O Don... Harold... please help me."

We tried to console her and settle her down, but she was soon up on her feet again and becoming quite agitated, "O dear it's coming again, the noises, the lights... fuzzy a bit... bobbing up and down... please gentlemen look... behind you... Don... Harold lights... real lights."

Vicky was suffering no delusion, there were two lights, flickering in and out of view way down below us. And also coming up to us in intermittent waves, a fully recognisable sound. Soon the great tractor came into view, reeling and waltzing to the growling, snarling, groaning strains of 'Fordson Major'. Up front could be seen the glistening blade of a snow sweep, and aboard were Harold's three country cousins, big rough lads who looked as though they were bred from a long line of Shire horses. On arrival they all boomed out at once a hearty greeting which, unscrambled, ran something like,

"Hey there 'arold lad, wher'st tha been lad, thowt tha musta gittin theesel' stuck ower t'moor or summat leyke, seyed glare o' sum leyghts 'bout an hour sine, went on and off a bit, just soort o' glare on th' tops mind ye, thowt betther cum up an' tak a leyeke, bit of a rough neyght up here 'appen, not sae bad at botthom. How ist tha lad? Whaat's this?"

"Am I glad to see you lot– welcome to the North Pole. Look fellas, sorry and all that. But I'm afraid Uncle's car's…"

"Buggered? Ney matter lad, s'lang as tha's alreyght eh." said the more vocal of the mighty trio, "And hey, wherdst tha pick this yannup? Bit o' lass isn't it? Bet tha muther dint knaw tha's cum out on a neyght sic as this yan, I warrants it, that I does."

"Specially wit that 'arold yonther. Naebody's dowter's ivver varry sayefe wit him abowt– aye," hollered the second giant, whilst the third one, who didn't seem to have speech, guffawed bestially.

Wasting no further time on their version of friendly greetings and introductions, and leaping as one from their mighty machine, the great three vigorously set to work on the stricken midget. Having thus far survived the buffeting of the storm, one wondered how capable she was of bearing up to the treatment being meted out by her rescuers. From somewhere aboard the tractor an enormous iron chain materialised. The great thing would have held down the Queen Mary in a hurricane. Vicky observed that this was a rather draconian measure, but her weak comments went by unheeded. A few minutes of super-powerful quarrying set the small one free, hoisted it back onto the level, and with the great chain attached to the shaky front fender, made fast to the rear end of the big Fordson. The haul downhill was terrifying. The wild antics of the little car as she was dragged unwillingly along the crooked track made by the towing vehicle were beyond belief. It was surely by means of some special providence that Vicky, Harold and I, who were jammed in an unseemly tangle in the cockpit, were able to remain aboard, for the car was rarely on all fours at any one time, and seldom if ever did she proceed on a vertical plane. After about an hour of this torture we made it to Duncrag Farm. The door was flung open and we staggered inside, shattered, shaken, and almost too weak from cold and exposure to show any visible sign of the great relief we felt. Here we met the remainder of Harold's large, boisterous, and extremely homely relatives.

"Sic a grand owld car an' all," Uncle Matt muttered repeatedly, "Whaat's tha deyene wit me Ten-Fower?"

"She'll be alreyght till mornin' faather, 'arold here says she's cowped a bit and happed reyght ower in t'sney– neybody'll ivver find 'er or try and shift 'er or owt leyke," assured the most vociferous of the hefties, "Ower risky to gaw back up t'bank– Hell up there."

"Hest had a leyeke at la'al yella yan in t'yard faather?" queried his brother, "Heyad fust in t'sney afore we dugbuggerowt. Gay lish yan that. Engine still starts, and lights still on."

"Nivver mind la'al yella yan in t'yard, meyne's not gawn tae bide all neyght on t'fell top, whaativver ye say abowt t'weather up there. If tha's all afeared or ower idle tae gaw back up, I'll tak t'spade and fetch 'er mesel'," emphatically declared a very determined Uncle, initiating a serious crisis situation. Auntie however skilfully switched the focus, beckoning loudly to the pathetic blue-faced figure huddled up on a ladder chair drawn so close to the fire that her sodden clothing steamed from head to feet.

"Just leyek at tha young lass, just leyek at tha. Soakin' wet tae the very skin tha is, cowld tae th'bone and shiv'rin' and shakkin' all ower. Poor bit luv, tha'll be gittin' tha deyath o' cowld if naebody does nowt gayly sharp for tha there. God bless tha, nice drink o' hot tea for tha... I've put summat special in it tae warm tha up a bit. Go on now me luv, just sup it all up and tha'll seyen stop tha shakkin'."

One sip at Auntie's special brew and Vicky exploded into a fit of coughing which nearly asphyxiated her, and put a sudden stop to the argument presently going on between the males. She was swiftly revived however by a session of pommelling and rigorous back-slapping from which she might have died from shock had she not been too chilled for feeling.

“Must be a bit ower hot for tha luv,” comforted Auntie, “Come on upstairs wi’ me... bring tha tea wi’ tha. Got a fair dash o’ whisky in it... gaws streyght tae tha bones it does... warm tha up reyght through. Hev tae dae summat abowt all them wet things tha’s got on, tha must be soaked tae the very skin. Cum on me poor luv.”

Exit Vicky, passively committed to the tender loving care of a very concerned Auntie. Harold and I promptly replaced her, close up to the enormous farm-house range, and tried to bring our trembling limbs and shattered nerves under some measure of control. The four noisy hulks left the room and resumed their family dispute in the farmyard. It must have been at least half-an-hour before Vicky re-emerged, smiling coyly, and her colour now restored to a rich rose flush. Completely re-kitted, she was splendidly arrayed in an odd assortment of too-large woollens and a pair of clumsy Wellingtons. She reminded me of a picture of an Eskimo I had once seen. I was unable to resist some mischievous inner speculation regarding the process by which this transformation had been wrought upon the person of the genteel Vicky at the practical and less than delicate hands of Auntie. The wild whim was instantly corroborated by the said lady’s loud outburst on entering the room,

“Here’s tha lass’s cleythes... ivry stitch, in-yans and outyans, wellies, stockin’s, bloomers, and all. It’s ney wunda she’s well nigh deyad wi’ cowld. Sic flimsy bits o’ things onyweys, and all damp tae th’skin at that, poor luv.” At which she deposited a folded bundle of damp unmentionables onto my knee before continuing, with extra emphasis, “Be gittin’ her deyeth o’ cowld, I’m tellin’ tha Mister, so just git her hoame sharp. I’ve lent her a few o’ my things tae tide her ower. Now just away and get ‘er tucked up in bed wi’ tha and keyep ‘er cosy and warm.”

“Do let’s go home my dear, I do want to go home,” whimpered Vicky, although making a very poor attempt at concealing the blush and somewhat wry grin on her face.

The journey towards the Athersedge homestead was through shallowing snow and therefore without any undue anxiety. The grind from the remains of the rope grips on the rear wheels offered some crude re-assurance that all was well at road level. The indomitable Vicky talked almost incessantly, except for the times when she would break off and hum a little tune.

“Happy Vicky? Well after ten you know... past your proper bedtime... and er... your daddy’s supper deadline eh?”

“Strange feeling Don... can’t quite understand... happy... kind of relieved... all sorts of feelings... and things,” she said, sighed, blew a puff of steam across the side of my face, then continued with her humming.

The Otterburn rug was still close by, for Vicky had cast it round about our shoulders and was holding it by two corners drawn together under our chins. It didn’t make driving any easier but it seemed to keep the inrush of cold wind at bay– and perhaps– generate other unfamiliar sensations. I drove right up the long drive when we reached her home, and set her down, in perfect gentlemanly fashion. I then accompanied her up to the front door of the large house, ostensibly to carry the bundle of damp cast-offs. All of the windows were lit up, and likewise the porch light.

"Mother and Father never retire until I arrive home, never," Vicky softly confided. Then there was an awkward silence as though she was having some problem in continuing.

"Very wise... very wise," I said involuntarily.

"Do come in, won't you?" she said, in a tone of voice which led me to fear that the lady had already reverted to her maidenly wistfulness.

"I'd love to Vicky, even if only to behold your mother when you present yourself in that glorious get-up."

"You would– would you? Well just you wait until Gina sees YOU. O Don– you look like an aborigine," she chuckled, then laughed long and heartily before checking herself abruptly with a self-conscious cough, and affecting a remarkable switch back to her normal propriety. It was a good try, but the former urbane lady was having difficulty in showing through her baggy, mismatched woollens.

"Well," I said, taking up the point, "I suppose it's now back to Miss Victoria?"

"Mr. Teviot– really– I beg your pardon. It is Miss Victoria Amanda Athersedge I would have you know. And don't you forget it my man. Do you hear me?"

"Sorry... I mean... beg your pardon Miss Victoria Amanda. But please allow me to thank you for your delightful company, and a most pleasant evening," I replied with suitable politeness and proffered the lady the formal handshake that was customary between ministers and distinguished members of their flock.

"Come off it... brother... dear dear Don. You know what, I wouldn't have missed today for anything in the whole world– thanks to you. Please dear Don, don't stand there holding out your hand. It looks so pathetic and unreal– so... unnatural."

Vicky leaned forward and kissed me on the cheek, only a brief, nervous snatch, the shock of her action seeming to momentarily stun her.

"Vicky!" I exploded, "Victoria Amanda! What has come over you young lady? Where are your... spectacles? I've just this moment noticed Vicky, you haven't got your glasses on."

"Lost them... long way back... shot off when the car tipped me overboard... somewhere in the deep snow I suppose. I didn't say anything at the time, because I realised you'd go and half kill yourself in trying to retrieve them for me. And I didn't want you hurt. Don you've done so much for me today, far more than I can tell, and I am for ever grateful to you. Brought me safely home through blizzard and storm, and lots more besides. Don, how can I tell you? You've helped me to be... to be... me."

"Then Vicky, Harold wasn't imagining it after all, and neither was I. You really are– an angel. You brought us home, and Vicky, we all love you very much."

She kissed me again, more resolutely this time, and turning swiftly, ran into the house without looking back.

I had a further two miles down the valley to travel to reach my own home at Lyndassby. On the low ground the wind and snow had petered out, and in fact conditions were similar to those prevailing when I had set off on my journey that afternoon. The damaged canopy, dangling at a crazy angle over the back of the car, heaved, squirmed and clattered alarmingly, and the knotted rope coils still bound unnecessarily about the rear wheels, beat out an ear-splitting percussion on the almost snowless tarmac road. But even this was comforting, for it signalled continuous, unimpeded movement, in the direction of home. I had drawn the Otterburn rug about my shoulders, and, for some sub-conscious reason, only half of it at that. It was not until then that I noticed– it was soaked through and through. On reaching home and penning our heroic little car, I staggered into the house, dishevelled and near exhausted. Gina did not rush out to greet me, for on hearing the arrival of the car she had, as was her custom, dashed into the kitchen to prepare a welcoming hot drink.

"Very late home tonight darling. Not had trouble with the car I hope. I know, invited out to nice big supper somewhere special I bet. Overstayed your... appetite. Lucky devil." Gina called out from the depths of the kitchen. "Bet you're a bit cold all the same... seems chilly out there... wouldn't be surprised if it turned to snow before the night is out. Got something nice and hot for you, so just get your feet up... not be a minute."

When Gina entered the hall where I was standing benumbed, with all my joints seized-up solid, and my eyelids refusing to blink, she almost let go of her tray in shocked amazement.

"Darrrrrrling– whatever have you been up to, whatever has happened? You're looking... just... ghastly."

"Ttttellll you all abbbbout it, affffter I gggget dried up, and thththawed out, and ffffed honey," I stuttered, "Ab'sssslutely Hell out there. Lllucky to ggget home at all. Blacrrrr... Broccc... Bwwwac... O dddamn it... Bbbblackrrrrock... newr again... never... here wwwwhat have we got on that tray?"

After a warm drink, followed by a hot bath, hot supper, hot water bottles, pre-warmed slippers, heaps of extra coal on the fire, total bliss was restored. Gina and I talked long into the night about the storm.

"By the way," piped in Gina at about 2.00 a.m. "You haven't mentioned Miss Victoria. I seem to remember that you were taking her with you this afternoon. Surely such a momentous event as that must have made some– er– significant impression upon you."

"O yes so I did. Impression? Well, kind of."

"She must have made some more congenial arrangement for her return, is that right?"

"Yes– and no. I remember taking the lady alright, and delivering her safely and on time for her appointment at Rewbeck. After that it's a bit of a tale actually."

"Oo do tell me– I'm all ears," Gina teased, snuggling closer.

"Mind you I did have a passenger to take home on my return journey this evening. And a very nice girl she was at that... very nice. Called her Vicky or summat leyke I believe. Eventful evening actually, let me tell you all about it, every detail, dot and comma."

"This second passenger– Vicky? That sounds cute. I'm intrigued."

"Fact is, I did go off on my round this afternoon, as planned, with Miss Victoria Amanda Athersage, a lady of considerable quality and grace, so perfectly poised, composed, formal, and staid a wee bit. But, by a curious twist of fate the passenger whom I brought back was a lovely girl simply called Vicky. Need to explain I'm afraid."

I then proceeded to describe the conditions and events on the fell top in colourful detail, including my problem with *double-entendre*. After some initial amusement, Gina mercifully passed this latter detail off as a symptom of acute hypothermia, that being a well attested cause of impaired judgement. She then went to great pains to re-assure me that under normal circumstance, as for instance now, I need have no fear of the return of the deadly trauma. Thus consoled, I continued the confessional.

"Conditions deteriorated by the minute up there on Blackrock, and we were growing weaker and less able to cope. We remained fully aware however of the extent of our peril. Even the possibility of our consequent demise was becoming a less remote idea. Possibly it was finally this that prompted us to indulge in a willing display of openness and frankness. I can in fact justly claim to have seen much more of Vicky Athersage than she is normally willing to display, the one concealed behind the image, attain some familiarity with... O darling forgive me, here we go again."

As I tailed off here Gina burst into a fit of girlish laughter, "Not very well put darling, was it. But I see what you mean by crude innuendo– must be the soldier boy coming out again eh! But surely, a thing can only be regarded as *double entendre* when it's intended as such, not when it's purely accidental. But don't worry pal, carry on– it's fun. Now tell me more about the blanket– that should provide a real trap for you shouldn't it– careful now."

"I'm glad you can see the funny side of things dearest girl, but nevertheless I'd have you know, there's a strong element of pathos in the whole affair."

"And that hasn't escaped me neither Don. Indeed my joking is most likely an attempt to dodge it. Poor girl, perhaps nearest thing to romance she has ever known. And she'll be past that before very long. So rigid, so precise, so demure– what a catalogue of insularity that is."

"I'm glad you're able to remain in sympathy through all this darling, because tired and worn out though I be, I am nevertheless very troubled... about my friend Vicky. And because of the deep understanding which you have shown, I want you to take half the load of a few sad revelations off my mind and share them. For, behind the cool, perfectly poised image there is a tragic figure, whether or not she has ever been able or permitted to recognise the grim fact. Maybe out of a moment of fear, panic, weakness, desperation, or some other emotion difficult to classify, Vicky has led me to strongly suspect that she is the hapless victim of a covert distortion of family loyalties. It would seem she is unwittingly held fast in some sort of bondage which is, albeit lovingly no doubt, administered by a doting mother and a proud despotic father. They have consistently set before her a cherished ideal of exclusive respectability to which from childhood she has been meticulously schooled to aspire and conform. Hence the prim and proper protegé whom we know as Miss Victoria."

"Poor poor Vicky. A cry for help do you think? Is there any chance at all of a break away? Sorry, sounds awful I realize, but—"

"For that we would hope and pray. But there is, I believe, one very serious complication. It is strongly implied that Vicky's substantial family inheritance is by some curious legal stipulation inexplicably conditional upon her perpetual spinsterhood. Alas our poor Vicky. What a cruel and callous imposition upon the love and trust of a noble and beautiful woman. Of course I suppose that one must allow for a possibility that there may be some pretty sound reasons, other than bizarre or just wantonly selfish, to which we have no right of access, as to why this state of affairs must be maintained, but I'm blowed if I—"

"Unless...unless," said Gina most lovingly, "unless another guardian angel comes along one dark and stormy night and firmly enfolds her to his bosom. And by the way my dearest Don, I'm not being facetious, I'm deadly serious. And what's more, I'm not jealous one bit. I'm proud of YOU."

"O yes, and another thing, which I think may come to you as quite a big surprise. Vicky is only twenty-nine."

"Coo. Only four years older than me, and one year your junior. But Don, she always seems so... so... senior... so... mature."

With that, sweet Gina smiled a radiant sunset, tucked me snugly into bed and kept me nice and warm, exactly as dear old Auntie back at Duncrag Farm had earlier prescribed for me and– Vicky!

POSTSCRIPT

The story of that wild escapade did not immediately become local currency, nor even did it enter the lively repertoire of the notorious bush telegraph. Yet by some queer quirk of subsequent historical recording it eventually passed into the colourful lore of the dale. Albeit with some significant apocryphal enhancement. And so, to this very day, when nights are dark and stormy, the cruel wind is blowing wild, and driving snow beats ominously upon the cold window pane, a strange tale is told over the cup that cheers in local hostelries, and where families huddle up to cosy farm-house fires, and mothers tuck away their children snug and warm into their beds. It tells of how on one awesome night, many a long year ago, amidst the fiercest blizzard that ever blew up over Blackrock Fell, a handsome young vicar and his beautiful missus were rescued in spectacular fashion by owld Jinny Scrawson's lads (there were three on 'em in them days). Aye, and summat else an' all. There was angels fleein' arowend on th'top on th'Rigg that awful neight. Aye that's reyght I tells tha... ask ony on th'owlduns, they'll tell tha. Aye, angels– proper yans– singin' and blawin' their trumpets and all that soort o' thing. And there was big flashin' leyghts in t'sky and alsoorts o' queer gawin's on. Aye. reckon th'good Lord 'appen laykes efter His owen in teymes leyke them... that He does... Aye!

An alternative version of the story relates to a mysterious 'Snow-Maiden' whose voice is allegedly clearly heard above the tumult by afeared and weary travellers in dire peril in storms over the Rigg. Whom, it should be said, she invariably guides safely home.

"Airrgh... Aye. It was sic a gayly rough neyght was that yan, and there's 'appen nivver been another yan the seame or th'leykes on it either afore or syne... Aye that there hesn't."

Chapter 15

IN EXCESSIVE GLORIA

"Tha'll beyth be joining us for t'carol singin' then?" Bob Askam's lusty voice made it sound more like a command than an enquiry.

"Maybe," I ventured with due caution.

"There's ney mebbies nor 'appens nor nowt leyke about it Ministher, we wants tha wit us... wants all t'noise we can git... aye and that la'al bit wife o' yours an' all - ivvry little helps."

Such a flattering assessment of our combined vocal worth could not be resisted, and sure enough, Gina and I turned up at the appointed place at eight o'clock prompt, to offer our eager participation in the great occasion.

"Leykes tae git stairted full week afore Christmas proper," Bob assured us, "Got a gay lump o' ground tae cover."

That was surely the understatement of the year. Covering that ground was going to entail long weary trudges in the cold and dark down endless country lanes, dragging ourselves along heavily rutted winding tracks which constantly threatened to peter out, clambering over hazardous shortcuts to reach isolated farmsteads up on the hillsides, or plodding over icy fields and rough frozen pastures. At some incalculable distance ahead would be that solitary flickering light, piercing the darkness and beckoning us forward with our glad tidings of great joy. On arrival we would disport ourselves in a crooked circle in the yard, and after passing round some whispered instructions emanating from Bob, we would burst forth with alarming suddenness into the selected carol. Whether the song had three verses or thirty, it would be rendered at full throttle to the bitter end. Bob however never sang a last verse, for he needed the respite to enable him to get up a sufficient head of steam to hurl us into a second 'choice' almost without losing a beat. On the very dot of the final word, a back door, or an upstairs window would be flung open from within, illumining the upturned glossy faces of this tough terrestrial choir. Greetings and good cheer would be raucously exchanged, in the midst of which a box on the end of a long pole would be thrust out to receive an offering of coins from the grateful listeners. Then Bob would herd us together and lead us off with urgent haste over hill and dale, moor and fen, long roads awinding, fields and fells, walls and ditches, bogs and thickets - at least that is how it was beginning to feel to me after the routine had been repeated more times than I was able to remember. Not so my companions, for their unbridled enthusiasm never wavered and their energy never flagged. These Spartans actually arrived at each port of call as if it was their first.

"They'll 'appen be waitin' up for us at Tolby's place," came the cry, just at the point where my wearied limbs and befuddled brain had calculated that we had completed our itinerary, and were heading for home.

"Only about hailf a mile fra here... gaw ower t'beck in t'bottom yonder... lot sharper... and up through t'copse."

And so it was 'ower t'beck' we went and ventured on what I began to suspect was another of those notorious 'short cuts'. The said beck was frozen over for most of its width, and the whole party, wearing Wellingtons, made easy work of stampeding through. Nobody seemed to have noticed, but I had been left behind, marooned on the wrong side. Carefully I picked my nervous way, slippery stone by slippery stone. Somewhere at about the middle of the stream, my ailing torch snuffed it. The next stone was a bad guess, or an optical illusion. As a matter of fact it was neither, but a patch of thin ice under which flowed twelve inches of very cool clear water straight from the North Pole. All very exhilarating, except for the fact that I was wearing my only pair of shoes. Two welly clad giants leapt out of the darkness to my aid, and with the deft action normally employed for hurling a wet sheep out of the dipping trough, whisked me up onto the opposite bank. Here a group of girls was frantically endeavouring to bring Gina out of one of her classical paroxysms of wild laughter. The next three hundred yards was agony, for all sensation ended at my knees, and from there downward I seemed to be lugging two prosthetic concrete posts.

"Ist tha up there 'arry? We've cummed... nice lot on us an' all... now what's tha wantin' us tae sing for tha? Summat special eh?"

Bob's greeting split jagged cracks into the brittle air of the frosty night. A small dimly lighted upstairs window swung open, Mollie Tolby's rosy face peered down upon us and her razor sharp voice peeled out, "Gi' us t'Bells ageyen Bob... tha knaws that's t'fav'rite."

And so it seemed, for we had already sung it more than a dozen times. As for the singers, their zeal for this number was never diminished by oft repetition. Besides, it sounded so 'native' to these fell folk.

While shepherds watched their flocks by night...
All seated on the ground... Sweet Bells...
The angel of the Lord came down... Sweet Bells...
They cheer us on our heavenward way... Sweet Bells...
Sweet chiming Christmas Bells... Sweet Bells...

This time the bells were nearly driving me batty. Either the choir was putting more gusto into this particular rendering, or tiredness was making my eardrums super-sensitive, for the volume and timbre were simply shattering. The cold night air gave the voices a keen metallic ring which echoed and rebounded around the farmyard like something gone amok. Gradually it built up into a deafening crescendo which must have sent up and scuttling every living thing for miles around. At one point it occurred to me, that if the heavenly host which flooded the cosmos with music on the first Christmas night had issued forth a sound like unto this, then surely it was no wonder that mighty dread had seized the troubled minds of those humble shepherds keeping watch over their flocks by night. Right through the song we sang, every verse, every chorus, every repetitive line. The shrill soprano voices of the girls vied with one another in off-pitch exuberance, the matronly altos boomed like bitterns, the tenors spumed and gasped and bayed, whilst big Bob and his lusty companions thumped out the bass like steam driven tubas. At the drop of Bob's hand the final 'bells' was resolved with an abruptness which inflicted a multiple shock on the nervous system, and at the same time got the laryngeal muscles into a kink. With a piece of superb timing, every window of the farmhouse lit up in one instant and the big oak door was flung open to devour the entire crowd. I began to suspect that this little spot of midnight drama had not only been prearranged but was part of a hallowed tradition of long standing.

"Tha should alweys answer t'carol singers fra top winther first," advised Mr. Tolby when queried on this fine point of etiquette.

An enormous log fire popped and crackled in the mighty grate, and there was plenteous warmth, light, and merriment all round. Large bowls of thick, hot, meaty soup were distributed and consumed with rapid relish, together with hefty hunks of fresh farm bread. There was strong milky coffee, lavishly buttered scones, hot obese mince pies, and massive slabs of luscious fruit cake.

"Ministher here fothers gayly well," came a coarse observation from somewhere in the room, but so engrossed was I in an unseemly display of gluttony that I did not immediately recognise it as a reference to me. That was, until I noticed that Gina had tactfully elected to distance herself as far away from me as was practically possible.

"Tha's gittin' theesel' some wet feet I reckons," was the next loud observation, but this time addressed directly to me. With this one Mollie, our host, caused a momentary break in the general hubbub, and all eyes were turned on me, freezing my champing jaws at mid-bite.

"Aye, that's reyght - tried tae walk ower t'top o' t'beck."

"Thowt he was that Sint Pether fella 'appen."

"Drinkin' ower much chapel tea... cowped ower slippy steyene."

"Better get tha feet dried up afore tha sets off again... can't have warm heart wi' cowld feet... not sing proper neither," broke in Mollie, at same time hustling me towards the great fire.

"Tha shoes is soakin' wet," and off they came.

"And tha socks... wet tae t'bone," and off they came.

"And just look at tha breeches... full o' watter," an awkward pause, a little cough and muffled chuckle, "Tha'd better stand ower t'fire and spin theesel' round like summat on t'spit and get dried up."

From that moment onwards, I couldn't have been a greater focus of attention had they been burning me at the stake. Clouds of thick steam and the acrid smell of singeing fabric well nigh suffocated me. More than doubly replete, the folk began to shuffle towards the door as though at a given signal. This action was soon to bring me the rudest shock of the night. My fond notion that the extra enthusiasm which had gone into the most recent rendition of 'the Bells' indicated a *grande finale* was totally misplaced. The idea that the sumptuous meal was some form of reward or recognition at the end of a mission well accomplished was but wishful thinking on my part. This call was but a pause in the way. In terms of time and distance it was but halfway. There were more weary lanes to trudge, rough pastures to stumble over, walls and fences to negotiate, and - Good Lord deliver us - more streams to ford. And there were many more renderings of 'the Bells' yet to come. By this time my voice had made the supreme sacrifice, and my legs were aspiring in the same direction. Otherwise I was now better equipped than before for the remaining rigours of this momentous marathon. The heavy woollen stockings which Mollie had rolled onto my legs would have fit a full grown giraffe, and the wellies were so many sizes too large that I had to take up what felt like two inches of slack with every step I took. And they smelled, how they smelled, both inside and outside, rich and vibrant with the pungent pong of warm cow dung. Gina still kept her discreet distance. More calls, more miles, and the long night wore on. Yet neither the zeal nor the vocal capacity of that hardy choir ever weakened. The journeys between calls seemed to be getting longer, and often took up more time than the call itself. But the pace never slackened. All was dark and quiet when we stole up on the Raylton's place, except for the gentle lowing and shuffling noises made by farm animals disturbed in the night. An upstairs window over the back door was ajar and a few inches of net curtain were spilling out. Bob aimed his opening salvo directly towards this spot.

"Ist t'Bells ageyen this year Matt?"

"Aye Bob lad, let's have t'Bells if ye can mind on them," Matt's muffled voice sounding as though he had already dived for cover.

Then the barrage went up, maintaining the same momentum throughout every verse, and every chorus, and every oft-repeated line. The great bombardment ended with the usual jar on the nerves and the sharp whiplash of echoing vibrations. The silent vacuum which followed enabled us to hear the creak of the window as it was opened a few more inches. When the light came on we saw that Annie peering out had got her pink halo of hair rollers entangled in the lace curtain, and Matt was skulking in the background.

"Thanks all on ye, that was real nice," the lady called timorously, "Where's t'money box? Happy Christmas all on ye."

The box on the end of the long pole was duly elevated, coins deposited therein, and greetings loudly returned. Then the Rayltons were suddenly re-absorbed into the darkness of the bedroom, the window creaked and closed, and an eerie peace was restored to Rowan Tree Farm. Now there was no lowing, nor the shuffling sounds which animals make when disturbed in the night. By this time my calculations had gone completely askew, and I had even lost the urge to grasp at any signs that the end was nigh at hand. I felt myself tottering at times, misjudging distances, misplacing steps, and the cold was beginning to find chinks in my thermal defences. Unexpectedly there came a whiff of warm steam over my shoulder from behind, and out of it came Gina's gentle whisper,

"I'm tired too darling, and I do wish we could go home."

But where was home? I had not only lost touch with time, but my homing instinct with it. My feet were turning into jelly, and neither they nor my brain would stay on course. I was occasionally plagued by an irrational urge to giggle disconsolately, or sit down on the cold ground and stare vacantly into space, but was unable to muster sufficient energy to attempt either. So unreal was the weird sensation that I imagined the sound of Bob's voice to be a delusion, and the flickering yellow light in the distance a sign that I was drifting into hallucination.

"Last call folks... yonder's chapel light... hope coffee's a-boilin' and pies is warm."

The initial Gloria In Excelsis which sounded from the heavens and echoed across the Eastern mountains and plains near Bethlehem could not have had a more divine sound. We were actually back to where we had begun five long hours before.

"Let's have t'Bells, just another yance tae wind up wi... sing up now all on ye... gi' it all ye've got... plenty singin' left in ye all yet. Aye!... come on Ministher, give us a strong lead."

I confess that even that rasping announcement by our conductor was not enough to offset the ecstasy of that sweet moment of heavenly bliss. And ere we entered the portals of that longed for haven of peace and light and warmth and rest, and hot coffee, and hot pies, both mince and meat, we gathered ourselves into a close huddle and sang 'the Bells' just this yance more, every verse, every chorus, and every repetitive line,

Sweet bells, Sweet chiming Christmas bells,
Sweet bells. They cheer us on our heavenly way,
Sweet chiming Christmas Bells,
They cheer us on o...

To my utter astonishment I suddenly found the will, the physical stamina, and the voice to sing with unbridled enthusiasm, every verse, every chorus, and every repetitive line.

I would not have missed that long night's merry ordeal for anything in this world or the next.

Chapter 16

CHRISTMAS CRISIS

The first Christmas at Lyndassby was a critical experience for Gina and me. This was perfectly natural of course, being our very first Christmas together. There were however other factors which made it equally traumatic. Household management had not yet settled into a regular pattern, and by reason of stringent demands upon time and purse, was not likely to do so for some considerable time to come. Our sparse financial resources ensured that we could not ever resolve the matter of simple budgeting with any peace of mind. Consequently, shopping lists were always meticulously scrutinized, and inevitably, drastically pruned. We smiled and blundered our way through, however, as young folk are wont to do, stoically assuming that it was the natural lot of recently-weds like us to have to endure such harassment, and want of so many basic necessities. All of which significantly affected our eager preparations for the Festive Season. Bit by bit we had built up a small store of culinary requisites towards the great occasion, so that even though there might be some shortcomings in terms of material provision, there was already no lacking in simple anticipation. It was during this period of preparation that Gina discovered to her horror and dismay, that her kitchen equipment was deficient of the essential large mixing bowl. Typical of her sex and status, she suddenly thought on the matter during a visit to town.

"It's simply a 'must' darling... absolutely and thoroughly... or there mightn't even be any pud, nor cake, nor..."

Now to my gastro-orientated mind, this was a crisis of no mean dimension. The notion of no pud and no cake was tantamount to the threat of no Christmas.

This matter must be dealt with urgently, on the spot, no holds barred now. Dredging my pockets at profound depth I came upon a half-crown, to which Gina managed to add from her purse a precariously preserved remnant of one-shilling-and-threepence. This as it happened, added up to the precise sum required for the purchase of one of those large cream and white earthenware mixing bowls seen in every kitchen in the land - except ours. Clutching the precious vessel closely to her, Gina sidled up towards the car, with a glint of triumph in her big brown eyes, like one who had just successfully pulled off a snatch of the Crown Jewels. With appropriate aplomb, I swung open the half door of the little sports car and Gina stooped down carefully to take her seat. We have never been able to work out what happened next, for the sequence ran through so rapidly that the main details were blurred. Gina's entire timing mechanism seemed to go haywire. Was it those over-large knitted gloves? Her coat sleeve got snarled in the door latch? Her foot slipped on something on the road? Perhaps the car maliciously leapt up at her? We couldn't tell how or why, but the shiny new bowl shot from Gina's grasp like a piece of wet soap or a slithering living thing making a lightning bid to escape. On the ground, by the side of the car, shattered into a hundred jagged pieces, lay the dismal wreck of the cherished mixing bowl, now as totally broke as we were. For a painful moment Gina simply stood there staring at the tarmac, crying silently with a thousand sorrows or more, as though the little girl she had grown up from had fleetingly returned.

"It's not 'cos the bowl's broke," she whimpered, "You're broke... and I'm broke too... everything's broke... I want to go home."

Gina was not to know it, but as a matter of fact I was not totally broke. With Christmas in mind I had long ago secreted away a hoard of thirty shillings, with the earnest intention of adding to it as the time drew near. This latter intention never materialised. My suspicions grew that Gina was harbouring some similar notion of presents, but with some poorly disguised urgency. On occasion, when I entered the room where she was sitting, a furtive shuffling motion and a ruffled cushion would betray a recent swift change of posture. Then there were the telltale fragments of grey wool which had drifted underneath her chair, and which I was obliged to discreetly ignore.

It was a drab and dismal Christmas Eve. It rained liquid ice, and the deeply penetrating cold set up agony in every joint and limb, and stiffened every muscle. I went into town, which was about fourteen miles away, ostensibly on business ("What - on Christmas Eve dear!"), but for the sole purpose of blowing my entire savings on the purchase of a surprise gift for Gina. I commenced my shopping spree with a quick reconnaissance of the main street shop windows, this to enable me to make a good and wise choice. The next foray was carried out slowly with a cool discerning eye. Then came a more thorough sweep, taking in some side streets, making a much more critical appraisal of what was on offer, and actually venturing into some of the larger shops. I trudged those wet, cold, and pitiless streets for what seemed like endless hours, until the movement of my feet became detached from my thinking, and my thinking got locked on a groove which led to nowhere.

I scanned those windows so many times that I could eventually have recited lists of their contents, such as in that futile party game played with a tray at parties. I got an acute feeling that my face had become transfixed into a gaping stare, and felt sick at its miserable reflection peering out at me from every lighted window. The misery was cruelly compounded by the reactions of some of the shop assistants, who would look at me askance, wag their heads apologetically, and address me with distant voices. It was not that I was difficult to please, or there was nothing suitable or desirable. On the contrary, for there was indeed an overwhelming abundance of eminently suitable and desirable gifts. But not at my price. The night was dark by now, and the persistent sleety drizzle combined with the glare from the shop lights began to hurt my eyes. The pain of frustration and self-pity was growing with the minute, and above all my pride was severely hurt. The assistants were by now beginning to display those specialised activities which signal that closing time is drawing near, and responded to my weary enquiries with polite irritation. And yet I continued to trudge that inhospitable street, until at length I had built up a tension which brought me to a grinding halt, reciprocating a cold blank gaze with my reflected image in a shop window. Then it came into focus, in stops and stages, until it stood out bold and clear, as though it had been placed there specifically for this great moment. It was not large, colourful, nor stylish, and yet it had strong practical appeal. It was enamelled in black, adjustable to almost any angle - a reading lamp. More significantly, and certainly most eye-catching, was the price tag - 'Reduced to clear - £1.10s.'

"Yes do wrap it up pretty please... present you know... want it to be a special surprise...thank you...very nice... no change... Happy Christmas to you."

With a lilt in my step, as though that once ghastly street had become paved with pure gold, I hurried back to the car park, where my faithful little friend waited, alone and forlorn, and her open cockpit awash. Put into motion and she purred happily all the way home. Tomorrow I would tell my lovely little wife that I loved her more than anything else in the world; the sweet sentiment amply reinforced with a thirty bob reading lamp.

Our modest preparations for Christmas Day had included most of the customary trappings, such as tinsel, greetings cards, candles, and dainty decorations. There was also the inevitable Christmas tree, which, small though it was, seemed to hold a mystique all of its own, as though happy childhood memories and far reaching anticipation were combined in its glittering magic. Santa Claus recognised that little tree on Christmas morning, for modest parcels neatly wrapped in fancy paper lay at its foot. Gina opened her parcel and 'discovered' her gift. Her girlish delight enhanced its value far beyond what it would have been if cast in silver and studded with rare diamonds. She fondled the little black lamp lovingly, gently stroking it as though it was all of fiction's Aladdin's lamps put together. I would never know how many hours, in secret, her clever fingers had worked on that Fair Isle pullover 'found' in the parcel bearing my name. That beautiful garment was a masterpiece of intricate patterns with rich love woven into every stitch.

The Christmas morning service was a perfunctory affair, with a congregation numbering well below the normal Sunday average. My sermon, which had been meticulously prepared with very special care was in fact wasted on the congregation there present, for it was indeed primarily directed at the unfaithful, the unbelievers, and the despoilers of the real significance of Christmas; the absentees! The obvious anxiety displayed on the faces of those present led me to make drastic cuts in the substance and length of the said sermon. The women were overtly suffering from visions of black smoke pouring forth from over-heated ovens way back at home, and the men were dreaming of things more pleasant to digest than my pious exhortations. In contrast Gina sat in the front looking so patient and serene that I wondered whether this might be an ill omen. Although well aware that she was capable of working miracles even with the limited resources available to her, and was adept at springing pleasant surprises, certain misgivings persisted. My worst anxiety was concerned not so much with what was cooking, as with what was not there to cook.

When I opened the front door on returning home that morning, the wholesome aroma of roasting fowl nearly sent me reeling backward.

"Came yesterday," chortled Gina, "while you were in town attending your special district church meeting. Sorry I forgot to mention it to you when you came back. Anyway you looked a bit done in didn't you."

"Church mee—? Ah yes, of course, bit of a drag it was actually and made me feel pretty fed up as well. Worked out alright in the end mind you."

"Yes, as I was saying, the door bell rang, and when I opened the door there was nobody there, or anywhere to be seen. But there was this large parcel that had been dumped on the step. I nearly picked it up and threw-it back over the gate... you know, the work of some sick practical joker or something of the sort. But curiosity got the better of me and I fetched it in and opened it. Gosh darling, I instantly began to modify my lost belief in Santa Claus. There was this great chunk of juicy, pink, home-cured ham, and this walloping big bird, already prepared for the oven. It's a real whopper... I wonder who—"

"We won't worry about who or what at the moment darling, except to remember that there are some wonderful people around us. Let's just believe for today that there is a Santa Claus after all and that he, or she, looks very ordinary."

"Or let's believe in Saints... It's said they hang around a lot at Christmas time. They look rather ordinary too, although ours of course was invisible."

"Some kind people prefer to bestow their gifts anonymously, but what a pity it is that they thus deny themselves the joy of witnessing the happiness of those at the receiving end."

Gina did in fact achieve wonders of culinary wizardry in preparing our Christmas fare; so much indeed that the most difficult item to digest was the feeling of disgust at over-indulgence. That bird, that whopper? To this very day we have never been able to establish whether it was an outsize chicken or a small turkey. But, as the local folk, and no doubt the mysterious donor would have agreed, it made 'good fotherin'.

Chapter 17

FOR TONIGHT WE'LL MERRY BE

It was one of the anomalies of life at Lyndassby, that the Christmas Party was traditionally held during the second week of the New Year. It would seem that a certain period of respite was required after the busy celebrations of the festive season, before this final fling. One suspected that another good practical reason for the two weeks delay was that this one needed to be 'talked up', many local people gaining as much pleasure from anticipation as from the event itself.

The party was scheduled to commence at seven thirty, yet within ten minutes of that deadline noticeably but a mere handful of people had arrived at the church hall. This last-minute complex was in evidence on all manner of local occasions. People in general displayed a marked preference for the anonymity guaranteed by arriving as part of a large group - sheep display a similar instinct. It was for this same reason that the name 'social' was the chosen designation for this particular institution, for no mature man of the soil would wish it to be known that he was going to a PARTY. Such were surely the preserve of those of tender years and delicate tastes - women and children for instance. Furthermore it could be observed that, by any other name, 'party' in the regular sense of the term, was hardly an apt description of this big annual event. In my estimation, neither was 'social', for this one surely featured a uniqueness which necessitated the coining of a new word, for example - Agrofling!

Like a surprise invasion, at about five minutes before starting time, the people arrived from every direction at once, in clamorously rapid succession, filling the large hall to capacity in a remarkably short time. From village large and small, distant hill and dale, lonely farmstead and shepherd's cot they came, for this was the great Winter get-together of the year, and if for no other purpose a splendid opportunity to talk 'lambing' with seldom seen friends and neighbours. The hall had soon exploded into a merry bustle of raucous voices and large bodies, lusty handshakes and full-throated greetings. All the guests were dressed for the kill. The girls were simply ravishing, with colour and style in abundance. Gathered together in such unusually large numbers they were obviously imposing some considerable strain upon young male equilibrium. The Mums, out of their drab farm fashions, had each shed several years in the process of dressing up for the occasion. Some of the men were unrecognizable out of gumboots and the motley assortment of tatty apparel which usually made up their working attire. Certain of the hill men were suffering apparent discomfort, and displaying some awkward signs of self-consciousness at being trussed up in unfamiliar style. They never seemed quite certain as to where they should position their hands, and were constantly bemused by the presence of their feet. The older men were farmers to the last, and in their smartly tailored, heavy tweeds, highly polished brown boots, and off-centre neck gear betrayed the well-known fact that their minds were never very far off the job.

"We—ellll, it's t'parson tae be sure. Ye knaw what mister, I hardly knew tha all dressed up leyke a proper man." Sarah Douthwaite had spotted my soft collar and colourful tie. "What I means is... well... I've never seen ye wi' none o' your proper cleythes on afore... If tha knaws what I mean le—" and realising that she had committed an irretractable gaff she checked and contorted into a bout of squirming, tittering giggles, soon to be joined by others of her kind.

Had I realised that my wearing of a collar and tie would create such a sensation mid-floor, I would have stuck to the old dog's-gear. I had considered that that might have been somewhat inhibiting for both the folk, and indeed myself, at a party - obstructs the letting down of the hair. Young and amateur in the ministry though I was, I had already begun to observe how the wearing of clerical dress was a sure means of eliciting a stiff respectable response, or of taking the shine out of normal conversation. Mufti notwithstanding, even on so informal an occasion as this, the older folk would insist upon conducting themselves as befitting my pious presence, albeit with not a little incongruity. This was maybe the Christmas Social, but it was a chapel social for all that. The loud banging of a massive fist upon a trestle table up front produced the intended shock wave, and George Randle's rasping voice cut an untidy swathe into the hubbub,

"Now then all ye foalkes, we'll ask t'Rivrent 'ere tae get us started off. Sooner t'bether I reckons."

Now, as I shall no doubt be constantly reiterating, for it is so central to my point, I was still incredibly green regarding the ways of country people. And so, this not so simple turn of phrase baffled me. Was it a request, an instruction, some odd observation, or what? Mrs. Randle however, quick to observe my predicament, solemnly corrected,

"Minister 'ere'll lead us all in prayer," and glancing reverently in my direction added the sweet injunction, "Grayess... you say it."

This one caught me unprepared, for I was still gazing with rapt wonder and anticipation at the good food weighing down rows of long tables that extended the full length of the hall. Unable to make a flash re-adjustment of my thoughts to my speech, I was blithely intoning,

"All good gifts around us are sent from heaven above, Then thank the Lord, O thank the Lord, For all His love."

"Should sung that yan if it wun't Christmas, or was 'arvest or summat leyke," raked an unknown voice in an amplified whisper, and whatever the intention, rebuke or display of weak wit, it came at me like a swipe with a blunt scythe.

"Onyweys," announced a more official voice, "now tha can all get theesel's sta– " The announcement was swamped mid-stream by the sudden onset of a din of clashing plates, sweeping knives, forks and spoons, gnashing jaws, crunching teeth, laughter and loud chatter, the happy sounds of people enthusiastically consuming large quantities of wholesome food.

"Likes tae put away t'grub fust," a nearby swain informed me, "then we can get on wi' enjoying oursel's proper."

When the meal was over the tables were cleared and dismantled with efficient haste. The guests disported themselves in groups and tight huddles around the perimeters of the hall, leaving the centre floor clear. It might have been thin ice, for no one deigned to venture out onto it. Eventually a petite solitary figure stepped forward and strode into the middle of the deadly arena. Young Madeline Bromley was an ex-Land Army girl, expatriate from Sussex, who had elected to remain in this area after the end of the war, and who had at this moment been unanimously elected as our Master of Ceremonies. The poor girl stood there long and lone, beckoning and pleading, at length lapsing into an embarrassed silence. The whole thing was beginning to take on the semblance of a seance got wet. She then tried to ease the logjam by offering carefull and elaborate descriptions of the game we were being invited to play, but this only tightened the resistance. Methought her alien accent, and a residue of Southern refinement didn't help. I myself made an attempt with some encouraging words to the group who had penned themselves in my corner, but this only served to heighten inhibition. It would seem that many of the country folk habitually invested the minister with an aura of superior detachment which was not his due, nor desire. The girls had by now shuffled themselves into coy giggly knots, and the boys bawled competitively across the hall with words of teasing encouragement and male bravado. With all of this pent-up rural energy and goodwill to hand, it was incredible that this party could not be got going. Country folk however were not prone to easy abandon, nor to exhibiting their feelings freely nor publicly, or by whatever name one chooses to excuse their native wariness in certain circumstances. This present situation required a hero, a brave soul to make the first move. Such a one was a long time in coming forward.

"Come on darling," whispered sweet Gina, "let's try and get things a-going." But for some lack of inner compunction, neither was I able to muster the necessary resolve and be that hero. Was it my so-called natural reserve, in which I took some secret pride? Or did I detect the onset of professional snobbishness?

Just when it appeared that all were becoming resigned to the painful stalemate, two halting figures presented themselves mid-floor alongside Madeline. Old Joe and Annie Brewster were veterans of many parties such as this.

"Let us younguns have fust go eh... come on luv, what's tha wantin' us tae dae now?"

There was loud general applause, but still no immediate rush for the floor. Much caution prevailed for some time, until one by one, and two by two, people began to sidle forward. It would be grossly inaccurate to suggest that from then onwards the party went with a swing. On the contrary; after the rules of each game or competition had been carefully spelled out, it would be pursued with deadpan seriousness, and joyless concentration upon getting everything just right. Certain of the items, especially those which involved such intimate frolics as kissing, or sitting on unfamiliar knees, were acted out like some dreadful ritual. The casual observer could be forgiven for suspecting that these lovely sons and daughters of the soil had grown up too far for their years, or had forgotten the art and spirit of play. They tried hard to make merry. Often the attempt was coldly precise, clumsy and crude. It would seem there was no escape from the dampening rural mist which hung over them. I wished that someone would introduce something musical, for there is nothing like music for loosening the limbs and breaking free the fettered emotions. Just then, as though my inclinations had strong telepathic power, a voice called out from somewhere near the stage,

"What about th'owld favorite... Grand Duke o' York or summat leyke?"

Oddly, I suddenly felt a strong bond of sympathy with those who were still huddled in the corners of the room. You see, I also am unable to let myself go at parties. And of course my now being the Minister and all that! I feel foolish when playing floor games, and am thus singularly adept at finding some plausible excuse for abstention from some frivolity or other. The piano is my favourite ploy, and to this refuge I fly whenever I am threatened with participation. There I am able to perform the extraordinary feat of sitting it out and being the indispensable centre of things in the same instant.

"Sumbody says t'minister plays piana," came a welcome voice from one of the huddles. (Gosh, that telepathic thing again).

Within seconds I was plonking out the monotonous, soul destroying routine of the Grand Old Duke of York, and soon wished he'd marched his thousand men over the top of a cliff. The game, as well as the music, is inane and painfully repetitive. Even so, I was utterly amazed at the way in which it aroused such spectacular enthusiasm amongst those stolid farmers and their kin, young and old. Gradually, the corners and the sides of the room began to empty and the centre floor erupted into two heaving lines of pitching, bouncing bodies, and stamping feet. Ah the magic of music! Eventually the silly charade began to take its bitter toll. Not on those indefatigable dancers, but on the pianist. My brain began to atrophy, and my fingers seemed to fuse together into a solid mass. I was stumbling over simple major chords, and breaking rhythm at every bar line. My confusion confounded the chaos already rampant on the floor, with all coordination broken and players colliding and stumbling into one shambles after another. My benumbed fingers blundered on, pounding the keys with mechanical imprecision, churning out that disgusting ditty with painful monotony. Well, I assumed that they were, that is according to the questionable perception of my befuddled senses. I never knew who, or what, initiated what happened next, but I swear it was not the result of any intelligent forethought on my part, because thought was a faculty which I had long since surrendered. Maybe it was Gina who had made or inspired that first move. She and her fifteen stone partner - a lively young bull - were at the time staggering down the ranks for the umpteenth time when, on precisely the same beat, as in the case of the unknown organist in the saga of The Lost Chord, my fingers wandered idly over the mighty keys and I found myself beating out the opening stanza of 'Sweet Little Angeline'. As though controlled by the same mysterious impulse to the very split second, Gina's dainty feet slipped with perfect timing into the first steps of the Palais Glide. The transformation was astounding. Within seconds the floor was filled with an orderly array of dancers in perfect rhythm and good heart. The shy ones began to slink out of obscurity and join in the fray, and clusters of hitherto gawping grinning youths broke up and joined in the dance, turning into men in the process. There followed the 'Dashing White Sergeant', performed with such vigour that Gina was flung about like the bait in the passing the parcel game. When it came to 'Stripping the Willow' I feared that she was seriously close to being dismembered or else that some of the dancers might be taking the name of the game a little too literally. 'Bumps-a-Daisy' was a winner which although it did little in the way of exhausting the dancers, almost paralysed the pianist. The middle-aged folk, not wishing to be outdone, dug out the 'Lambeth Walk' from retirement, and the older ones came in with 'The Charleston', for me as well as them reviving nostalgic memories of war time merriment. It is true that farmers' feet are not designed for dancing, neither are their limbs formed with fine movement in mind. Even in the slow waltz they tended to drive the lady around like a tractor. Foxtrots were executed with as much elegance as sheep- dipping, and dances involving ranks or rows invoked the kind of concentration employed in ploughing a straight furrow. Whatever may have been lacking in finesse however, was well and truly made up in wholesome enjoyment.

It was precisely at the termination of one of these epic endurance tests, when I was sinking back into my chair and trying to muster sufficient strength to enable me to raise up my broken wrists from the keyboard that I felt a firm cold hand laid upon my shoulder. Making a half turn I found myself looking straight into the marble face of George Jarvison. In the affairs of the village, George was the undisputed elder, and in the business of the chapel, he was next to God.

"Dancin's not permitted on chapel premises," and for at least half a minute we regarded each other starkly before George let go his second salvo, "Now tha's t'minister, and tha's gawn tae hev tae stop them afore it gets ower far."

Had I broken the rules - not George's - the official ones? Our faces remained mutually transfixed like those of two contestants working out the next move.

George's face - marble remember - was within but an inch or two of mine and was completely obliterating my view of the body of the hall, and the bodies assembled therein, and what was worse, denying me the chance of observing the reactions of the folk to this encounter. I habitually go blank in confrontations like this, and I wished that the man would say something and stop staring - any old thing would suffice, just to break the impasse, or give me something to tag onto. Patience paid off however - a knockout inspiration. In deep legal tones I found myself citing the relevant official regulation,

"The said Standing Order implies unequivocally that, whilst dances as such are not permitted on our premises, the act of dancing as part and parcel of any other social programme is totally acceptable. Note a clear distinction between organised dances, and the act of dancing."

George kept his awesome gaze firmly locked on me, but having for a moment gained the initiative I intended to hold on to it and not give him a chance to prepare his next round,

"So you see Mr. Jarvison, we are not out of order. This is not really dancing proper. It's games - all part of a games programme - games to music if you like. We're all joining in rhythmic musical games, our feet are moving to music and our hearts are leaping with joy."

I fancied that I detected some vague muscular activity in George's features. Whilst his lips kept a smile securely stitched up, his eyes let a little bit of it leak out. Then the dear old sport turned about sharply, and performed a magnificent vanishing act, merging somewhere into the crowd of revellers. The interruption had given the dancers the opportunity to recoup their spent energy, and to my dismay, they were ready for more. And more they got, and kept up the frantic pace right up to the Epilogue called by Mr. Jarvison (had the last word after all) at ten o'clock prompt.

This unfortunately was not to be the end of the matter. To the mischievous delight of some, and the consternation of others, word soon spread among the villages, hamlets, lonely hillside farms, cottages, markets and moors. There was in the area a large residue of leftovers from a former age of joyless non-Conformity, who became wary and suspicious of this modern young minister, who jazzed up everything that he put onto the keyboard, and who had a pretty young wife whose dainty feet had rhythm in them. A sure prescription for leading the dale to the devil.

I had always been directed to believe that one of the most significant contributions which our denomination had made to the thinking of the Church as a whole, was our emphasis upon joy. It was variously described in outright biblical terms like 'unspeakable', 'full of glory', 'overflowing', and was regarded as the inevitable by-product of a freedom of the spirit which only faith can bring about, and nothing in this life deny us. I was therefore finding this difficult to reconcile with the dour strictures and drab countenances of some of the local exponents of our evangelical message. These were they who would only permit the expression of 'joy' in severe terms more fitting to undertakers at a burial service, than to the true worship of Him whom we claim is the supreme source of all true happiness, and 'soul of all our joys'.

All was not lost, for Gina and I were thenceforth enabled to establish a more positive rapport with a wider cross-section of the fellside community. We began to discover that happiness and holiness are in most instances close companions. Remembering our 'calling', it became our earnest hope and striving that many would arrive at faith along the road of happiness, or at sound happiness along the road of faith.

Chapter 18

MATERNAL BLUES

"Is th'minister at hoame? Fetch 'im sharp... I've got tae have sum 'elp... it's reyght awful it is... get 'im sharp... please." The frantic caller at the back door was Ben Matfen, a near neighbour. His wife Nan had recently borne their first child, a big bouncing boy.

"Steady Ben-steady... easy lad," I called out from an airborne position half-way down the stairs, "Come and sit thee down lad... nothing can be all that bad... getting all worked up like that."

"Better both calm down I think," said the unshakeable Gina, drawing up two chairs, "What is it Ben? Do tell me."

"It's Nan, my poor Nan, think she's gone off 'er rocker or summat awful. She's gittin' howld on t'big carvin' knife, and she's waving it about summat terrible. Can't git close up on her nor nowt. Just cummed runnin' out o' t'kitchen wi' this horrible thing and—. Look I din't want tae say owt mare wi t'missus standin' there... would ye mind gawin' out sumwhere for a minute or two missus?"

Gina dutifully vaporised, leaving me alone with Ben, and the knowledge, communicated by a furtive wink, that she'd remain close on call.

"It's Nan, she's gone mad. Got howld on this big carver, nasty pointed sharp thing her mother used tae use in t'pig killin's, and she cums streyght towards me wi' t'point to t'front leyke... scared t'wits out o' me she did... din't knaw what—I'll— "

"Alright Ben, alright, now really there's nothing for you to get all worked up about. She hasn't done you any harm, has she?" I said stallingly and not believing a word I was saying.

"But she's bawlin' and shoutin' all ower t'place she is, and gaws slashin' this thing about leyke. I just laughed at first... thowt she was havin' a bit o' fun or summat leyke. Ye knaw the way summonem gits a bit daft and playful after t'first babby. She didn't want this yan in fact... nivver... until it cummed... and now she's all ower it."

"Good, just a spot of high spirits eh. Probably got over it by now... had her little bit of fun... scared you out of your wits... she'll be laughing her eyes out back there. Better slip back in case she thinks you've bolted for good."

"Just stood up full length leyke," Ben persisted, "Says nowt but just meks queer pantin' noises, and hissin' awful. And her face... nivver seen owt leyke it afore, all hangy and twitchy... couldn't howld bottom jaw up proper... and eyes... all glassy and glarin'"

"Good gracious Ben, that doesn't sound like a joke. What did you do... I mean how did you c— ?"

"Nowt. I couldn't, I was that baffled. Just stood and stared back for a la'al bit... couldn't move... or say owt."

"How dreadful," I understated.

"Then she moves a bit, streyght at me. And I off . Cums reyght sharp down here. Couldn't think o' neywhere else... sorry. What can we dae?"

"Now look Ben, this is no prank is it. I mean it looks pretty nasty, and just not like Nan at all. There must probably be something amiss somewhere." I was so pre-occupied with this evasive recital that I did not notice the re-emergence of Gina.

"The baby Don. What have you done with the baby... Ben?"

"She'd just gotten 'im put down for th'afternoon nap... afore this—"

"The baby Don, the baby, do something quick, come on." Gina shrieked and shot out through the door as though there was gelignite in her shoes. Ben and I were soon close on her heels, and it must have been by accident rather than by design that I arrived in Nan's kitchen first. Nan was a big, strongly built girl of about twenty-nine. She was standing with her back to the sink when I entered, having turned about to face me. Her features were frozen solid, her eyes wide and immobile, her lips twisted into a sinister sneer, and she was holding that evil knife.

"What are YOU wantin' holy Joe? Cummed tae pray wi' us 'appen? That's just what we wants, mare prayers, mare prayers, proper yans an' all, proper yans. Nay tha hasn't. Tha's cummed tae tek my babby away, hasn't tha. Well tha can have it back, if tha can find it. Mare prayers is what we want, mare prayers."

I was standing still, somewhat stunned by this opening, when Nan caught me by surprise. She made a sudden lunge, straight at me. Luckily my well-trained reflexes were swift into action. I moved one quick pace forward, affected the appropriate feint and accompanying yell, kicked the elbow of the knife-holding arm, and fixed a shoulder lock which brought us both painfully to the floor, the knife being flung wide.

"Honestly I wouldn't have... I couldna," poor Nan sobbed, her stockinged legs still poised full length upwards, "I would've dropped the thing... nivver want tae hurt anybody... nivver... nivver." Poor Nan was so torn up in hysterics that she was as yet unaware of her bruises. With a somewhat undignified struggle we got her up into a chair. In the excitement of the last few minutes we had not noticed the silent departure of Gina. Then she re-appeared smiling in the doorway, and lovingly holding baby Charles in her arms.

"Here Nan, baby's wanting you... been crying. Brought him down 'cos I think he's wanting you to give him a big cuddle. There you are darling, got a nice big chuckle for Mummy then."

Nan had quietened down considerably by the time Gina and I left the house some two hours later, although she remained somewhat incoherent. This factor may have been due to the sedative administered to her by the young doctor when he arrived. Methought the potion might have been more appropriately prescribed for Ben, who continued distraught and in severe shock.

"Simple case of Puerperal Psychosis," the physician assured Ben and me as he departed, "Post Natal Depression, or better known as P.N.D. Quite common actually... nothing to worry about... soon clear up. Give her one of these morning and evening and that'll do the trick - 'Bye."

This was all very fine, except that Ben didn't appear to find either the diagnosis or the prognosis very re-assuring. "Baby Blues," I foolishly jested in a vain attempt to bring a smile onto his face.

Gina and I returned home to an unsettled evening, and a restless night, with frequent nocturnal brew-ups. I was, as yet, unaccustomed to dealing with the full range of such shocks as were part and parcel of a pastor's lot. I did not relish a repeat of this one. There was however the consolation that the incident would for my part pass into the realm of routine, and perhaps be forgotten by Nan and Ben as they grew strong again. As it turned out this was but a vain hope. The change which came over the Matfens, and particularly in their subsequent behaviour towards Gina and me, kept the issue painfully alive for us for many weeks to come.

"They're just not friendly any more dear. Nan actually crossed over to the other side of the street as I approached her this afternoon. Never as much as a smile." Gina was obviously distressed, and anxious for Nan.

"Nan's not quite better yet darling. Takes a long time in some cases I'm told. Can become quite melancholic for a time, some of them other kinds of 'olic' as well. Some indeed, nev—"

"Poor Ben. Seen him lately?"

"Yes - unfortunately. Avoids me like the plague. Remote in his talk. Even at a distance, casts rotten glances in my direction."

"Must be that nasty throw you had to give poor Nan darling. Pretty rough stuff you know... glad you're a bit gentler with me. And I bet you'd be casting more than rotten looks to anyone who'd treated me like that, would you not."

"No Gina lass. Although I don't think it's precisely that, I have been giving the matter some thought recently. Features of my old war- time training I wish I'd never encountered."

"Like unarmed combat and such vicious things?"

"Yes, but worse. Probably never fully grow out of it. Comes to hand too readily I fear. Can create a kind of reckless arrogance in one."

"But it only comes when on the defensive Don, you know that."

"And that my dear is precisely what is wrong with the Matfens. They've gone over onto the defensive, and this is their unfortunate and irrational way of dealing with a painful memory they are unable to eradicate. To add to their miseries they have acquired an acute persecution complex."

"That's taking it a bit far dear. Mightn't it be a simple case of extreme embarrassment?"

"Either way, it's part of the same process. And I suppose our close involvement in what might have been a private domestic issue leaves plenty of scope for embarrassment, doesn't it. No need for it neither. Actually that young doctor, a bit professionally off-hand maybe, but he did try to take the edge off it a little for Ben. Gave him a useful lecture all about poisons in the bloodstream, temporary hormone imbalance and the like, told him it was unlikely to recur, even with a second pregnancy, and all the usual stuff. But Gina, something nasty and traumatic happened to Ben also that day, and he's still brooding."

"You know what I've been thinking Donny boy? Perhaps we all over- reacted right from the start, got excited too quickly, or just plain scared, and we carried things a bit too far. I fear Nan's sore arm and bruised shoulder are not the only injuries left over from that day. Nor is fear of a relapse of her trouble. There could be complications like wounded pride, loss of dignity, even some painful remorse. What a shattering experience for any woman."

"We've got to do something - desperate."

"S'right, and you know what you often say and are sometimes too ready to put into operation, according to your own admission, 'Attack is the best form of defence'. A quote I think. So, how about you taking a bold initiative then? Like going across and facing Ben and Nan head on about the matter. After all, you ARE the minister, and Ben DID trust you in the first place. You must make the opening move towards restoring that trust. and preserving it."

On that same evening, I took me along to the Matfens' place, and on arrival at the door gave the bell a long and less than nervous ring, "Hello there Ben, how are you? Just thought I'd call in passing and see how you three were getting along - our paths don't seem to have crossed for a week or two." My opening remark was typical of my rare flare for queering the pitch.

"Fine... OK... Aye," mumbled a steely-faced Ben.

"Nan? Keeping well? Getting along fine and all that?"

"She's alright... nivver felt better... thanks."

"And Baby? Bet he keeps you going eh."

"Babby's alright an' all. Nan's busy... bedding him down... can hear 'im crying... better be gettin' in," Ben was curt and shifty.

"Ah well I'm so glad to see you... just thought I'd call... you know, in passing. Better be getting along... see you again sometime," I said with an inward sigh, and walked slowly away feeling defeated. I had moved but a few feet away when I heard the door clunk behind me.

There was a moment the next day when Gina gave me cause for serious concern. I noted that she had provided herself with balls of fine white wool, and that every spare moment she could grasp, she would be knitting frantically.

"Baby booties," she replied to my unuttered query.

"Nice... very nice indeed... you mean—?"

"Yes, baby booties... for a baby of course."

"But Gina dear, you won't be needing anything like that... yet."

I felt perspiration gathering about the rim of my clerical collar.

"O yes I do, and pretty soon at that. So just run along Donny boy, get on with your work and don't hold me up in mine." With this sweet rebuke I was summarily dismissed from the hallowed presence, disturbed, but by a pleasing admixture of unfamiliar emotions.

When I returned later in the afternoon, Gina had completed her happy task. "Aren't they just sweet dear, with little ribbons? Like them?"

"Lovely... but I'll never get them on... bit small."

"Silly man, they're not for YOU."

"Are they to put away? Somebody's little bottom drawer perhaps. Stop teasing darling. Is there something I should know? What are you hiding from me? Are they really for—"

"Yes they are. For little Charles. Nan's baby. Got to make a break through somehow."

One fine afternoon later that week, the plucky Gina ventured forth. Nan herself subsequently supplied me with the information for the rest of the story.

"Hello Nan, so nice to see you. Couldn't resist the urge to come up and see young Charles... sweet little fellow... don't mind I hope."

The ensuing conversation was at first difficult and restrained, but although Nan was still somewhat surly, Gina refused to allow herself to feel unwelcome, and patiently vied for kindly advantage - a simple matter with her soft voice and such appealing large brown eyes.

"How I do envy you Nan. Must be simply heavenly spending so much of your time loving a sweet little cherub like this. May I hold him?"

"It is. That is, 'cept at nights. Not very heavenly when he starts playin' up at three in the morning. He's wet by the way. Hope you don't mind."

"Keeps you awake in the wee wee small hours then?" This wee pun melted the ice.

"Nay, not a lot - I don't alweys wek up. Ben's leyght sleeper and sees tae t'babby most neyghts. Dab hand wi' nappies. Nivver thowt my Ben would tek tae owt like that soort o' thing. Just leyke fish tae th'watter," and Nan rocked with laughter, her defences crumbling to pieces. Gina's timing was perfect.

"So that's it Nan. Ben's tired, not getting sufficient sleep. Been wondering... Ben's so uncommunicative these days, not his usual—"

"Sae bad tempered an' all. Shouts at me a lot. Nivver used tae be like that. He'll not gaw out onywhere, nor talk much tae onybody. Droppin' off gawin' tae chapel as well. I was wonderin' if men gets this P.N.D. whats-it as well as women?" Nan broke off into a short interlude of restrained sobbing before continuing, "It's not just that he's tired or owt, it's mare than that I think. He fancies iverybody's looking at him and whispering. Says they all knaw about my little 'do' the other week. I think I went la'al bit crackers or summat, but honestly I couldn't help it, I just couldn't help it. I knew what I was doin' alright, but I couldn't stop meesel'. I just hadn't ony control. Honestly, I wouldn't have hurt onybody, not a-purpose onyweyes... I just couldn't st—"

"Nowt o' this would ivver have happened if your man hadn't gone around tellin' iv'rybody about t'knife and all that." Ben had entered the room unobtrusively, and spoke through clenched teeth. But Gina, strong and tender, resolute to a fine-degree, remonstrated,

"Ben, poor old Ben, you've both had it pretty rough I tell you. Nan had her little upset, not a crime, not even a tragedy - that is unless you choose to make it such. There is no reason at all for feeling any shame - do you hear? Fact is, you've tried to dispose of your own feelings about it by projecting them onto other people. It's all in your own mind Ben Matfen, and if you don't shift it, people are going to begin to speculate as to why you've become so touchy. And that could become very nasty. And Ben, do be doubly assured, nobody knows anything about the little upset, absolutely nobody. Only Nan and you, Don and me. And nobody shall ever know... nobody... never... take my word for it"

"What about that doctor, wi' all his fancy talk?"

"Ben my friend, don't you understand?" Gina pleaded, "His observations were reserved exclusively for you. He's a doctor Ben, and doctors don't talk loosely. You might have to trust that man or his likes with your own life one day. Or don't you trust anybody at all, not even yourself? All our lives are full of mutual confidences Ben, and our own happiness is nearly always in the hands of some other. That's what friendship, loyalty, and love are all about. Ben are you aiming to ruin other people's happiness by destroying your own?"

Nan had sat down, sobbing quietly into her hands. The undemonstrative Ben stood erect and motionless, his features set at neutral. Gina stood her ground also, but with more grace.

"Have you no feelings at all man... or are you so ashamed of them you have to cover them over with bitterness? Is there no feeling of love inside you, no tenderness, no sympathy? Or do you consider that to be unmanly? In reality Ben, you're behaving like a perfect wimp. Shouldn't you be wanting to come over here and comfort Nan in some way, for surely you have noticed her distress. Come on man, what about putting an arm about her? That's what a strong man's arms are for you know."

Gina said no more, but stood there in total command, letting the ensuing silence sink in. Then her sweet face filled with the world's loveliest smile, and, dipping her hand into her carrier bag, she held out a pretty little pair of white baby booties with blue ribbon ties and bows. She kissed baby Charles, she kissed Nan, and she kissed Ben. She took her leave immediately, and everything fell into its proper place again.

Chapter 19

OLD SOLDIERS NEVER DIE

The heavy fall of snow was a winter afterthought, for March was already well established. Being out of season, the snow caused greater havoc than it would have done had it been expected. Some cars which had been caught out by it were slithering about in the street, and there were fewer people afoot than was normal for this time in the early evening. The Knotty Stowp however, was fully lit up in anticipation of business as usual. Landlord Matt Bretherton was frantically clearing a way through the snow up the steeply sloping drive towards his welcoming front door. Now Matt was built for neither speed nor power; the entire range of his physical resources was required simply to move his enormous bulk at a steady pace on the level from A to B. His face had acquired the rich red and deep purple hues of a full-blown fuchsia, he was sweating like an over-wrought draught horse, and the long drawn out wheezes from his heaving thorax sounded like a thousand death knells.

"Take it easy Mr. Bretherton," I called out as I passed by, "Easy lad, what's all the rush about anyway?"

"Seyen be... time tae... oppen 'appen," he gasped. "This slope's ower slape... nivver... gi... nivver ghit up on it... got tae... got tae... bluddy hell... I'm abowt knackered... proper knackered... nivver ghit... this lot shshif... phew... gimme few secs tae ghit me puff will th... phew."

"Better let a younger blood have a go," I chipped, swapping the rolled up cassock I was carrying for the shovel which was dangling limply from Matt's huge hand.

"Hey, it's t'young parson is it not? Hell I wouldn't hev said words leyke 'bloody' or 'knackered' or owt if I'd kent it was thee. I beg your pardon Mister... not let it 'appen again 'appen."

"Well well well, how about that then? Now just you stand back for a bit and let me get cracking on this heap. I'm in need of some exercise anyway."

"Nay Mister, cannae hev th'parson shuvllin' sney up or owt leyke... s'not proper... not reyght at all. It'll ghit me a bad name it will... not dae thee ony good neither 'appen."

"O come off it brother, I'm maybe divinely appointed, but I'm no more divine than anybody else. I have limbs and joints and muscles and things the same as any other man, and for the same purpose - good ones, strong ones at that. Whatever are they for if not for pushing snow around and such things?"

"But what'll yon chapel foalkes say if they cums alang and sees tha shiftin' sney from outside pub door?"

"And lead us not into temptation, but deliver us from evil," I swear that mischief slipped out before I could check it. However back into a more serious vein I continued, "I could quote some appropriate scripture Mr. Bretherton, something about 'prepare ye the way of the Lord, Make straight in the desert a highway for our God'. Personally my friend I don't give a damn - sorry I shouldn't use rude words like damn should I when talking to you, but it comes from the bible as well you know. What I mean is, I don't care who nor what sees me. Am I committing some sort of crime?"

"Tha's a bit of a bulldozer aren't ye - in mare ways than one. They'll be wantin' ye on their farms afore lang - lot cheaper than runnin' a tractor."

After about twenty minutes of very hard labour (mind you I had deliberately laid it on a bit) I had cleared a way from the road-side up to, and around about the pub door, which on being pushed open exhaled a warm beery blast that completely enveloped me.

"Now tha's done a gayly good job there Mr. Minister, and I thank ye. I tell ye what, I think this calls for some refreshment. Cum on, cum theesel' inside a minute, let's see what we can knock up for tha."

'Well well' methought, 'There is obviously room in this Inn for me but Gosh - whatever will any of my guardian angels at the said chapel be thinking, if they're watching?'

Assuming his official position behind the bar, and official voice, big Matt boomed out of his jolly face "And what's yours?"

My instant "Coffee please," seemed to take the landlord aback, but he soon recovered and shot off to the kitchen to prepare the welcome beverage. Rarely inured to the interior of common hostelries, I became greatly fascinated by the contents of this one. The rugged, blackened, ancient oak beams, never far above the head, were studded and festooned with a glittering array of discarded horse brasses. Shelves along every wall held trophies and insignia, many whose significance had paled into antiquity. There were old pewter drinking vessels from the days when hygiene took second place to the strength of the brew. Now they had become highly exalted to the status of ornaments. Other relics bore silent witness to the good old days of illicit gaming, and nocturnal fishing. A large specimen entombed in a glass case above the bar bore the legend, 'Biggest yan ivver gaffed in the Lyndass'. In a tight enclosure at a far corner of the room there was enshrined the original Knotty Stowp, renowned to be the actual gnarled gate-post which had had to be removed to make way for the building of this place which was given its name, way back in the year of Our Lord, seventeen-hundred-and-sixty-three. Two of the walls were occupied for their entire length by massive settles, large communal seats with high plywood backs peppered with small holes in intricate patterns. There was a cavernous fireplace at one end of the room, accommodating a large fire, crackling and popping a warm welcome for the first patrons. Moving towards the opposite end of the room, I took me to examining other large items at close quarters, with particular reference to an old Bechstein grand piano which was crushed forlornly into the corner, with the top down and the keyboard closed. Furtively, I opened up the instrument. It was not long before my exploratory tinkering took on the pattern of a familiar tune, albeit somewhat dated. Then the single notes began to resolve into chords, my left hand was beguiled into joining in, and my rump found its way onto the stool. One old number followed another, until the old banger and I were getting along like long divided pals. Presently Matt peered into the room, and coming up on me from behind, discreetly placed a large mug of steaming hot coffee onto the piano top. The gesture had a strange nostalgic effect upon me, and in an instant I had slipped back a few brief years, and was back on my stool in the NAAFI, thumping out those eternal singables for crowds of lads whom I would never meet again. And a thousand wartime memories good and bad, happy and horrific, came crowding in on me all at once.

"By gum lad, that's champion that is. Keep it gawn - that owld piana's nivver been played in years. Wonder it's still in tune. Reg'lar piana players are bad tae cum by these days."

"And I haven't played for a few years neither. We haven't got a piano at home - can't afford one neither. Got to keep a wife, and for the job run a car and all that."

"In that case I'll tell tha what. I've just had a good and practical idea - our mutual advantage I'd say. What about mekin' theesel' a bob or two up here yan or two neyghts a week. Get this owld piano warmed up a bit. I'd pay tha of coourse, and tha'd seyen be buyin' yan of tha own. Now how's that proposition sound tae tha?"

I was obliged to use up my entire stock of polite excuses, about time and opportunity, pressure of my work and the like, not to mention the devastating effect it might have on in-church relations. Casting these torments aside, I played on in selfish delight, as though the music, and perchance something added to the coffee, had rendered me unwilling and unable to tear myself away. Lost among the magical sounds, I had not noticed Matt move away and unbolt the front door. Nor did I notice the immediate entry of the first customer. When I inclined my head slightly to the side I saw him shuffling towards the bar. He was well dressed, and yet somewhat bedraggled. His attire was stylish and well cut, yet there was an oddness about the way it hung on him. He would I guessed, be over thirty and under forty, but already there seemed to be no sparkle left in him, and certainly no light in his limpid eyes. He drew a long-legged stool up to the counter, removed his soft trilby hat, unbuttoned his long coat, performed a perfunctory grooming of his forelock with the palm of his hand, slammed down his elbows, and completed the ritual with a long loud snort from his nose. I was still tinkering with the final notes of 'A Nightingale Sang In Berkley Square' when the man turned towards me and muttered,

"Bloody wartime rubbish - sentimental crap - time we forgot all that lot - isn't it Matt, eh?"

I gestured an apology, and left the piano, feeling slightly ashamed, and not a little out of my element.

"Let's have first one Matt make it a mild," the man called out, scrutinizing me disdainfully as I moved towards the door. As I passed by him however, my folded cassock slung loosely over my arm, I was seized by a strong compunction to stop and talk to him, if for no other reason than common courtesy. But what if he wanted to buy me a drink. Would he be awkward to fob off with 'Coffee Please'? I tried every tag I knew, the weather, the state of the nation, world affairs, football, family, but nothing would engage this moribund fellow. I soon began to suspect that he would be as glad to be rid of me as I would be of finding a decent excuse for making a discreet disengagement. The landlord, seeing my embarrassment, accompanied me to the door, and walked a short distance with me down the drive.

"Sure ye wouldn't want tae cum and gi' us a few turns on t'piana now and again? Customers would leyke it - good for your popularity as well."

"Didn't seem to work out very well with the first one, did it?"

"Ah, Coulston... tek nae notice o' him... harmless fella... means well enough... just... well... problems. He's alweys fust in and last out every night, sometimes afternoons as well. Often hev tae git sumbody tae tek him hoame on a night."

"Bit of a soak?"

"Aye, ye can say that. No good for t'place... not much good tae hisel' for that matter. That man's 'appen gawn tae crack up yan o' these days I tells tha. He gits me fair worried at times."

"Chronic alcoholic?"

"Summat leyke that I suppose. Cummed up here fra somewhere down in't Midlands, seyne efter t'war. Started off on a bit of a building business. Seemed tae be not very short o' brass - at start onyweys."

"Employ any local men did he?"

"O aye, a few. Still got yan or two I think. But nowt seems tae have gone right for t'last year or two. Lot o' bother ower 'is men. Then t'wife left 'im... went back tae mother in London they say. He was bad tae live wi... stopped out a lot at nights... worse for ower much drinkin'... he's a reyght mess that yan I tells tha."

"He certainly doesn't like nostalgic memories does he."

"Doesn't leyke very much at all 'appen... 'cept glass in 'is 'and. He'll be up there till closin' time I tells tha, then he'll stagger tae t'doo-er, and sumbody'll hev tae see 'im ower t'roaad, or mebees help 'im all t'way hoame. They're gittin' a bit sick on 'im in there. He'll be gittin' hisel' hurt yan o' these neyghts I tells tha."

"Which reminds me, so will I if I don't put a move on and get myself away down home. My wife will be wondering where I've got myself to."

"Bet she'll nivver guess," chuckled Matt with a foul grin.

"Haven't been home for tea yet... it's a fact." Thus saying I beat a very hasty retreat.

Arriving home I was greeted with "Wherever HAVE you been dear? Tea's been waiting over an hour and a half. And so have I."

I should have replied with my usual jest about jam and bread going cold with waiting, but Gina seemed to have already perceived that I was troubled about something - not a rare observation in clergy wives. When I told her of my adventures with the shovel, in the pub, the coffee and the piano, she threw up her arms in mock horror, then almost fell about with merry laughter. Then I mentioned Coulston.

"Gosh, did anybody see you? Anybody of consequence - you know the types I mean? What would they say if they had, I wonder?"

"Darling, I don't give a da-I mean I don't give a piano recital free... of course, do I now. And the pay is good...very good... and the company is genial." So saying, I was still wondering whether my casual reference to Coulston had gone completely over Gina's head.

"But you won't be going back any more, will you? Heaven knows, the money would be useful, if only to keep the car on the road, or get us a few necessities. But unfortunately you can't, can you? Rightly or wrongly, it could cause a great deal of misunderstanding, couldn't it?"

"I suppose so. But if we had to publicly explain ever—"

"But darling, it's more complicated than that... unthinkable."

"Dearest Gina, you always get it right. You see, that is precisely the trouble - unthinkable. I can't get something out of my mind... that man at the bar... that miserable wretch... Coulston."

"Now you can't just go running after him dear... probably wouldn't be very welcome anyway. What would you propose to do about him anyway, or say to him? He's so sullen and uncommunicative."

"You seem to have heard of him before."

"As a matter of fact I have. Sometimes heard the women discussing him, not in very complimentary terms neither. Funny temper... had a bad ulcer a while back... started hitting his wife a lot... went on long drinking sprees... then to pieces... pretty pathetic. She fled for good."

"Well I'm sorry my love, but I've got to tell you, something deep down inside of me is driving me to want to help that man. It's maybe not your business, or even church business, but it's mine. I tell you what honey, I'm going back up there to the Stowp at closing time, and I'm going to organise an encounter with this Coulston fellow. I'll try and contrive to assist him safely to his home. And I don't care who sees me, nor whether they approve or not. We cannot stand by and see a man destroy himself. Remember General Foch, 'The best form of defence is attack.'"

"Bravo Lieutenant - there goes my soldier boy again." called Gina, throwing the most elegant salute I had ever seen.

Needless to say, the encounter with Coulston was a failure, for once onto the street, he sourly scorned my assistance. Even on those occasions when I had to raise him up off the ground, he cursed and complained. My visit to his home on the morrow, when I expected him to be sobered up and perhaps more amenable to friendly conversation was equally disastrous. The aggression had gone, but the man had sunk into a mood of deep melancholy. Every attempt to make conversation fell flat on its face. Frustrated by the result of this brief foray, I attempted a tactical diversion, that of introducing a pretext for being in some urgent haste, having just noticed the time. I made for the door, opened it myself, revealing the car parked at the gate. I was surprised when Coulston accompanied me, for I hadn't deemed courtesy to be his forte.

"Hey! What's that little yellow sport there? Not yours is it?" he slobbered, falling over his words and some unfamiliar enthusiasm.

"Mine alright. Like it? MG - J Type - 8hp Overhead Cam - '37 I think - well some of it is - I think."

"You're doing a lot of thinking. Aren't you sure?"

"No I'm not actually. Bit like me I'm afraid - bit of a bas- - - I mean made up of bits and pieces from all over the place. Good stuff though."

The immediate effect upon Coulston was sheer magic. Revived in health and vitality, he shot down the steps from his front door, and began to fondle our little pride and joy from end to end, and inside out.

"Wow! O yes. Marvellous! Genuine article this alright, and I should know. Used to have one of these myself... red... lively... fast... incredible little bomber she was. Now them were the days. Don't want to sell her do you? Sell me soul for one of these."

A few more minutes of fond eulogising, and Coulston was unable to resist the urge to step into the cockpit. He began to tinker with the controls, purely for old times sake he explained, and in doing so just happened to draw the starter switch. The faithful little lady sprang instantly to life with an ear-splitting roar, so inviting that Coulston moved over to the passenger seat and gestured for me to take the wheel. For the next hour I conducted him on the fastest, windiest, bumpiest, noisiest, coldest, wildest spot of motoring he had enjoyed for many a year. Whether it was the invigorating effect of the icy blast streaming through the open car, the physical shake up, or the exhilaration of lively nostalgia, I couldn't tell, but I delivered back to that house a far different man from he who had set off with me but one hour before.

"Strong coffee," he announced when we had found a place to sit in his grossly untidy house. "Always keep plenty of strong coffee... addicted to the stuff you know."

The said coffee was so potent that I imagined that it must have been brewing slowly for a week, and the first gulp of the disgusting stuff set off a gastric explosion.

The query did cross my mind, that if this concoction was intended for the sobering up of soaks, what would be its effect upon the abstemious, such as me? Was it a stimulant (a kind of shock therapy)? Or would it induce stupor, or delusions perhaps? Was the man really talking with me? He was indeed, in fact he was still enthusing. But he was talking, actually conversing. It was perhaps too early to presume that we had achieved a breakthrough, except, that Coulston's final remark as I left him seemed to make such sense,

"Have to have another wild trip some day, if you please."

Without appearing to push the issue, I ensured that this 'some day' came around very soon. Thus began a series of MG runs, and home visits deliberately calculated to assist this man in blowing his cover of bitterness and depression. He talked readily now, but never without constant prompting, and any apparent encroachment into certain specific areas would cause him to clamp on the restraints. He told me about his ulcer, his business misfortunes, his drinking, and his wife - in that order. But he invariably addressed these issues from the point of view of the victim. He never saw himself as the possible cause. He was on the whole very articulate, and yet there was intelligent caution in his choice of words. He would fidget incessantly, fumble with a cigarette or, whenever he felt that something was slipping out too freely, push it between his lips and indulge in some long pulls. Sometimes he would abruptly alter the subject, and seek refuge in a switch to some more congenial subject, such as motor talk. This man was acting out symptoms rather than stating a case. Patience therefore was the order of the day; the man had to be drawn somehow. The idea once occurred to me that the quirks of the little yellow MG might provide some useful bait to this end, for so far that old jalopy was having a curious effect upon Coulston. A trifle unorthodox however, considering that my concern was strictly pastoral, but nevertheless a passing thought to smile at, then discard in disgust.

I saw Coulston frequently during the next couple of months, even though it was usually when I contrived to be passing by the Knotty Stowp just after closing time. I would use such a 'chance' meeting as an excuse for escorting him home. There were other occasions when, to his obvious delight, I took him away for what he termed a 'blow out' in the much venerated sports car, which car had now become the vital link between Coulston and me. It had the power to loose his tongue, and how I envied the strange rapport which had sprung up between them. There still remained the more official calls, purely duty and pastoral of course, although heavily camouflaged. In this mode I would note how Coulston flaunted his withdrawal symptoms, if such they were. I would react true to form by trying to insinuate into the conversation all the classical incentives in which I had been recently schooled. None seemed to work on him, for the simple reason that Coulston was not a classical subject. Business worries of course? Health matters? Some secret personal anxiety, or serious family concern? Unresolved infantile fears - a childhood trauma? Thwarted ambition, rejection, unexpired rage, unmitigated hate, anger? Something black and sinister at work in the subconscious? Then of course there was that sure winner and absolute must in any sound analysis of personality and resolution of emotional problems - his sex life? No, that one was a trifle personal for Coulston, and taboo for me. What about repressed guilt? Guilt transference? Projected guilt? Guilt - but that was surely verging upon the religious, and to trespass in that direction could, in one tactless move, destroy all that had so far been built up between us. Thus it was that over a period of many weeks I expended my professional best in an effort to probe the cause of this man's hang-ups. I doubted whether Coulston was receiving any benefit out of the exercise, for it was threatening to destroy my own self-confidence. For one thing, and I knew it, I was talking too much; which is what I habitually do when I have nothing to say, or am feeling hopelessly vulnerable. The taciturn Coulston would respond by peering expressionless into my face, or indicate his agitation by fumbling and fidgeting with a well-worn cigarette. Occasionally he would venture on a mumbled comment, but if it didn't peter out before it made sense, it would be swamped by my ever-ready zeal to keep the sound going. I had not yet learned that there is nothing amiss with prolonged contemplative silences. Silence can be golden, is rarely sterile, and may open up ways and means which are tightly closed against all other prerequisites. It was during one such period of silence that it began to dawn upon me that the error was entirely on my side. I was, in effect, striving desperately to win over from Coulston his trust and confidence in me. Perhaps I should endeavour to reverse the order and become less questing. I should make my trust in Coulston become the operative factor in this enterprise. Forget this psychotherapy stuff, at which I am but a poor amateur anyway. This spiritless approach on a purely academic level would never do, the classical approach, the professional touch, and even that hardy misnomer, pastoral concern. Whether any of these qualities were of any positive value in the circumstance in hand was open to conjecture. Let me try the one thing I'm good at– friendship. God make me this man's friend, to share equally, to endure each other in the same measure. Let me therefore be less patronising, and if it is possible for me, to love the unloving and unlovable. Surely if one is trying to save a soul from whatever, it is well to remember that tolerance and friendship get nearer to the heart of a man than all the preaching and counselling in the world. And so, with one so insular, suspicious, and withdrawn the first priority must be to establish a mutually effective friendship. Well, I did say earlier that a period of silence could be useful!

It was on one stormy evening, so stormy indeed that Coulston had neglected his routine visit to the Knotty Stowp, that seeing his light on, I called on him 'in passing.' He was in a sullen mood, having had to make do with a couple of 'flats' from his warm cupboard. I responded as usual, over-vociferously, groping for a conversational hold. I had little success, and when tension had built up out of frustration to an intolerable pitch, I attempted one of my futile break-off bids,

"Well nice to see you old man, but really, got to be moving along down street. As the Yanks would say, 'I'll drop by again sometime.'"

"You mean you have to call at some other house in the street?"

"O yes, on the present errand all of them in fact - just a sort of quick stop off you know. Sometimes reminds me of the old house-to-house stuff during the war.

Officially called mopping up... sometimes had to deliver a present... ghastly business... drop it in sharp and run like H—"

"House-to-house?" Coulson seemed to get these words entangled in his vocal mechanism, "House-to-house did you say?" At this an astonishing change came over the man, he became agitated and began to perspire.

"Are you alright Mr.Coulston?"

"Yes, yes, OK. Just get these hot flushes now and again. It's all alright though, nothing amiss, nothing to get all het up about."

"Change of life?" I jested.

"O no, too young for that yet. Everything's OK. Only had a couple of halves over at the Stowp this afternoon. O yes, and some whisky... was feeling a bit cold. Had some sardines for me tea, couple of tins, and some pickled onions. So it's digestive eh. All in the guts."

I began to wonder whether both Coulston and I were in fact getting our figures of speech quite wrong here. In reality, had something in our immediate conversation exposed a raw nerve? A chance word perhaps, or passing thought half-expressed? Had we accidentally laid a bogey? I decided to continue in the same vein, just in case I had dropped a wrong one in a wrong place. This should make it easy to veer off without notice, if it became necessary or expedient.

"As I was saying," I began, "this house-to-house stuff... the war you know... was a soldier... seven years. Commando units most of the time... pretty horrific at times. Think we'd better find something more pleasant to talk about. Let's change the subject."

"No, no no, by no means. Do carry on soldier, it's right up my street, I'm telling you, right up my street." Did I imagine it, were his eyes gazing wildly?

"Your street... house-to-house you mean?" I said facetiously.

"O hell, sorry about the pun. No, the war, up my street. Your rank?"

"Tuppence-ha'penny lieutenant. You know... everybody's mug eh! Commissioned clanger-dropper-can carrier... sandbag... section leader and all that."

The outside of Coulston's face smiled, but the inside didn't; his eyes shone, but there was no light in them. He held out to me his right hand and as I grasped it, I felt that it had no grip of its own, and it was trembling slightly.

"635, Sergeant Coulston Sir, Royal Gloucesters. Comrades! Comrades!"

Although one cannot report a sudden or dramatic change in the conversation, a detectable spirit of camaraderie began to lighten the atmosphere. In no time at all we had forgotten the horrors, the terrors, and the pains, and our exchanges had descended to the indelicate levels of barrack room humour. There was the inevitable succession of literary gems from our respective collections of lewd militarabilia, and spicy old hardies retold with gratuitous delight. Unseemly? Unbecoming? Crass? Perhaps, in some circumstances, but here like a strong purgative medicine they worked wonders.

"You were saying - about mopping up I mean?" Coulston brought in from nowhere.

"O yes, this house-to-house thing - that what you mean? We seem to have got a long way from that during the past half an hour."

"Well we're back aren't we. I suppose things like that are not all that easy to shake off," mumbled the sergeant, "By the way you seem to have got yourself mixed up in a spot of this street scrapping yourself. Have you?"

"Well... a bit... sort of... now and again... I mean a war's a war isn't it... sometimes things don't turn out right... get out of control... bit savage and inhuman at times. Never otherwise I suppose."

"You can bloody well say that again, that you can," said Coulston, with some huskiness of voice, "Kick in the door, pull the pin, let go, duck like hell - and - WHAM." Now why was it that I involuntarily winced just then? But I did, and Coulston noticed it.

"Sorry Lieu, shouldn't be talking to you like this, should I? You're not a fighting man now, all that's behind you for good. Peace and love and forgiveness and all that jazz now isn't it. Sorry again mate." Actually I had myself begun to wonder whether the present trend was consistent with my holy calling. Of course it was, every whit, for with a soul in peril surely everything goes.

"No, no, it's OK with me. Got to get it all out of our system have we not, some way, somehow. Going to take some guys a long time I reckon, and be a hard grind. You ever flung one in?"

There was no immediate reply to this one. He seemed to run into some trouble with dehydrating lips, and when he finally got his words out they sounded as though his tongue had turned into a stick.

"Yea I have, and more than once. Thought I'd actually put all that lot clean out of mind. That is until you come along you old blighter and start remi– Never mind though, no real harm done is there. It's all OK. Old soldiers never die, eh?"

"Nor do they ever forget, even when they think they have." I was unable to pitch my own voice above the level of a hoarse whisper. We sat for long, peering at the floor and our twitching toe ends, both at a loss for appropriate words. Then Coulston broke in, his voice little more than a vaguely vocalised thought,

"Thrown lots of eggs I have... lots of 'em."

"So have lots of other blokes, lots of 'em." All this follow-on did was to exacerbate the awful impasse, which was clearly working to Coulston's severe discomfiture. Noisily clearing his throat as though bracing himself, he went on slowly, and with strained deliberation,

"Yea, tossed lot's o'them in... now and again... here and there, had to I suppose... not sure about that, I forget. But...one special one... one very special one... one bloody spe—"

"Good for you - it got Hitler?"

"Don't joke Lieutenant, don't joke. I wish to hell it had, or some other wicked bastard... or better still - got me."

"Come on Coulston, what's this all about? Out with it man, the whole lot. Something rotten's on your mind and it won't do. It'll destroy you... come on now. I reckon the war's still going on for us two, and thousands like us. Got to stop it, and enjoy the peace we won. Alright?"

“I suppose you’re quite right - in a way. Much easier for you than for some no doubt. But as I’ve said, old soldiers never die.” I perceived that whatever Coulston was trying to bring to the surface it was giving him pain.

“There are many things that old soldiers can understand about each other. Nobody else can appreciate their problems. War has compelled us to participate without thought in reprehensible deeds in the line of duty and name of survival. Must try and forget.” I said.

“I suppose you’re right. But no, not this one... can’t trouble you with this one... man of peace and love... cushy job... pretty young wife and all that. No... it’s all over and done with now... all forgotten until you got me going. Had some whisky earlier on as well - should’ve kept my big mouth shut, shouldn’t I - better for us both.”

“It’s an order Sergeant - out with it man. For your sake, for mine, and for everybody who has to do with us. It’s like having a primed grenade in your pocket. Out with it man before it blasts us both to Hell.” Tension was beginning to run high, for a thousand inexplicable reasons, and we were each driven to take cover in silence, each hoping that the other would be first to speak.

Coulston it was, dutifully, and with some pathos in his voice,

“Pulling rank eh? Well, maybe civvies now, but an order’s an order for all that. So here goes SIR, seeing you seem to like your little war stories.”

“My friend, it’s not like that at all. It is just that the only way to get some things out of our systems is to talk them out with... er somebody we can trust - the experts would say, exteriorize them.”

“I hate to admit the damn thing, but I have a feeling you’re quite right. I probably kind of respect you. Nothing to do with erstwhile rank mind you. And certainly not just because you’re a parson - hell no, not that. Kind of affinity somewhere I think - in spite of that. Not a word to anybody else about this mind you.”

“Glad you’ve noticed that this soldier has never died neither.” I said, having found Coulston’s last comment as hard to swallow as he had found it to cough up. Consequently another painful silence ensued. I was not fully aware of the exact moment when he resumed speaking, for I came in somewhere mid-sentence at... “mopping up, after mediums had softened them up, and RAF boys had pulverised them a bit. Lot of houses and things still standing though - after a fashion. Only a small place, Leibschaffen or something the name was. Lot of trees, some still standing with leaves on. Caught the Jerries by surprise we did. Some of their armour had been hiding among the houses. Ordered to creep up on the bas— Well you know the drill don’t you.”

“Rotten risky business. Plenty of cover I hope.” I asserted with an air suggestive of vast experience in that particular stratagem.

“Not much as a matter of fact. Plenty of cross stuff coming from cellars and windows and such places, and just had to blast the guts out of them. When it all began to settle down, me and three of the lads got to this row of cottages... just like some of them around here, but battered a bit of course. Got myself up to a door, kicked it wide open, and delivered my message - WHAM! When things stopped flying about, pumped in a few rounds from my Sten for extra measure."

"That should have settled them down for a bit."

"Sir. Hell. Please. You always seem to say the wrong thing in the wrong place, don't you - good grief," Coulston turned his face floorwards, and wagged his head as though in bitter anguish.

"Look, I'm sorry about that. It's a universal defect of the cloth I'm afraid, a bit verbose all the time, and so we're bound to slip up some of the time. Come along, you carry on regardless, if only to keep me quiet."

"You don't mind me shooting a line then? Sure you can stand it?"

"Come along, out with it. All the horror, the fear, the look back in anger, the lot. I'm absolutely unshockable. And don't forget, I went through the thick of things as well, I'm quite at home with your talk. Gosh man, I'm already getting a vivid sensation that I was right in there with you. Comes back you know, at slightest provocation, so real." This bold assertion brought about another temporary lull in conversation, which was oddly reminiscent of that deadly hush which preceded an opening barrage, or the cold paralysis which came in the wake of a lost battle.

"Sergeant! Keep it going will you. It's nothing to do with sordid nostalgia or morbid curiosity. It's but an expression of true comradeship which could be beneficial to both of us." I tried to sound brotherly and stern in the same instant.

"So, orders being orders, I'd better keep going. Well, you asked for it. Anyway I know now that everything's safe in your hands."

"Safe as houses. O heck I'm sorry about that," said I, instantly wishing that I could pull that one back in.

"Mess and stour and stuff got cleared up a bit... all quiet inside the place... rushed in... few more rounds from my Sten as I went. Was right airless and dusty in there I tell you. Shouldn't have rushed in like that... but you know... excited a bit... or scared more like... and damned risky anyway. Fell over something on the floor... soft a bit... came a hell of a cropper... hoped he was stiff... no knife or gun or anything. But he never moved. Felt about where his face should be... was wet... and warm... he'd copped it alright. No helmet... bloody hell... and... long straight hair, wet as well... down to shoulders..."

"Hair? And so what, a bit long, but so what?"

"Yes... hair... long... straight... went through my fingers... made them tingle. Damn it, why am I telling you all this? You've surely got enough troubles of your own." Coulston was beginning to lose his soldierly calm. I sat back let the silence happen, and waited for him to continue.

"I came out of that cottage, and called some blokes forward to clear the place a bit. There wasn't a living thing in that house. The boys dragged her out. O God... a woman... mangled... just young... bleeding all over the place... fair hair... long, straight fair hair. And they dumped her in the row beside the—"

"Take it easy mate, take it easy. You've got perfectly good reasons for sharing this one with me, and I fully understand."

"And listen Padre, there's some more, and worse. Her right hand was still tangled in the chain of a crucifix on her neck."

"She died praying," I agonised to keep my voice level and my face set to neutral as I spoke. But the pain was as much as I could bear.

"Can you take any more? Thing didn't stop there you see."

"After years among that sort of stuff, I can take anything," I said.

"The lads - rough a bit some of them - mostly young... just like that poor girl... bit upset... unusual I thought... but only human."

"Only human... aren't we all? That is until... the corporal was down there doing his usual going over, and he shouted 'Hey Serg, got a wedding ring on, maybe there's some kids about somewhere.' I wish he'd kept his flaming mouth down." Coulston was obliged to pause here to deal with an obstruction either in his throat or his sensitivities before going on, "Well, to cut a long story short, they went back into the house, and they fetched out two kids - little Jerries - dangling all limp, and bloody, and dusty in the soldiers' arms."

"Have a rest here me lad, this is a bit rough on you."

"No, let me keep going - get it all over with. The boys put down the little kids on the ground by my feet, sort of gently as if they didn't want to hurt them. Believe me, the only marks on them were fresh bullet holes."

"What we call the fortunes of war I suppose."

"Good grief Padre, is that all you have to say? Can't you see what it means? That brave young lass died shielding her two little kids from a bloody lunatic like me - from my grenade - and she had succeeded it would seem. That is until I had burst in and riddled them with a Sten gun - big brave Sergeant - two less Nazis to worry about."

"Bloody Hell," was all my lips could echo, my feeling utterly inept.

"Well one consolation. I suppose it was all OK in the end - in YOUR book anyway," said Coulston bitterly, "She died praying didn't she."

I simply had to attempt some kind of deflection here, for my own sake, and without being seen to break into retreat. "By the way Sergeant, you seem to have forgotten something. Then, I was not a padre - I was a fighter like yourself. So you see I understand this lot from both sides of the problem. Another thing I'd like to know. Where were the Jerries you talked about while all this was going on?"

"Gone - vanished - crept out - crafty bastards. Gave us the slip and left us blasting at the civvies. Dug themselves in farther up the road and waited for us."

By this time Coulston was emotionally exhausted, sore distressed, and so was I. For a long time we sat speechless and staring into space; space which was not empty, but full of horrors which it couldn't dissipate. We realised to the full - and this was our main source of comfort during these tragic moments of bitter remembrance - that there is no greater comradeship known to man, than that between two soldiers when they stagger out of the fight bearing each other up. The time had surely come when it had become necessary to try and alter course. I wondered whether this might be the opportune moment to introduce an element of evangelism. But surely that would be a callous act of hitting a man while he was down. At any rate, the stock clichés of our redemptionist religion had no rightful nor meaningful place here. How do you preach forgiveness to a man who is unable to forgive himself, even for a dark deed which was thrust upon him? How can you talk of reconciliation with God to a man who cannot be reconciled within himself? How can you dole out the standard stuff about compassion to a man who has known only one side of Calvary? Not out of faintheartedness, nor unbelief, but from wise necessity, I opted for the healing virtue of silence. That silence was long, and deep, and sacramental. Now perceiving that Coulston was moving about, I raised up my head from my cupped hands, and found that he had poured two small drinks - of what I did not know, but being from Coulston's hand, they certainly would not be of distilled water. Again in the cause of inspired tact, and total abstainer though I was required to be, I gladly shared that one with him. After sharing with a comrade in arms so much that was far more potent than alchohol, what odds? The clear chime of those two little glasses as we clinked them together rang in the beginning of breakthrough.

I tossed and turned that whole night through. The anguish I suffered vicariously, coupled with the torment of my inadequacy to deal with Coulston's problems, just would not dissolve into sleep.

"Not sleeping dear - something bad on your mind?" Gina had recognised the signs. We talked long into the night, and I shared with this beloved girl many of the dark memories from which I had hitherto tried to protect her.

"The wounds of the soul, often unseen, undeclared, and alas unrecognised are sometimes resistant to the normal healing processes. They work their secret havoc of shame, remorse, guilt and disillusionment behind a shabby cover of arrogance or self pity, and when the collective guilt of a whole section of mankind rests upon the conscience of one individual, perchance in the shape of the ineradicable memory of one dark day, or an accident of circumstance into which he was inexorably drawn, that burden is agony to bear, difficult to share, and impossible to decisively cast off."

"It may surprise you Don, but I know all about it. Your little lass has kept close watch throughout all the years she has known you. Now get strong my darling... after all you've been through, and especially now that the memories have been rekindled. Get strong... there are maybe lots of battles to help people ahead of you, so don't go down at the first fence. Look my soldier boy, there's a man out there badly hurt. Got to go out and get him haven't you? He's no common dipsomaniac that one I'm afraid. Badly hurt, and you know why. Strong now... strong..."

Gina fell asleep even as she spoke the words. I looked at her lovely dark tresses draped about her pillow, and worshipped them. Good Lord long hair. That poor man's bitter anguish came flooding back in on me and I strove to beat it off for what seemed to me like many long hours of the silent night. What could be done to try and eradicate the dark shadow from this man's soul? What could I do? Something pretty drastic, but what? Unorthodox, irregular, outrageous, crazy, but what? Something sacrificial, but what? My proper calling, of course, I'm being tempted to forego my calling - and I was back to evangelism. In my half sleepy state the very word conjured up the notion of the threats, forebodings and solemn warnings of those latter day Gospel frenetics who are the self-appointed custodians of truth, and administrators of divine judgement. No, this was surely no place for the spiritual pride, loveless aggression or crude cant of the classical revivalist. The said Gospel testifies that Christ's single method was to love the fallen into the Kingdom... so must I... so must I... but how? So easy to say... or think... nice feeling... but how? Practical... how? Something old... something new... untried... different... daring... devious... daft ...that's it... daft... da... ? And I must have fallen off to sleep.

As a rule, I did not implicate Gina in my more intimate pastoral confidences, wise and loving counsellor though she was. I felt however that I must needs bring her in on this one. Her tenderness, practical common sense, and her womanly intuition calmed me, and greatly assisted me in getting Coulston's problem into proper perspective. I would not even try and work out a scheme of action. I would forget all the potted psychology I ever knew, there would be no intimidation, either by skilful argument, preaching, or 'bible punching'. I would simply come alongside him within the context of the friendship and trust which had now become firmly established betwixt him and me.

I was sitting in the car, which for some reason or other I had parked near to the Knotty Stowp, when Coulston happened to approach. I went straight to the brutal point, "I'm not on house-to-house calls today."

"What's it today then - old women's meeting I bet? Better come in here with me and help me with my 'refill' eh. More worthwhile and do you a world of good. Come on man."

"Nothing so boring - as a women's meeting I mean. Should really be out at one of the villages today, but, can't make it I'm afraid. Never told you about the eyes did I? Sometimes have spot of bother with eyes you know, not serious, but bit of a nuisance. Usually happens when I get down on things a bit... another one of those old war stories... you know... and wouldn't want to bore us with that. I don't reckon to drive very far like this. Stopped here to decide whether or not to go back home and get my bike."

"Villages, on your bike? More than you'd get me doing, even on a job like yours. That's it then, if as you say, you're down in the dumps a bit, come in here and join me in my afternoon session - buck you up no end it will."

"Sorry, duty calls. Got to keep to my priorities you know, discipline and all that. Actually, what I was thinking - I was wondering that is if you'd be so good as to - or able that is - or if you had nothing else on - nothing pressing you know - or could perhaps change your own plans and—"

"O come on padre, what are you stuttering about? Out with it man."

"OK, straight on target then. Would you be so good as to drive this old girl over to Mossguthrie for me?"

"Great, fine, OK, you're on. But what about my usual?"

"Afraid we can't have it both ways can we? Two precious lives and an even more precious little jalopy at stake here isn't there."

"Haven't felt up to driving for quite a while you know, so I might be a bit out of practice. The lads look after the lorry and any driving that's to be done. Tell you what, OK, but not unless it's an order - Sir. Then if anything goes wrong, you take the can."

"Sergeant - to Mossguthrie, pronto! schnell! sharp!'"

"Alright then, move over you old ba—sorry again Lieu, padre, or whatever... O blast... Don. The name is Don isn't it? Anyway, move over, let a real driver have hold of this thing. Needs a few cobwebs blown off all round I reckon."

The ensuing journey had a full and mixed quota of scares and thrills with Coulston driving the car as though it was a Bren carrier, and enjoying himself intensely. There was never much breath to spare for talking, but at one point I did let slip the tactless observation "Quite intoxicating, isn't it" Arriving at Mossguthrie, we stopped alongside a row of five neat, low-roofed cottages. Purposely selecting the end one, I walked along the narrow path towards the door, and beckoned Coulston to follow me. I was a little shocked to realise that I had done so by using the up-and-over arm wave familiar to advancing troops. My swing of the heavy cast-iron knocker was hardly necessary, for the door was slightly ajar. I pushed it open gently, "Anybody at home?"

"Oo you giave me a reyght freyght there tha did," came a voice from about the level of my knees. Madeline was down polishing an area of floor almost immediately inside the door. Rising swiftly to her feet, she was seen to be the perfect archetype of English rural charm; tall, elegant, young and fair. She smiled a smile which was as radiant as the roses of early summer. Her kindly voice had that attractive metallic ring which was so typical of the women of the dale, and it seemed to linger with you a while after she had spoken. The result was that you invariably tended to delay your reply. For at least half a minute we stood still, exchanging smiles and happy thoughts. Coulston's involuntary cough indicated that it was time for some introductions.

"Madeline Messenger - MM for short. Victor Coulston, old war colleague of mine. O by the way - VC for short."

"I'm just an old colleague," chuckled the sweet lass, with the emphasis on the word 'old'. "Come in now - had ony tea? Owld soldiers leyke their tea - nivver loss habit. Minister here doesn't. Regular visiter - can smell teapot ten miles away."

Coulston entered sheepishly, but chiefly I thought, on account of the low beams and his six feet height. No sooner had we sat down luxuriously by either side of a cheery log fire, than the door directly opposite Coulston opened furtively, and from it emerged two bright-eyed little children. When I stood up to greet them they flung themselves onto me, so that I was left holding them up, one under either arm by my sides. They glanced shyly at Coulston as they made their giggling exit by the front door. The subsequent conversation got off to a bad start when Coulston launched in with,

"Husband working locally?"

"Harry died on D-Day. Arromanches I think they called t'place," the brave girl spoke with quiet control.

"Marines," was all that I was able to contribute, but surprisingly Coulston was quick on the uptake,

"Sorry about that - so sorry - shouldn't have asked that. Blasted war - such a waste. You must feel bitter at times towards th—"

"It's odd I know, but actually I don't. Him or them that did it were only doing t'same as Harry, carrying out their duty, unwillingly maybe. Can't attach ony individual blame to them can we? I suppose they were just fulfilling the impersonal assignments of war."

A twitch in the corner of Coulston's mouth seemed to indicate that this one had gone down deep, and he said gravely, "Generous thought, but it doesn't lessen the hurt does it. What I mean is, it's hard to make the cause justify the effect, whatever way we look at it - War."

"O well, I've learned tae cope - haven't we Minister? Get sad a bit sumtimes, but got tae keep looking on t'breyght side haven't we. Got me man... not going to let them get me down as well, nor the bairns"

"You're a very brave lady," said Coulston with some feeling.

"Well our lads fought gayly hard for victory in th'actual war, so it's pretty well up tae us tae keep victorious in the aftermath, isn't it. I mean we should nivver let the sadness and regrets and bitterness and dark clouds and things grieve us beyond repair. Got tae build our lives on the happier memories, then 'appen the sad ones'll crumble away. Hitler couldn't beat us wi' all his bombs and rockets and things, and we're certainly not goin' tae let 'im beat us wi ' worries, or owt else for that matter. Are we now?"

"Sad regrets, rotten memories, black shadows, don't wear off very quickly do they, if ever at all. They'll always keep coming up." This cost Coulston dearly, and his sudden break off indicated a cry for help.

"Victor's witnessed some ghastly scenes in his time Madeline, like many of us I suppose. In fact he was much involved in some of them. Hard to shake off, especially when other things are getting you down as well."

"The only cure for dark shadows is plenty o' leyght, that's what I say. So the best way for t'future is tae keep lookin' on t'breyght side. There IS a breyght side you knaw," said the girl with irrepressible charm. Then turning her sparkling blue eyes fully in our direction she went on, "I reckon t'same power o' darkness as took away my Harry from us, and all them nasty shadows we talk about, are still at work. That is if we let them get away wi' it. Can destroy your soul mister, mess up your life, and lot's o' other people's wi' it."

"That's just the point at issue Madeline, if we let it," came in the preacher, "Must keep on fighting I suppose... resisting. Easier said than done of course." A futile interjection I know, but it came only because I was beginning to feel futile alongside the noble stature of this courageous young war widow.

"Still lot o' nice things in life ye knaw, and you fellas fought and suffered tae keep them safe for us all. Like love, and hope, and trust, and things tae laugh at. Indestructable things these are, and naebody can tek them away from us... the things that nowt can kill."

"You're a wonderful example to us all Madeline, although I suppose you must get a wee bit sad and discouraged sometimes. You've still got your memories haven't you, which even though pleasant, can at the same time hurt. Sadness and joy are not necessarily opposites are they?" I found it difficult to look the girl straight in the face as I voiced this platitude.

"Well, happy or sad, good days and bad ones, I'm learning tae cope. And I'll tell tha summat else - I still nivver forgets me praying... levels things out a lot you knaw... perspective I think it's called."

A sideways glance and I noticed that the trend of this conversation was becoming somewhat tedious for Coulston who was fumbling with the matchbox in his jacket pocket. I was not surprised therefore when he affected a deviation onto a more congenial topic.

"I noticed as I came in Madeline, that the lintels and pointing on the front of the house are looking a bit tatty. Need some attention."

"I knaw, I knaw, but I din't knaw when I'll be able tae get them put reyght. Poor Harry, he was alweys talkin' about trying to fix it, and just as alweys putting it off another week. And well, he just nivver got round tae the job. On his last leave he was sayin' that'd be his first job when t'war finished, mending things about th'ouse."

"Just that I was thinking... well you see... I'm at a bit of a loose end these days... could come over and try and fix it for you..."

"Victor's in the building trade," I butted in.

"Very nice of you tae be sure Victor... but... well... at th'moment well... it's t'money actually... kids growin' fast... breadwinner—"

"Not to worry Madeline, this one's on me," said Coulston, his eyes flooded with tender admiration, "Do me good... getting lazy... need a bit of exercise... good for the soul I reckon."

More tea, more pastries, but alas the conversation began showing signs of drying up. Just when we were preparing to take our leave, Victor began to enthuse once more about the necessary work on the front of the house, and it seemed that the finer qualities of the encounter were to the larger extent squandered. When we set off for the journey home, we did so quietly. Even the little car seemed to comply, with her normally noisy exuberance damped down somewhat. It was as though we were taking our leave of holy ground. For the first mile at least, Coulston drove the car at an untypically steady pace, and it was some time before he seemed ready for the resumption of conversation. I ventured cautiously for I feared lest my lack of tact should spoil this beautiful moment.

"Nice girl. Blue eyes, china doll complexion, fair hair down to shoulders - gives her that perfect country look doesn't it. Tremendous fortitude. A fine lass. Worth dying for."

"Worth living for," my companion corrected.

"People like that put a bit of reason back into life, don't they."

"I've been wondering what was getting me. It's sort of uncanny you know. Reminds me of somebody... from the past I'd say. Yes I know what - my old mother of course - yes. Bit religious... Church of England... wonderful woman for all that. Died in '40, soon after the war started. Brought me up on her own... old man killed in first one... Somme I think."

"Sorry to hear that, well the last part anyway." I said solemnly.

"Always lecturing me she was, about life and all that, as though it was chock full of dangers and pitfalls. When I first joined up she said she'd always be praying for me. In fact, tried to get me onto this praying lark she did. Didn't go down too well I'm afraid. Actually tried but soon had to go the way of all flesh."

"This praying lark you mean?"

"Naturally. I suppose it's alright if you're a bit inclined that way - which I'm not - or if you're not very practical, haven't much up top, or prone to turning a blind eye on some things. But hey, it's not right for me to be saying things like this to you is it. Praying's really part of your job - your duty I mean."

"Praying's never but a duty my friend, nor anyone's job, and there's nothing terribly exclusive about its application neither. That's what corrupts it. It is more like as you say, a natural inclination. When we make it otherwise so that it loses its spontaneity, I'm afraid it can become a meaningless mechanical habit, a fetish, and even a bondage."

"Like Army discipline you mean - nuisance, but sometimes useful, even necessary. But in the wrong hands though, absolute bu— sorry - *bovine excreta*."

"I liked the admission of 'necessary'. But seriously, didn't the idea of praying ever hit you suddenly in a moment of panic? Sure you must have had plenty of them in your time."

"Like the squeal of a rabbit, whimper of a child. Soon over and forgotten, instinct, reflex action, sudden surge of adrenaline, purely pathological, devised to make one dive for cover or get the hackles up. Don't know why religious folk have to be so sentimental and superstitious about it."

"You know what, there's more truth in what you've said than perhaps you realise, or even intended. Mind you with regard to this prayer lark, I've experienced some rather odd co-incidences which I'd like your help in explaining sometime."

"On the other hand," Coulston asserted, "I've seen some pretty horrific happenings in spite of it - in fact in the very face of it. This praying stuff's maybe alright for some, like something to feel good about when everything's going well, and hide behind when it isn't. But, if one's got any practical reason, or solid down-to-earth common sense left in him, it offers pretty poor consolation. And one needs something more substantial than that to get out of the messes you and I have sometimes been in."

"I suppose we should call that 'checkmate'. Think you'd like to re-set the sights a bit, down on elevation eh?"

"O yes," Coulston went on, with an air of relief, "now getting back to this Madeline friend of ours..."

"And those gorgeous twins. By the way Harry never saw those kids you know. Were born sometime in the February following D-Day. Tragic."

"Reckon there were thousands of blokes who never lived to see their kids - on both sides. And lots of kids that never saw their fathers, and some even their mothers. But look, about this job on the house. I'm going to do that you know - no kidding - hundred percent repair. For poor old Harry's sake if for no other reason."

"And Madeline's of course. She'll certainly appreciate the gesture, and the spirit in which it's made and all. You're a great guy, buddy."

"How's the driving? You haven't commented. You know what - this little bitch and me are getting along fine. Have to get to know each other better."

"Nice handling V.C. - nice handling. Have to flog it to you one day - better start saving up."

"I'll have to get back to taking the lorry out. cost me a tidy packet that thing did... lads are knocking it to bits... nice run over here isn't it." Thus saying, Coulston's right foot went down to the floor, and the little yellow bomber responded in the usual fashion.

Except for the occasional street encounter, and a number of calls at his home, although rarely finding him in, I did not see a great deal of Coulston during the following few weeks. I did observe however that his physical bearing, his turn-out, and his general demeanour were improving markedly.

"Don't see ower much o' your owld crony in t'Stowp these days, teased the fat landlord, "Place'll be gawin' bust. Must be findin' better ale sumwhere else 'appen. Better for that yan if he took hesel' in hand a bit. That's 'appen what he's up tae. Sum on his lads says he gits up tae t'yard a lot of'ner an' all lately. Picks up th'truck and sum gear and gaws out on 'is own. Din't knaw what's cummed ower 'im. Still pops in on a night, but nivver teks much mare than yan or two halves."

"Dark horse that yan Mr. Bretherton. Wonder if he's up to summat?"

Thus the weeks went by with evidence of Coulston's self-rehabilitation becoming plain for all to see, and some to rejoice in. One evening near the end of September when it was unusually quiet in the Knotty Stowp, he called in for his chat over the counter with Matt, and his now usual single light ale. He had got about half-way though his drink when, dropping the glass, he slumped forward as though suddenly struck by intense pain. He then staggered groaning to the centre of the room before falling unconscious to the floor. The doctor, and me, both having been summoned by Matt's wife Nellie, arrived on the scene almost simultaneously. But Victor Coulston was beyond the help of either, and died held up in the arms of a very distressed Matt Bretherton. Looking up and slowly wagging his head the doctor made his pronouncement. Then a most remarkable thing occurred, the memory of which disturbs me somewhat to this very day. It so happened that I was standing beside the faithful old Bechstein at the time. It also so happened that - and this was rare indeed - the lid was open. I swear that the action which followed was totally involuntary. My right hand was somehow drawn towards the keyboard, and my fingers, wandering idly over the keys, tapped out the notes of The Last Post. There was a long and solemn silence in the Knotty Stowp. Then Matt moved across to the bar counter, struck one soft peel on the bell, mumbled - 'Time fellas' and closed down. It was but seven-twenty-five.

A mere handful of locals were gathered at the churchyard down by the river for the funeral. The undertaker said that 'they' had not been able to contact any relatives, but had been through all of Coulstons' available papers. As far as he could see, he 'hadn't any proper religion nor nowt' so therefore he would have to be buried Church. For some reason understood only by the terrestrial powers ordained to make celestial judgements, the entire service took place at the graveside, and was a prime example of ecclesiastical perfunctoriness. The smooth-faced, whining, anaemic fob of a curate who was brought in to do the deed was in the true succession of that out-moded brand of the king's clergy whose habit is to 'never mind the spirit, but be diligent in fulfilling the letter'. Like a badly adjusted talking machine he scurried through the Office with some garbled prayers, mumbled mumbo-jumbo and a high-pitched stream of abstruse jargon phrases, addressed to no-one. Then peering blankly upwards towards some invisible object in the tree-tops which seemed to be enthralling him, he launched into a desultory diatribe of pious platitudes and trite tributes taken randomly from straight out of stock and guaranteed to be totally irrelevant to all particular situations. This ending abruptly, he shifted back into intoning mode with a restrained cough of the classical clerical kind, and without so much as shifting his entranced gaze from the mystery object in the tree-tops (or perhaps beyond!) he put my friend away, casually committing the body of 'our dear braathar hear departeed to the ground, and his soul to the merssay of Almightay God'. Scooping up a minute morsel of earth with a highly polished trowel handed to him by the undertaker, he poured it down into the open grave, intoned the final formula (still gazing piously into the tree-tops), 'Dast to dast, airshes to airshes...' mumbled the Benediction, turned about, and was gone. The only semblance of reverence I witnessed that day was in the four of Coulson's workmen who bore him down the grim churchyard, and laid him in his lonely grave. When it was all over Gina stepped out from a small group which included landlord Matt and his wife Nellie, and an elegant young woman with fair shoulder length hair. Close by her side were two small children. Without any premeditation I joined the group to walk slowly up to the graveside, where, also without any premeditation, I threw up the smartest salute of my whole career.

Moving to the head, Gina tenderly laid down a large bunch of deep red and gold chrysanthemums. And all that was written on the card it bore were the words,

'Old Soldiers Never Die. My love V.C. - Gina.'

Chapter 20

SPRING SURPRISES

'In Spring a young man's fancy lightly turns to thoughts of love'. So wrote the bard, and in the nature of things it is probably one of the more predictable facts of life. But in this idyllic patch of England's green and pleasant land there was an exception, for here a young man's spring fancy was customarily totally pre-occupied with the more practical business of lambing. Consequently spring weddings were rare, inconvenient, and suspect. This understanding was causing me no small amount of misgiving as I made my way to the lovely village of Saltersgarth on a sunny Saturday morning for the first Spring wedding of my career. There was also the knowledge, already well substantiated, that at this place any event which entailed a departure, even temporary, from the regular run of things, like for instance a wedding, was sure to be highly hitch-prone. It is a common maxim that one should be prepared for unscheduled shocks and shocking surprises at any wedding, and so, as the car spluttered and faltered all the way to Saltersgarth, I began to wonder whether she was actually sharing in my uncomfortable premonition of a grim concentration of nuptial nasties.

Saltersgate chapel served a wide area of countryside in the upper reaches of the Lyndass valley, and accordingly was larger and grander than average. The place was already well filled when I arrived, and that air of shuffling excitement typical of all weddings had taken hold. So had the heat. April weather being so unpredictable in these elevated Northern parts, it was normal practice to prepare for the worst. The caretaker, true to form, had therefore stoked up his boiler at full blast from the night before, and was now nowhere to be found to locate and close down the appropriate valves. Something else was greatly amiss, and it was quite some time before I was able to place my finger upon it. There was no music.

In fact there was no organist. Where was the faithful Annie Mitchelson? It was well known that the good lady was less confident than competent, especially when faced with rare or special occasions. Had she taken fright? Members of the congregation were now casting furtive glances backwards towards the open door, and setting up a flurry of expectant fidgeting each time the sound of an approaching car was heard. The waiting bridegroom, seated in the front row was becoming more agitated and pale-faced as time dragged on, scrutinising his wristwatch several times per minute, frequently gathering up his socks, or twisting his trouser bottoms. The best man was no more composed, and appeared to be having some trouble in reconciling a perspiring neck and a tight collar. By now the bride was ten minutes behind schedule, and elderly men began to weigh anchor with their pocket watches. The mounting tension was blown with some shattering abruptness by Jack Vasey, on guard at the main door, who aimed his stentorian voice straight down the aisle to the point where I was sitting,

"She's 'appen 'ere Mister - aye, she's 'ere."

This pronouncement was intended as a signal for the organist to rapidly resolve whatever she was rendering at the time, and bring in the opening strains of the Bridal March. I stood up, the bridegroom stood up, the best man stood up, the congregation stood up, but the organ stood silent, its long shiny stool stark and vacant. Meanwhile the flustered bride waited anxiously outside for her marching orders, but none came, and the magic moment was about to be lost in cruel anti-climax. With all thought of due dignity abandoned, I shot across the front of the apse towards the organ, performing a splendid trip act over the hem of my cassock en route. I mounted the high organ stool with such clumsy commotion that I scattered an assortment of tatty old books which had been piled precariously on one edge. The sliding glass doors enclosing the console refused to open, and my frantic efforts to prise them apart bent back my fingernails, setting up some excruciating pain.

"Annie genrilly what keyeps t'keys on t'ledge ower th'top o' tha heyad." came a mystic voice from somewhere in the depths of the congregation here present. Fumbling for the elusive keys with numbed fingers I knocked them to the floor with a loud 'PING'; which would not have mattered a great deal had they not landed between 'G' and 'G Sharp' amongst the pedals, and had the boy behind the curtain at the blowing crank not already got up a hissing head of compressed air. I had heard of this particular organ's reputation, and simply dreaded the moment when I put down my fingers for that vital first chord. Some of the stops were dead, some would have been better dead, and others had strips of pink sticking plaster holding them closed lest they should be accidentally resurrected. Most of the pipes were in need of a re-bore, and others should have been stuffed with concrete. It was not at all surprising therefore that when I set down my hands and my left foot, the sound which came forth was like the 'Lost Chord' come home drunk. The intended work was Lohengrin of course, but it presented as a swinging combination of imperfect memory and irreverent invention, with profound apologies to Wagner. Nevertheless with a smile of smug satisfaction I turned my head to witness the grand spectacle of a beautiful bride making her triumphal entry... moving gracefully down the aisle to my music. But the aisle was empty, the doorway was empty, and so were the faces of the bemused congregation. The quick-thinking Vasey, not knowing what might happen next, had, before the organ struck up, ushered the bridal party back into their car and sent them on a minor excursion until he was certain that matters had got properly organised inside the church. When the bride arrived with her father some five minutes later, having shed a few tears, and some loose blossoms from both her bouquet and her cheeks, but otherwise unabashed, she was to have her great moment after all, for the swinging parson was at the console. The bridegroom had resumed his seat after the first shock, and now attempted to get back to his feet. He petrified half- way up, lost whatever morsel of composure he had left in him, and rendered a performance not unlike that of a frightened heifer trying to rise on wet cobbles. The bride was a picture of elegance and exquisite charm as she moved slowly down the aisle with dainty dignity and perfect poise; that was until her father, at least two inches shorter than his daughter, but walking by her side with incredible panache, stepped briefly onto her train. The resultant pause for re-adjustment of both step and hem was so efficiently executed, with mutual bows and flashed smiles, that it would have been easy to suspect that the action had been anticipated and rehearsed in advance. The bride safely installed beside the groom at the rail, I ended my jazzy improvisation (bearing a vague resemblance to Lohengrin). Climbing down from the organ stool with clammering inelegance I walked across and stood before them in clerical splendour and a pretence of composure. A few whispered greetings and re-assurances, and I proceeded to announce the first hymn - selected specifically for this one occasion the inevitable 'The Lord's My Shepherd' to the equally inevitable tune 'Crimond' of course. The announcement duly made, I must needs cross the apse again and in doing so repeated my classic cassock tripping act on the way to the organ stool, which mounting thereupon, I committed another loose pile of tatty books to the inclination of gravity. The congregational singing was so loud, hearty and uninhibited that for a few moments at any rate my fear of this weird instrument was banished.

Returning to the rail with leisurely stride and a feigned air of competence, I gleaned some moral support from the sight of that bride and groom standing there, she radiant as a princess and he handsome as a guardsman prince. And they were waiting for - me! I took a deep breath and was about to launch into the formularies when I realised that I still had two-thirds of a Fox's glacier mint rolling around in my mouth. My bid to bolt the offending confection unobtrusively nearly brought disaster, for it became lodged internally at about the level of my second rib, from which position it never budged for the remainder of the ceremony. Now every precedent dictates that it is during the next and most solemn juncture in the marriage service that most of the ecclesiastical jinks and classical difficulties arise, oftimes augmented by a mischievous crop of awful impediments. Whining babies were either swiftly smothered or noisily removed, but how to deal with the distracting proclivities of bored small boys, and with infant girls who would butt into the brief silent periods with shrill piercing voices to address intimate questions regarding the bride to their mothers or aunties, was quite another matter. Now and again an explosive "Shshsh." would cause greater distraction than the childish transgression it was meant to pre-empt. And why is it that by tradition grandmothers and elderly maiden aunts have to occupy the front row of pews for the sole purpose of enjoying a good weep or run a gravely whispered commentary on the bride's attire, and the groom's performance, and their respective relatives, past, present, and future? In terms of performance, this particular bridegroom was no exception to the general rule, for the local lads never fared well on public display and more especially when called upon to speak. In the vocal responses this poor fellow stumbled and stuttered, and finally developed lock-jaw. I whispered a few re-assuring words into his ear, for my benefit as well as his, and remarkably from then on, all proceeded smoothly. That was, until the arrival of an uninvited guest. A very large wasp joined the bridal party and buzzed frantically about the bridegroom's face as though his after-shave might contain some vespine aphrodisiac property. It then found his deep red carnation buttonhole to be similarly attractive, before moving towards his mouth to investigate what he had recently had to drink. It was precisely at this point when the poor man was struggling with considerable difficulty to repeat the words, 'I do solemnly declare... that I know not... of any lawful... imped... imped...' that he simply froze solid. In utter desperation I aimed a murderous swipe at the horrid creature, felling it either to the ground or amongst the bridesmaid's voluminous flimsies. All continued well for a few more minutes however, until an intermittent muffled buzzing sound indicated that either he had recovered and was making an illicit exploration, a frantic bid for freedom, or that he had been joined by an accomplice. It was during the bride's shy responses that the monster re-emerged, and was instantly attracted by either her sweet voice or her lipstick. That brave girl battled on without faltering, until the wretched insect made a too close reconnaissance about her head before entering fully into her visor veil. Deftly following it through with the little black service book which I was holding in my left hand, and at precisely the right moment slamming it shut, I brought the offender to an inglorious liturgical end. The odd thing was that this entire drama seemed to escape the congregation's notice, for they stood there stolid and unsmiling. Not so the bride, for I was about to witness a spectacle which I had never seen before, nor have ever experienced since. She began to chuckle, and before long the sweet lass was almost beside herself with unrestrained mirth. The bridegroom joined in, the best man joined in, the bridesmaid joined in, and finally, without a clue as to what they were laughing at, all joined in. The funny thing was that throughout the whole episode there was never the slightest hint of irreverence or triviality. As for me, I struggled valiantly to maintain the dignity of my office, and some kind of fixation of my features.

Now followed a period of reasonable normality, with all concerned back into a settled state of mind. Then came the sermon. Specifically prepared as an erudite dissertation on the blissfulness of the state of holy wedlock, its delivery turned into near disaster. In my attack on the naughty wasp the little slip of paper containing my 'headings' had slipped from the service book and vanished. From now on I had to go along free style, and that in my present harassed state together with my obvious amateur status was going to be a considerable disadvantage, and no less to the congregation who would have to endure my unguided periphrastic ramblings. The lachrymose elderly females in the front row were soon in full cry. Then a fat maiden aunt broke out into a wheezy coughing fit which persisted in volume and momentum until someone from behind leaned forward and administered some form of oral analgesic - probably a Fox's glacier mint. Battened down small children became increasingly fractious, and bluebottles wandering about among the rafters occasionally came down to examine the odd face - particularly mine.

By far the most serious distraction came from the direction of the organ where the blower boy, partially concealed by a curtain in his appointed small corner, punctuated my rhetorical silences with disgusting long drawn-in pulls on his snotty nose. The bridesmaid wriggled and squirmed throughout the duration of the sermon, as though more than suspecting that the mischievous wasp was still on the rampage among her petticoats. The main door, which opened directly onto the road, was left open, presumably because of the heat within the church, but also because it was the regular custom at local weddings - probably contrived as an ancient foil to secrecy. The occasional passer-by, or clutch of giggling small boys, would appear in the doorway, gawp for a brief while, and then pass on. Even this was reasonably tolerable until some local with an untimely sense of judgement drove a flock of ewes and lambs down the road. Some of the men in the back pews, sensing their approach, made a brief move to prevent the entire flock being penned among us. The gentlemen however were soon back in pews, lost in rapt attention to the wisdom emanating from the pulpit, or in their own musings on better things to come. Soon however a bunch of shaggy break-aways re-appeared in the open doorway and gaped at me vacantly, in similar manner to the congregation. The men of the back pews were on their feet again, dispersing the creatures with bucolic expressions known only to shepherds and their charges, to the effect, I believe, that they were not welcome here, and had best be moving along. I struggled on regardless, churning out gems of marital wisdom from out of my vast store of experience, acquired over exactly one year of wedded bliss. All seemed to be going down well, until the aftermath from the passing flock percolated through the entire building and eventually reached my nostrils, elevated though I was in the pulpit. The congregation was not displaying signs of having noticed anything out of the ordinary, either in the atmosphere or in my now rather peculiar behaviour. It was then that a large crow, whose fancy had also likely turned to thoughts of love, began to proclaim the fact from a high tree by the side of the road, raucously hailing every winged creature for miles around. The sermon ended as it had begun, that is at the same place except for the position of the hands on the clock, and in a splendid faux pas, in which I bestowed on the happy pair my pious wish that every day of their lives forthwith would be as memorable as this one.

Now it was back to my peripatetics, an unceremonial dash across the apse, stumbling indelicately over the hem of my garment as I went, and toppling a massive rumpled edition of 'Moody And Sankey' as I clambered aboard the organ stool. But lo, no sound came forth from either pipe nor reed, nor did any wheeze spring from the bellows. Dismounting, again with characteristic inelegance, I pulled aside the curtain to behold the said blower boy totally engrossed in the latest edition of 'Beano'. The hymn, again inevitably, 'Love Divine All Loves Excelling' to the inevitable tune 'Blaenwern', was sung in typical style with spirited enthusiasm. Now down from the organ once more, I escorted the bridal party to the vestry for the registration formalities. This completed, having taken up every minute of half-an-hour, I made another frantic dash to the organ to brace myself for a crashing rendering of the processional, which as it turned out was another jazzy improvisation of an Impromptu vaguely approximating the Wedding March by Mendelssohn.

"Tha's deyene reyght champion for us Minister, that tha 'as. Pity we hadn't ony bells mind ye - tha could've rung them an' all," came a kecking voice out of a fat rosy face, which turned out to belong to the bridegroom's father.

The photographer was a fearsome character, long past the capability of smiling convincingly, even though his 'professional' antics raised many a smile on the faces of the onlookers. His equipment was likewise fearsome, and seemed to date back to Daguerre. His complicated verbal instructions, hurled out like battle orders, his constant gaffes and false starts, together with his quaint little wife's long sessions of pummelling and prodding at the girls' dresses produced an unphotogenic group of nervous wrecks. I hastened away from the scene to seek refuge in the vestry. And there was sitting poor Annie, the absentee organist, sore troubled and greatly distressed.

"Fine day it was, so thowt I'd just cum ower tae t'village on t'bike. Gat meesel' a pumpture half-way ower, and had tae start walkin'. I did try and run a bit for sum o' th'way... but I still gat here ower late. Onyweys, tha seemed tae be enjoyin' theesel' on th'organ when I gat here. It sounded reyght grand it did. Din't knaw what they'd done wi'out tha. Thanks fra me onyweys, and everybody else an' all."

In one thrilling moment all my fears and regrets melted away, and in my own mind this had become a great and memorable occasion, and I was quite a remarkable fellow. The greatest thrill of the day however was to witness the joy of that lovely couple, and in some measure to participate in it. Surely, I thought, even the minor calamities of today will merge into a cluster of choice jewels to add to their treasure of precious memories. I confess again to some proud satisfaction in having been a part of it all, albeit in my own clumsy way.

"Tha'd better cum theesell ower tae th'Reception for a la'al bite tae eat Mr. Minister. Tha's 'appen worked gayly hard for it today," called out the bride's father down half the length of the village.

I declined the kind on the spot invitation however, although less publicly. I preferred that my last pleasant observation would seal for me the remembrance of my first Spring wedding, without being in any way affected by the spectacle, and sound, of so many who were 'unaccustomed as I am to public speaking' or similar trite wedding reception manners.

It would surely be a far far better thing to return immediately home, where Gina would be anxiously waiting to launch into her post-wedding interrogation.

Chapter 21

SHOW TIME

The second week in May could be deemed an odd time for the holding of a country show. It was just another one of the anomalies of life here among the Pennines, and particularly in the Lyndass Valley. There was however at least two good reasons for this arrangement. Lyndassby Show was dated to coincide with the end of the lambing season and the beginning of hay time, both being periods of extra work, long hours, much anxiety, and uncertain results. Furthermore, it was not a show within the strict meaning of the term, but, although modest by any standard, a general fun day. Nevertheless, it was greatly anticipated, widely discussed, and enthusiastically prepared for during many weeks beforehand. It was so deeply integrated into the life and culture of the region, that as the date drew near, the parting greeting was invariably 'See tha at t'Shaw then'.

Even I, off-comer as I was, had become infected with the fever of eager expectancy, to such an extent in fact that I could not resist the urge to take an early morning stroll up to the two fields of rough pasture, opposite the chapel, which on this fresh and sunny day would be the venue for the great occasion., On arrival I saw that preparations were already well under way. Groups of local men were erecting what looked like barriers or stockades, and a baffling variety of other structures whose purpose was not obvious. Other men were laying out cordons of rough posts and the ubiquitous binder twine, or setting up flimsy frames of white painted laths into enclosures of varied shape and dimension. At several points, pairs of burly fellows with beefy arms and massive hammers, were driving in a motley assortment of pegs and stakes with such urgency that one feared an invasion might be imminent. A large, tatty, brown tent was already erected, after a fashion, at the far end of the field, and was doing its early morning deep breathing exercises. Some neighbouring specimens, smaller, pitched perilously, had the appearance of a clutch of fledgling birds making their initial experiments in wing flapping. It was presently explained to me that the large tent had been acquired from Army surplus; from which I assumed that it must surely be a relic of some war or other, although of which, it was not patently obvious. The range and quality of a country show is often epitomised in the style of its canvas,and these rag bags didn't augur very well. By about eight a.m. all the properties were duly assembled and proudly presided over by that shabby shambles of a brown marquee, veteran of many such shows and both allegedly and obviously survivor of many battles.

"Toilet for t'lasses," mumbled Jack Sneaton over the back of his hand, having observed my fascination with the relic. "Airrgh, we'll 'appen hev tae git sum mare pegs arowand botthom - not deycent all flappin' upandowan leyke that - not deycent." Then after a self-conscious flip-over cough devised to alter the subject, he went on with a flourish of enthusiasm, "They'll be fetchin' t'big yan in a la'al while - reyght on t'stroke of nine - hev tae finish gittin' t'patch ready— S'long."

Having dashed home for a hasty breakfast, I made sure to be back at the show field for that crucial moment. As forecast, on the very stroke of nine o'clock, the sound of many rattles, squeaks and clanks signalled the approach of Matty Sisterson's aged Bedford two-tonner. The battered old crate rolled and cringed under a shifty over-load as she perilously picked her way over a stretch of terrain which resembled a solidified section of mid-Atlantic. Perched precariously atop the heaving load, and clinging to anything that would give a hand or foot hold, were half a dozen local stalwarts, looking for all the world like first-time camel riders. This ramshackle arrival set up a fresh spate of lively activity, as eagerly excited helpers converged on the lorry from all parts of the field. This must surely be the showpiece supreme - the 'big yan'. With dexterity swift and efficient the great white sheet was spread out on the grass, then picked up and ceremonially marched to its allotted position. Lines were uncoiled, intervals paced out, and wielding huge wooden hammers, groups of thick-limbed hefties pounded large stakes into the ground. Within less than thirty minutes the canvas was hoisted, and like some gigantic white moth emerging from the chrysalis, with its gleaming wings filling out in the morning sunshine - behold the big marquee. The ostentatious satisfaction of the crew on completing their mammoth task, and the resultant applause of the bystanders aroused in me the suspicion that the delivery and erection of the great tent had been purposely delayed until this hour so as to ensure maximum publicity. I was mistaken however, for I was subsequently to learn that, as a matter of fact, the said tent was hired on an hour by hour basis, and these extremely practical country folk had so planned their programme that no expensive hire time would be wasted at either end.

"We'll 'appen be takkin' it dowan cum five o'clock exact," old Seth Manston told me, which intelligence was demonstrably borne out by the fact that even before the flaps and frills had been fitted, a busy bustle of men, women, and children were moving towards the great tent, bearing tables trestled, forms and chairs various, stands assorted, boxes miscellaneous, parcels, bundles, pots, and tins of every shape and size.

“Beer Tent - nay lad - tha should knaw better than that,” scolded Seth with feigned disgust in answer to my furtive query. “Nay mister, it’s nowt o’ that soort or owt... ower mony chapel foalke about for that.” At which point he nearly got his intestines into a tangle with wheezy diaphragmatic laughter.

The old man had, although no doubt unintentionally, hinted at a notable historic fact. This Gala Day had originated many years before, when the said chapel folk had considered that life in the dale consisted of too much ‘all work and no play’, and accordingly set about doing something practical to redress the balance. The ensuing years had seen many changes in the structure and purpose of this annual event, yet a large proportion of the organisation remained firmly in the hands of the so-called chapel folk. Consequently some traditional imperatives remained, such as the formal opening ceremony, complete with prayers, speeches, showy platform party and all. And it was more than doubly imperative that the minister should be included in that platform party, if for no other reason than to ‘lead us all in prayer.’ The vicar could also come up on high, if he wanted to, or didn’t mind appearing superfluous. In either case we both felt like misplaced wet rags. On this particular occasion the opener was the long, lean, and effusive Colonel George Mannington, MC, DSO, ex-of the Royal Regiment of Artillery. It was never disclosed to me why this gallant, whom I had never heard of before, had been invited to perform this singular honour. It was whispered to me however that he had some kind of reputation for impartial generosity, a fat cheque book, and rousing speeches - surely a useful combination of attributes in the present circumstances. Rising majestically from his ex-NAAFI folding chair, the good colonel encountered some initial difficulty in extracting a small notebook from the inside pocket of his heavy tweed jacket. After a few preliminary rhetorical coughs in ascending order, he launched directly into the main substance of his speech. To my ears, well attuned to verbal militarablia, his effort was richly reminiscent of the pep talks of doubtful sincerity given to troops just before a battle. Otherwise, although in places blandly prosaic, the speech was quite charming, and it drew a satisfactory applause. Much encouraged, the gentleman, after more statutory range-finding coughs, and some periphrastic peroration, formally declared the Show open with the cheerful exhortation,

“Now let us one and all, forget our cares, our work and all that damned sort of thing - to He... what I mean is, well, let us all be carefree and let our hair down.”

This was all fair comment, until it was observed that the colonel himself was as bald as a fresh egg. The trim matrons who accompanied him on the platform were pale with shock. Realising that he had committed some kind of gaff, the brave soldier simply reloaded, re-aligned, and let blast with,

“Now let battle commence... everybody to your posts... give it all you’ve got... make this a great day. Forward!”

The order did nothing but confuse the crowd, most of whom confessed to never having heard a show start off ‘wi’ owt t’leykes o’ that.’ The people simply sat still, not knowing what it was they were supposed to do next. The whispering, murmuring stalemate persisted until a portly fellow stepped forward and strained his thick neck in order to bring his mouth into some sort of approximation with the microphone, which had obviously been adjusted for the convenience of a giraffe. His lips were seen to move, and a cacophonic cascade spilled all over the field, which a lady sitting next to me interpreted for me,

"Says naebody's tae gaw into t'big tent yet. Judgin's still gawin' on or summat leyke."

Something perverse inside me whispered that this was a splendid chance for me to make my escape from the official party, and make a bid for the big marquee before the rush was eventually turned loose.

"Only judges and committee members," boomed the hairy giant who was guarding the tent doorway, "Where's tha official badge?"

"Badge?"

I tried the old clerical collar ruse, stating categorically that this was the only badge I needed, but the massive one remained steadfast and unmovable. When however, I solemnly informed him that the people inside would probably be waiting for me to conduct some official prayers, he meekly yielded, doffed his cap, and bid me enter. The interior of the big marquee was like another world. The bright sunlight, diffused as it penetrated the white top-sheets, the dulled ambience of sounds partly absorbed by the walls, the sweet smell of trodden grass, and the overall aroma of oiled canvas blended together to create an atmosphere which belonged only to this place. The bank of tables set up towards the far end of the tent looked like a mighty altar to Providence, being lavishly adorned with pampered blossoms, bloated early fruits and vegetables, rare gems from the kitchens, treasures wrought out of long hours, or even weeks of eager toil, watching, and waiting. The patient skills of hand and eye were on display also, in cleverly worked design and craftsmanship.

Presently, a commotion at the main doorway indicated the arrival of Gina, accompanied by a fearsome entourage of meaty matrons and spindly spinsters. She appeared so fragile and petite at the head of this formidable host. Yet she was not lacking in importance, for in the lapel of her smartly tailored jacket was an obtrusive red disc in cardboard, bearing the awesome inscription 'JUDGE'. When I tactfully enquired of a member of the show committee as to why they had elected Gina to perform this onerous duty, I was obliquely informed that 'We gently tries tae git t'wife o' sum rather prominent person of soorts tae act as judge for t'cayekes, and jam, and stuff leyke that - puts a bit o' edge on t'show ye knaw.' Now if this really was the case, then the said Committee had in this instance a shock coming to them. In addition to being 'T'wife o' sum prominent person o' soorts', although they didn't know it, their present young novelty choice just happened to be a very highly qualified teacher in Home Economics, and already at twenty-five, an experienced judge in the culinary arts and crafts to boot.

"That spunge's Mary Ouston's tae be sure - can tell be t'culla," blurted out the buxom Nellie Bagguley.

"Aye, and she alweys gits them ower big, and dropped a bit in t'middle," subscribed another.

"Jinnie's gitten hers reyght nice again, 'esn't she," came a thin voice from out of a thin face. "That she has, reyght neyce reyce cayeke if I meyght say sae."

"Gat a first at Kestendale last week, and Baxterbrigg t'week afore."

"Ower much fav'ritism around them pa—" The remainder of this comment was swamped in the hubbub it initiated amongst the committee ladies.

"Shhhhhhhh." Gina's stern scolding finger (left index to be precise) was pointing upwards, "Shhhh - please - no external comment."

The dart went home, the voices and the faces froze solid. Producing from out of her bag a flashy new kitchen knife (recent wedding present) Gina deftly cut out a small portion from each cake on display, thoroughly scrutinised it, smelled it, palpated it, and broke it. A pause for thought, some characteristic stroking across the dimple in her chin with that same left index finger, and the appropriate award cards found their targets. Then, with an air of quiet efficiency, she took out some dainty little sheets of notepaper, wrote upon each a few comments relating to the basis of her judgement, and deposited one with each winning exhibit.

"For future reference, and guidance," she sweetly mused.

Still the voices of the ladies did not unfreeze, although their muscles did, as they broke into some strange form of surd communication which entailed the slow writhing of their bodies and features. The Show must go on however, and so to the home-made jams. These were subjected to similar exacting tests. Removing the paper cap from the top of each jar, Gina tested the product for aroma, held it up to the light to examine clarity, and to the apparent horror of the onlookers, gave the pot a swift sideways tilt for consistency. Bottled fruit was traditionally the great speciality at all the local shows. Although rather early in the season for this particular exhibit, it was the ambition of every kitchen wizard for miles around to pin up a few 'Firsts' in this category. The visible apprehension of Gina's support group was amply rewarded when they arrived at the 'Bottled Stall'. Again she followed her standard procedure, but with one additional feature. Calling for a male bystander to unscrew the lids, she then held up each bottle by the glass cap. Any which revealed the slightest trace of air bubbles were summarily disqualified. The effect was devastating. The ladies stood aghast, and not without cause. Gina had calmly and efficiently foiled a custom which had, from time immemorial, been perpetrated among the local shows. Reputed but usually self-appointed 'experts', and social favourites were in the habit of hawking a single exhibit from show to show, often hogging the competition, discouraging and even barring the way to newer local talent. It so happened on this occasion that some of the items which had been disqualified or downgraded by Gina, had already won awards at other recent shows. Probably this was why Gina dropped points for the failure to display date of origin.

"And now to the wines please." Gina chirruped, turning her winning smile towards the stewards.

The effect of this request was quite dramatic, as though she had accidentally trodden upon some hidden alarm button. The ungainly gaggle of assorted matrons who accompanied her erupted into agitated chatter and gasps of dismay, while the male stewards hissed with stifled laughter.

"Weyne? Nay luv, we 'appen nivver show owt leyke that as a rule. Well... you see... well sum on us chapel foalkes dint gaw in for... that soort o'... you knaw what I mean... " and Sarah Cowan's rather embarrassed little speech fluttered off before completion.

"That's all t'judgin' ower," broke in an extremely large, loud and fripperous lady with carousel headgear, "Thank you very much young woman. And I'd just like tae say, that is on behalf o' the ladies' Committee, we've nivver seen it done owt leyke that afore - leyke breakin' stuff oppen and lookin' on th'inside, cowpin' up jars and bottles, smellin' them, tastin' them, pummellin' them around - was just leyke t'menfolk tryin' ower th'stock at auction mart 'appen."

"I'm so sorry if it seemed irregular," Gina sweetly replied, "but I assure you I go through all those motions for precisely the same very good practical reasons as the men at the auction." Thus saying, Gina braced herself accordingly.

The very large woman was smiling now, and looked considerably less belligerent. The other ladies were smiling also, and seemed to have pulled the ripcords on their stays.

"And if I might add," announced the forthright Mrs. Dunholme, "on behalf of the Committee and all the ladies here also, thank you young woman, we are most grateful to you. Indeed we are unanimously agreed that today we have witnessed the fairest and most efficient adjudication that this show has had for many a year. So once again we all want to give you a big Thank you Miss...er... Mrs. ...er... Teviotdale.

Out from amongst the coterie, now chattering excitedly in closed session, there emerged a slender one wearing a wide-brimmed hat with a herbaceous border. She bore in her hands an enormous bouquet which she presented to Gina with a quarter curtsey and a shy cough, before vanishing back amidst the group from whence she had come. And here ended the judgement.

That part of the great event which could be rightly designated 'Show' occupied but a small proportion of the day, and soon was to give way to the bean feast. By eleven-thirty a row of black Sawyer stoves were belching dense pillars of blue and yellow smoke skywards, and were producing strong tea by the gallon, at about the same rate as it was about to be consumed. "Meyest onnum genlly what cums for t'fancy fotherin' 'appen," one elderly bystander confided to us. The sight of big men lustily consuming hefty sandwiches, large wadges of slab cake, and an incredible range of wholesome home-made confections by the hundredweight gave considerable credence to the old man's claim. It should be mentioned here that the aforementioned great sandwiches were sufficient of a Show speciality to merit the accolade 'Lyndassby Landmines'. No dainty cucumber whimsies these, for each consisted of two one inch slabs of firm country bread with equally substantial fillings which required lashings of rich farm butter to hold them together. "What abowit a splash o' nice mustard on this yan la'al Missus?" proffered Lizzie Broomfield as Gina took precarious delivery of a big ham block buster. Incongruous as it may seem, but the local version of the meringue was the other notable speciality of this great feast. These large luxurious puffballs, bloated to the limit with thick cream, were to be seen in large numbers on stalls in every part of the show field, being ever in great demand. Inevitably the efforts of some of the lesser refined hill men, with fingers as nimble as cow udders, to negotiate these fragile dollops often ended in disaster, and created a good deal of unscheduled entertainment. It was during my own awkward pre-occupation with one of these fripperies that Gina and I mislaid each other.

"She telt us she was gawin' across hoame cos it's time for la'-al puppy dog's feed - says it's just leyke la'al babby," volunteered a small girl who claimed to be on special terms with Gina. That piece of intelligence was quite plausible, considering Joo Di. This minuscule parcel of canine high explosive was in fact a smooth fox terrier which we had recently acquired from the R.S.P.C.A. for the princely sum of ten shillings. Already she was evolving into a delightful combination of whirlwind mischief and rare charm. But my secret worry was that she was beginning to take precedence over me in some quarters.

"Can't have a show without Joo Di," mused Gina on her return to the field, with dog in arms. "See what I mean!"

An ear-splitting blare of unintelligibility from the loud speakers had the effect of an air-raid siren. The people distributed around the field instantly cutting short whatever they were engaged in, and hastily converged upon the cordoned-off area at the centre. The garbled super-diction then seemed to invite us to make ourselves as comfortable as possible, and settle down for an afternoon of real sport, competitions, plenty mare tae eat, and it was hoped, some good entertainment.

From that moment of the Tannoy's thunderous summons, all semblance of 'Show' had departed from this auspicious event. It was hereafter to be referred to as 'our Sports Day'. Being such, we would all maintain that noble spirit of fair-play, good sportsmanship, and uncommon courtesy for which we in these parts were noted. And therefore, blasted out those terrible horns, it would be, as our custom always is at this here show, the ladies first please, for some of the gentler sports, so would t'lasses line theirsel's up for t'grand tug o' war please. Thank you kindly."

Two teams of belligerent beauties rushed forward into the arena with frightening impetuosity. They came in a variety of ages, shapes and sizes, but each one vibrantly confident in her unequalled strength of limb. Heels were pitted, teeth were gritted, and each team slammed itself into reverse gear. The stout white rope was raised up from the ground and the tension was on, the starting pistol poised skywards. The sudden appearance of a pair of brightly coloured flimsy intimates, which some practical joker had substituted for the marker rag at the middle of the rope, had a devastating effect. The teams fell apart in a wriggling giggling shambles, and the great moment was lost. With some difficulty the girls were eventually brought back into a semblance of control, and the fight was on in earnest, the only change being that a sombre-faced middle-aged committee member had rushed forward and exchanged the dainty distraction for a neat white handkerchief of her own. The starting pistol failed to go off, but the sharp click of the trigger was sufficient to hurl the ladies into this grim fight to the death. I had never before realised that the female of our species was capable of contorting its fine features into such ferocious grimaces, nor that soft throats could emit such fearsome sounds of savage fury. From the very start, this contest was no mere fun spot. Some of the girls were well nigh hysterical, and others wept with wild passion. The said contest however, was brief, and to say the least, one-sided. The local team had obviously not bargained for the presence of Nellie Oundle, strategically positioned at the tail end of the visiting team. The extremely formidable Nellie simply stood there chewing gum, and with two turns of slack coiled about her copious waist. They may as well have made an attempt to dislodge the nearby solid granite mass of Snarlston Crag. One bystander tersely remarked that even if they had succeeded in budging Nellie, her feet would have gouged out two furrows a yard deep.

Women are essentially ladies nevertheless, and our country maidens are singularly prone to gentle femininity. At least that is what I had been brought up to assume. I began to wonder however, whether certain stresses, such as a country sports day, cause them to recall from our common ancestry traits that are not ordinarily discernible. The Ladies Football Match did much to reinforce this notion. Whilst it was easy to suspect that this event had been organised by the all-male sports committee, and was being staged primarily for the amusement of the men, there was no doubt that the ladies were entering into it in a spirit of uncompromising partisanship. The two teams, 'North o' t'Watter' and 'South o' t'Watter' lined up, all clad in a colourful assortment of borrowed football gear.

"Leykes 'em wi' nice thick thighs... an' nice an' round o' t'rump... not ower much on," observed a grisly grey rustic well past the time of sexual decay, "Ney shin pads or owt leyke... and all wearing them breeches far ower far up t'legs an' all... not deycent."

The mischievous streak native to my constitution had already led me to note that in any case, Mother Nature had adequately equipped most of these her daughters for the efficient absorption of physical shocks. And well she needed to do so, for from the very first peep of the whistle this was a furious all-in, everything-goes, no-holds-barred flurry of flailing limbs and storm tossed hair. The noise was incredible, with a high proportion of it coming out of the players. Despite the wild energy being expended in every direction, the ball, except for the odd occasions when it was booted at random or lost amongst the spectators, tangled up in a melee of writhing legs, arms, hands-knees-and-boomps-a-daisy, rolled free. This phenomenon was due, I adjudged, to the fact that the two sides were so much pre-occupied with the destruction of each other, that possession of the ball was of secondary consequence. These Nordic maids were apparently aware of the rule pertaining to the handling of the ball, but were notoriously indifferent towards the one about handling one another. Some of those borrowed shirts would never fit snugly about their rightful male owners again. For that matter, neither would the shorts. Not surprisingly a dispute broke out mid-field, and there was a savage tit-for-tat between two curvaceous forwards, vocally aided and abetted by their respective team-mates. The male referee indulged himself in some sensual pleasure in his unnecessarily prolonged efforts to separate the two damsels, who then lost interest in each other and directed their combined wrath against him. Regaining some measure of control over himself and the game, he ostentatiously ordered the more aggressive of the two ladies to leave the game. To the accompaniment of a loud cacophony of boos and cheers, she stomped off the pitch, remorseless and defiant, but lovely even in dishevelment. To my own horror and shock, as she drew nearer I saw that the rebel was none other than the sweet Mabel, my cherubic organist from Fellsyke, who had always impressed me as the very quintescence of rural feminine charm. Mabel flashed a wicked wink at me as she passed me closely by. Needless to say, the match ended with no categorical result. Although allegedly many goals had been scored, there was wide disagreement as to how many, by whom, for whom, and which side had totted up the greater number.

The ladies having had their fling, it was now time to get down to the more serious business of the afternoon - the Mens' Sports. The loud speakers boomed again, this time directing the crowd to a tight enclosure for the Greasy Pig Contest. To much applause from the spectators and with strident protests from himself, the young victim was hustled into the straw-strewn arena. The pig was notably of some rare breed, seldom seen in these parts. It was completely hairless, of a fair complexion and had a skin so shiny that the animal had the appearance of an out-size piggy bank. It had been greased overall with pure lard (compliments of one of its late relatives) and looked as though it would be as easy to hold as a wet fish. A self-styled inspector then entered the ring, gave the hapless creature a cursory going over, and pronounced it 'fit for owt'. The human contestants were now lined up and subjected to what for these manicure sensitive farmers was the indignity of an inspection of their talons.

"Summonem used tae growum for months aforehand at yan time. Now they maks 'em shear 'em afore t'stairt." said the man on my left, a little too closely to my ear.

The principle was to grasp the writhing animal with both hands, and whoever held on to it longest in this fashion was the undisputed winner. The prize was the pig itself so, although the metaphor may appear a little dubious, there was much at stake. One would have expected that these swarthy hill farmers, who could seize hold of a full-grown ram, flick it over and hold it in a grip like a vice, or bring down a bullock in one deft throw, would be a sure match for this squealing young pig on any count. Not this specimen however, for the group of senior cognicenti who were still engaged in a prolonged dispute regarding its far from obvious pedigree had established one clear fact; this pig had quick-silver in its breeding.

"Hoddum!... hoddum!... hoddum!" chanted the excited onlookers, which. expression I took to be a local form of the "Ole'!... Ole'!... Ole," of the Spanish bullring.

Tom Swithanbank managed to 'hoddum langest'. That was after twenty or more pairs of grappling hands had stripped away most of the lubricant from the pig's back and under belly. And this lucky little pig went instantly to market, for on receiving his prize, the enterprising Tom immediately set up an impromptu auction on the spot.

Meanwhile a long jagged line of swaggering swains had drawn up in front of the large marquee to participate in the greatly renowned Fell Race. This was a feat of endurance specifically suited to those possessed of an unnatural surfeit of stamina or congenital madness. Appropriately undressed for the occasion, the sinewy striplings danced on their toes, or performed similar rituals of impatience as they awaited starters orders. At the slobbering report of the pistol they were off, as though sprung from a mighty catapult. The initial momentum soon wavered, for the runners encountered rising ground even before they were clear of the field. All too soon they would have to negotiate Lyndassby Fell, which ascended in rough degrees seeming to vary between one-in-ten and one-in-one. The entire course would traverse the Southern aspect of the mountain, and so with a pair of sharp eyes, or good binoculars, the runners could be kept in sight for most of the time, even as the many ad hoc commentaries indicated. But for most of the folk in the show field, once started, the fell race was of no further consequence until the first runner was due to stagger home in approximately one hour's time.

"Charlie Mecca's lad'll 'appen cum in fust again I reckon... alweys does... ivvry year t'sayeme... faather was t'syeme an' all... still runnin' ower t'fells when he was mair than fowerty... until that lad o' his grew up an' beyate him... beyate his owne faather he did," speculated an elderly sage nearby, "Airrrghhh... poor Charlie...dee-ed seyen after."

"Nae bettin' Joe," chided a poker-faced fellow, turning briefly aside from a suspicious looking huddle of men by the corner of the tent. "Nae bettin... that is... official leyke... what's yours Billie... unofficial leyke?"

Nothing very spectacular happened for another thirty-five minutes until a multi-barrelled sonic boom from a cluster of loud speakers immediately above my head, although totally unintelligible, set up a stampede in the direction of the largest cordoned-off area of the field.

"Cuddy Rayess - Cuddy Rayess," gasped the man when he collided with me as he dashed by. I thought I recognised a similar sound coming from the announcer, even though it was totally baffled by ear-splitting audio feedback.

"The Donkey Derby," a smartly dressed lady who spoke my language translated for me.

In an astonishingly short time, the entire population of the field, and one suspected of the whole valley, had concentrated around the perimeter of white rope. Expectancy and excitement were already running hot and high. The stewards had mistimed this one, so it seemed, and nearly created an unseemly anti-climax, for unexpectedly, and out from nowhere, a solitary, bedraggled figure staggered into the ring. Using up the few ounces of energy remaining in him to hold up his arms above his head in triumph, he reeled twice before collapsing in a limp pile at the feet of the stewards. There was hilarious laughter all round, until the crowd gradually began to realise that this was indeed the first fell-runner home. The laughter converted to cheers, loud at first, but louder still when on being raised to his feet it was seen that this runner was not indeed the predictable Brian Metcalfe, but the young Nick Sedgely. We were subsequently informed that, even when advancing and overtaking to take the lead for his classical final spurt, the truly sporting Brian had dropped out to give assistance to an injured rival.

The notorious public address system was manned by some over zealous amateur who was obviously intent upon making this his very own field day. He sounded off with such shattering frequency that it gave one the sensation of being stranded on a busy railway station in Hell. The next blare-up was to state the obvious, and inform us that the Great Donkey Derby was about to commence. Or was the man being over-optimistic? No sooner had the clashing echo scurried off into the hills, than a bizarre assortment of gladiators processed falteringly into the arena, clad in a crazy variety of odd garments. Then the hapless asses were ushered in, neither willingly nor unwillingly, but displaying that stoic indifference to mocking abuse which is their wont. That the donkey is a creature of unpredictable manners must undoubtedly be the under-statement of the century, for the creature can certainly be relied upon to confound any man-made situation. True, it is highly prone to creating unsolicited comedy, but often at the expense of man. Resistant to force, scornful of cajolery, this humble little animal with unviolent ways of subduing humans, has an uncanny genius for setting up situations in which human beings will unwittingly make a mockery of their own kind. Indeed the essential nature of the donkey may provide adequate grounds for honest doubt regarding the accepted Biblical premise that the Almighty, in His great wisdom, at the initial act of creation gave man to have dominion over all the beasts of the field.

Incidentally, where did all these donkeys come from? Except for the three scruffy specimens kept by the eccentric 'Irish Jim' right up at the head of Scragdale, there were no others in the area. It was while I was ruminating in these fields of thought, that a fierce argument broke out among four Tannoys that were unstrategically placed within earshot of one another. When I managed to adjust my tympanums to this latest decibelic bombardment, I suspected that what I was hearing was a catalogue of donkeys, their origins, capabilities, and, without any qualification, their riders.

"Says sumonem's been browt fra Blackpool, and sumonem's fra Morcum, and sumonem's reyght fra Egypt or summat." After a short pause in which to absorb further explosive intelligence, my informant went on, "Says there's got tae be nae bettin' nor owt leyke... not official leyke." At which he twisted his toothless face into an exaggerated wink, and dug a bony elbow deeply into the side of his fat companion.

"All t'sayeme," rejoined the portly one, "I'll bet tha hafe-a-crown owd Billie Atkinson gits in fust... always fetches his own cuddie."

"Now I telt tha... gamblin's prohibitated... shhhhh... bet yon parson fella's list'nin' ower yonther. How much did tha say Jackie?"

Like their bi-pedic counterparts, the donkeys came in a variety of heights, widths, and length of leg. This enabled the handicappers to introduce an element of callous comedy, in the shape of deliberate mismatching. At least fifteen minutes were expended on efforts to marshall the stubborn animals into some semblance of simple order, like a straight line, all facing in the same direction, and standing reasonably still. Another ten minutes were lost, due to the inability of some of the riders to remain mounted. The donkey is notoriously individualistic, and no two of the species will ever react in the same way to any given situation. This factor was already throwing riders and organisers into idiotic confusion. The exact moment at which the race got under way was difficult to assess, for the starting pistol went off unexpectedly with a soft muffled 'pooff' as though the shot was damp, or it had fired accidentally in Tom Raine's trouser pocket. The higgledy-piggledy assembly of donkeys showed no instant reaction to the signal, but simply carried on higgledy-piggledying. The over-enthusiastic, sharp-eared public address announcer did re-act however, causing overhead loud speakers all over the field to split the air with a sudden, too-close-to-the-microphone, "THEY'RE OFF."

And that is just what at least two thirds of the riders were.

And were painfully deposited on the ground for good measure. These castaways were destined to spend the remainder of the race pitting their wits and athletic prowess against all the tricks which asinine wisdom had devised for the keeping apart of man and donkey. This wily animal has been endowed with a peculiar talent for complicating a simple issue; like a line from A to B. Straightforwardness is not a trait for which it is noted, and it has an uncanny aversion towards getting to the point. The corpulent Will MacAlister had moved about three paces from the starting line when his shaggy mount affected a solid seize-up on all four brakes, which stance it steadfastly maintained to the bitter end, irrespective of all manner of bribes, coaxings, pattings, pettings, cursings and threats. A sprightly white specimen was going well until it abruptly decided to pause for refreshment mid-course, making a lengthy meal out of a meagre morsel of vegetation which had caught its eye. Sid Bates was off and on so many times during the first ten yards that he abandoned his charge and fled the field in pain, and not a little temper. His elderly mount had long since perfected the art of jettisoning an unwelcome load, by a simple technique of an upwards and sideways jerk of the rump at irregular intervals. One large animal, with a small jockey aloft, began the race with a resolute dash in a direct line for the winning post, but due to the frantic cheering of the crowd it lost its nerve and comatosed within but a few feet of the finishing line. From that station it could not be budged, until the race was over, at which point it quietly strolled away of its own accord, having spent the entire duration of the race standing with a silly grin on its face and nodding tantalisingly at the man with the chequered flag. Soon there was the inevitable log jam in the middle of the field, but a sudden diabolic exclamation from the loud speakers caused it to explode with donkeys bucking, riders sprawling, and stewards tearing their hair out. The long, lean Joe Wilkie, on a shortie, was proceeding splendidly, feet on the ground, hobbie-horse fashion. The ingenious method was showing great promise until the donkey, a male, paused en-route to answer a call of nature. For Joe, this necessitated a wider spread out of his feet. Amply relieved, the creature moved off unexpectedly from beneath him, leaving Joe standing splay-legged and looking for all the world like an abandoned Eiffel Tower on a very wet day. It was thought that Andy Windlass was revealing some hidden talents as a stunt man, or was plainly showing off, until it was realised that his frantic antics were but his desperate efforts to remain on board, or halt his super-charged donkey. Jack Cowan's large grey steed had turned to concrete soon after the start. The bemused Jack sat motionless on its back, whilst the faithful animal stood with its head bowed solemnly to the ground, the pair striking a statuesque pose reminiscent of Napoleon's Retreat from Moscow. The last we beheld of Harry Boscomb's short-legged beast was when it ran amok in the direction of the ladies' Toilet Tent, with the short-legged Harry in tow.

Nobody knew where it came from, to whom it belonged, or how it arrived on the scene in the first place. But enter a large riderless male, trailing behind it a long length of ragged rope. Trotting vigorously onto the course, head held high, it pursued, and attempted to mount the first moving object it encountered, which just happened to be the dainty little Jenny with Ned Keston astride. A well-timed back kick from the little lady despatched the randy male into shamed retreat, and in the same instant launched Ned into several feet of free flight. Meanwhile, old Jack Sneaton, who seemed to have appointed himself as her chaperon for the day, was bamboozling Gina with a low-voiced impromptu disquisition on the sexual proclivities of donkey stallions. By this time, the entire catalogue of possible calamities having become expended, the event began to take on some semblance of a race, and this in spite of the frantic attentions of the priapic male. The animals that were still in motion, in various speeds and modes, seemed to have overcome their aversion to the direction of the finishing line. It actually began to look as though the event, no longer a rodeo, could reach some kind of logical conclusion after all. Indeed it might have accomplished just that, had one donkey not paused to gape just opposite the point where Gina was standing with her small pooch in her arms. And that is how things might have remained had the ass not opened its great mouth and delivered a tremendous HEE-HAW in her direction. Now there is only one other animal in the whole of creation which is more proficient than the humble donkey in making havoc among a crowd of humans, and that animal is a five-months-old Fox Terrier whom an ass has insulted. In a split second the small dog turned into a live missile and launched itself into the arena on a wild escapade of pandemonium, intent upon destroying every living creature in sight. The first casualty was poor Ric Beckleton. Facing his charger head on, the bundle of miniature fury hurled a spate of hot canine invective straight at it. The donkey bucked violently and deposited its rider in an ungainly heap about its hocks. Transferring her evil attention to the next in line, young Joo Di ran circles of yapping fury about its feet until both mount and jockey were totally disorientated and unsure of the direction of gravity. On now to a cluster that were running confidently down the middle of the course. They bolted, reeled, hopped, skipped, and jumped in terror, treating their riders to the thrill, or the tumble, of a lifetime. Now Joo Di had arrived at the place where MacAllister's shaggy little female was still standing stock still, and resisting all efforts to move her on. A savage torrent of yapping, snarling and screeching had no effect whatsoever upon the donkey, which continued to stand its ground, nonchalantly nodding its head as though all was well with its world. Several spectators entered the fray, but only added further complications by their efforts to salvage what was left of the Mid-twentieth Century Donkey Stakes. The crowd was paralytic, and poor Gina was screaming "Joooooo-Diiiiiii" so frantically that some people thought that she was having some kind of fit. Next thing, Gina herself entered the lists, and added more havoc to the confusion. The last word however just had to be with the public address man, and the celestial voice boomed out in a thunderous cascade of exploding glottal stops,

"Wiltownerolalpuppydogtryangittitoftfeyeldorsummatpleasethenkye?"

Whatever strange tongue this was, the announcement had quite a decisive effect. The donkeys were left in abeyance, and the great race was transformed into a catch-the-dog marathon. In howling panic young Joo Di made a direct line towards a white, wind-blown bell tent which was giving itself airs near the winning post. She was promptly followed inside by a whole regiment of foot. It was all over within seconds, when out of the resultant heap of canvas, strings, and bodies, there emerged shattered, one Gina, hugging her precious canine bundle close to her, and followed by a disordered procession of dishevelled gallants.

The stewards and the few competitors remaining on the course were by now conferring together as to how to proceed from then on, when a loud burst of applause went up from the crowd. This greeted the sudden re-appearance of Harry Boscomb who had last been seen when his donkey bolted off the field, dragging him behind. Returning from its pleasant excursion into the distant moorland, with Harry seated sedately aboard, the little animal made its triumphal entry into the ring, with those short, dainty steps so typical of donkey locomotion. The near hysterical applause hushed as the plucky pair passed confidently through the tape - from behind. The ever present, ever obliging Tannoy was swift to settle the issue,

"Mr. Boscomb, riding Bessie, is er... disqualified. And therefore the winner of this year's Donkey Derby i—"

"Hod your stupid moothe ye silly bu—" came some harsh audio interference, originating from rather too close to a microphone. Unfortunately the vital information, and fortunately the subsequent comments were instantly swamped by the tumult of a herd of humans gone berserk.

A poem which I had long since learnt at school, now beyond recall, had been vaguely taunting me throughout the crazy proceedings of the past hour. Now true to present form it came in backwards, and the last verse sprung back at me crystal clear:

'Fools! For I also had my hour;
One far fierce hour and sweet:
There was a shout about my ears,
And palms before my feet.'

C.K.Chesterton, of course.

******

"Tha'll be stoppin' for t'big race, wiln't tha not?" a low pitched voice let loose on the free air.

"Means thee, minister - aye. Didn't tha Sid— ?" came another.

"Airrgh... big do that'n... ivvrybody stops tae see t'Big Run... cross country soort o' thing... tha'd enjoy it." added the chorus.

The Big Run was indeed the Grande Finale of this day's events, and a prestigious affair, to say the least. The run was coursed around the far boundary of the two large fields occupied by the Show. Although the well-meaning organisers had never intended it to be an obstacle race, Mother Nature obviously had, for she had spent several millennia in preparing the course with all the necessary hazards, and had also thrown in a number of unnecessary ones for luck. Most of the spectators bunched up near the start, but some, more Spartan, ran out to disport themselves at various vantage points along the route.

"All t'runners on t'line," went out the command, and various athletic looking men, appropriately kitted out, presented themselves to the official handicapper. This extremely imposing gentleman placed them at irregular intervals away from the starting line, presumably according to each man's age, station, kudos, and certain other undeclared factors. This event was clearly regarded in a category all of its own, a very serious affair, and a very fitting climax to the Great Lyndassby Show. That is... official like.

"Gaw-on have theesel' a go minister," came a low-pitched wicked voice, "We all knaw tha only works on Sunders, but this is special."

"Aye, gaw-on ministher...we'll all put a dollar on tha... or mebees mare... 'appen sumbody up there'll help tha alang a gayly bit eh."

"Gaw-on ministher," sounded a rude chorus of assorted locals, and before the echo had died a tale-end voice called out,

"Parson 'ere's wantin' tae run Bill... give 'im a line will tha."

"Gaw-on, it'll dae the cause a lot o' good ye knaw," confided a nearby church official into my ear, "We knaw ye'll maybe not dae nowt, or owt leyke, but just for t'fun on it... or 'appen for t'Lord eh."

'Just for t'fun on it'. Now those words hit me really hard, and called up one of those parsonic dilemmas which troubled me much during those early noviciate days; the difficult matter of public relations. Would it be scrupulously politic of me, a respected man of the cloth, to parade myself before a crowd as a spectacle of fun? Yet wasn't it Saint Paul himself who elected to become a fool for Christ's sake? But that was different of course. He didn't mean a clown, or idiotic exhibitionist, did he? Mind you right up until recently I had been an enthusiastic amateur sportsman, with cross country running, University football, some boxing, swimming, squash, all part of my list. And of course, there was seven years as a fighting soldier, physically and mentally trained up to the hilt. Then again - I wasn't a minister in those days, was I? That phase of life is past and over. And there was yet another area of doubt. 'We'll all put a dollar on tha' the man had said. As the Non-conformist Minister should not I be seen to question the ethic of participating in any activity which entailed gambling? The debate was going well towards getting me off the hook, when the sweet whisper of Gina wafted softly, and as was invariably the case, persuasively, across my right shoulder, "Go on darling, show your true metal, give them some fun. They'll simply love you for it... and so might I... go on my old sport."

Although that suggestion knocked me cold, the mischievous shine in the big brown eyes of the girl who made it was sufficient to transport me full of smiles and regrets to the starter and present myself for the race. I had been too hastey, and immediately began to feel very foolish indeed. I prayed for a sudden thunderstorm. The hilarious applause from the spectators indicated that serious though this race was meant to be, they were nevertheless fully appreciative of the inclusion of a comic element. I must surely have appeared to them as just that, formally attired as I was in my clerical greys (my only suit incidentally), immaculately positioned dog collar, and a white carnation in my lapel.

"Tha'll hettae tak them booats off Mister," bawled a hefty man with a gun in his hand, promptly stooping and relieving me of my brand new shiney black shoes."

"He'll 'appen not be needin' them breeches neither Matt... and owt mare as is gawin' tae be gittin' in 's wey," taunted a shrill voice from the edge of the crowd, setting up a gurgle of course laughter. This however came over to me as a challenge and I held on to my equilibrium, and my clothes. Then came the final mockery. The big pompous handicapper, wad of papers in his hand, set me right back to the utmost rear of the starting box, loudly proclaiming, "Dint waant tha tae be gittin' in tae t'rooad of t'proper runners or owt leyke."

I was striving to enter into the sporty spirit of things, yet some strong misgivings persisted and I wasn't quite sure about the expression I was forcing onto my face. There were minor traces of snobbish pride still to be disposed of. But the folk were laughing... at me... making sport out of me... taking the mickey... and they were really enjoying it at that. Something snapped and a nasty admixture of emotions took hold of me; a volatile compound of temper, indignation and determination. And yet of what I was determined, I hadn't the faintest idea. For a few agonising seconds I felt myself go red, inside and out, and for me that is usually a sign of the supercharge switching on, for better or worse. Then quite suddenly the fever passed, I took a deep breath, the proud young clergyman was banished, and I felt myself becoming me again...

"Ppffftttttt." Tom Raine's pistol spluttered off prematurely as usual. But we were off, including the man in my clothes.

Whatever emotions had broken loose inside me, they had somehow affected the muscles of my legs. At that muffled report, something propelled me forward like a bolt from a crossbow. My pace seemed to quicken with every powerful bound. I lost all concern for appearances. I became insensitive of the agony and destruction being wrought in my shoeless feet. My misplaced pride in being set up as a joker vanished into the air streaming past me. The passing glimpse that I got of Gina jumping up and down with girlish excitement supercharged me with such a surge of red-hot energy that I thought I would explode. Soon I had caught up with the main body of runners and was overtaking them one by one.

"What's all t'hurry Vicar... divvil chasing tha or summat?" came a sardonic voice as I overhauled its owner.

"Nay lad, I'm chasing t'divvil," I hurled back, "It's me job you know."

That was not entirely true, for as a matter of fact, by now I was chasing the only runner remaining ahead of me. He was a dark haired, sinewy young man with a stylish stride. He was wearing white shorts, a bright red vest bearing some impressive insignia and, to my utter consternation, he was running in spiked pumps. A strange thing happens inside of me whenever a challenge is narrowed down that far, and it is a profoundly unwholesome feeling. I actually came up on this greyhound, and for a few hundred yards I kept him parallel company. We occasionally exchanged breathless smiles, words of mutual encouragement, and rude goadings. He ran with uncanny confidence, and as we were so far ahead of the rest of the field, I began to suspect that the man was but using me as a pacer. His intention was surely to stay with me until near the finish, when he would make a spectacular spurt for the winning post, for with this man victory was a foregone conclusion. It gradually began to dawn upon him as well as me however, that we were so equally matched that neither was able to wrest an inch of advantage from the other. Nor was either showing any sign of yielding to fatigue. My adversary's occasional sideways glance with mischief in his eye signalled that he had spotted my attire, by now so drenched with perspiration that I looked like a high pressure boiler on the point of blowing off at any moment, and he seemed to take encouragement from the observation. Two thirds of the way along the track, and we came to a long run downhill towards the beck. Even here, neither of us was yet prone to either yielding or gaining a single footfall. The stream was about eight feet wide at the well marked crossing point but it nevertheless took us both by surprise, our minds being fully concentrated upon other matters. When we reached the edge, simultaneously, my companion waded in with a high powered splash which for an instant blotted him out from view. Whatever happened to me next was neither premeditated, calculated, nor expected. Either it was a simple case of brake failure, or the phenomenal transference from the subconscious to the body fibres of some colossal psychic energy - but it just - happened. I threw every nerve, bone, tendon and muscle into a flying leap which landed me clean over on the other side, and to my shocked surprise, and his, almost three feet ahead of my opponent. There was not far to go by now, and with every ounce of energy I could muster or borrow, but certainly not command, I hung on desperately to my advantage until I fell through the tape almost senseless. The crowd went berserk, but I was unable to hear the din above the loud bangs in my head and chest. When my eyes began to focus, the first object they fell upon was Gina, still jumping up and down in unrestrained excitement, the little dog in her arms being almost shaken lifeless. No sooner had I been helped to my feet, incidentally by someone whom I seemed to have met before, than my grand opponent grasped my hand in a vigorous handshake,

"Want to congratulate you lad - tha's a good sport - and a gayly good runner if I may say so. Tha's certainly gi'n me a good run for me money. Onyway, I'm Fred Nuttall fra Wassellborough, county cross-country champion. At least I was... until a few minutes ago."

My humility was dealt a shattering blow by this, and even more so when an indecipherable super-phonic roar (except that it had something which sounded like my name in it) from the loud speakers sent the crowd into wild acclaim. I hated my enjoyment of the luxurious sensation which the moment gave, but alas I could not shake it off - nor was I certain that I wanted to.

"Does this mean that Donni's the new champion?" I heard Gina's clean, clear voice enquire.

A dispute now broke out amongst a group of official looking gentlemen with huge lapel badges. The dispute waxed into a general discussion, and the discussion was adjourned to a committee meeting in the white tent with the airs and graces. Returning in a remarkably short time to the makeshift podium adjacent to the tent, the most important of the gentlemen, he was wearing the largest badge, was handed a microphone. The sound of his throat clearing was like the derailing of an express train, and the rest of his announcement was totally incomprehensible. But my interpreter was once more conveniently to hand and unscrambled the message, her word for word translation being,

"It's the unanimous decision of t'Sports Committee that as this is not a soort of official race, and Ministher here wasn't entered as a proper runner, or owt leyke, tha all knaws what I mean I'm sure... well what I say - that is on behalf of t'Committee - Fred Nuttal being still t'real champion leyke, and wel—"

When the near riot which this broken announcement incited had sufficiently subsided, Fred was called to the podium. A voluminous and fripperous lady, wearing a flamboyant hat with a balcony all round it, had the greatest of pleasures in presenting Fred with a handsome cut glass fruit bowl. As he must have done on numerous similar occasions, with appropriate modesty and a well practised look of wonder in his eyes, he had great pleasure in receiving this trophy. No doubt it would be added to the many such trophies already adorning his shelves. But this was not to be, for silencing the rather restrained applause, he called out in a loud voice,

"Come tha up here sir, I wants tha up here aside o' me."

And for a moment of history the oft presented became the rare presenter. Handing the precious prize to me, he grabbed the hand-mike, (loud booms and deafening crashes) and addressed the audience,

"Parson here's not only good sport, but he's proper runner alright... better'n me onyroad... but I still say... I still say... and I mean what I say... he's t'real champion... official race or no... it was a fair contest... must be that fancy collar he's wearin'."

Fred's magnanimity earned him a delicately discreet kiss from Gina, whereupon amid enthusiastic cheering, a group of handsome opportunists began thrusting themselves to the fore and calling out, "Hey lass, I say parson's t'real champion an' all, aye."

The moment of glory was short-lived however. By now the time had got to half-past-four, and as though at a given signal, the crowd began to gravitate towards the gate. With routine foddering and milking to be done there was some spontaneous urgency about the departure. Having temporarily lost sight of Gina, and being in a shattered state of body, mind, and dress, I decided to make for home with urgent haste also. Now a fit and sprightly young athlete like me had no need to delay his exit by moving with the slow queue at the gate. After all the drystone boundary wall was but a mere four feet high. This confident bid would have worked out splendidly had I not dislodged a large topping stone on the way over, which, landing at the same instant with me, cut a deep gash into my right knee, and left an ugly contusion in my precious trousers. Now, methought, the former champion will be safe for the next few weeks. I was still sprawling in the grass by the roadside, pondering the impossible in working out an explanation to Gina re trousers, when a large green car drew up.

"We see tha's worn theesel' out wi' all that stupid running aye," raked the puny voice of old Charlie Doughty, "Better be gittin' inside and I'll gi' tha a lift to tha house, aye."

Perched proudly in the back seat of the car was Gina, clutching a very subdued puppy dog in one arm and a shining crystal bowl in the other. For reasons unmentionable I chose to join Charlie in the front seat, contriving to locate a hand over my right knee.

"Tha's lost a gayly lot o' money for sumonem this efterneyen, ye knaw that? Who'd ivver thowt." And Charlie broke loose into the deep throated kecking which he substituted for laughter. Turning his head fully about to face Gina, he chuckled,

"Tha should have put a bob or two on tha man young missus... tha'd have deyen alright... that tha would. Could've gittin him an extra suit... or 'appen sum runnin' things." More kecking.

The last word was, as usual, with Gina,

"I always put everything on my man, and he's a good safe bet."

Chapter 22

MAKE HAY WHILE THE SUN SHINES

"Tha might as well tak theesel' a holiday for t'next week or two mister. Naebody'll be wantin' owt tae do wi' owt at haytime - not wi' parsons or prayin' or owt leyke that onyroad," advised old Bert Fenton.

The warning was timely, for of all the seasonal regulars of the farmer's lot, hay-time was the one fraught with the most hazard. Very critical it was, for so great a part of the farming economy during the subsequent year was contingent upon its success. Such devices as the field baler, crop drier, and the new agricultural technology which came with them were not yet in general use, so that in the matter of hay making, the age-old, labour intensive, time consuming methods were still followed. From field to barn was a long drawn-out process, with the various stages of mowing, strowing, gathering and setting up into long- standing pikes, each providing its quota of frustration and potential for disaster. As in most matters agricultural, the weather was master, and in hay-time it was more so. It was no wonder therefore that the day of leading and stacking was hailed with such great relief and enthusiasm. It was indeed the grand finale which brought together in one place all available hands, including neighbours, perhaps on the larger farms some extra hired hands, and sometimes a few volunteers. When the barn was filled up, the remainder of the crop was built up into outdoor stacks. These structures varied in size and shape, some being made in the round and placed in groups reminiscent of African kraals; others large and house-shaped, were usually situated in near proximity to the farm buildings, or at corners of nearby fields.

It was one of this latter variety which was under construction when I arrived at

Blaeweltonrigg Farm. I was never altogether sure as to what got into the farm folk during these great occasions. The urgent enthusiasm with which each went about his or her allotted task, the self-abandon and incredibly loud conversation gave the whole affair an air of happy celebration. Perhaps what had got into them was a surfeit of that strange soap-suds-coloured womp which the farmer's wife dispensed in copious quantities throughout the day - traditional (innocent!) and home-made of course, especially for the occasion. Maybe the noisy goodwill was a symptom of the eager anticipation with which the workers contemplated the massive feast prepared for all at dusk when the work was complete. A decrepit old Fordson tractor stood anchored to the ground near the gate, and was connected by an extremely long drive belt (relic of the former days of steam power) to an equally ancient elevator. The belt flapped and slapped ominously, and the oily old tractor, in addition to belching out dense puffs of noxious smoke laden with paraffin fumes, had an ear-splitting exhaust report which sounded like a giant corncrake. A procession of horse-drawn low loading hay bogies, and tractors with forked sweeps brought the hay pike by pike from the fields, to be hoisted aloft by the conveyor then spread out and trampled by the men atop the growing stack.

"Alreyght... ivrybody stop work... nae need for ony o' us lot now... here's the very man we've been waitin' for..."

"Good afternoon," boomed out the master of Blaeweltonrigg. The announcement greeted my arrival on the scene, and was instantly supplemented by an eager babble of practical suggestions.

"Leykes 'orses... gi' him a go wit owld Sandy," shouted one with an evil twinkle in his eye.

"Nae lad, just lake at them arms - strang enough tae draw t'bogie hisel', din't ye reckon."

"Spoil his nice soft 'ands though... not can mak 'is sermons wi'em or nowt... might git them grubby a bit an' all."

"What about 'is la'al yella motor yonther? Reckon that can fetch a few in gayly fast for us - come on minister, fetch 'er ower 'ere."

"I'm sure Mr. Teviot would be better suited to one of the tractors," protested the farmer's more genteel wife, "Onyweys, I din't think it's reyght at all, it's not proper nor nowt... shouldn't expect our highly respected minister tae—"

"But that's precisely what I've come here for today," I broke in opportunely, although not particularly willingly. "Actually got my old overalls with me in the car. Where do I start?"

"Gi' him a fork afore he changes 'is mind," commanded big farmer Smeaton, "Can help t'lasses rake up t'bits at bottom o' elevator." He wasn't aware that I had observed his corner of mouth aside to his son, "Git 'im that big yan out o' t'byre."

Johnny dutifully fetched, and duly presented me with the biggest hay fork I had ever beheld. It must surely have been as wide between the points as a highland bull's horns from tip to tip. The hot June day wore on, and the stack grew slowly higher. To my surprise, and to the visible astonishment of others, my energy never seemed to flag, even though, purely from motives of show-off, I loaded my great fork to full capacity every time, and in spite of the fact that Mrs. Smeaton would only lubricate me with pure water. Eventually I got round to removing my shirt, not merely because of over-heating, but chiefly to demonstrate that parsons usually have all the things with which other men are endowed, including well developed muscles, and hairy chests. There were many amusing incidents and unscheduled complications during the course of the day, but one in particular caused greater disarray than all the rest put together.

Leaning wearily against the stack during a temporary lull was the gorgeous, alluringly rounded Jennie Skelwell, fork in hand, and wearing one of those flowery, flouncy, form-flattering cotton frocks which are brought out on hot hay making days. Risque? In the present circumstances, I would say - just a little - perhaps - depending upon the way you look at things. The overhead view however presented a tantalizing temptation to the droll Wally Peterson who was standing high up on the stack immediately above Jennie. He was holding aloft by the tail a live harvest mouse. Wally's eyes stood out like chapel hat pegs, as they focussed on some mischievous design. With precise aim and perfect timing, he let go, and the hapless creature made a perfect plunge directly into Jennie's ample cleavage. Suddenly everything in the stack yard went completely haywire. Jennie wriggled and squealed and squirmed in near hysterics. Eventually she froze rigid in abject terror, as the creature began a slithering rampage about her equatorial regions. She frantically appealed to the ladies for help, but none was willing to run the personal risk of having to come into close quarters with the wee monster. At this point several swarthy swains with bared hairy forearms and meaty stretched out hands rushed forward and enthusiastically proffered their efficient assistance, but the prospect sent Jennie berserk.

"What about t'minister," called a course voice of sweet reason from up above, "He's proper gentleman and 'appen 'armless isn't he?"

"Aye!... aye!... cum on ministher, dae your stuff... git your 'and in," shouted another in quick succession.

"That's ower personal. Hod her up be th'ankles ministher, that's t'proper way... mouse'll drop out."

"Not if it's gittin' fast in her breeches or owt," gargled a very earthy specimen.

"'Appen hesn't ony on." chirruped another. Not savouring the drift of this conversation I then made the splendid suggestion that Jennie should perhaps retire into the house and attend to the emergency in private.

"O no! O no!" she screamed, "Can't touch it... might get out... run all ower t'place. It's started a-crawlin' up me back... sumbody... hurry. sharp... help me... dae summat sumbody... quick—"

Like a genie out of some Aladdin's lamp, a sinister figure materialised immediately behind the girl, swiftly ran a crooked hand around her midriff, and locating the invader through her dress, squelched it hard against her back with a long, slow slam. Jennie promptly swooned, and even more so when she turned and came face to face with her rescuer.

"Tap o' the maarnin' tew you aall now," said the genie. "Now tew be sure isn't it jiust loike old Pathric tew arroive at the roight toime."

"Just in time tae dae a bit o' work for tha livin' and earn theesel a crust ye idle owld bu—" came a unanimous response.

"Now tew be sure, that's not precoisely whaat Oi had in moind. Just passin' the toime o' day so tew spake. Moind yew, if Oi could have a drop o' sumting for this almighty thirst o' moine, Oi'll be able tew tink a bit more clear tew be sure."

Patrick was one of a choice breed of vagrants who used to roam the highways and byways of the valley, sleeping rough in hedgerows, or putting up in farm outbuildings. Nobody knew to where they hibernated in the winter. Occasionally they would perform some token task about the farm for a meagre levy of hard cash, but preferably for a small reward such as a simple meal, a packet of fags, or the use of a hayloft on a chilly night. The said Patrick was a disgusting specimen, over-clad in an assortment of ragged garments, and with face and head so overgrown in matted black hair that only his sharp, beady eyes and his nose-end were visible. On this occasion he hung around for the rest of the day, now and again performing futile work gestures. His main concern of course, was to be around at the time of the grand evening feast.

During my sojourn in the Lyndass Valley I witnessed many spectacular gastronomic feats, but never anything on so mighty a scale as this. Sandwiches like landmines, blockbuster pastries, and blocks of cake from which fortifications could have been constructed. Such wholesome fare was demolished by the hundredweight, and strong tea, served in large mugs, was consumed by the gallon. There was great merriment, and everyone was in good heart and voice and stomach. Harvest-time tales abounded, bringing forth frequent flurries of ribald laughter, especially those which it seemed necessary to relate in subdued voices with the climax passed down from ear to ear. From this I suspected that today's story of Jennie Sewell and the naughty mouse, with the addition of a few spicy variations, would loom large in local hay-time lore for many a year to come. To me the whole of the feast was uniquely impressive, as indeed was my own unprecedented gluttony. There was a feature however, which disturbed me greatly. In spite of the hearty goodwill that was overflowing in all directions, the hero of the day was not present at the festive table. Poor old Patrick, true to his humble station, sat on a bench at the far end of the farmyard, although generously provided with choice victuals, and surrounded by cadging chickens. But no dogs?

As the local sage, old Emerson Slack had once told me, 'hay-time—is hay-time, and when it's hay-time 'nowt else matters. They din't even bother tae git married, born, or dee for a few weeks until it's all ower, the thatchin's on th'top, and even then they talk about nowt else until th'time cums round tae git corn in.'

I quickly discerned that the best way to evade that 'in-the-way' feeling was to lend a practical helping hand here and there. That day of hard graft at Blaeweltonrigg proved this point beyond all doubt. And more, for as a result of this policy I gained useful experience in all things farming, from driving tractors, handling horses and other animals, and even to carrying out simple running repairs on dickey farm machinery. I also acquired an enhanced appetite. But above all was the rapport gained with the fellside folk.

Returning home one day some weeks later, I announced my arrival to Gina by calling out through the echoing portals of our too-large house, "Sorry to be a wee bit late for dinner darling... car's been playing up... gosh I'm famished. I say, something smells a bit strong... not got burnt with waiting I hope."

"Sorry... I mean sorry you're famished... because you see…"

"Now don't you worry dear, we all have our little accidents don't we."

"It's nothing like that I'm bothered about. Dinner's not got burnt anyway. You see... well... the truth of the matter is... there's no dinner for you... that is... you see."

"Alright then love, dinna fash yourself, even if it's back to the old jam pot. There'll be another day won't there. By the way, what happened... forget to switch on the oven or something?"

"No Don, nothing like that. You see, there was this old gentleman called - he's still in the kitchen actually - and he said he hadn't had a bite to eat for over a week. He looked ever so pathetic and... hungry... and... Well you see, dinner was just ready at the time, and well, I just gave him some of mine. He ate it all up in a flash, and said he was still desperately hungry. So I'm afraid I gave him some of yours too... and some... more. Well that's it you see. So I'm afraid that… for today perhaps…"

"Shure now that was a foin repast... the saints will shure shoine broightly on yeou young missus," a voice of earlier acquaintance burst forth from the vicinity of the kitchen. "Not havin' a woife of me own to spake of that is, sumtoimes me mails is not so reg'lar as Oi'd loike. Well now, if it's not the young Faather hisself. And whaat in faith brings yeou here moight Oi ask?"

"I live here Patrick. And feed here - sometimes."

"Now Oi'm shure plaised to hear that. Very hospitable Oi'd say."

"O Gina, this is Mr. O'Shawnighan - hangs out around these parts. Nice of you to call Patrick. Once helped me to build a haystack."

"Now Oi loike to kayp an oye on aall me friends, so Oi'll call on yeou often to be shure. Now before Oi get on me way... Oi seem to have mislaid me waallet. Do yeou think yeou could see your way clear to lendin' me a smaall sum loike a couple o' shillins to toide me over. Oi hate beggin' moind yeou, so this is only borrowin' see. Thanks now, and the saints assist yeou to be shure."

"Careful what you do with that Patrick. It's my petrol money for the whole of this week. I'll have to walk from now on."

"That Oi will Oi will. And I was wunderin' if this charmin' yung woman would loike to wrap up a few sandwiches for me supper... there's notting in the shops Oi fancies to be shure."

Well financed, victualed and satisfied, Patrick gathered his grubby clouts about him and took his protracted leave. We were not sure whether our outburst of laughter was as appropriate as it was spontaneous, but simultaneously we stopped, sniffed at the air, and dived for the Flit spray.

The act of dubious charity gave us a good feeling nevertheless, and so it might have continued save for one thing. Soon after that day we were plagued by a succession of vagrants and weird characters at our back door, every one of whom hadn't eaten for a week, had helped the father to build a haystack, wished to borrow a couple of shillings to tide him over, and would like a few sandwiches for his supper.

Chapter 23

THE COMEDY OF ERRORS

"Looking a wee bit gloomy today we are," observed Gina between two dainty sips of coffee during breakfast.

"Feeling rather gloomy actually - most likely digestive." I moaned pathetically, "Nothing else wrong that I can think of. Just this... some kind of premonition I think. I just know somehow... no reason or logic in it... but I just know somehow... there's going to be no fun and games anywhere today. It's that queer feeling I sometimes get... dark foreboding... like morning cloud on the hill-tops... can turn to anything before the day is out. Yes, one of those difficult days, I know it... I can feel it com—"

"More coffee dear? Extra sugar?"

In spite of my sombre forecast, the morning passed by as normal as any other, and four hours routine work in the study were without special incident. The afternoon was to be given over entirely to pastoral visitation, which on this day would be carried out within the confines of Lyndassby and consequently, on foot. The weather however matched my mood, being dull, dismal, and sultry.

My first call was on Gavin Osterly. I confess that this was from the call of duty rather than out of special preference. Gavin was either a very old sixty or a youngish ninety, and he lived alone. 'Alweys been a scraggy owld sod,' summed up the local estimation of him, and beyond that nothing else was certain. One thing was beyond all doubt however, and universally attested; Gavin was the world's most pessimistic pessimist. He had a photographic memory of astonishing range, but which only reproduced negative images, and those were usually out of focus. Scandals reaching back into the distant past, exploits which had come to no good, characters who had deservedly come to a sticky end, vain hopes, lost causes, unresolved mysteries, unpaid debts, unrequited loves, tales of deceit, disgust, and dishonour. And so the list could be continued, for this was the morbid stock-in-trade of this master of misery. Being more of a born optimist than he was, I would try and counter with some morsel of good cheer, but all in vain, for Gavin's eyes were so accustomed to peering backwards into the darkness, that he dared not turn to face up to the light of the present or the brightness of future hope.

"What a glorious start to the afternoon," I soliloquized as he ushered me into his den.

"O aye, good on ye tae call... nice tae hear your crack... cheer yan another up a gay lot 'appen. O aye... aye... aye. O aye, now there was summat else I was wantin' tae tell tha, and it's geyen clean out o' my hey-ad ye knaw, clean forgat. Now what it?"

"Perhaps it'll come back another day - next time maybe," I gabbled whilst moving with some urgency towards the door.

"O aye - aye - airrgh - aye - yes - it's just this minute cummed back intae me hey-ad. Aye, I'll tell tha what it is now aye. Neighbour o' mine - cummed tae live here a year or two back. Used tae be a scheyelmeyster or summat leyke in Southern parts sumwhere. Reads an awful lot o' beyeks an' whatnot - Aye. Gayly bad he is - aye. Not gawn' tae be wi' us for much langer is what I reckon. Telt us when I was in seein' him yestherdey as he'd leyke tae hev sum parson fella or other tae call on him yan day. Nivver said what for nor nowt. He's mebees writin' out his will or summat and wants tae mek summat out for t'Chapel... nivver knaws dost tha? Or mebees it's just sum queer fancy that's gittin intae him - aye. Nivver been yan for gawin' tae church or chapel nor nowt leyke, but well... when tha's startin' tae get near th'end, that 'appen din't matter ower much... if tha knaws what I mean. Well, as I telt tha, he wants tae see a parson, and I reckons tha'll be as good as ony."

I duly called upon Mr. Thornton, a very sick man who, as his loyal neighbour had suspected, was obviously sinking. I tendered the customary introduction, all the conventional absurdities concerning the weather, a perfunctory enquiry regarding the poor man's present state of health, which I trusted was improving, and a thoroughly tactless lie about his looking well. At precisely the moment I considered to be appropriate I enquired,

"You wished to see me I believe?"

"Ah yes. Now the reason I requested a parson visit was... well... I really don't know. You see, I've never felt either the desire nor the necessity for doing that sort of thing before... but... well... O for God's sake Minister, come on and stop stalling. Let's get on with whatever... come on get on with it and do your professional stuff and all that, and let's get it over and done with it man."

The unexpected request, painful and slow, yet rendered in the manner of a command, threw me into immediate confusion. There followed one tragic impasse after another as I found it well nigh impossible to establish any measure of rapport with Mr. Thornton. His general concepts were so materialistic and unspiritual that I was unable to manoeuvre myself towards any form of working communication with him. All my classical theological clichés fell upon stony ground, and my 'comfortable words' felt puerile, slipping lifelessly past my lips like so much hollow church jargon. My scriptural references, whenever I chanced to proffer them, invariably fell wide of the mark, for ambiguous logic is no less baffling because it is biblical. I was indeed confronted with the sobering realization that the church's common vocabulary, and its basic assumptions are meaningless outside the context of faith, and must often appear pathetic and ridiculous when separated from the accepted formularies of official religion. I suppose that I could have, or ought to have, pointed the poor man to that brighter beyond; except that according to my book he did not specifically qualify, nor did he conspicuously share in the Christian hope. I was therefore forced to fall back on the old parsonic defence, "We'll have a little prayer, shall we?" But the attempt at prayer was likewise sterile, as it always is when praying is contrived. The man, his face pallid and drawn, continued to stare blankly into the area of empty space which was occupied by my equally empty features, and the entire encounter began to take on an atmosphere of mocking irrelevance. Unlike certain other denominations of the church, mine made no provision either in doctrine or practice for the imposition of mechanical grace. Neither did it, as they, equip its clergy with set formulae by which to stage manage situations such as this, nor any dramatised symbolism or oracular rites and rituals with which to fill in the spiritual vacuum.

"Goodbye," said Mr. Thornton, softly and courteously, as I left him. Perhaps to slip away alone towards an empty eternity?

As I strolled woefully away from the house I began to realize that the pathetic farewell had irrevocably shattered something vital inside of me. Its echo grew more persistent and shrill as I proceeded up the road until it seemed to call out from the hollow depths of a lost eternity. It was as though it contained disastrous implications both for that poor unchurched stranger and this poor over-churched me. I was gradually overtaken by a searing torment of shame, remorse and sense of inadequacy. I sat me down on a low wall by the roadside and wrangled with my rebellious thoughts, hoping that sound logic and cool reason would hasten to my aid. Surely, I thought, the application of divine grace is not conditional upon some parson being up to his job, and a soul does not have to be lost to all eternity because some incompetent cleric has missed out on the contingency of a moment in time. Are spoken words the only vehicle through which the mercy of Almighty God can be effectively conveyed? Can the salvation of the soul be only appropriated by means of clerical esoterics or the hallowed mechanics of mediaeval church ceremonial and its latter day counterparts? Good Lord, with what celestial magic the rite of Ordination has endowed us! *Salus extra cathedra non est* - what monstrous presumption is this? Saviour of the world deliver us Thornton and me. For 'What but Thy grace can foil the Tempter's power.'

With heavy heart and unwilling feet, I trudged to my next call. According to my prepared pastoral list, this would be a family who had very recently moved into the village and my simple duty was to bid them welcome.

"Good afternoon. My name's Teviot. I'm from the Chur—"

"Ah yes I see... Oh... well... look will you hold on just a minute and I'll see wh—" and the lady, a large specimen with a bold thoracic frontage, turned about and scurried back into the house, leaving me to hold on to the open door. Returning after a few minutes and wagging her head she continued, apologetically, "O... er... look Mr... What's-the- name... Cheviots did you say... I'm very sorry but I don't seem to have any small change at the moment. Another time perhaps eh... tomorrow perhaps. I'm sorry, 'cos I always like to do me bit for the church you know."

"Good lady, I'm not wanting your money. As a matter of fa—-"

"But you ARE from the church aren't you?"

"Madam, the church has better things to do than go round the houses begging. It's not your money I'm interested in. You have something far better than that to offer I am sure. Now if you'd just like to invite me inside for a wee while I'll explain"

"Invite you what? One of them eh? I've heard all about your type. Now look here mister, too many o' your sort around the place, bloody creeps. Back door an' all... think nobody'll see you eh? Now just hoppit before me brother..." The crescendo built up until her eyes flashed wildly and her lips quivered speechlessly.

"What's like the trouble then?" A large comfortable-looking fellow appeared in the doorway from out of the shadows.

"Ah Mister? Mister... ?" I croaked.

"Nettlesworth, Bill Nettlesworth, just moved in yesterday. Sister Jean...you've met her I believe. Well-meaning girl, but bit of a man hater, gets all worked up for nowt, touchy you know, but really harmless and good-natured," said the man with considerable calmness. "I see you're parson. Don't usually go round upsetting folks you fellas do you, especially the women. Now what d'you reckon's set her off?"

"Seems like a bit of a misunderstanding Mr. Nettlesworth. Your dear sister seems to hold the all-too-common notion that the church always comes cap in hand and that it's habitually only interested in your spare cash. I was merely trying to explain, rather badly it seems, that the opposite is true. You are new here, and I simply came to give myself the privilege of being the first to bid you welcome, that's all. I want nothing from you, except your friendship in exchange for mine. And by the way, also to tell you that if ever you need us for anything, there are two churches in this village who have much to give, indeed much that money cannot buy. That's all I came for."

"O yes...well... alright...thanks and all that. Maybe better luck next time eh?" said Bill, as a very red-faced brother and sister sank back into the house and slowly closed the door.

Close at hand lived Joe Meridon, a school teacher who was one of my younger church officials. I was so sickened by my afternoon calls so far that I was sorely in need of some good cheer. Joe and his charming wife Susan were just the pair to deliver it. To reach the front door of the house I had to pass across the large window. A casual glance as I did so showed Susan in a deep snooze, stretched full length on the settee, with trailing hand and open book down to the floor. Realizing that Joe was due home at any minute, and would expect his tea to be ready, I treated the door to a mighty knock. The instant response was the sound of much scuffling and calls of "Coming Joe...coming." Susan flung open wide the door, and in the same instant her flared skirt, the waist band of which she had unhitched for comfort before her relaxed read, draped itself neatly about her ankles. Susan froze but for a brief second, but long enough to let me come to the rescue with a life-saving pun,

"Nice slip!"

Susan shot behind the half-closed door, struggling to re-instate her decorum, reputation, and propriety of dress.

"Alright, I'm terribly sorry, but you shouldn't gi' foalkes shocks leyke that ye knaw. I knaw it was me own fault, but ye could've turned away. Didn't leyke t'wise crack neither, bit ower intimate fra one such as you. Suppose tha'd better cum in onyroad, and wait for Joe if it's him tha's wantin' tae see. Should be in ony minute."

"Tomorrow perhaps. Just thought... have an urgent call to make further up the road...bye for now." I called from the gate towards which I had beaten a panic retreat. But turning swiftly I collided with Joe, pausing only long enough to say "Whatever Susan tells you, it's not true. Do you hear?"

Another failure, and this time even my emergency wit had not paid off. I paused for brief reflection at the corner, and decided that in the circumstances it would be better for me to quit my present duty, and make for the safety and security of home. On the other hand, if I was a man at all, I could take out my notebook and scan the lists, perhaps for an easy option. Which is precisely what I was doing when old Vicar Teal, the interim replacement for the late and venerable Father Rhos had chanced to be passing by on the other side. When he crossed over and joined me, I sadly poured out to him my recent woes, and beseeched his solace.

"First call I was impatient, second totally ineffectual, third one brash, and fourth, well, it just had to happen to me. The whole afternoon a downward spiral of crass incompetence. And what do we offer? Some have made a fetish of the cross, others an unintelligible set of formulae out of liturgy, and others of us a simplistic farce out of the doctrine of free grace."

"Young man," the vicar began kindly, "beware the moment you feel equal to your godly vocation, or more precisely, to quote that is, 'Alas for you when all speak well of you' - Luke six, twenty-six. Or when you feel all wise and faith ceases to be an unfathomable mystery to you. In that moment - resign. Because, it indicates that you've not only chosen to put your trust in man alone, particularly the man who inhabits your body, but that you've ceased to be sufficiently humble to let God be the judge of your every endeavour. Not precluding patience at every stage, for there are skills to perfect."

"Theoretically very sound and wise, Vicar. But in practice..."

"Ours is but a pilgrimage young man, and a steep uphill road at that. No man living can bear on his mind and within his soul the pains and sorrows of others and remain himself unscathed. Every time you address yourself to the aspirations, needs, and failures of your people, you will become more acutely aware of your own, and another little bit of you is spent. If this is not so, then you have set yourself above them and beyond them, which is sin. The true discipline of the loyal and faithful servant of God is to be in constant encounter with questionings for which only Eternity will provide the answer.

"But surely we may share their joys and successes also?"

"He who shares their sorrows will partake equally of their happiness, and he who joins them in their happiness will be entrusted with their woes. Remember, it is YOUR faith which will continue to inspire them, and YOUR sanctity which will lead them towards aspiring onto higher things. Beware of accidie. You may not yet have developed immunity from this scourge of our calling."

"The Sermon on The Street Corner! Strikes me that even in our weakness and in the face of God's generous mercy, ours is at all times a pretty awesome charge. And thanks for those inspired words old friend. They'll not be wasted on me, I can assure you. So, back to the grind in fresh heart. Let me see, where next?"

"You seem to be in some doubt - perhaps looking for an easy one? Now I wonder therefore if you would be so kind as to assist me? I'm having a rather tiring day myself, and the old legs are beginning to flag somewhat. Perhaps you would care to relieve me of my next call? Task for a younger man than me anyway."

"Your instructions good brother, I'm all set."

"Please go down and call on the unfortunate young couple who live at Rose Cottage. It's about three-quarters of a mile down the Pikerigg Lane there. Slackston's the name I think. Cot death - such a tragic circumstance - need our ministrations to be sure. She was confirmed as a child, according to my register. Seen little since. Married at Registry Office last year. Husband, hardworking - unsophisticated."

Nellie Slackston stood softly weeping, as she gazed blankly upon the sweet face of the sleeping child who had not wakened up. The only word she could utter without choking was a repetitive "Why? Why? Why?" Some friends and neighbours with good pious intentions had too readily answered her agonised question with old wives tales, pathetic anodyne, and sentimental slosh about it 'all being for the best - who knows?' Others had spoken without caution about the will of God, who loves us and knows what is best for his children, Jesus needing some little angels to augment His choir up there, and all such pseudo-religious codswallop. Spiritual placebos, in whatever form they are administered, and by whomsoever, are dangerous medicine. It was no wonder that that poor girl was beside herself with blinding grief compounded by crazy confusion.

"Why?" she whispered again, looking straight at me, "You should surely know why"

My heart was just about to break, but I was spared both that trauma and the pain of having to provide an instant or provisional answer by the sudden appearance of the young husband, a physically awkward and slightly uncouth fellow who was showing no outward signs of grief or of loss, nor did he demonstrably exude any excess of loving tenderness toward his young wife.

“Plenty mare where that yan came frae, that’s what I keyep on tellin’ her,” he blurted, and departed from the scene as abruptly as he had entered it. The stricken mother fixed her sorrowing eyes upon me again, and her lips made the shape of the only word left to her, “Why?”

“Well why?” I secretly asked myself over and over, and the only semblance of an answer came in the form of a chain reaction of torturing inexplicables. Deep frustration threatened to burn the soul out of me as I searched, even for one, single, effectual word of comfort and reason. The girl apparently perceived that I shared her dilemma, and that for me was some small consolation. The moment was delivered to the hand of fate by a sharp rap on the front door. I let in a nervous young doctor whom I presumed to be a first year assistant to our local general practitioner. His clumsiness in handling the situation which confronted him revealed that he was no more practised in the art of professional detachment than I was.

“O hello there Mrs... er... Sl... Eleanor isn’t it. Just called in passing, got the Certificate for you, already signed... I think... O yes...all complete I see. O and while I’m here, I may as well drop these for you - some tablets. One every two hours should be alright, settle you down a bit, and maybe help you sleep a bit. Ah well, I think that’s about everything for now - ‘bye now - and Vicar.” Swiftly, like a genie which had evaporated in the middle of a spell, he was gone. And I would readily admit, he had my complete understanding and sympathy.

Those drenched eyes again, looking directly into mine, and the lips quivering as they moved into the now familiar shape. I did not have to think out my next move, for some overpowering compunction simply caused it to happen. I moved across the room towards her and placed a strong sympathetic arm around her shoulders. She buried her head upon my shoulder, and for a timeless moment we kept profound and healing silence. When I walked slowly away from that house I did so with my emotions in dreadful turmoil, the aftermath of sorry failure clinging onto the inside of my mouth like an evil taste which would not wash out. Should I turn back, face the issue head on, and make some kind of amends for my tragic omissions? But whatever I had possessed of self - confidence was by now completely shattered, and my very faith was caught up in a whizzing whirlpool of confusion. On the more practical level, that visit had also upset my time-table, it was past tea time, and Gina would be waiting - sufficient justification there for me to press on. Given my state of mind and spirit however, the three quarters of a mile walk back to Lyndassby was fearful to contemplate, for the journey would occupy my troubled thoughts as well as my hesitant feet for at least another twenty minutes. There was a short cut of course, over the fields along the bottom boundary of Johnny Beccle’s spread. This would be a kind of trespassing, but only a small trespass, a locally acceptable trespass so long as one wasn’t spotted. In any case, the risk was well outweighed by the urgency of the cause. Besides, for the most part of the way there would be little likelihood of my meeting anybody at this late hour of the afternoon. The dry-stone wall gave me adequate cover from the road, and the footpath quickly descended into a dip where it was completely obscured from the distant farmhouse. Time was of the essence, and so I elected not to trudge to the gate near the copse at the bottom of the large field, but to make use of one of those points in the wall where recent collapses had lowered the height. My leap was executed with all the agility of a sprightly young buck, but unfortunately not the foresight. Once airborne I had no way of evading the twisted end of thick wire which was protruding upwards from out of an unruly pile of discarded fencing posts on the other side. The cruel barb took a firm hold on my trouser leg just below the level of the knee and ripped the fabric wide open up to the line of the belt. Mercifully, or miraculously, my tender hide was spared. But it felt cold, and so frightfully immodest. A sudden flash of panic, guilt, and shame sent me scurrying, head down, along the wall in the direction of a nearby field barn. Entering cautiously, I only part closed the battered old door behind me, for otherwise it would be rather dull inside, the only other source of light being a narrow slit in each of the walls. The old place was dry, dusty, and the ancient rafters were draped eerily in obsolete cobwebs. But it was secluded. The floor was cobbled, but for the most part it was cluttered with derelict agricultural machinery, and there was a neat pile of hay at one end. I sat me down on the studded iron wheel of a clapped-out binder and laughed myself into near hysterics. I ceased with a painful jolt however on suddenly realising how preposterous was my predicament. Even taking the short cut into account, there still remained a portion of my route which would take me out onto the road and along the main street. Gosh! If seen in this condition I could be charged with indecent exposure. I could think of only one solution to the problem, and that was to hide out in this place until the onset of darkness. A dashing flight of martins, taking their evening constitutional, made frequent sorties into the barn to tease me with twittering laughter, and a restless huddle of young beasts stomped and shuffled outside, occasionally lowing mockingly in my direction. I attempted to occupy my mind in a bid to rationalise the experiences of the day, excluding my present situation of course, but concentration was difficult with a disgusting area of pink raw thigh peering up at me. Remarkably, it was some time before I thought on making some effort to close the gaping rift. If I could find a morsel of thin wire somewhere about the place, I could perhaps draw the edges together. Maybe there would be a length of the ubiquitous binder twine amongst the junk which littered the floor. Eagerly I moved forward to open the decrepit old door in order to let in some extra light when, to my utter horror, through a crooked gap between two of its boards, I caught a glimpse of Johnny Beckle, approaching rapidly. A battered old meal chest in a far corner offered my only chance of concealment, and so with a painful vault, I landed myself tightly packed behind it. I heard Johnny move the big door slowly, his heavy hobnailed boots as he trod over the cobbled floor, and the prolonged swish as he strewed the heap of hay. I simply presumed that he was preparing their evening snack before shutting up those young bullocks for the night, and would therefore soon depart. Not so; for sitting down upon that very iron wheel which I had so recently vacated, he lit a cigarette which, judging by the time it took him to smoke it, I estimated must have been at least a foot long. Considering how ridiculous was my plight and becoming more desperately aware of my excruciating discomfort, I resolved to make a break, come out from hiding, and confront the man. So far as I knew, Johnny was a reasonable and innocuous fellow anyway. His long hard day was no doubt as greatly in need of some comic relief as mine had been. Johnny would surely be so highly amused that he would overlook the trespassing part - after all, as aforesaid, it was but a small trespass, and in a worthy cause at that. But my splendid intentions were rudely forestalled, and just in the very nick of time. There came the sound of light footsteps, running on the soft grass and coming to a halt on the cobbles of the barn floor. The old door slowly creaked to a close, and some heavy object was drawn up against it.

"Tha's a bit late gittin' down t'neyght ist tha not," Johnny said condescendingly.

"Aye, la'al bit. See'd stock in t'field bottom and knawd tha wouldn'd be down here yet. So stopped a bit langer and offered tae help Missus git all t'chickens in. She bides in that place a gay lang time - still there when I cummed away." The voice was unmistakably that of young Netta Peters, a simple bit lass, but physically every inch of sixteen, and who worked as a daily help at the Beckle farm.

"Mak it a bit late, and seyen be dark," chided Johnny sportingly.

"S'alreyght - browt me torch - neyghts cuttin' in a bit. Me muther says your missus is gaw'n tae hev tae let me finish a bit sharper. Should be payin' me ower-time or summat she says, 'cos extra time means extra work," and the girl dissolved into silly giggles.

Good Lord, had I accidentally stumbled upon a clandestine rendezvous? Was I about to be forced into a nightmare of involuntary voyeurism? I instantly developed some difficulty in breathing noiselessly, and my mouth dried up so that my swallowing was making clicking noises. I nevertheless felt some security in my cramped hide-out, for I could not be seen, not unless either of the pair should chance to look over the top of the meal bin, which was unlikely, for the sound of rustling hay indicated that they were prone, and thoroughly pre-occupied with other matters. Neither could I see them, which was a mercy, for I had no strong desire to be an eyewitness to this disgusting debauchery. Nor did I wish to acquire yet another item for that store of sights which I wished I had never encountered. This was all very virtuous of me, except for one serious snag. My mind inadvertently got to work on some unseemly imaginings and lewd interpretations of current sounds, which were hard to fight back. And worse, for this led me to speculate as to whether, by virtue of my holy calling, I had a moral duty towards these two lost sheep and foolish sinners. Yet on the other hand, I had to concede, in truth I had no divine right to intervene, nor even so much as to remonstrate with them.

"Hod your feyace still lass, I'm tryin' tae kiss it," said Johnny in a coarse farmyard voice.

Apart from such crude romantic outbursts, the conversation was for the most part garbled, Johnny's contribution being rendered in husky mutterings, and the girl's vocabulary being limited to gurgles, shrieks and high-pitched giggles. The few snippets which were more legible were certainly not poetry, and by any standard of decency were thoroughly offensive to the ear. I wished that I could go deaf, fall asleep, or pass out, or that a large hole would appear in the wall behind me. I began to feel some sore distress at having to be party to such disgusting intimacies, and more especially as I was at the same time wrestling with my sense of pastoral duty mingled with a feeling of social concern. I found myself agonising in logic as twisted and contorted as my enforced unnatural posture between the meal bin and the jagged stone wall. I reached a point where I almost decided to throw my pride to the wind, spring out on them, break up their little party, reprove them, and swear to them an oath of silence in return for their undertaking to 'go and sin no more'. Johnny may well and truly deserve the consequences of his misdemeanours. But I had to do something for the sake of his wife and children, for if this was allowed to go unchecked, how they would suffer. And of course there was this silly young girl, innocent victim of his wily seduction. But surely such action of mine would entail unthinkable risks, for all concerned. It would surely be a far far better thing for my part, to suffer in silence. Mine was to dispense the love of God, and not to administer His judgements. And yet, this could indeed be a cowardly, though beautifully pious, evasion of my calling? And so the debate continued within my mind, which by this stage was totally blitzed, baffled, and bewildered.

"Gittin' layete a bit," the girl mumbled. "Hens took a lot langer tae git in, didn't they. Me muther'll play war again - tea's gittin' cowld."

"Aye, t'same wi' meesel'...took a lot langer gittin' t'stock penned up or summat. Wife 'appen finished hens lang syne. Be waitin' s'pose."

What happened next was so swift that any reason behind it is beyond my comprehension. All the wise restraint which I had built up during the past half-hour simply vanished, without forewarning, into thin air. As though propelled by some irresistible impulse, I shot out from my hiding place and stood before the guilty pair. In an even swifter move, young Netta gathered herself together, fled through the door and dissolved into the encroaching twilight.

"Bloody hell– what the– where the– who the– what the hell are ye deyin' in here meyght I ask? Bloody tootin' that's what. What soort o' sod's put tha up tae this then eh? I'll bloody we—"

"You'll bloody what Mr. Beckle? Now before we go any farther, calm yourself down man, because I think you may be in real trouble. O and above all, cut out the threats, because despite their noisy vehemence, I assure you I don't find them very frightening. Alright? O and also, by the way, I don't know what your immediate plans for dealing with me are, but perhaps I should remind you that I am still able to make it a bit difficult for you, and in more ways than one. So steady man."

"Blo— hey it's t'minister isn't it. Well I be blawed. I meyght ha' knawn, all that fancy talk an' stuff. Well now we do git sum big supprizes sumteymes din't we - gay bigguns."

"Or shocks Mr. Beckle?"

"Tha's t'one what's gittin' t'shock. Ye see, tha's not only not mindin' tha own business, but tha's trespassin' into t'bargain. Tha shouldn't be in here, or on my land at all for that matter. Now I'm tellin' tha just yance, git movin' afor—"

"Threatening again Mr. Beckles, now please don't scare me. And as for the trespassing bit, well now, that puts you and I pretty much in the same boat doesn't it." I peeled rather gratuitously, at the same time stepping right out into the open. The sudden appearance of my naked pink thigh protruding from my riven trousers set Johnny into a bout of loud earthy laughter, right up from his disgusting beer belly.

"Nivver see'd owt sae daft afore... nivver... nivver..."

"Alright, you may have your little laugh Mr. Beckle, I admit that in this case it does look a bit funny. But surely the sight of a length of bare thigh is not entirely untoward in the present circumstances." Whether it was the shock of this crude observation, or my demonstrable putting up of a bold front and exuding my sense of physical invulnerability, qualities with which my war time training and career had embued me, but something seemed to cause the man to sober up somewhat.

"Well there's lots of things we hes tae turn a blind eye tae isn't there Mr. What'sit... ivvrybody's entitled tae his bit o' fun sumtimes. It's his own business... naebody else's."

"But not at the expense of somebody's young daughter. Under age you know. Of course you know - you employ her. And as for minding one's own business, isn't protection of the young and innocent a public duty - everybody's business?"

"Nivver deyne t'lass ony proper harm oneyweys, I knaws when tae gi' ower and all that soort of stuff."

"Only a matter of time Mr. Beckle, you're not infallible. Besides, that's not the point, there are other serious implications you know."

"Din't cum that high-falutin' stuff mate, and git back tae t'proper business, tha's trespassin' and I wants tha off - sharp - wi'out ony more argument. I'll tell tha yance more - tha's trespassing"

"So what? You must know that the Good Book tells us that whenever we want to think of other people's trespasses we should first take a good look at our own. Sort of keeps a fair sense of balance you know. Yes Mr. Beckle, I do mean yours, by God I do. In any case my little trespass along the edge of your field has done nobody any harm, except you man, and that's what's eating you - the possible consequences. O yes of course, and it's cost me one of my only two pairs of trousers, and the embarrassment of having to sit through your rotten escapade, neither very pleasant experiences I assure you. I've got to face my wife with my breeches. I wonder what you might have to face yours with?"

A foreboding sneer came across Beckle's face, and his mouth twisted.

"O aye, Good book, now that's a lark for tha. Oneyweys them's your rules not mine. And we'll not be needin' ony o' your preachin' thenks, cos it's not Suntha onyweys. Mind you, I could alweys tell ivvrybody what ye did wi' your breeches, couldn't I"

"And I could tell everybody what you did with yours," I retorted.

"Why ye cheeky bas—. Nivver mind... neybody'd believe tha in ony case... supposed tae be sweet innocence an' all that muck isn't tha... hear all, see all, say nowt, an' if ivver tha daes owt for nowt..."

"No, I wouldn't dae owt leyke that, to be sure. Besides the way you live your life is no business of mine, except that is, at those points where it impinges adversely upon the lives of others. And it's very much the business of those who love you or trust in you - like your wife and children, and that poor girl yonder - their whole future, and for that matter, yours. Now Beckle my man, if that's what you are and not a beast, whether you want preaching or not, you're getting it, and some good common sense, because God knows, you need it."

"Christ Almighty man, tha's gittin' tae preachin' sermons again, 'tsall ye blokes are ony use at - tellin' other foalkes what they're 'sposed tae dae and not dae. Ye kens, I think's tha's enjoyin' this."

"I was going to say 'Let's keep Christ out of this' Mr. Beckle, except I've suddenly remembered that whether we like it or not, He's very much in it. But at any rate, we'll be a little more careful in the use of that name shall we. If not reverence, then a little respect eh?"

"Respect leyke hell. Din't believe in things leyke that onyweys, nor that bloke neither, all superstition... your property not mine."

"Whether you believe in Him or not is not the question at issue Mr. Beckles. The thing that matters at the moment is whether this Christ bloke has any good reason to believe in you."

"What'll happen if ony o' this lot does git out ye reckon?"

Maybe it was pure wishful thinking on my part, but I fancied that Beckles had calmed down a little.

"I dread to think of it man. You may have your little laugh over a jar with your mates up at the Stowp of course, about my ripping my trousers and hiding in your barn, but there'll be the risk of blowing the lid off the other bit won't there? But let me assure you, for my part, not a word will get beyond this door. There is one very serious consideration mind you. If young Netta Peters blethers - not got much natural cunning has she. Bit silly and unpredictable at that age aren't they, especially when they become scared, or get to feeling guilty, or some fool gives them too much to drink. Loosened tongue - dangerous. Mind you on the other hand, I think the fright she got a few minutes ago should keep her out of further mischief for a wee while."

"So tha's given me tha word then - tha'll say nae mare about what tha seed tae onybody."

"Conditionally, yes. O I say Mr. Beckle, do get your fences put into better repair will you - all of them."

"Aye better be gittin' away up t'field... t'wife'll hev tea ready lang seyne... be wundrin' where I've gitten tae. All settled then and done wi'. I'm trustin' in tha tae keep this lot under tha hat."

"And I'm going to trust you, no bragging in drink, and above all, stop meddling with that kid - or else. But afore ye go, what about this mess I'm in - the trousers I mean. Should really charge them up to you - had I not been in theory, trespassing. I ripped them on some wire jumping one of your walls, just innocently taking a short cut. Risky business springing forbidden boundaries isn't it Mr. Beckle?"

"Just hod 'em tegither till tha gits hoame. Bet tha can tell that wife of yours a likely story when tha has tae, eh. Keep hands in t'pockets."

"Time to settle for a spot of sweet reason Mr. Beckle, if you're capable of such. Have you got a couple of safety pins, or a piece of fine wire or summat leyke?"

"Nowt at all - just hod two hailfs tegither leyke I say - pockets."

"I noticed you were wearing an old raincoat when you came in. That was strange, I thought, on a dry clammy evening like this."

"Was I? O aye, mebees I was - aye. Of coourse, why man here it is... musta fallen on t'floor or summat... nigh forgat about it. I'll just slip it on again tae gaw up t'field... meyght be startin' tae put in cawld a bit. T'wife see-ed I had it on when I cummed away fra th'ouse, 'cos she asked me if I was expectin' rain or summat, and I had a bit laugh tae meesel'. Onyweys tha wouldn't want tae put it on... got a few things in t'pocket I carries round... soort o' private an' personal leyke."

Stooping into that old meal bin of recent ill fame, Johnny fished out a large sack, "Here, see what tha can mak out wi' yan o' these, he blurted rudely, tossing the tatty thing to me, and then sweeping himself swiftly outside, giving the arthritic old door a mighty slam shut behind him. Easing the door back a fraction and peering through the gap, I observed him swaggering away, and could hear him kecking smugly. I held him steady in my sights until he had dissolved into the thin blue haze of the deepening twilight. God forgive me, but for one loathsome moment, how I hated that animal's guts. Poor fool, he didn't yet realise that, in spite of his assumed self-assurance, his fate lay in the unsteady hands of that simple wench, who in any subsequent contingency would be bound to place her own interests first. Not very safe custody. For Beckles the consequences of this little episode may be far from over and done with. Now I busied myself with some frantic experimentation with that smelly sack, in turn trying it as apron, coat, kilt, cassock, but to no avail. In a hot surge of inspiration the idea struck me that if I stuffed the thing, I could carry it before me, thus concealing the mighty rip. Satisfied with my plan, I perched me down on that iron wheel of earlier acquaintance, and waited for the dusk to thicken sufficiently to cut down the risks in my making the unavoidable public appearance. During this recess I fell into pondering with some modicum of objectivity over the events of the past hour, and was much troubled thereby. Had I reacted with appropriate wisdom and grace, or merely taken illicit pleasure in getting the better of an obnoxious man in argument? Had I displayed elements of arrogant pride? Whose interests had I endeavoured to safeguard anyway? That somewhat inadequate girl? Those of the unsuspecting Mollie Beckles and her four children? Or, and the very thought be damned ere it forms, the unsavoury interests of that wretched man himself? Or even worse, those of that other wretched man - myself?

Eventually I dismissed my painful scruples and ventured forth from the barn, concentrating all my resources upon the effort of not being seen, and carrying the dusty sackful of hay in front of me, as though it was a fragile burden. Struggling along thus, I had the immense misfortune of being overtaken by the kindly Mike

Brotherwell, who insisted upon trying to relieve me of my burden, stating emphatically that I 'shouldna be carryin' that filthy owld bag next agin your nice clean clethes aye.' After a polite tussle of words and gestures I succeeded in getting out of that one by inventing an urgent appointment to deliver the sack by the back door of a house conveniently situated by the roadside. And from there I did not creep out until satisfied that the man had gone. The remainder of the journey was without any further trouble, except for the growing anxiety of having yet to face Gina.

The dear girl greeted me warmly as I entered the house. "Have a nice interesting afternoon darling? Delayed a bit I see, and tea's been waiting ages. What have you got there... not another hare I hope... or rabbit perhaps? Looks more the size of a whole sheep if you ask me. What's in the sack Don...nice surprise for me eh? Dare I take just a little peep? Please."

"Just some hay darling... keep legs warm... local device...git's a bit chilly towards evening this time of year you know. No leave it alone... only hay I've told you... don't tou—"

"GGGGGGooooooddddddfd Grrrrrrrrrrrrieffffff... DDDDDDon... O...no not again. That's the second pair of trousers you've ruined in months... beyond repair this time. Soon be left with nothing to wear but your kilt...not very good for these chilly evenings."

"All in the eager pursuit of pastoral visitation dearest, a trifle too vigorous maybe, but some of these visits turn out a bit rough you know."

Once we had settled down, I related to Gina the story of the fatal short-cut, the wire, the hide out in the barn, and, omitting names and unsavoury details whilst spicing it with as much humour as I could muster, the horrible sequel. Gina laughed and laughed, "I say what a magnificent leg - Whoopee!"

The humorous interlude soon evaporated however, and looking me straight in the eye Gina said, "Not been all fun today, has it dear?

"Just like any other I suppose, it's had its moments."

"What kind of moments? Your joking just now came over pretty hollow; hollow Don. You can't kid me you know. Something troubling you isn't there? Come on dear, get it off your chest. It's obviously hurting."

"No, nothing really...only myself...not up to things today that's all... just temporary thing. Come on, let's have tea, I'm fair famished."

Gina listened lovingly and patiently as I poured out my load of anxious care. "By now dear you must surely be well acquainted with my astonishing adroitness in the fine art of blunder, and the conflicts and crises my errors and hasty judgements lead me into. All the frustration and self-disgust, disappointment and disillusionment which I constantly bring down upon myself, you know all about that don't you'? Worst of it is that I just cannot help it. It's the raw - me."

"Fings just ain't turned aht the wye you expected 'ave thie Donny boy. More tea."

"And this afternoon everything just seems to have come to a head. I feel condemned, and mocked. Take for instance that poor old fellow Thornton, dying you know, and without a hope in this world or the next, and certainly none from me. I just couldn't rake up a morsel of anything relevant to say, couldn't get onto his wavelength or speak his language. Just stood there dumb and embarrassed I did. I did so want to spend myself in this, but I found I had nothing to spend."

"You're exaggerating a little darling - you tend to do that when things don't seem to be going as you expect. It's just one of those days when things look blacker than they really are. Who knows, but your so-called display of weakness perhaps did more for that man in his weakness than if you had been bold, brassy, and cock-sure. You got on a par as it were, and he no longer felt a stranger in distress."

"And what about Susan then? I made a right mess of that lot I did, didn't I? Tried to be sharp, witty, and the darned thing back- fired on me. She and Joe are always such good sports and game for a laugh. But not today thank you. Got me all wrong she did. She's rattled."

"She hadn't properly wakened up dear - you know what I'm like at that stage. She was still confused from the shock of your sudden knock."

"Rather by her skirt about her ankles you mean, and of course my clever quip. Didn't realise Susan was so sensitive."

"Of course she isn't. And not unreasonable neither. Just you wait until you see her next time, you'll find everything OK. I bet she and Joe have been laughing themselves silly over the thing."

"Alright, I suppose so. But that poor lass who's just lost her baby's not having a good laugh to put things right, is she? Gina darling I just can't get her off my mind. I stood there like a stuffed dummy and a bible in my pocket at that. The very Word of life they say. Well it wasn't burning a hole in the lining, nor screaming to get out."

"Don, dear Don, I love you dearly, and I think I understand what you are trying to tell me. But first let me assure you, that what you are suffering are mere growing pains. You cannot be a master of the cure of souls in a day. It requires a lifetime of ups and downs, surely. And another thing; have you ever realised that there are times when even golden words would fall futile, and there are situations in life when even the finest speech, superbly delivered, could be fatal, because in spite of all our clever calculations, it is not timely?"

"Especially if they're my words, my speech. Better for me to learn to keep my trap shut after all, for when not dumb, I'm stupid."

"Please don't get me all wrong dear, nor get yourself all wrong. Of course there must be times when keeping mum would be appropriate, and that goes for everybody, and not poor miserable you alone.

"Yes I follow. Anything else your wisdom has ordained? Floor's all yours my dear, carry on."

"Of course there is, and plenty. For example, take the case of that poor young mother who's lost her baby - and listen, I am speaking not as a theorist, but as a woman. Do you not realise that your silent sympathy was a more vital source of strength and consolation to her than all the sermons you'll ever preach, all the lectures you'll ever deliver, and all the words of counsel that ever fall from your lips, put together? When you communicate shared feelings, empathy, as YOU can - charisma I think it's called - by simply being at hand, words are totally superfluous, and would destroy the healing of the moment. I don't wish to appear cynical Don, but often actions speak with more power than words, yes and I dare say it, even the so-called word of God."

"Maybe you're perfectly right my love - perfectly right. After all, even the Word which you speak of was never fully effectual until it was made flesh and dwelt among us."

"Clever boy. Now, about Natalie Slackston again. That strong arm of yours, and that broad shoulder to cry on. Nothing we ever say can substitute for those things. Given the circumstances - and I don't mean to be irreverent - as I say, given the circumstances, and a strong bond of sympathetic human understanding, they can be as mighty as the arm of the Lord."

"You're sure a treasure Gina, both in word and deed."

"And as for the other two experiences this afternoon, no more needs to be said. I think you acted wisely and discreetly on both occasions, and time will tell."

"Yes time will certainly tell, so long as we remember that this arbitrary conditioner of all things not only heals but can destroy."

"I really liked what old Vicar Teal said to you, about when you begin to feel confident et cetera. To which - if I may presume to append my little piece, which is to advise you to hang on to that sense of weakness and failure dear. You see it may keep your head and your heart in correct perspective and proportion, and also keep your nature natural, and you'll never need to stumble home again in sackcloth and ashes."

"Well now, I shall have to take time to try and sort that one out. But that poor girl, alone, wonder if they've removed her baby yet? That'll be the real crunch."

"Husband?"

"I'm afraid that lad has been presented with a situation with which his frail moral constitution is unable to cope. He'll be up at the Knotty Stowp just now, as usual, seeking escape by the only means he knows."

"Then if that be the case, you and I will take a little walkies shall we, down to Rose Cottage - about a mile did you say? And we'll spend an hour or so with Natalie. We'll not use the short cut over the fields of course. Just don't want to run the risk of getting my pants caught up on a wire, nor your only remaining pair of wearable trousers ripped up, do we?"

"Great idea darling. Only - traditional priorities you know - I'm afraid you'll have to go it alone, for I've got an urgent meeting of the Church Finance Committee at half-past seven. Which, is in about five minutes time... 'bye."

So long as I lived I would never forget the sad rebuke in my young wife's big brown eyes as I hurriedly departed.

Chapter 24

A TALE OF TWO BROTHERS

The battered old car was so thickly overlaid with mud and coagulated cow dung that none of the features by which its vital statistics could be assessed was visible; even its outline was obscure. And it was standing on the road by my front gate. On entering the house, the sounds which fell upon my ear indicated that Gina was entertaining visitors. She herself seemed to be conducting the greater part of the conversation, for her slightly out of character, whilst her guests, of whom there were at least two, were doing little more than uttering affirmatives in a brutish tongue, “Mbaa, Mbaa, Mnnn, Mnnn.”

“Mbaa,” came the bucolic voice, “Thisn’s thatn’s yonther.”

“Mnnn, mnnn,” said a young bull, “gayly lish lass an’ all and sight betther than that yan he’s gittin hisel’ howd on... dost think?”

“They look like a pair of very nice girls to me,” Gina’s voice was heard to say, “You’re lucky fellows I think. Any more photos?”

“Hello there,” I burst in from the doorway, sensing that Gina might be in need of a rescuer, or an interpreter, “So nice to see you.” I found myself addressing the two Matfen brothers, hill farmers from way out and beyond. Both in their late twenties or early thirties, they were good-natured and rugged, each with a unique brand of rustic quaintness. It transpired that they had recently ventured beyond the pale, or at least beyond the range of their domineering mother’s ever watchful eye. And they had discovered ‘Woman’. The experience had unsettled them, and they were having some difficulty in coming to terms with emotions hitherto unfelt.

“Thowt tha meyght gi’ us a bit advice or summat leyke.”

“Mbaaaa, mbaaa. There’s these two lasses ‘appen... see-ed them at t’Mart ower at Claversdale yan Mondtha, and gat on talkin’ soort of. Wurst thing is sumbody’s geyne an' telt me muther." At which awful confession both men became agitated and even more uneasy than before.

"Mnnn, mnnn. Thowd lass's gittin' hersel' all wurked up and fratchin' on all day. Says she's gaw-in' tae tak coos intae t'Mart hersel' fra now on."

"And what about the two lasses? Expecting to see them again?"

"Nay, it's not t'lasses we're worrit about - it's t'coos."

"Aye, that's reyght. Owld muther's gittin' a bit past that soort of thing, buyin' an' sellin' and that. Not much use on t'pricin', and knaws nowt about t'way they gaws on at t'Mart these days."

"It means you're both going to be a bit hamstrung doesn't it. Seems to me that you've got to have a cow or two to put in for sale in order to see the lasses. That right?" Which notion, though true, caused the boys to break out in crude coy giggles.

"Forget the coos," chuckled Gina, "Go for the lasses, surely."

"Mbaaa, that's reyght, t'lasses. What's tha think mister?"

"It's surely what you think that matters lads," I answered, "What have you got in mind about the lasses? Serious I hope."

"Mnnn, aye - I've been gittin' tae thinkin' this last day or two. A good strang lass would be gayly useful up at oor owld place, aye."

"Coos gittin' a bit ower much for only two on us, wi' mare sheyep than ivver out on t'fells. Hev tae build up bigger flock leyke."

"Me muther thinks we've gawn soft in th'eyad or summat. Says we should keyep t'place seyame as father had it afore he dee-ed. Nae good at all, we said - hev tae keyep up wi' th'times hest tha not."

"But she'll not budge wi' nowt. Should've heeard 'er when we wanted yan o' them new Ferguson TE tractors. Mak us idle she says. Faather nivver grumbled about owld Fordson, had it for years and still earnin' its keyep she says. Th'owld Fordson, now that's a lark, even when it gaws at all it's nae use."

"Seyem wi' th'owld car. Fallin' tae bits it is, wi not mony bits left tae fall off now 'appen, and what's left rattles summat bad."

"Want a new un...yan o' these new Land Rover things, wi' a trailer. Hest tha ivver see-ed yan?"

"O yes, very nifty, and just right for the job. Rather like the Jeeps we had during the war... they'd go anywhere and stop at nothing. Which reminds me, what about those lasses you were talking about. You've soon got away from the subject haven't you? What's up then eh?"

"Mnnn, argh, aye, t'lasses... din't knaw what ta—"

"Taboo isn't it? Bit scared of the idea aren't we?" I quizzed.

"Mbaaa, aye, if tha says sae... but... well... tha knaws what it's leyke wi' us leyke."

"Yes fellas, I think that I do. You see, you're looking at it all the wrong way - coos sheep - stock - tractors. - Land Rovers - trailers - lasses all in one breath, as though they are all the same to you, and all equal parts of the same big deal. No good chaps."

"Well if tha says. Must be reyght. But all t'sayeme, me muther'll not bide ony talk about them lasses," said Sammy almost under his breath.

"That's reyght," concurred Josh; "shuts us up streyght away."

"Look here my friends, I wouldn't like you to misunderstand me, but I see the position like this. You've met two girls, and if the love bug has bitten you - gets at us all eventually you know - then coos, sheep, tractors, Land Rovers, trailers, and Muther, may have to go slightly by the board for the time being," I said emphatically, Gina choosing that to be the appropriate moment to effect a tactical withdrawal on the pretext of getting up some coffee. "What I mean is, and again please don't pick me up wrong, if this is more than just a silly flirtation or mischievous lark, and frankly you're both getting a wee bit past that kind of thing, you've got to start deciding whether these ladies are the ones whom you'd like to get to know better, and eventually share the rest of your life with, as equal partners at that. And by the way, seeing I've got the floor, don't you think it's about time each of you two guys started doing things on your own? You're going to get in each other's way one of these days you know, especially with a couple of lasses to cope with."

"Mbaaa mbaaa."

"Mnnn mnnn."

The conversation would doubtless have become well and truly penned-up had Gina not pushed in her trolley at that instant. The two hill men were at considerable unease by now, and soon got into difficulty with their coffee. Sammy's massive ploughman's fists didn't match up over well with the china coffee cups, and when Gina proffered to relieve Josh of the cloth cap which he had been clutching throughout the evening there was near calamity. That same Josh committed the lushest slurps I had ever heard, and his embarrassed efforts to modify them only made matters worse. Gina however, true lady of quality, and perfect hostess, tactfully contrived to set the lads at ease, so that 'ere long they were quaffing repeated cups of strong coffee, downing heaped plates of home-made scones, and conversing freely. It was almost as though the coffee had been 'doctored'.

"And what's tha wantin' us tae dae about these lasses 'appen?" burst in Sammy through a shower of scone crumbs.

"Aye, tha hesn't telt us owt leyke that yet," subscribed Josh, surfacing from a deep draught of hot coffee.

"That's not the question. The real point at issue is, what do YOU want to do about these lasses? The encounter's obviously made a profound impression upon the pair of you."

"Well, din't knaw leyke. Only see-ed them the yance, efter t'Mart," said Sammy bashfully.

"And what did you do, talk to them, go walk with them, treat them?"

"Nay, they did all th'talkin'. Proper chatther-boxes."

"All women are like that - you'll learn we men just can't get a word in for most of the time."

"Correct," concurred Gina from the silent shadows.

"They cummed ower tae t'ring wi' us, but nivver said nowt about th'stock or owt - din't think they knawed ower much," enthused Josh.

"Went across tae a cafe place for a drink o' tea afore we walked them across tae t'bus."

"O aye, sum tea, and a cayake, and they paid - for ours an' all."

"Very romantic to be sure. Good grief, Sammy, Josh, I just don't believe it. Why a couple of aborigines from the Australian outback would have done better. You've got an awful lot to learn about how to treat the ladies haven't you? They're not just jokes you know, playthings, chattels, stock, or cheap farm hands. At your age fellows, they should be seen as potential wives, and... er... mothers." Gina chose this moment to effect an urgent exit.

"Mbaaa, mbaa," mused Sammy.

"Nnnn, mnnn," mused Josh, almost in shock.

"Gosh lads, you'll have to learn to say more than that if you really intend to go courting these two lasses. What on earth will you say if one of them just suddenly spouts out that she loves you eh?"

"S'nowt leyke that or owt," giggled Josh through his teeth.

"Hey, hey - tha's a good yan mister - bit of a lad tha is, a reyght bit of a lad." laughed Sammy.

"Scared of the idea of love aren't you. That threw you didn't it? Well lads let me tell you something it seems you need to know. See that bonnie lass who's just gone out through that door? Have you noticed all the happiness she has to share with us? That's what having someone to love, and to love you, gets for you. You've got your ideas all bogged down, or kessened or something. Animals mate, we marry. Animals conquer to possess, we give ourselves in love. Animals breed, we generate into families. Human love is of the heart, the soul, the whole person, and is not a mindless pursuit of one of the instincts. It effects your life in every aspect of it and totally alters your direction. It's the whole of you that's reaching out, wanting to live, and love, and be yourselves." This fine outburst took my breath away, and left the lads staring blankly at me.

"Me muther'll be wundrin' where we've gittin tae. Cummed here streyght fra th'auction," ventured Sammy.

"Leykes tae knaw where we git tae on a neyght if we stops out langer than usual." murmured Josh, "Alweys askin' a lot o' questions when we gets in. Nivver gaws out onywhere hersel', not much, 'cept for chapel and t'shop. Funny sumtimes these owld muthers, I reckons."

"Fine lady your mother... not had a very easy life. She only wants to see the best for you two...all she's got you know. She maybe has some rather odd ideas as to how to go about achieving it mind you, and like you I'm not sure she is always right. But look here...surely you're old enough and wise enough to start deciding what is right for yourselves. But - straying a little I think - if I judge correctly, it's these lasses you really came to talk about, isn't it?"

"O aye, t'lasses. Sharon's that yan," confessed Sammy coyly.

"And t'other yan's name is Shirley, she's t'yan I fancies. Big strang lass that yan, Oo aye." boasted Josh.

"Looking at this photo...very nice indeed. As a matter of fact I think I fancy both of them myself."

"Now tha's deyne alreyght for theesel' mister, what mare dost tha want. T'missus yonther's a grand la'al lass and nae man could've been luckier than thee," Sammy hastened to assure me, winking wickedly, but yet at the same time causing me to suspect that I had got the lads onto the right track. It was probably time to proceed a stage further.

"I thoroughly agree with you Sammy, you obviously know a goodun when you see one. But however, if you're still wanting some advice, let me suggest that the next time you see Sharon and Shirley, that will be at the Mart on Monday I presume, take some steps to break out of this off-chance meeting stuff. Make a firm arrangement to see them again, but under different circumstances, not at the Mart - not a very romantic environment is it. Something special. It's called a date."

"Mnnn, mnnn."

"Mnaaa, mbaaa."

"Take them a walk, and talk to them about all sorts of things that will be interesting to them, and remember it mightn't be coos and sheep and tractors and the like. Take them somewhere nice for tea, and this time make sure it's you who do the paying, for them as well as for yourselves. Got to look kind of prosperous, and generous you know, as you are.

"Mnnn, mnnn,"

"Mbaaa, mbaaa."

"What about taking them to the pictures one evening?"

"Me muther doesn't believe in t'pictures nor owt leyke. Might start cuttin' pocket money if she gat tae knaw."

"Well, a decent dance. Lots of good hops around the village halls you know - the girls would like that I'm sure."

"Nae good at th'dancin'...nivver knaws where feet should gaw."

"Or what tae dee wi' t'hands neither. Went yance and yan lass said I was nippin' her summat rough, and t'bloke wanted tae fight."

"Aye, that's when we went tae t'dancin ' at Browtonshields last Chris'mas. All t'lasses just stood a-starin' at us and laughin' leyke owt. Not be gawin' back there in hurry, 'till I learns tae dance."

"Well just find out where they'd like to go, get to know them, they might begin to like your company, and you their's. You'll see, it'll all come natural to you before long."

"Din't knaw about that," the brothers groaned simultaneously.

"It will, I assure you. You see fellows, your trouble is that you've spent too much of your time up on the high fells - far, far ower lang - just like those sucklers and strays you have to fetch down in the back end, a bit out of place and shy at first. But once among the herd, soon you can't pick them out from the rest."

Duly enlightened, and somewhat over-awed, the Matfen boys made their departure, leaving Gina and me to consume the few remaining fragments of coffee and buttered scones.

"Did a thoroughly bad job there." I confessed.

"Not really. Indeed I thought you waxed pretty eloquent at times, and I actually thought you were getting a little carried away."

"Waxed eloquent - too eloquent I'd say. What a splendid substitute for wise counsel, or even worldly wisdom. Never mind the content so long as it sounds well."

"What price wisdom if it is not clearly communicated, and whither eloquence if it's not adequately informed?" declared the young sage.

"But what a terrifying onus to put upon the parson. Whoever created such a crazy custom, and why? Behold your Minister, the Omnipotent, Omniscient, Infallible - next to God. Is this how we are to be regarded and is this how we are expected to perform? Some of these dear folk entrust much of their vital decision making to types like me. 'Which way?' they ask. 'How? What? When? Shall I? If I? Does it? Will it?' and go out and venture confidently in the direction we have set for them in accordance with our own personal whim and vaunted wisdom."

"You're over sensitive my love," said Gina, "And in this, over the top a bit. What you tender is surely advice not instruction, guidance not direction, assurance not insurance."

"Maybe so, but do you realise that those lads have gone out there in all their unsophisticated trust, perhaps to follow my words - some even spoken in half jest - to the very letter? I fear they may not possess the background experience nor the necessary emotional equipment for handling the situation they just seem to have stumbled into. They might even make fools of themselves, or get hurt in the process, or both. Gosh, I'm not God."

"No dearest, but you speak and act in His name."

"Why do you say such terrible things? And why should ordinary people, many with much wider and more complicated experience of life than I, let this pompous young whipper-snapper direct them in the way they should go, for no other reason than that I wear this shining white celluloid halter about my neck?"

"Or put them on the road to happiness? Don't get bigheaded my dear Don, for in reality you do not impose anything upon them. You merely share with them as a hallowed confidant in their decision making, a safe repository for their doubts and fears, a consoler, encourager, and dearest friend, and all on terms more equal than you think at that. And whatever way you may regard your Ordination, to them it is a most sacred thing, not to be treated lightly, for it is of divine institution. Pastor - shepherd. Minister - servant. Priest - bridge. You - that three in one."

"Good God - how dreadful is this place."

At about that period I was being sorely troubled by a sad complex of negative self-appraisal, and persistently harried by oppressive feelings of dire failure. I began to realise more strongly than ever, that whatever my worthiness or otherwise, I had been entrusted with the cure of souls, the work of a spiritual leader. Now I was beginning to fear that the essential content of my judgements and counsel was often sadly lacking in 'spiritual' incentive. The more personal aspects of my work routine seemed to follow a miserable pattern of shameful evasion, brushed off challenges, wasted encounters, and forfeited opportunities. The Matfen brothers and their problems were a case in point. What could I now do to try and make it up to them? Not a great deal actually, for except for their now very rare Sunday afternoon appearances at the little chapel at Keldhoff village, they were rarely seen in public for the next few months. I occasionally met their mother on the first Monday of the month when she would emerge from the wilderness to call on the local branch of Lloyds Bank, allegedly - according to *vox populi*, to deposit a stack of notes, but rarely to withdraw. I fancied she looked upon me askance and disapprovingly. There was however some small consolation for me in the knowledge that Mrs. Matfen was not usually prone to wearing her emotions on her face. Her attitude, true or imagined posed no threat to me until I began to couple it with certain murmurings here and there that 'them two Matfen lads hes gittin theirsels mixed up wi' a couple o' town dollies hangin' about t'Mart'. Tales of their alleged goings on proliferated throughout the village, at the local stock marts, and the humble hostelries. Some would be hyperbolical, the lads being easy butts for such humour, and yet the telling of them, as well as providing some light amusement, often betrayed some small anxiety. Such concern was well founded, for a remarkable change had come over these two innocents, affecting their work, social attitudes, attendance at their church, and, so it was said, was reeking havoc upon the peace and happiness of the little farm way up over the hills. Current rumour conjectured that the girls in question were but a pair of unscrupulous pleasure seekers who, finding the two unsophisticated rustics to be easy game, extraordinarily responsive to flattery, and flamboyant in parting with their loose cash, had led them into wild escapades of unprecedented prodigality. The lambing season might have been a total disaster but for the two hill men's tough resilience, hay time would have ended in calamity but for their inherent capacity for enduring exacting hours of hard work with sparse rest, and all may have been loss but for the powerful drive of their indomitable mother. Eventually even this latter force began to lose its effectiveness, as these two hardy inseparables started showing signs of a growing independence from each other, and from their possessive parent. It was said that they had now established their right to a proper wages structure in place of the irregular pocket money which had hitherto been the only source of ready money available to them.

******

One miserable wet evening our peace was disturbed by the noise of intermittent revving up of a car engine outside our front door. This was closely followed by a hesitant knock, and the sound of muffled voices.

"Howistha Rev... can I see tha for a la'al minute or two... not tak lang...summat else I wants tae ask tha about... sorry tae bother tha leyke." gabbled Sammy Matfen, holding out his hand in exuberant greeting. I coaxed him right into the house before he continued, "How's t'wife then? Not seen her for a lang teyme... tell her not tae bother wi' ony coffee nor nowt if she's in. O aye, and that la'al motor o' yours? Still gawin' strang I bet. Lish la'al packet that yan... wadn't mind yan like it meesel if I needed it."

"The lady?" I enquired, observing the rather over-dressed, fair-haired young woman standing rather incongruously by his side.

"O aye, tha still calls your la'al car t'lady I sees. Nae lady that yan is it...ower fast... wild... ower sharp off t'mark... dangerous a bit for t'leykes o' me 'appen. Still waldn't mind it meesel'."

"No Sammy, this lady. Man you haven't introduced us yet."

"O argh, aye. This is t'lass I was tellin' tha on a bit back. She's soort o'... er... well onyweys I've browt her tae see tha... that's if tha din't mind leyke."

"Sharon... Sharon Murgatroyd," the girl spat out impatiently, with a voice like breaking glass. "Quite new to these parts... heard a great deal about you though... belong Liverpool... got a job in the sock factory in town...not bad... good money at least."

"So nice to meet you Sharon, and I hope you're settling in well. Now Sammy, Sharon, is this a purely social call, or is there something very special? Hope there is, but in either case, it's a pleasure to see you. So whatever, come on in, and let's out with it."

The unintentional brashness of that invitation blew back any reply which may have been lingering on Sammy's lips, and it took him at least half a minute to recover sufficiently from the shock to proceed,

"Aye, well what it is leyke... well I din't quite knaw how tae put it...what I mean is..."

"Come on Sammy, what's the matter with you, surely it's not as dreadful as all that? One would think you'd come to confess to a murder or a bank robbery or something equally heinous."

"Aye, well you... well it's... well t'lass here...what I was saying...well you're a proper gentleman and all that, and 'appen we shouldn't cum here talkin' about things leyke—"

"Sammy let me assure you, I ain't no gentleman. So if there's anything you want to say, however wild, or rough, or just plain crazy, I can take it, and especially if it's something where I can be of any help. If it's bothering you, it's my business also."

An atmosphere of severe tension was beginning to build up, the girl reacting by fidgeting impatiently in her chair. "Tell you what Sharon," I said tactfully, "I don't know what Sammy wants to tell me, but it's sure to be man talk, and it would probably bore you to tears. Why not slip through to the other room, Gina's in there sewing, and I'm sure she'd be glad of your company, eh?"

"I'm having a baby, that's what he's spluttering on about," the girl exploded, "and that yokel's the father, that's what."

I had already learned from previous pastoral escapades that in situations such as this, one must not outwardly indicate shock, surprise or disapproval, inwardly harbour rash judgements, nor too readily dole out slick advice or pre-packaged remedies. And yet overt caution can create the impression of evasiveness, indifference, or incompetence, which are all equally as risky. So, I had before me yet another test for my raw ingenuity as a shepherd of souls.

"Not the end of the world, is it?" I slipped in unobtrusively, "I'm sure that between us we can bring a happy issue out of this little situation. So, let's start by stopping worrying."

"Like what?" said the girl, now threatening to weep, while Sammy sat engrossed in gazing at the floor through his straddled knees, and vigorously stroking a full day's growth of stubble on his substantial chin, intermittently emitting hissing sounds from between his teeth.

"Well now, before we begin to offer any suggestions, have you anything in mind, any plans of your own? Surely you must have talked the matter over a great deal between yourselves before coming here."

"Not much, hardly at all," Sharon burst forth, "He's always too scared to talk about it, changes the subject, blabbers on about stock breeding or some stupid farmyard talk. Have to get married I say, even if it's only to give the baby a name. It's got to be born proper an' all, hasn't it, we don't like bastards where I come from."

"A's not gittin' married nor owt leyke," muttered Sammy, still pondering over the space between his boots, "Onyweys, a's not t'faather on it, so it's neyne o' my business I tells tha."

"O yes you are," snapped Sharon fiercely, "Who else? Anyway I can easily prove it you know - plenty of witnesses."

"Canna prove nowt lass, that's what." responded Sammy brusquely, yet turning a pair of pathetic eyes towards me, "Onywey, a's nivver done owt wrang or owt leyke, nivver, nowt leyke that."

"What about the time you were blind drunk? Went at it like somebody fed you on raw meat, like a flaming animal. Forgotten that time haven't you, and that was only one of the times wasn't it. Proper randy one this when he picks up the smell of the barmaid's apron, that's all it takes with him, and he's unstoppable. Don't let him kid you Father."

"Nae she's wrang there... I've nivver done owt...started the drinkin' an' gawin' into t'pubs an all that... but nivver nowt else."

"I'm not telling lies Father, nor trying to accuse him out of hand, nor trying to mess him up. I'm just wanting fairplay, that's all, and this is the only way to make him listen, by telling you. We've got to. I'm willing to...want to...get married...that's all. It's the baby I'm thinking about... the baby... the baby." And Sharon wept.

"Mbaa, mbaa, alreyght tha sayin' things leyke that, but baaby's not mine nor owt, and it's nae use tha bubblin' on about it, cos that doesn't mak me t'faather. And there's gawin' tae be nae mare talk about gittin' married or owt leyke." squawked Sammy in off-beat aggression.

I found myself inwardly praying for the strength of Samson, the patience of Job, and the wisdom of Solomon, but all to no avail, for the pair cut proceedings short at that point and prepared to leave, with the matter unresolved and me dumbfounded. As a parting shot the girl put in one further complication,

"By the way, I'm a Catholic, so I think I'll go to Confession this week, haven't been for a while, and I can ask our own Father for a bit of advice while I'm at it."

The visit left me perplexed and much disturbed in mind and heart. Calamities like this are no less tragic when they are delivered in a comic wrapper. I decided upon the inevitable, which was to await whatever outcome Sharon and Sammy would unamicably arrive at, yet fully realising, to my dismay, that whatever the outcome, some innocent child could be destined to suffer. Besides, they would be back, I felt certain of that, yes they would be back. For days I waited, lost sleep, lost confidence, and much self-esteem. But Sammy and Sharon did not return, and to all practical purposes I lost touch with them, and presumably their dilemma.

One evening, about a month later, I returned home to find a neat, gleaming black sporty-looking car at my gate. "Why Josh, what a pleasant surprise to see you... had Sammy here a week or two back. Come on in."

"Mnnn, mnnn, browt Shirley tae see tha. Meynd me tellin' tha about Shirley, on th'photo, meynd? Thinkin' o' gittin' married, and just called tae ask tha how tae gaw about it and that."

"Better go inside hadn't we," said I, trying to stave off a sudden attack of foreboding which was weakening my knees. "But by the way, where is the lady, your lady?"

A tall handsome young woman emerged from the car and presented herself with outstretched hand, "Shirley Denton, foreigner I'm afraid. Father farms on t'other side o' hills, near Ripon. How d'yi do Sir."

Entering the warm, brightly lit drawing-room into which Gina had ushered us, I was immediately taunted within by that age-old adage, 'However did the likes of 'er...?' There were strong traces of a quality in the girl which, to my mind (may God forgive me) was somewhat incongruous with her present relationship. Like some gardener's pride and joy which, in spite of the loving care he has lavished upon it over many seasons is nevertheless reverting to the wild. Although Josh displayed his characteristic resistance to an invitation to be seated, I otherwise noted some remarkable changes that had come over him since I had last seen him. He even seemed to be at ease in his now stylish apparel and fine shoes.

"I believe you mentioned getting married," I ventured with calculated audacity, for I was still mindful of brother Sammy's ill-fated visit some weeks previous. And this time I determined to take the bull by the horns. Well- not literally - Mnn! But I was forestalled.

"How d'ye leyke t'fresh car then? Just bowt it forthneyght sine, wi' me ain money an' all. Reyght goodun - Triumph - reyght bewty on t'road I tells tha."

"Very nice Josh, smart, bit of a cha—"

"Gits a gayly move on when tha's waantin' tae an' all. T'lass here leykes fleein' alang in't - din't tha luv."

"Certainly an improvement on that smelly old banger he had I must say. Needed to wear overalls just to ride in the disgusting thing. Know what somebody'll get their self killed in that stinking heap yet, and it won't be with speeding neither. Falling to bits even standing still," laughed the girl.

"Mnn - aye - our Sammy's still running around in that yan. Suits 'im. Belanged tae me faather. Bit owld fashioned 'appen."

"But Josh, Shirley, you didn't really come here to discuss the merits and otherwise of various models of automobile did you? I presume that the intention was for us to get down to some wedding arrangements."

"O aye - mnn - mnn - aye - that - well- aye - that's reyght 'appen. But din't knaw how tae put it soort o'." An awkward pause, then he blurted out from somewhere at diaphragm level, "Onyweys betther be seyen as we can - seyen as we can if tha can oblige us Mister."

"O listen Vicar he didn't put that very well did he. It's nothing like you're maybe thinking, and I don't blame you. Just - well we mean business, so no point in waiting. Not getting any younger are we?"

"No doubt you've sorted out all the details between yourselves to your mutual satisfaction - such small matters as da—"

"O yes, and I think we know what we're doing. Some pretty big changes needed on both sides of course, but I think we can manage once we get started, can't we Josh."

"Your mother Josh?" I ventured timorously.

"Hostile," snapped the girl before Josh could switch on.

"Din't leyke th'way a's gawin' on she says, and she's creatin' and frattin' all day lang."

"Won't have another woman about the place. So that's me out."

"Hevn't knawn t'lass lang enough she says. Fra far ower far away, and tha nivver knaws what they git theirsel's up tae, or what soort o' foalke she's out of."

"Led poor innocent Josh astray and all that, got him into bad ways, too much time off the farm, and too much money to spend on... me of course. Really doesn't want to lose him, that's the main trouble. Gets all the work done on the cheap - stop me somebody, stop me, it's clean pathetic," Shirley said mockingly.

"She'll not knaw we've cummed down here... start gittin' vexed wi' thee an' all if ivver she finds out we've been talkin' tae tha."

"Can't you help the poor dear, Vicar. And O come on Josh my man, and stop behaving like a great big soft boob."

"Our Sammy fell out wi' Muther," came in Josh's voice from somewhere obscure, "He's talkin' about shiftin' out or summat. She'll not let him fetch t'lass hoame or owt. Doesn't want tae see her, an' that's that, she says."

"O yes, Sharon, little Liverpool lass. I've met Sharon, when she and Sammy called to see me a few weeks ago. On similar business to yours - in fact. But I suppose you know all about that," I reeled off.

"Want to get married you mean?" mumbled Shirley, "Well I never."

"I don't want to risk breaking any confidences, but, you do seem to know that there's a little problem."

"Little problem you call it, you certainly hit the nail on the head there Vicar. Little something else actually - she's pregnant dead sure - starting to show. And they seem to have brought you into it. Well let me tell you something important before you go rushing into anything with Sharon - seeing as how we're trading in confidences, and if you want to look after your own reputation. That bun was in the oven before Sammy came onto the scene I'm telling you. Poor twit, poor gullible Sammy."

"That's a pretty serious allegation Shirley. I do hope you realise the possible consequences of what you are saying." I said gravely.

"Listen Vicar, Sharon's my best friend, and I wouldn't wish to get her into any more trouble than she gets herself into. But I don't want her to go hurting anybody else neither, and that includes yourself."

"Meaning precisely what?" I queried.

"Well to be quite frank and honest, as it would seem this is called for; Sharon's a grand lass in lots of ways, but when she's downed a few glasses too many... well... let's say, a bit easy going. So you see, there's plenty of others. Am I making myself clear?"

Josh had withdrawn from the discussion, and was scrupulously examining the toecaps of his highly polished tan shoes, conversing with himself in low bovinic murmurs. There came an uneasy stalemate, eventually broken up by Shirley, "Have I put my foot in it? Honestly Vicar, it's just that I don't want to see anybody badly hurt. You see Sharon's desperate, and a bit indiscreet, and—"

"Perhaps," I interjected, with calculated tact, "we should break off at this point eh? Meanwhile I'll be seeing the other two again I hope soon. And you two, get on with some definite plans, I'm at your service. And, come and see me again, about details - soon."

We adjourned for the inevitable coffee and cheese scones, half an hour of small talk, in a lighter vein, before the couple left. The cowardly element in my nature made me relieved to see them go, and yet something noble in that girl Shirley caused me to hope that they'd soon return, especially when she called out from the car,

"Thanks Vicar, you're a real sport you are and I like you. We're going to be busy for the next week or two - I'm all excited. .'Bye."

At about five o'clock on a Saturday afternoon, two weeks later, I answered a bold knock on the front door, to find myself face-to-face with a very grim looking Police Constable Littlejohn. "I'm wantin' a little bit o' help wi' a case Minister. Can I cum in - t'wife's not in earshot is she?"

"No, no she's not actually. But what's this all about? I'm not in any kind of trouble am I? Not aware of committing any breach—"

"Nay, worse than that. I'll get straight down to t'business if ye din't mind." The policeman was uncommonly distressed. "It's that young Josh Matfen - I tek it ye knaw him well enough - fresh car, sporty thing - nivver been used tae nowt but his faather's owld Minx— fast a bit this new yan—Josh bit wild sine he gat this lass."

"Not in trouble over it already is he?"

"Aye, hit milk lorry - full head on - cumin' round t'bend down at Lyndie Bottoms yonder. Cor, sic a mess as I've nivver seen, sic a mess - nivver seen owt as bad afore sine I came into th'force."

"Is Josh badly hurt or anything?"

"Dead...clean as a whistle...t'lass wi' him an' all... smashed tae pieces...sic a sight."

"Mother?" I gasped, out of an unutterable confusion of emotions.

At this point the shattered constable invited himself to a seat, setting himself down heavily.

"That's just what I'm wantin' ye for. Can nae mare gaw up there tae tell her meesel' than flee in the air. Cum on, we'll both ha' tae gaw up togither. It'll tak us both... an' mebees t'good Lord an' all if He's 'appen on our side."

As my little yellow MG two-seater bumped, roared, rolled and clattered up the tortuous track towards the old hill farm, I wished that she would bog down, seize up, put on a delaying tantrum, or turn up something mean and final, if only to relieve us of the awful moment which faced us when we reached our destination.

"Afternoon Mrs. Matfen. Sorry to trouble you, but Mr. Littlejohn and I have come to tell you... er... that—"

"We're nivver in any kind o' trouble up here thank ye, so whativver it is tha's gittin' tae t'wrang place. Nivver had t'poliss up here afore. Din't see ower much o' t'minister neither, cum tae that."

"We've cum about your Josh," hastened the Law coming to the swift rescue of the Church.

"Josh? Now tha knaws very well, my lads is nivver in ony soort of mischief... been brought up better. Where is our Josh onywey...time he was in for t'milkin', hest seen him 'bout place as tha cummed in?"

"Mrs. Matfen please sit yourself down just for a minute, and if there's any tea in the pot, pour youself a cup, and we'd like to sit down for one as well." Reluctantly the lady complied. "You see," I continued, "we've really come to tell you that Josh has had an accident on the road, with his car. And... well... I don't know how to put this, but you see... well it's going to be a bit hard for you... but we know you'll be very brave... and so—"

"Mrs. Matfen, Josh is dead. Mrs. Matfen, are you listening? Josh has died." once again the long arm of the law reached in and saved the moment.

"That lass... that bad, bad lass... she's—."

"Mrs. Matfen, Shirley has gone with him - together," I whispered.

The stricken lady took a sip from her cup, and slowly stood up. Her complexion suffused with a grey like that of her hair, and she looked straight at me with a face which was at once haunting and full of rebuke. Nodding her head, she uttered but one word, "Aye."

"I'll just pop outside and see if I can find Sammy about t'place," said the constable with some urgency, "You'll bide with Mrs. Matfen I warrant?"

Presently, Sammy, who had been gathering in the milk cattle, came crashing into the kitchen.

"What's up here then? Poliss's out there. Sent me in tae th'ouse and stopped in t'byre hissel'. Says he'll git on wi' t'milkin' for few minutes till I gaws back. Summat queer gawin' on here. What's tha wantin' here an' all minister. It's still got nowt tae dae wi' that ye-knaw-what if that's what's botherin' tha."

"Sammy, I want you to sit down. Forget the milking for a minute, Littlejohn's looking after that. You're a man, a good one, and a pretty strong one at that. And so, what I have to tell you I'm going to say straight out - OK? Sammy, your brother, Josh, is—"

"Aye, where's he gittin' tae. Was cummin' tae your place to see about weddin'...said he was cummin' tae your place... said ye wanted mare details about t'weddin' or summat. Hest tha not seen him? Ony roaad, wherivver he's gettin tae, it's time he was back for t'milkin'"

"Sammy, steady now. Josh has died. The car Sammy...accident... bad one... and Shirley... by his side... gone with him."

There ensued a long painful interlude during which not a word was spoken, and the silence was not of this world. The mother sat pallid and statuesque, staring vacantly into the inexplicable. Sammy stomped aimlessly about the flagged floor, wagging his head, and as he always did when under severe stress, breathing noisily through clenched teeth. I stood stark still, and wept secretly deep down within. Here was no place for sweet anodyne, nor the dutiful dispensation of pious platitudes, however golden they might be. It was a time for prayer, at greater depth than words. Mingling with my immediate distress were strong feelings of remorse at the thought of my own part in the events which had led up to this terrible day. There came a moment when Sammy ceased from pacing the floor, slumped slowly onto his knees in front of the large settle, and buried his head deeply into his massive rough hands. I knelt down by his side. What transpired in that farm kitchen from that moment cannot be told, for the memory of it has sanctuary within the deepest depths of my soul. And when I looked up to rise from my knees, I saw P.C. Littlejohn kneeling humbly alongside Mrs. Matfen. Surely the perfect assimilation of law by grace.

As the policeman and I drove slowly away, I chanced to look back. The sun was beginning to set, and the Western sky was bathed in sombre red. I took to wondering whether the sun would ever rise again in joy over that tragic little farmstead. If the story had ended there I would never have told it, for it does me no credit.

Mrs. Matfen bore her sorrow as stoically as she had handled every other tragedy and crisis in her hard, sad life. At least so it seemed, until another crisis loomed up and drastically altered the order of things at the Matfen homestead. Sammy went off and married Sharon, quietly at a Liverpool Registry Office. To the immense astonishment of all, Sharon became a tirelessly efficient farmer's wife, and a truly devoted daughter-in-law. The baby duly arrived, although obviously not Sammy's progeny. I baptised him at the little chapel in Keldoff village. That baby totally transformed Mrs. Matfen, who became fully absorbed in smothering him with love and tender care. And with her own particular brand of possessiveness.

Chapter 25

VERY HIGH TEA AT THE RECTORY

The rough narrow road between Rickmansgarth and Coppleby possessed a peculiar aura, which induced in travellers along it a pleasant mood of aimlessness. It didn't seem to matter where the road had begun, nor to where it led; it simply wandered on regardless. There was no readily apparent reason for its gentle meanderings, except to facilitate the getting of a short way in a long time. This was the road on which Gina and I elected to travel, to nowhere, and spend a quiet afternoon together, doing nothing. The sky was bright blue, and there was a sharp nip in the air, so that ambling along in our MG Midget Sport we were inspired with an exhilarating sense of abandon, akin to gliding aloft. Then came a rude shock, immediately after we had negotiated a double bend ('One good turn deserves another' according to Gina). A blue Singer Nine saloon stood motionless at a crazy angle across the entire width of the road. Standing alongside, and frantically waving his arms about like a string puppet gone haywire, was a scrawny fellow of not more than five feet and a small fraction tall. We had scarcely come to a halt before he had clamped a fumbling hand upon our windscreen. He was wearing a loose fitting suit of ageing tweed, and an extraordinarily large clerical collar which gave the impression of someone peering up out of a hat box.

"The Reverend Theodore Tansie, Rector of Attleby with Coppleby," announced a booming clerical grey voice which was completely out of proportion with the rest of the man, "I wonder if you would be so kind as to assist me in my time of trouble? It would seem that my beloved Annabella here is unable to proceed."

"Run out of petrol... ignition snuffed out perhaps... battery... plugs?" came the ever-ready voice of Clever-sides occupying my driving seat.

"O no, no, no, no, my dear, dear fellow. I have diligently conducted all the usual formularies, and have eliminated all such rudimentary impediments. Such lowly vices just do not become Annabella."

Gina and I had clambered out of the cockpit of our two-seater and joined the quaint little cleric alongside his stricken non-mobile.

"There is, however, one other thing which fills me with despair and despondency," his Reverence intoned, "I have indeed with my own hands raised up the lid, and have beheld a most awesome sight. I do believe that I observed the machinery."

"But my good brother," I laughed, "you were bound to see the machinery or whatever under there, for that's where it's normally kept."

"No, no, no, dear young man, you don' t seem to comprehend. What I saw was unfamiliar machinery."

With some foreboding I looked into the engine compartment, and my worst fears were emphatically confirmed. Some of Annabella's most intimate parts were exposed stark naked and shiny. A large section of the crankshaft was in full view, and pieces of bright broken metal lay on the ground directly beneath the engine sump. The whole grim aspect was pervaded by the sight and odour of black, sizzling, spilt engine oil.

"O dear, O dear, and if you would care to look down upon the ground, you may observe that the dear girl is bleeding somewhat profusely," the rector's speech now affecting an echo of some distant cathedral close.

Before I could get a grip on discretion, I heard myself blurting out with, "You'd be bleeding profusely as well, if you had as much of your g—I beg your pardon—inside hanging out as this."

"It is all so frightfully ghastly to look upon."

Gina nudged me before I could make the obvious follow-on, which I promptly rendered as, "Big end gone vicar... bad show... jolly unlucky for you...very bad one I'm afraid...very bad indeed... smashed right through the side of the crank case... wrought absolute havoc on its way."

"You would seem to be very well versed in the rudiments of automobile anatomy young man. Tell me if you please, what in your opinion, is the probable prognosis?"

"Bad, very gloomy. In fact, without being over pessimistic, I would say, even from my limited experience in such matters, quite frankly - well - I think your engine's wrecked, ruined, beyond repair, that is...con rod's shattered... smashed through crank-case... and heaven knows what else... anything can happen when that— what I mean is, you'll need a new engine, or if you're lucky a reconditioned replacement. This one's had it I reckon."

"That is a most dismal nomenclature young man. But for the moment, what am I to do? Ah, perhaps you could be so ki—" and before he completed what we suspected he was about to suggest, I chipped in with, "Better push the old girl off this narrow road away from that blind turn. Come on all hands, onto the grass with her."

His light assistance with the necessary push flustered the puny fellow alarmingly, and he staggered to and fro for a while before regaining his equilibrium. During the process of pushing, the rector's wide-brimmed black Stetson had toppled off, revealing a mature cranium as bald and shiny as a pink balloon. My attempt to grasp the escaping headgear only succeeded in deflecting it underneath the car, where it came to rest, brim down, in a pool of warm, black engine oil.

"A piece of stout rope would verily make all the difference," gasped his exhausted reverence, regurgitating an idea which I had abruptly caused him to swallow earlier in the conversation. To which Gina and I crashed in simultaneously, "We have no rope."

"O dear, O dear, however am I to return home? I will be so terribly late for tea, and my dear Emma will become so fretful and distressed. Such a sensitive soul she is, and... aha, I perceive that you also young sir, are a brother of the cloth." My large striped scarf had unwound during the car pushing operation.

"Wherefore, kind brother, you will most graciously assist me?" he did earnestly pray and beseech me, and as many as were here present, in exquisite Cranmarian mode.

"We would rejoice and be exceeding glad to do so dear friend, jump in to yonder chariot, and we'll get you home safe and - er - sound. Regretfully I'm afraid, we must needs leave your pride and joy to languish alone by the roadside."

Now anxious and overwrought, Tansie sat down rather precariously on the off-side wing of the MG. Gina's mischievous glance indicated that she as well as I had observed how, in that attitude, he so closely resembled one of those ornamental garden gnomes. I was so pleasantly pre-occupied thus, that it did not occur to me to enquire as to how far away his home might be. And as we had now solemnly committed ourselves to conveying him thither, there was a small complication. We had that day spent our last few shillings on putting one gallon of petrol into our hitherto empty tank. Expected mileage, approximately twenty-five.

"When we reach your home," I continued, "you'd better 'phone your garage to come out and take your car in. She's due for a long holiday I'm afraid."

"So unfortunate, so unfortunate. You see we do not possess a telephone for we have never had need of such. But let me see, I must needs thank you two dear, dear young people. It is so extraordinarily kind of you to undertake so willingly for me, and I fully appreciate that you will finish that which you have begun," whined the gentle parson in highly sanctimonious tones, his heart being unfeignedly thankful.

This small cloisterphobic, with a strong accent of the High Altar, was not only out of his element, but was equally out of his generation, and at the moment, almost completely out of breath. Opening the meagre side gate onto the passenger seat of our car, Gina bade him enter. This he prepared to do as though he was about to board a state carriage. He hesitated half-way through the motion however, stroked his exposed scalp rather ruefully, walked smartly over to his own car and, without sacrificing a morsel of aplomb, he stooped to retrieve his oil-sodden hat from underneath, meticulously wiping the brim on the grass. Then, still with minimum damage to his dignity, he firmly set himself down into our low profile passenger seat, planting the said hat fairly and squarely upon the dashboard shelf.

"Ah, the dear young lady. O deary me, what must we do?" wailed my extremely grateful passenger, having noticed Gina still adrift on the grass verge, and that our conveyance was only made for two.

"I could climb in and squeeze up tightly on your knee," teased my young charmer. Seeing the instant shock which this suggestion precipitated, she reacted swiftly, making a clean vault up onto the rolled-up canopy on top of the locker, finishing the move with her shapely legs wedged immaculately between the rector and me. It soon became clear that the poor man was finding our unluxurious mode of travel a trifle terrifying. He constantly fumbled about for something permanent to hold on to, and shuffled to locate a safe anchorage for his feet. Now and again he would cast a wistful glance backward toward the place where he had left his dear disembowelled Annabella desolate and alone. Unfortunately the windblown Gina unavoidably presented a dubious distraction, confronting him with an alluring array of flying flimsies. Whereupon the lady, suspecting that the main objective of his peering vision was not Annabella's plight, would treat him to a deft push to the side of the face with her dainty left foot. Once settled down however, we nevertheless struck a bizarre spectacle, with me pushed closely up to the steering wheel, his eminence clutching his stark naked cranium, and Gina perched perilously aft, clinging grimly on to her unruly clouts. There was no conversation during the first two miles, although Gina made some attempts at slip-stream singing; alright except that she would insist upon such ditties as 'Those Daring Young Men In Their Flying Machines.' Once as we brushed past an insignificant hamlet the rector announced in a high quality stentorian, "Attleby, this i... er... was. Only another mile, church and rectory on right."

The church and parsonage stood in unsplendid isolation. This location so we were informed, was chosen not primarily to ensure privacy nor remoteness, but for sound strategic reasons that were something to do with the geographical heart of this sparsely peopled parish. The house was a large, bleak grey stone edifice, situated at the head of a long leafy drive, and surrounded by geriatric trees and unkempt gardens. The heavy studded front door opened with an ominous groan, and closed behind us with a no less ominous clunk. The initial impression was that of a sombre cavernous interior, pervaded by an oppressive atmosphere of old drapes and musty books.

"Emmmmmmmmaaaaaaa," called out our holy host in a voice which echoed through the portals like a grand 'Amen'. "Come, come, come my dear, surprise for you-ooooooo."

Whatever form the affectionate bidding had caused our mind's eye to anticipate, the image was quickly dispelled by the sound of approaching footsteps on the oaken floor of a long passage; not unlike the approach of a foot patrol of the Nazi SS. Dear Emma appeared almost explosively. She was a smartly groomed lady of vast proportions, sculptured features which did not appear to be designed for smiling, and a harsh brassy voice,

"Aha, aha, aha...so we... have... visitors... have we not?"

"Emma my dear, I bring you sad tidings. Dear old Annabella is very sick and alone by the roadside three miles back. This very kind young man, and this most charming young lady," here a pause and fleeting glance over Gina which either disturbed or delighted his reverential sensitivities, "appeared and have delivered me out of my distress. O I am so sorry, my friends, so remiss of me, but this is Emma, Mrs. Tansie... my dear wife that is." The little man was, quite literally, overshadowed by his wife, and, as we were soon to discover, not a little over-awed by her vibrant verbosity and power-packed presence. The round diapason of his former conversation had already given way to a meek pianissimo. The dialogue between the pair invariably followed a litanic pattern of versicle and response, the former usually being the prerogative of Emma. Their verbal exchanges were made as though we were not present, except when indirect reference was made to us. Eventually the conversation inclined towards us, although even then we were invariably addressed in the oblique.

"I am sure that your two young friends would just love to stay to tea Dorrie dear," Emma fanfared across the hall.

"They have indeed already decided my dear, I'm sure... of course."

"It's so very kind of you," I began, "but actually we—"

"Aha, that's it then. As a matter of fact it's all ready... been so for some time actually, but nothing spoiled." and before we could show any response, Emma was gone, and charging down another grim passage. So, as the lady had said, that was it then. We were trapped.

Presently we were led into a spacious dining room, which was dominated by a monolithic mahogany table at the centre. Scattered about the place was an assortment of odd chairs, ancient and modern but mostly the former, and in sufficient number to seat a medieval banquet. Only one half of the great table was furnished, but with an array of exquisite Victorian table-ware, which must surely have been in the family, or the Rectory, for two or three generations. Food was provided in considerable bulk; a point which was not lost on Gina, judging by her dark eyebrows, now curved upward like accent signs. Emma was proud of her culinary capability and what was maybe lacking in refinement was clearly made up in the mass and wholesomeness of her products. Her mode of hospitality was generous to a fault, but over zealous in the extreme, exuberant and overwhelming. Rough hewn pastries, and confections which would confound the digestive system of a dinosaur were heaped upon me in quick succession, until I had almost surrendered the will to live. The apple pie was a case in point, fabricated in the ratio of four thicknesses of dough to one of apple filling.

"I'm sure our dear friends would like another helping of this lovely apple pie," Emma addressed to me via her spouse. With an indestructible hunk of the former offering still trying to book a passage through my gullet, my polite 'No thank you' was sufficiently delayed to permit the lady the opportunity to slam down on my plate another mighty portion of the dreaded delicacy. Neither did Gina escape this avid generosity, and was indeed a little harassed by it, trying hard to strike a compromise between keeping up the pace, and preserving her natural daintiness.

"Aha - plate's empty. Macaroons? Haven't sampled my macaroons have you?

Love these you will... my speciality... pass them over Dorrie dear."

The said macaroons were fearsome beasts which appeared to have been made of an aggregate of course coconut chippings and other non-malleable materials. I was not surprised therefore when dear Dorrie flunked in the act of delivery, and caused one of them to fall with a heavy thud upon Gina's plate. Emma's deft handling of the teapot was beyond belief. She was able to carry out the operation of filling your cup at the same time as performing some other totally unrelated task, such as offering a dish or plate towards the opposite side of the table, and all the while engaging in an animated conversation with any who would listen. Our cups of tea were maintained permanently at boiling point, for each time Emma observed that the level had fallen an inch below the rim, they were topped up instantly. At long length, the gastronomic marathon ended, and our ebullient hostess adjourned down the long passage towards the kitchen, loudly beckoning Gina to accompany her, 'While the men retreat to the study for a little chat'.

At the first hint of freedom, Theodore executed a rapid about turn, and hastened in the direction of an oak door immediately adjacent to the place where he had been sitting. Opening it with some panache he signalled for me to follow, at the same time lifting up his rich liturgical voice and saying unto me,

"Behold, the study."

Here was another out-size room, but its spaciousness was partially relieved by the unruly array of bulky furniture cluttering the floor. Three of the four walls were totally occupied from floor to ceiling by bookshelves, overloaded beyond safe limits, and stacked so precariously that one was inclined to move about gently, and talk quietly for fear of precipitating an *ex libra* avalanche. Having suspected various shades of eccentricity in the man I began to wonder whether I was in the presence of a super-academic or a harmless libramaniac. The fourth wall was dominated by a gaunt mottled marble fireplace, drawing attention to a relatively puny fire. Nevertheless, temporarily delivered from the imperious solicitations of dear Emma, I was now able to feel somewhat at ease. Not for long unfortunately, for no sooner had I set me down in a voluminous well- worn old chair than my knees were invaded by a mangy feline, and the grey woolly rug laid before the fire metamorphosed into the shaggiest canine I had ever seen in my life. These loathsome creatures set about vying for my undivided attention, each according to the habit peculiar to its species. The old dog, much in need of a bath, a comb-out, a more strictly controlled diet, and some regular exercise, smothered me with affection, disgust, and loose hairs. The cat, having secured my special attention by anchoring itself firmly to the flesh of my thighs with its full compliment of recently honed talons, responded to my grudging fondles with loud catarrhal purring, treating my hand to a savage bite each time I attempted to withdraw my attentions.

"I observe that you are very fond of our animal friends dear boy. Such knowing creatures, and so responsive to our loving care," said the rector, with the affected *tremolo* of Sung Eucharist.

Eventually the ordeal by pets became so intolerable that I resolved, should their owner turn aside for but a brief second, I would swiftly kill them. In desperation I sought some means to extricate myself by a feigned fascination with the contents of one of the great bookshelves. I stood up with well-timed abruptness and made off in haste towards the most distant wall. The old dog took the hint and skulked off into the shadows, but the cat didn't succeed in completely unhooking itself until I was halfway across the room. Meanwhile, back in the kitchen, Gina was struggling to remain friends with Emma, who had discovered verbal perpetual motion, and also assumed that all modern educated young women were now totally lacking in the finer skills of domestic management. The heavy beating tones of Emma's voice seemed to emanate from all over the house at once, they were omnidirectional, neither could any door keep them out. The noises off never seemed to trouble Theodore, who seemed to have other things on his mind, and was busying himself in a corner of the room with a large dark bottle.

"Port - glorious Port. Only very special occasions mind you, and er - only very special guests - ahem."

Taking note of the two glasses which he had perched precariously at the edge of the table, I politely informed him that for reasons of health, habit, and calling, I was totally abstemious. Cheerfully unabashed he elected to go it alone; magnanimously I thought, vicariously he intended. "Jubilate," he called, raising his glass in a reverent toast to us both and all others like unto us, and flashing a demonic twinkle in his eye.

"Only one glass mind you... matter of principle... moderation in all things...only one," said he, addressing the words directly to the fat bottle as though it was a bishop. He never drank his glass to below the halfway mark, but in the course of his 'only one' made frequent toppings-up. Within a short time this 'one glass' seemed to precipitate some remarkable changes in the little man's deportment. There was an unaggressive boldness, and his manner of speech became less formal and not so markedly ecclesiastical. The magic potion had lowered the rector's churchmanship by a spectacular degree, and such was the transformation that at one point I wondered whether the object which stood before me was indeed a genie which had arisen from out of the great dark bottle.

"You must be new here, stranger to these desolate parts?" he splurbed, scarcely raising his half-submerged lips from his glass.

"Yes, a fresher actually... less than a year that is... won't be remaining long though... about three years... probably less... actually."

"Nice bit of a girl you've picked up there what...very, very nice indeed...very, very nice. Should try and hold on to that one if I were you... good advice from one who knows... kind of alright I'd say... got an awful lot of... of...plenty of what it takes... proportions... oomph... er... personality that is... lots of—"

"My wife actually, and nice girl, as you say. The best there is actually. And I assure you, I really do mean to hold on to her, actually."

"Ah - Oxford! One cannot mistake it. Why the very manner in which you annunciate 'actually'. Yes, yes my man, thy speech betrayeth thee. Oxford to be sure."

"Wrong! Saint Andrews, and Durham... actually."

“Not remaining here for long you say? he queried with his lips awash.

“We are invariably itinerants. It’s the custom with us, especially in the early stages of ministry. Hierarchy likes to keep us moving along to broaden our experience. Good habit, gather no church moss.”

“Ah me, then you’ll be spared my grave misfortune. Twenty-six... I beg your pardon twenty-seven years, or more... no feelings left on the matter I suppose... what’s time anyway? Yes twenty sseven long years... sstrile you know... fruitless... grown roots in dry sand... bogged down... ossof... flossiplied... plossif-”

“Ossified?”

“That’s right... crucif... fucifosed... O damn it... plain stuck,” he affirmed, affecting a rasping rake-out of the laryngeals so greatly in-depth that it also cleared up his befuddlement. Sinking into a cavernous chair opposite to me the little rector poured forth the sad testimony of a lonely, disillusioned man. His voice never wavered, neither did his eyes ever shift from their fixed gaze upon a distant corner of the ceiling. His voice though grave, was totally void of passion; the tone indicated naught but loss of spirit. Not once during the ensuing twenty minutes did he pause to top up his glass of rich red Port, so totally pre-occupied was he with pouring out his woes and frustrations. Shunted early into an obscure rural living, he had gone to ground, and forfeited both the will and the acumen to press for change. At a wicked moment I pondered the thought as to whether this quaint couple, seen as a potential embarrassment to the Establishment, had been thus edged-off to the backwoods, marginalised, etcetera-ed, or by whatever term this shameful process is appropriately described. On the other hand, this could be a classical chicken and egg situation, posing the obvious question as to whether this gentle fellow’s ineffectualness was the cause or the effect of this isolation. And could not the same have been said with regard to his wife’s stridency?

“Begun well you know,” he continued, in a more colourful vein, as though sensing the nature of my ruminations, “Ah yes... Oxford First and all that - actually. Married a bit late. Emma picked up a doctorate you know - biophysics. Never put it to any practical or academic use I’m afraid - not much scope for it in the parish - or kitchen eh. O, and of course, no children.”

We luxuriated silently for some five minutes or more on the body- swallowing chairs. My tormentors returned without invitation, grovelling dog, and savagely amorous cat, lavishing upon me their unwelcome affection. The small cleric eventually broke out again with his woeful recital of dismay. But the sadness in his voice had now diminished significantly, and he seemed to be building up to a crescendo of bitterness and wrath.

“Always had preference for a University town you know, or a good urban parish. Both of us could have got in some teaching. Persuaded to fill in here on temporary basis. Got stuck, left out, voice crying in the wilderness. Square peg in round ho— round peg in squ— O I don’t know— just some sort of odd peg in some sort of odd hole eh.”

I wondered what dint of fate had compounded the miseries of these two dear people by denying them the affectionate regard of the local populace, that one factor which would have partially compensated for their abandonment by the powers Ecclesia. I trembled inside with anger and resentment toward 'them' or 'it' or whatever institution, influence, or intuition it was which had misdirected them into their pitiful plight. Equally painful was the frustration I felt at having nothing worthwhile to offer the man, out of my youthful inexperience; naught perhaps but the rare commodity of a patient, sympathetic, listening ear.

"You may have already deduced that the local folk don't in any way appreciate me here... never wanted me in the first place... have often made more than strong hints at that... don't blame them... never did fit in. Fine people mind you... kind... frank... gracious with it... all so busy... church too far out... inconvenient. So good and so kind, but so charmingly indifferent. Rarely see any other clergy out here... all so busy as well I suppose, or stuck down in their patch. Town men say it is too remote. Do their souls good to come out and take a long rest it would. Ah well... get a bit like this sometimes you know. Just exist for the purpose of existing... ghastly futile eh?"

"Sundays?" I managed to wedge in.

"Routine - routine," wailed this lost cause incarnate, "Just a never ceasing round - Matins - Evensong - Matins - Evensong - world without end - Amen. Now and again, but very rarely, someone will die, and that adds a bit of variety. Or get married, again very rare, and make it big for one day - at least get the bells clanging. There's the odd baptism - day for great family celebration - including ten minutes at church."

"Confirmations?"

"Once in a blue moon. But then, the Bishop and his entourage come in and take over. All glory laud and honour." The Reverend Theodore was sliding deeper into despair, and I felt helpless to check him. What was needed at this moment was some powerful intervention, something like a thunderbolt. And it came - miracles do happen.

"Sorry to interrupt you gentlemen," came the voice of creation's sweetest thunderbolt from just outside the door, "But if we don't get a move on Don, we'll be too late to call at the garage and send them to attend to poor Annabella." An exasperated Gina had broken loose from captivity in the kitchen, and had come to my rescue. I urgently extricated myself from the man-eating chair, and hastened for the hall, with that hideous feline still firmly attached to my trouser leg. We were followed close at heel by Theodore and Emma - the mere mention of dear Annabella's sad and lonely plight was sufficient cause for our ill-mannered departure to be overlooked.

"Well goodbye young friends," pronounced the rector with the combined accent of sound churchmanship and full-bodied Port, "And thanks awfully for your splendid assistance, and for coming to tea. Thank you Mr. - er - er - do you realise that I do not know your name? Frightfully remiss, but no-one has yet introduced us - actually."

A burst of gravelly laughter from Emma, which seemed to set up a vibration in the oaken wall panels, was fortuitously timed to lighten the atmosphere, for the rector, after a deep rubrical cough, had begun to revert to his most splendid ecclesiastical self.

"Don Teviot," I managed to slip in through a gap in the cloud.

"The Reverend G. MacDonald Teviot, B.A., B.D." subscribed Gina, more in keeping with the atmosphere.

"And this most charming young lady? Secretary of course, what? Sister perhaps? Ah, or a very special acquaintance I hope?" quizzed Emma with characteristic lack of tact.

"My wife - Georgina G. Teviot er - B.Sc."

Emma's sudden outburst of ponderous laughter almost overshot the runway, "Whatever's gone wrong with us? We've all become so formal."

Both Gina and I felt an uncomfortable twang of guilt for so much as desiring to discharge ourselves from our neighbourly obligations toward this desolate pair. And yet that door continued to have drawing power.

"Is your parish far distant from here?" said Emma arrestingly.

"No parish, as such, actually. I am a minister of one of the non-Conformist churches, and cover a fairly extensive circuit, with pastorates along the full length of the Lyndass Valley, and up the fellsides."

"Almost the dimension of a diocese - must be wonderful." What was that jarring note in Emma's voice? Was she being patronising? Or was she betraying a trace of sincere envy? Or purely accommodating? Perhaps it was time to switch the subject.

"We were out together for the afternoon, a rare opportunity I should add, and such a beautiful run," chuckled Gina with that twinkle in her eyes which was capable of defusing a landmine.

"O dear, dear me," sighed the rector in plainsong, "I trust that we have not stolen your precious day off. Non-Conformist did I hear you say?" A small note of paternalism crept into his voice methought, but an abrupt blurt from Emma checked any potential drift.

"My grandfather was a Wesleyan local preacher. But of course, that was a very long time ago."

"The family fortunes have improved significantly since then?" chirruped my precocious helpmate, "But you do have an excellent pedigree and you must surely be proud of it. We also belong to the Methodist Church."

"Of course, I have a superb pedigree," boomed the large lady, arousing the suspicion that this might be a sensitive area. It was time for yet another rescue, and this one was for Theodore.

"We have had a superbly glorious afternoon, with you young sir, and this exquisitely lovely young lady."

"And as well as your delightful friendship, a superbly wonderful tea," I briskly contributed in the cause of tact.

"And a thorough-going womanly heart-to-heart in the kitchen. This dear child and I have discovered we have such a great deal in common." said Emma, much to our consolation and relief.

I marked Gina's slight wince as those words fell on her ear, and instantly wondered whether Theodore had found a similar compatibility with me.

"One final request," he solemnly intoned, "please speak our fond affection to dear Annabella as you pass."

"I assure you brother, we will not pass by her on the other side, but will pause and minister to her immediate need." Foolish talk, but I was beginning to appreciate that old Annabella was, after all, a thoroughly sentient creature and must therefore be regarded accordingly.

"And please do return soon, and often as you wish," added Emma with exuberance. "We're surely good for one another. And what is more, I'll be sure to have a good stock of your favourite macaroons always to hand for you."

"I'm not sure about those macaroons darling," I muttered to Gina as I let in the clutch to tear ourselves away, "But that other one's correct, we are mutually good for one another - in both directions. Nice old guy isn't he - lost his way a bit - wilderness - in more ways than one. Madly fond of Emma though - quite uxorious in fact - infantile dependency."

"Poor Emma," said Gina, "Great big noisy hulk, but pure, solid gold. Still in rough ingot form perhaps, but good stuff. Let's come back darling - often. - we'll call this old dump The Gold Mine eh?"

And so, we rounded off that fascinating afternoon with twelve more exhilarating miles of happy laughter, yet mingled with some trace elements of sadness, deep down.

Incidentally, we did not speak Theodore's fond affection to dear old Annabella as we passed. She was not there. Only a pool of black engine oil marked the place where she had languished. Arriving at the garage we discovered that some passing parishioners had come upon her, and she having woefully explained her troubles to them, they had kindly towed her in, and in compliance with local custom, not said a word to anyone.

And further incidentally, our own little buggy ran out of petrol within a mile of home, and was towed in by Matt Jordan's tractor.

Chapter 26

ANGELS UNAWARES

There is a certain reaction to the arrival of the parson, which is typical of the lady of the house, the world over. I first encountered it amongst the wives and mothers of the fellside farmers. It originates in that element of house-pride which almost every woman possesses, and of course denies. The moment you cross the threshold, she will draw your attention to all manner of irregularities which otherwise would have completely escaped your notice; articles of furniture temporarily displaced from their normal stations, ornaments askew, things which her inconsiderate family hadn't put away after them, an open book other than the Bible, and a fine layer of dust on a polished surface, although only visible to her. Tact is not always readily to hand, for after being most careful to explain that the present chaotic state of affairs is thoroughly out of line, she will go on to inform you that had she known that you would be calling, she would have had the place all neat and tidy, which of course, except for this present instant when, for some unknown reason, it just isn't; is it?

This brings to mind a particular afternoon, when I called on Maggie Nethergill, the wife of one of my country stewards. Immediately upon my arrival the recital began, and even while I was still making my entry I was forewarned that, only on this particular day mind you, many items would be found amiss in the small living-room of that cosy cottage. Now Maggie was just everything that a fine woman could be, and all of it in good measure. In her early forties, she was tall, of elegant posture, outstandingly handsome, and her flaxen hair showing but a vague hint of greying. Her rosy cheeks would strike two seductive dimples each time she smiled.

She was unaffectedly modest, winsome, and shy to the point of coyness. Her voice came over in a clean clear ripple; gentle yet there was a firmness in it which signalled that she was no waster nor manipulator of words.

It was a cool drizzly day, and it was Monday, yet, for some inexplicable reason which had nothing to do with necessity nor regular habit, Maggie had done her washing. She went on to assure me that she customarily hung out her washing in the garden, but today, for yet some cause unknown she had brought it to dry indoors, and although normally she never used the thing, today she had cluttered up the pulley rack suspended from the ceiling. Confident that she had assured me today was in all things an exception to the domestic rule, Maggie not only pointed out the offending laundry, but immediately busied herself in removing it with grasping haste. Being tall of stature she had no need to lower the structure, and it was this factor which caused the mishap. A vigorous tug at a stubborn woollen at the end of the rack opposite to that under which I sat, sent the entire contraption into a wild wobble which dislodged and draped over my head and shoulders the largest, longest, most voluminous, and prettiest pair of pale blue bloomers I had ever beheld. Maggie froze solid, blushed almost purple, then stood staring aghast. I am not one for quick thinking in the moment of catastrophe, but I nevertheless realised that in this particular instant I must in no way appear to reciprocate Maggie's embarrassment. With measured discretion, I removed the offending intimates from my person, and deftly folded them into a neat bundle, which with some mild aplomb, I presented to the lady. At that point I lost a little of the grip on my deadpan features, and a slight twitch at the corner of my mouth betrayed a suppressed smile. Simultaneously Maggie and I exploded into loud, uninhibited laughter, mine almost choking me and hers rippling like a mountain stream. I was in fact delightfully surprised at the sheer spontaneity of Maggie's merriment, and its loveliness. That day, a young, inexperienced country parson was to learn a lesson as to what firm rapport can be forged out of such ordinary human material as shared laughter.

Composure eventually restored, Maggie set up a small table between us in front of the enormous log fire crackling with joyful abandon in the grate. We ate a dainty tea, and chatted long about many things, all seemingly thrown into the conversation with random ease. There was the little chapel in Alstondyke village, and the business of the leaking roof and some woodworm in the organ panels. There were items of fresh local concern, some farming chatter, the matter of husband George's new job with the Ministry of Agriculture, and much small talk besides. At length there came upon us a long silent fascination with the glowing fire. That period was neither amiss nor intolerable, for Maggie was very proficient in the management of silence. Eventually she broke up the interlude with a nervous little cough,

"I hope you won't mind or owt...but there's summat very dear and close, and sacred to me... I've nivver telt onybody about it afore... in fact I din't really knaw what makes me wan-—"

"And of course you wa—-" Why am I so readily inclined to jump in with a prompt each time someone seeking help pauses for breath or hesitates for thought?

"Well...as I was sayin'...if you doesn't mind that is, and I have a feeling tha wun't... summat that bothers me a lot... a bit intimate mind you... be a secret... would leyke tae share it just with you... feels ivvrything will be safe that way. Should mebees hev telt it tae a woman, but no... I thinks you're t'proper yan tae ask and all that."

Young fool that I was I threw the magic moment away, in my usual fashion. My mouth suddenly dried up, and likewise my courage to listen. I sought refuge in consideration of my professional status, which, I concluded to my immense satisfaction, was being recognised at last. Consequently, my mind instantly formulated the classic reply, "My bounden duty of course dear lady, and what can I do for you?" But my lips refused to handle the words, and so it came out as, "Thank you Maggie, thank you. I'm indeed honoured... what I mean is, it's an undeserved... well a sort of privilege... I mean, well to share... to be... you know what I mean... O come on Maggie lass, come on, let's both stop stalling, out with it."

Even the lively fire seemed to cease to crackle, and a soft stillness fell over the room. Maggie spoke in little more than a whisper, slowly and deliberately as though in prayer, looking me straight in the face as she disclosed her soul's secret. I had never seen a countenance so serene as was hers in those moments. Yet, though gentle, there was a power and pungency in her words which would be lost in print, and dulled in the re-telling.

Maggie had lost the only baby she could ever bear, and was lying gravely ill in an isolated cubicle off the corridor of Ward 5 at the County Hospital. She was in fact, at death's door, and what was more, she knew it. She knew also that everything that could be done for her had been done, and so far all had failed. It was only a matter of waiting, of time, and the time was drawing to a close. She had picked up some garbled clinical intelligence from a mumbled outside the door discussion. Voices, and one standing out clearer than the rest, "Only matter of time - so sad, very sad. Only a matter of ti..."

"In fact, I felt the time was already here, because I could feel mesel' drifting away into a kind of ecstasy, a sort of peace that was all unnatural leyke. Tranquility it was, real luvliness all over about me, over the top and underneath me. Everywhere was flooded wi' a strange soort o' light - you could feel it, warm, and penetrating, right through. Soothed away all the pains it did. From inside as well, all the doubts and fears and worries. I wasn't even freyghtened ony more, of owt, because this warm light took away everything and left me filled wi' the peace and joy of everlastingness. I was full reyght up wi' the happiness of living, and living, and living - wi' everything tae live for. I knew I had passed ower... O I knew that alreyght. And tell ye what, I wasn't sorry, or sad or owt leyke that. Just alive, alive, alive, and absolutely nowt tae stop me being alive. Well... I was just on bracing mesel' tae tek in as much o' this Heaven in one go as I could stand when and I swear this is true - I heard a voice. No earthly voice was this - nivver had ony doubts about that. It was the voice of an angel. O yes, and there was nae mistakin' it for owt else neither.

Sweet and gentle, and yet at t'seyame time loud and clear... soort o' echo wi' it, coming from ivvry direction at once. Din't get human voices leyke that does tha? 'Like a nice cuppa tea Maggie luv?' it said."

Maggie had to pause at this point for re-charging, and there ensued a long contemplative silence during which any sound would have been profanity.

"'Like a nice cuppa tea Maggie luv.' Well that's what it said, this strange... voice. Now I thowt on a bit, and I realised that wonderful though Heaven meyght be, they're not very likely tae bring tha cups of tea in bed there. And the shock o' this silly thowt jolted me up a bit. That bad in fact, that the vision, or experience or whatever I was havin', just soort o' faded away, and I felt mesel' fair and square back on earth, in this life - just a-lyin' there on that bed. But it seemed tae feel a bit different sumhow. I oppened me eyes just tae mek sure... and I gat sic a freyght I did. The angel was there... standin' reyght there by t'side o' th'bed... cuppa tea in her hand... unworldly smile on her sweet young face... didn't just see it - you could feel it. 'Come on Maggie my love, look I've brought you a nice cup of tea. No, no, now don't you try and sit up, just leave it to me, I'll hold the cup for you... just little sips now.' she says."

Although recognising the exercise to be crassly vulgar, I spent the next silent staring-into-the-fire interlude in theorising within my mind, formulating a rational explanation of Maggie's 'ethereal' experience. It was after all, but one of those precious fantasies of an over-pious imagination, an uncomplicated case of simple hallucination (note the imagery!) probably induced by heavy medication. Maybe it was a classic example of the kind of pre-death syndrome which the subconscious mind will devise to tide us over the loneliness and uncertainty of the final moments. Although I hated them, I was helpless to stave off such irreverent meanderings of my cynical mind, or to quell the shame which they brought in their wake. I had desecrated a moment most holy.

"Thinks I'm crazy din't tha...bonkers?" Maggie broke in sadly, "And I can't say I blames tha one bit. Sorry if it's troubled tha at all, but just had tae get it' out o' my system - it's been a few years you knaw. Knew you'd try and understand. I feel better already."

"Maggie, dear Maggie - I'm so glad you've shared it all with me, and not a little humbled that you've counted me worthy to do so. Let me tell you that my whole life from this moment would have been the poorer if you hadn't. And, that lovely young nurse standing there - sweet angel - O yes, angel. Typical of one of those tangible facts of life which we may encounter during the normal course of any day, and don't always recognise it for what it is."

"Tha's just called her an angel. But she was only a nurse wasn't she... only... a nurse."

"Only a nurse? Maggie my dear, if we are to get some sparkle into life, we've got to rid ourselves of this curious habit of projecting Heaven into the realms of the beyond, hereafter, and fantastic. And we've got to stop conceiving of angels as overgrown fairies or nebulous super-women. Heaven is all around us Maggie, life is full of angels, and to those with faith, everywhere is hallowed ground. The

Kingdom of God is people, and His angels are usually people, people Maggie, people - like you."

"This queer experience, vision, or whatever I had, you'd say it was just sum genuine kind o' dream, special and all that, very pleasant, even scary a bit, but only a super dream?"

Good Lord, what had I done? Destroyed something beautiful, made a rip-off of careless rhetoric from an earnest confession? Pragmatic prig! And worse for me; had the sensitive Maggie seen through to the pedantic pride which forbade me to see wonder in anything? Good Lord deliver us, and that right early.

"No, no, no Maggie, not at all. You know what I think, quite honestly and truly; this sort of thing is not easy to explain away, and if we could, then it would cease to be wonderful, heavenly, or a vital factor in our total scheme of things. It was real to you, make no mistake about that. We have shared it, heart to heart, soul to soul, and so now it is equally real to me, and will always be cherished as such. What I really think is that the good Lord just for a wee while drew you rather close, let you have a little peep, just from the edge, and then sent you back to share your little bit of Heaven with us for a while."

"And what about the angel... that turned out to be but a nurse?"

"Nothing surprising in that Maggie. Lot's of angels turn out to be nurses, just as lots of nurses turn out to be angels. Ministering angels, their selfless care a lively link 'twixt earth and Heaven. No you didn't just imagine any of it Maggie. Isn't it the writer of the Epistle to the Hebrews who says that some have entertained angels unawares? And if I may presume to add to that, I'd say that some people have been angels without knowing it." As these words tumbled out, I felt a sudden release from the oppressive feeling of piety which had held me hitherto, and an exhilarating sense of realism came flooding in.

"What about George?" I continued from out of the blue, "Does he know anything about it?"

"Well I did tell him at the time. Didn't laugh at me nor owt, but didn't seem tae tek it very seriously neither. Just summat leyke I'd get ower it in time... wear off leyke ivvrything else. He's nivver mentioned it since...and neither have I."

"So then, nobody else knows, except me? And Maggie, I give you my sacred and solemn word for it, there it will rest. I'll cherish it for always, and whenever my spirit is down a bit, and things seem to be ge—"

"No, I'll tell tha what. You keep it safe for a bit, just 'tween thee an' me, an' the good Lord Hissel'. And if in the years tae cum, He taks me afore thee - nivver knaws does tha - that'll be t'time for tha tae fetch it out fra t'secret places o' tha heart. Just tell it far an' wide. Tell it specially tae onybody it might help or bring them cumfort or healing, them that's lonely, or sad, or sick, or maybees getting tae feel that God's ower far away to reach, or doesn't care about such as them. And tha's gonna meet plenty of foalkes like that afore tha's finished aren't tha. Well, you just tell them 'bout your friend Maggie, that yance gat reyght close tae Heaven, and at the seyame time bide on earth, and that she was close enough to entertain angels unawares. Now promise me you'll dae that for me... please."

For many years since then I have been honoured with the custody of Maggie's solemn secret. Until now. Sadly, the time has come for me to fulfil my promise to her. I am now able to tell you Maggie's story.

Chapter 27

THE LETTER KILLETH

"A penny for your thoughts dear," coo-ed Gina, observing my blank gaze into the dying embers of the evening fire. "Do you hear me? Penny for your th—"

"Eh - what - O - nothing significant love. Kind of self-analysis I suppose. Good for the soul they say. Have to confess though, I usually find the exercise somewhat depressing."

"Ah I see. But really Don, it's not your personal fault you know. Other people most of the time, and things, and dint of circumstance and such adversaries."

"You mean, I'm always on the receiving end?"

"That's right - trouble prone that's you. You poor old chap."

"I guess I must be just that— trouble prone I mean. Or how else would I have met YOU, and married YOU, and—"

"Naughty! But seriously Don, what I mean is; if there's an accident looking for somewhere to happen, it'll search you out; if a cause is destined to be lost, it will start with you; if there's a fight taking place in the quietest spot on earth, you will chance to come upon it; and if there's an unfortunate lying helpless by the wayside, you will stumble over him in the dark."

"Quite a spiel eh. Thanks a lot. I take it you mean that I'm a kind of magnet for trouble?"

"Of course you are. That's why I am singularly attracted to you. Come on dear, have this coffee, you're tired, that's all."

Admittedly, I had been ruminating on the past week's quota of miseries and finding the exercise depressing. There was for instance the church family picnic at Kelpington Grange, a picturesque area of unfarmed parkland about eight miles down river from Lyndassby. A geriatric Leyland bus with many rattles crawled up to convey our party of parents, children and others to the spot. The journey was an adventure in itself, and the fact that we arrived at our destination nothing short of miracle. As a matter of fact, I had not experienced so rough a ride since my D-Day crossing to Normandy during the war. For the most part, the afternoon proceeded according to plan, with the customary programme of chaotically organised games, contests and entertainments, and the mid-afternoon binge of sandwiches, buns, and pop. This was followed by exhaustion and the inevitable stalemate, when the adults sat in small bored groups on the grass, and bands of children roamed the surrounding area in search of some mischief for idle hands to do. Eventually the frustration boiled over, and with spectacular spontaneity the field erupted into a wild melee of all-in, no-holds-barred, noisy, limb-flailing, everything-goes, if-it-moves-kick-it-if-it-doesn't-destroy-it 'football'. This frantic escapade of mob-violence seemed to take in every man and woman in sight, of whatever age, station, shape, dimension, or physical condition. To our profound regret, Gina and I were politely excluded, for local propriety would rule that the minister and his lady were not expected to become embroiled in such vulgar frivolities as this. Ordination is a terrible, terrible thing. So, as popular preference dictated, Gina and I sat demurely on the grass, with legs respectably crossed, raising a restrained cheer for goodness knows whom or what now and again, but yet dividing our attention between the riotous spectacle up on the field, and some children who were playing down close by the river-side. They were mainly our own children, but the group had been augmented by some local boys who were ostentatiously demonstrating their superior daring in negotiating the boughs of a fallen old tree at the water's edge. The shock came at a moment when Gina and I had turned about, resuming our fascination with the mad frolics on the football pitch.

An ear-splitting 'CRACK' and a flurry of frightened screams suddenly jarred every fibre in my body, reminiscent of the effect of a starting pistol. It was for me as if the whole thing had been anticipated at the level of the subconscious, for before I was aware of what I was doing, some frantic instinct had sent me racing madly down towards the river. Still fully clad, and without a second's pause for observation or reflection I hurled myself from a high bank in a power dive which thrust me directly to mid-stream. On surfacing, collecting myself, and some breath, I spotted my target, for the first time. Some thirty yards ahead a child was thrashing the water in wild panic and being swept swiftly downstream by the powerful current for which the Lyndass is notorious. Although straining every nerve and muscle in the strongest strokes I knew, it took me much longer to overtake the imperilled child than I had anticipated. He had stopped screaming and struggling, and when I made my all-in desperate grasp on him, I was shocked to find that he had become limp, offering neither assistance nor resistance. The current would not permit me to either haul him or nudge him directly towards the nearest bank. I therefore had to opt for allowing it to sweep me by its own momentum towards a convenient turn in the river farther downstream, and here I renewed my fight. Looking back at one point I noted that there was considerable chaos in my wake, for Gina, without any forethought had impulsively dived into the river after me, shedding only her sandals, and was valiantly striving to shake off the pursuit of a swarm of swarthy swains who had jumped in to 'rescue' her. An excited group of anxious people had beaten me, on foot, to my landing point, and began to declare with great relief that the boy 'wasn't yan o' ours'. He was a stranger, about twelve years of age, and he was not breathing. "Artificial respiration - onybody knaw how tae do artificial respiration?" went out the urgent cry. But the only response was a nervous shuffling of feet, and some distressed muttering.

"Come on dear - quickly - you can do it - O do hurry," gasped a near exhausted Gina, as she emerged bedraggled and distraught from the torrent. Swiftly I rolled the boy over onto his face, and commenced to administer artificial respiration, by the then better known Schaffer's method. The onlookers gathered closely around, grave and silent. Nothing would avail however, and I could detect no sign of restored breathing, and there was no discernible heartbeat. Without pause for thought I flicked the boy over face upward, tilted back his head, held open his lower jaw and proceeded with the then seldom used mouth-to-mouth method of resuscitation, interspersed with short spells of cardiac massage.

"Indecent, thoroughly disgraceful, that's what," a crabby old voice in the crowd was heard to observe, "These modern parsons that gaw around kissin' la'al lads and such outrages wants puttin' away, that's what I says. That laddie's de-ad onywey, and that immorality's not gawin' tae help him. I tells tha, summat should be done tae stop it sharp, are ye all just gawin' tae stand there?"

"But there's a good biblical precedent Mr. Marfitt," announced Gina sweetly triumphant, "I might have known it was you - there's no-one else this side of perdition who would think like that. Just you go home and read about Elijah and the widow of Nain's boy. Second Kings, chapter sixteen I think. And by the way, how dare you - and just how dare you?" Marfitt's pale mean features registered no reaction, his acid drop eyes never blinked, and his drop-corner mouth didn't flinch. This miserable dropout from some odd sect had attached himself to my church and appointed himself as the village moral watchdog. He came back fighting,

"Nivver mind your fancy talk young woman. It's just not reyght I says, not reyght, and that's all there is to it. Sodomy... Si—"

"Belt up ye religious owld bugger - piasty-feaced owld sod - tha's alweys interferin' w' things as hev nowt tae dae wi' ye, and pokin' your snotty owld nose intae other foalks's business. Tek nae notice on him minister, naebody else ivver daes." And the big rough man with the big rough voice came down on his knees alongside of me, to try and lend at least some moral support. "Hey leyek. Leyek! Listen... T'lad's acumin' round I tells tha. Leyek... moved a la'al bit... jersey at top... and feyace... breathin' tae be sure... breathin'—" and the big man choked off with emotion and rubbed his eyes without shame. True, there was a slight stirring, then a little quiver. No denial, the boy was breathing.

"Tha's done it leyke, tha's done it, t'laddie's startin' tae breath proper and gi' a la'al cough... just leyek at 'im. Minister... God bless tha lad... if tha hadn't lowped intae t'watter and gittin' him out, then gittin' down an blawn all t'watter out on ‘im, that laddie would’ve dee-ed alreyght... that’s tae be sure... God bless tha lad...God bl—” the big man sobbed. Regaining his composure he then called out, “Hey ye lot, what he needs now is a la’al dash o’ brandy or summat leyke. Onybody got ony brandy or owt on ‘em? Wants it here, and sharp.”

“Listen here ‘my man, these are all good chapel folk, and none would carry with them such substances,” came back the stern crabby voice of old Marfitt. “Besides, I forbid you to expose an innocent child to the evils of alcohol. Have you not read the Scriptures? And you especially young woman there, ‘If anyone cause one of these little ones to stumble, it were better that a great millstone were hanged about his neck and he were cast into the dep—’” the loathsome voice was suddenly drowned in an anguished cry of indignant crowd protest. The big rough man, now worked up into a furious temper, rounded savagely on him,

“There gaws that crazy owld bible puncher ageyen. Now just tha hawd your stupit mouth will tha, afore sumbody cums an’ braes it in for tha. What’s tha knaw about bairns onyweys eh? Tha’s nivver had ony o’ tha ain, and tha’s freyghtened mare o’ other foalk’s bairns away fra Suntha Scheyel than tha can keyep count on - mesel’ included. I wants the brandy for t’minister, ye silly owld bugger - can’t ye not see, he’s shivverin’ all ower wi’ wet and cowld and shock and things?”

“And his la’al bit weyfe, just leyek at her,” enjoined the very large woman who accompanied the big man. “Hey leyek Charlie, here’s t’bus driver, fetched his bottle o’ whisky as he keyeps under his seat, big bottle wi only a la’al sup left in, but it’ll dae - gi’s it here.”

“Our ministers are required not to indulge in alcoholic substances under any circumstance whatsoever,” our crusty tormentor persisted.

“Now look here brother,” I croaked, rising to my feet with some difficulty, and gladly committing the care of our casualty to the women of the group, “We’re dealing in real, tangible matters of life and death here, not some particular church’s custom and policy, nor some individual member’s personal prejudices, so, begone you reprehensible fellow.”

“I would have at least expected you, a man of the cloth, to pray,” the tin-pot elder, now pale faced with self-righteous indignation came back at me with a sickly sneer.

“And what do you think these people standing around have been doing all the time you old serpent, while I breathed life into the boy and you stood by in judgement - not divine judgement I might add, - yours?”

“I heard no-one praying.”

“No you didn’t, not even yourself. Neither did God.” I retorted. “God does not ‘hear’ our prayers brother, He feels them. You probably wouldn’t appreciate that, your religion so-called being one of externals, and your own dowdy expression of piety.”

“I shall certainly report this matter to your superior, and in my official capacity as—”

“Report it to Satan himself,” Gina burst in vehemently, “I’m sure you’re on close speaking terms with him. You grizzly old rascal, you disgusting old hypocrite.

What a charming display I must say. It sure does no credit to you and whatever you stand for. Now listen to me, that is if you're capable of listening, or reasoning, or even thinking. This boy was as good as dead, and is alive again. Look that one up in the scriptures, for it is a well-known quote - Saint Luke chapter fifteen actually. He's alive I tell you, and who cares by what method or means? If he were your son you certainly would have no scruples."

I had never known Gina to become so agitated and cross; her outburst was quite frightening. During the noisy furore which followed she and I took the opportunity to slip away towards some nearby woods, soaked, bedraggled, and badly shaken. There we would find a hidden place to strip off and wring out our clothes, and perhaps sit quietly for a while to try and regain our equilibrium.

"Some shooting going on in there," whispered Gina as we searched out a suitably secluded spot, "Are you sure it'll be alright?"

"Pigeons - gamekeeper probably - cull them at this time of year. Might even be no more than a clay pigeon shoot going on up at the Hall."

All was going well for us until quite suddenly, from out of nowhere, "Mr. Adam and Eve I presume?"

"Where are you, you filthy Peeping Tom?" screeched Gina in panic. Come out and show yourself."

"Which is precisely what you are doing. I'm right over here. And what on earth are you two young scoundrels up to in there?" demanded a firm cultured voice.

"Only drying out our fig leaves," chirped Gina in mock innocence, with only her big brown eyes showing over the top of the thick foliage, which was fortunate, for we were clad in nothing but our wrist watches.

"O yes. Then let me tell you, whatever you're up to, you're trespassing...do you hear, trespassing. This wood's very private property."

"Then we're in good company my celestial friend. That is of course, if we really are Adam and Eve, in which case isn't trespassing in somebody's garden perfectly in character?" So saying I raised up my head to find myself looking straight at a tall middle-aged man, immaculately dressed in heavy brown tweeds and a matching deerstalker perfectly poised on his head. He was holding across his thighs a magnificent 12-bore, and a shaggy wimp of a dog was skulking at his heels.

"Now look here, damn you, who the devil are you? I'll have your names and addresses to start with."

"You have them," said Gina at her most pert, "Adam and Eve, address, Garden of Eden, probably Mesopotamia. O, and er - Mister and Missus."

"Well whoever you damned well think you are, you're trespassing, and by Jove, I'll have you out of there if I have to blast you out." We had been mistaken in assuming that the intruder was in jocular mood, for by now he had become heavily flushed and irate. "You're bloody well trespassing I tell you. That plain enough for you to understand? Now out I say, and your rags with you, before— before—"

"Now, now kind sir," I said with calculated calm, "As I judge you to be a man of substance and good breeding, might I suggest that you conduct yourself in the manner of a gentleman."

"Particularly in the presence of a lady," scolded Gina, holding up her right wagging-finger.

"Lady did I hear you say? By Jove sir, one can quickly see the type of 'lady' you are, you impudent young hussy." This remark so infuriated me, that on impulse I came crashing out from the thicket intent upon destruction. Incidentally we had by now made ourselves partially decent. The sight of the two shiny barrels, although still pointed groundwards, had an instant sobering effect upon me.

"Listen here my friend, if I am correct in my judgement as to what you are thinking, and I assure you that to read your mind isn't a particularly complicated business, let me frankly explain—"

"You've done all the explaining that is necessary, there's nothing more to be said, so—"

"As I was saying, before being so rudely interrupted; we have not desecrated any part of your private wood with any loutish conduct or brutish behaviour. This charming young lady is my wife, and together being of a modest and decent disposition, we've merely concealed ourselves in here for a short time in order to dry out our wet clothing. We've been in the river... dived in as a matter of fact... we've be—"

"Fully clad? You, you crazy young fools, just the kind of thing modern young idiots like you would get up to I suppose. In the river you said? Then that is trespassing also. That stretch of Lyndass is strictly private, no fishing, no bathing. You must be crazy - it's damned dangerous as well. If you want to get yourselves drowned, then not on my estate, you hear?"

"But sir, will you please let me continue, I think you'll understand when I tell you the circ—"

"I understand all right, as much as I need to, you blasted young liar. Can't bluff me I say. I know all about your little games."

"So easy with a gun in your hand isn't it. But let me tell you my friend, that in no way intimidates me, and neither does the man behind it." I said threateningly. Collecting myself, and dropping my voice, I continued, "Alright then, I think some apologies may be called for at this point; from us for carelessly trespassing in this wood, and from you sir for behaving like an uncouth ill-mannered snob, without such minor graces as a sense of humour, courtesy, or elementary decency. Listen now, and don't speak until you are called upon to do so. We were wet, very wet. Cold, very cold. Shocked and badly shaken. And all for a very good cause - we've both been i—"

"Now look here, I don't give a damn where the Hell you've both been, nor for what reason, and I'm having no more of it. Now I'm warning you, for the very last time, just get out. Do you hear, get out. Ah, Dobson, what the devil are you doing down here?" At this point our adversary raised his gleaming ordnance ominously to waist horizontal.

"Would you come back to the Hall if you please my Lord, it is a matter of some urgency." Dobson's politeness was beyond belief.

"Can't you see I'm busy? Damned trespassers here Dobson, dam—"

"I beg your pardon my Lord, but it's Master Richard - accident - the river my Lord - please come quickly," and before the faithful footman had completed the sentence his Lordship had bolted and was crashing through the undergrowth towards the Hall like a rogue elephant.

"Mr. Dobson," I said on emerging from our leafy bower, fully clad and in my right mind. "His Lordship didn't get our particulars. Please be kind enough to present this my visiting card - while it is still wet if you please. O, and also, respectfully inform his Lordship please, about his 12-bore - I had noticed it was not loaded - I know about guns you see."

Arriving back at the riverside after an absence of more than an hour, we found the place deserted. Returning to the roadside we saw to our dismay that the bus, although a private hiring, had departed ahead of schedule. According to some picnickers the children had become unsettled and the outing had been called off prematurely. It was a long and miserable trudge home, but it served one good purpose in drying us out, calming our shattered nerves, and providing a thoroughly imperfect end to a thoroughly imperfect day. Next day was Sunday, that hallowed time of rest, recreation, and gladness, bringing to me the opportunity of tempering the delayed reaction to the previous day's events with the hassle of three open car journeys in the rain, four church services, and the onerous chore of delivering four half-prepared sermons.

It was on the following Monday morning, at about eleven o'clock, when Gina's urgent call sent reeling the normal peace and quiet of the Manse.

"Don - Don - Don - come quickly. Big black car... Daimler... limousine I think. Stopped right outside our front gate... fellow just getting back in... driver... kind of uniform... breeches... black leggings all polished... livery of course. Go catch him Don. What's he been up to? Hurry Don, he's moving away."

The car had disappeared by the time I got outside the front door. But just within the front gate, neatly deposited to the side, was a large wickerwork hamper. It bore an ornately inscribed label to 'The Reverend and Mrs. G. MacDonald Teviot, Lyndassby.' Gina chuckled merrily when we opened the great mystery box, for it was packed full to the brim with a choice selection of highly volatile goodies, all contained in shapely, elaborately labelled bottles.

"Such a profound waste," Gina kept on chortling, "Such a pitiful waste, I mean with our being teetotal and all that. Can I cook with it?"

"Listen dear, I don't want his Lordship's disgusting largesse, especially in the absence of some normal good manners. How much more humanly gracious would have been a courteous, simple, personal 'Thank You'. We saved his boy, he's more interested in saving his face." I said bitterly.

"Ah yes darling, quite correct, and I thoroughly agree. But surely," she went on - irreverently quoting Saint Paul, "while the letter killeth, it's the spirit that counts every time, isn't it."

Gina began mock fumbling a large dark green bottle, and then convulsed into unstoppable laughter as though she had consumed its entire contents.

Chapter 28

IT'S ALL IN T'BREEDIN'

"Ah gat that yan owta fust yan, and them two yonther fra t'third yan, and there's three mare ower th'other place, ah gat them three owta second, and there's been nae mare for a lang time syne 'appen."

There is something about leaning on a closed gate that is conducive to relaxed conversation. That is precisely what Eb Newbury and I were engaged in, whilst at the same time observing the cattle grading activity which was taking place in his extensive farmyard. In the circumstances, it was some time before I realised that the subject under discussion was not bovine genetics after all. Eb was indeed referring to his six 'all good, strang, and lish lads', sons of whom he was justly proud, 'ivvry yan o' them, wuk gayly hard, and nivver complains nor nowt'.

Ebenezer Newbury was a large, cumbersome man, with slovenly speech, and a very red face which was reminiscent of a fully matured fuchsia. During his seventy five years he had been widowed three times, each spouse in her turn bearing him a clutch of sons in quick succession. All of the lads were grown up by now; none had ever shown any inclination to depart from the family farmstead, leaving the service of their father, nor chanced to marry. It was a well-known fact that Eb was an excellent and prosperous farmer, for over the years his spread had kept on spreading until he now farmed one of the most extensive acreages in the county. There was the small matter of economics of course, and it was also general knowledge that his overheads were relatively below average. Rumour would have it that he didn't pay his loyal workforce of sons wages at official rates - that is, 'not proper yans, if tha knaws what I means leyke'. Nevertheless they always seemed to be a contented family, although their creature comforts were 'plain', and they sustained a single-minded dedication to the land. On the domestic front, the household had been efficiently managed by a succession of housekeepers, none of whom had remained for more than a year or two before retiring worn out from the task of tending so mighty a herd of humanity.

"Aye, what ah was a-wantin' tae see tha about... well ah suppose it's... well aye...it is soort o' chapel business... depends on t'way tha leyeks at it... I mean... well ivvrything's chapel business when tha's talkin' tae t'minister about it isn't it."

"I'm not quite sure that I understand what you mean Mr. Newbury. Is there something troubling you?"

Eb did not respond readily, thus giving me time to recollect that 'Chapel' was a very comprehensive term in Eb's reckoning, and very much his business, next to the concerns of the farm. So much indeed that the little chapel at Sneaton Burn was affectionately referred to as 'Saint Eb's', for he controlled its affairs and provided the larger proportion of its finances. Even in church circles affluence and influence belong together, power and pence are concomitant.

"You were saying Mr. Newbury?"

"O aye, O aye. Well ye see, a've gittin' this housekeyper, they ca's her Billie. Queer soort of name for lass... had her a few months now... grand lass she is an' all... aye. Alweys dresses herself up gayly fine - nowt wrang wit a bit of powther and paint on a woman is there? Aye, and she fothers us all up a treat, and keyeps t'lads in their place an' all, that she does. Aye, reyght alreyght is la'al Billie. Gittin' tae be yan of t'family she is an' all - just leyke yan on us."

"Delighted to hear that Mr. Newbury, and so glad the lady's settled down so well. It must make life much easier for all of you. Do you think then that the lady will remain a bit longer than—?"

"O Aye, that she will. Says she's gawin' tae bide wit us for alweys. She says it's her duty, 'cos God's called her tae it - telt her in a vision or summat yan neyght - wekened her up wit an awful stairt. Now as tha knaws, I'm not yan for believin' in all that soort of thing, but all t'seyame, A've got a queer feelin' about this yan - seems genuine eneough tae me. Aye."

"How do the lads feel about it?"

"Well as lang as she fills their bellies and mends their socks and suchleyke they'll not hev owt tae say. Time summonem were leykin' for a woman of their ain onyweys. Meesel', A've gaen through three and nivver rued the day."

"Well I suppose a man can do many a worse thing - than get married."

"O aye now, A's glad tha's mentioned that, 'cos that's just what A'm cumin' tae. Ye see th'ousekeyper - Billie that is - well ye see, she's a widda hersel', and she's been thinkin' things ower a la'al bit lately, and thinks it meyght be a lot better if she soort o' belanged mare tae the family - ye knaw, proper - official leyke."

"Perhaps she's had another nocturnal vision?"

"Nay, nowt leyke that. Ye knaw, she's been reyght sensible about it an' all - talked it ower wi' me a bit."

"O I see. Got her eye on one of the lads has she? She must be about the age of the two elder ones."

"Nay, nay, nowt sae daft as that. They wadn't knaw how tae meyake out onyweys.

Nay, th'lass hes better ideas than that."

"You don't mean...?"

"Aye, tha's queyte reyght. Lot o' life left in this owld dog yet 'appen. Aye, I'm t'lucky fella alreyght. Says she wants tae comfort, honour, and obey until de-eth us do part and all that, and that leyeks like a gayly lot o' sincerity tae me. Din't ye think sae ministher?"

"Far be it from me Mr. Newbury, I mean a young whipper-snapper, a mere stripling youth, to presume to advise a man of your years and experience in matters matrimonial. You surely know your own mind, and indeed have made it up. It's just for me to... well... string along with you isn't it?"

"Aye, well, that's just what I was wantin' tae knaw leyke. It'll be down at t'chapel of coourse, pretty seyen 'appen - Billie's 'appen stairted gettin' her things togither already. Nae point in waitin' ower lang is there, meyght be in bit o' hurry mesel', aye."

With this final assertion, Eb pushed open the big oaken gate, and ushered me through to the inside of the stockyard. Leaving me there he strode away hastily towards the house, which he entered and closed the door behind him - an unusual gesture about a farm. It was then left to me to circulate freely among Eb's beasts and his offspring. The more I pondered over the matter the more troubled I became. Had old Eb become so wildly besotted with this younger woman that he had lost his reason? Was this another case of a phenomenon which as yet was quite new to my experience? In such cases marriage seemed to be expedient chiefly as a biological arrangement, or had something to do with agricultural economics. And the woman herself, Billie, shrewd, scheming, ambitious, plausible, indiscreet? Perhaps none of these things, and yet, out of my few brief encounters with her I had already dubbed her 'different'. Vociferous in the extreme, she gave the impression of one who could lie with a clear conscience - a mythomaniac? And all the while I was disturbed at the thought that here was perhaps another one of those local situations which were operated through maxims with which I was not yet familiar. I must therefore be careful to reserve my judgement.

"What's th'owdun been whisperin' in tha ear ower th'yat this teyme then?" enquired the sardonic voice of Newbury the elder, as he emerged from the shadows surrounded by a strong odour of organic farming.

"O nothing... weather... time of day... stock prices... chapel affairs... local gossip... that kind of things."

"Nowt else then?"

"Listen Jake, I'll come straight. You surely don't expect me to report all my private conversations to all and sundry do you? And that has to include you I'm afraid, good friend though you be. I'm a Minister."

"Private eh? If tha talk hes tae be private, there's summat wrang wi' it, that's what." Jake was so overcome with rage at this point that his speech left him and he turned swiftly about and bolted for the nearby shippon. On entering he slammed the door behind him with such violence that it set up noisy panic amongst the entire farmyard population.

"What's gittin' intae his nut this roaad?" enquired young Steve, the third in line for the throne, as he temporarily set down a milk churn which he had been waltzing across the yard.

"Nothing... I mean... he seems a bit upset at something, doesn't he?"

"Summat ye said 'appen - gits upset ower nowt our Jake, it's his liver! Just soort o' snaps, and ye nivver knaw what ye've said or done as hesn't suited him."

"By the looks of it Steve, it's more likely to be something I didn't say, something he maybe wanted me to say."

"Didn't mention that Billie did he - th'ousekeyper? Sore point wi' our Jake that is ye knaw."

"Billie? She seems to be very efficient, and industrious."

"Tha can say that again Minister," said Steve dissolving into loud laughter. "Here, cum in here wi' me, and I'll tell tha summat," he went on, and beckoned me towards an annexe off the milk parlour, where on entering I found other four of his brothers systematically skiving, and smoking furtively.

"Now that tha's mentioned this here Billie, I should tell tha for a stairt, all ower th'owld man she is... not deycent...pampers him tae de-eath she does... not let him dae owt for hisel' nor nowt."

"Owldun's all ower her an' all he is...summat shameful," snapped Ossie.

"Randy owld sod," muttered young John, "Owld eneough tae be her faather twice ower."

"I'm sure your father may mean well," I protested, "Perhaps he's just trying to demonstrate his appreciation for her good services and he—" My unintentional *double entendre* was cut short in mid-flow by a general round of caustic laughter which was a long time in fizzling out.

"Summat not reyght gawin' on atween them two ah tells tha, plain as a pike stack that is...all ower their feyaces, and t'way they leyeks at yan another when they're suppin' their tea." The rare voice came from an obscure corner where young Jimmy was sitting precariously on an upturned pail. Jimmy had a reputation for silence. Indeed it was known that at times his voice would never be heard during the course of a whole week. Unfortunately when he did choose to give vent to speech, he was unstoppable, usually producing a preponderance of words with no corresponding abundance of ideas. Jimmy was the classic brooder, but rarely hatched anything of significance.

"Owldun wants tae marry t'woman Ah think, that's what these lot say. She wants tae marry him mare leyke, I say, rule the roost then wiln't she, feather her ain nest into t' bargain." Jimmy had got going.

"Is that what's eating Jake?" I managed to squeeze in rapidly so as not to betray the fact that such suspicions had not evaded me.

"Aye, that's it," bawled big Ossie, "Wants her for hisel', 'appen."

"Cum off it," corrected John, "Our Jake wouldna' touch that yan wi'a muck rake... heerd him say sae mare than yance."

"Matter of fact," said Steve resolutely, "Our Jake's afeared that if owt happens tae faather, well... ivrythi—"

"Hod tha stupit gob our Steve, tha's alweys spekin' out o' turn tha is," checked Ossie as though flaunting his seniority.

It was at that very moment that big brother Jake made his appearance, "Cum on ye lot, time for t'milkin'. stop larkin' around." At this command the entire assembly broke up and each went his separate way, including Jake. Much to my relief, I readily confess. And I promptly went my separate way.

The weeks went by, with the astute Billie continuing to lavish her excessive ministrations and tender care upon old Eb, managing his household, and his sons, with ostentatious efficiency. I have to admit that during all this time I gave the Newbury farm a wide berth, having no strong desire to become embroiled in what held promise of being the break up of a hitherto closely bound family. The wedding was duly arranged so that willingly, or otherwise, I was implicated once more. To my amazement, the very public announcement elicited neither shock nor surprise in the neighbourhood. It was common enough practice for widowed farmers to marry their housekeepers, for perfectly genuine reasons of true love. There were situations however where it was not easy to ignore the suspicion of such material considerations as economic advantage for the man, and pecuniary ambition on the part of the lady. A wide disparity in ages was not a relevant factor.

The arrangements for the grand wedding went ahead unabated, and although not with indecent haste, certainly with widespread publicity. As expected the Sneaton Burn chapel was to be the venue, and invitations went out far and wide. Eb's sons were putting on a brave show, as though accepting the inevitable with quiet acquiescence. Not that their resentment of the invader was unknown. If discussed in village circles, it was always in a soft, eyes-sideways whisper. As for myself, not yet accustomed to such heavy stuff, I continued to anticipate the event with no small misgiving. There was the easy acceptance of the affair by the local populace, the restrained but real antagonism of Eb's sons, and his own apparent indifference to what motives, respectively, lay behind this union. Helpless, I found myself beginning to respond with a degree of patronisation, and even condescension. Surely a solemn reminder of the fact that the moment you feel superior to your subjects, you've immediately branded yourself their inferior.

But alas and alas, the great day was not to be. With but one week left to go, and without any preliminary indications, Ebeneezer Newbury suffered a massive stroke, and died within a few hours. The funeral was a grand affair, with people gathered together from far and wide. Billie turned out in heavy drapes of deep, flouncy black, topped by a wreath-like hat lavishly adorned in a voluminous veil. The lady was distraught with grief, and laid on generous displays of histrionics whenever the audience was right, and splendid theatrical faints whenever the man with the brandy bottle was within close range.

Eb proved to be as capable of producing shocks and surprises in death as he had been in life. In his elaborate will he had bequeathed his entire estate to his eldest son Jake - that was the one he'd 'gat outa the fust weyfe'. Whether there were any practical provisos in favour of the remainder of his sons, or what furore was created within the family I was never to know, and for that I was grateful. On my subsequent pastoral visits to that bereaved family I was careful to avoid the subject, for what was done, was done. Surface appearances would indicate that the lads had willingly transferred their loyalty (or servitude) to their elder brother. Billie carried on, although by no means regardless, for she had exchanged her cosmetic smile for pitiful spasms of synthetic grief, again whenever the audience was right. She displayed a fearful anorexia at meal times, in spite of which she continued to show no outward evidence of impoverishment. Her moods varied by the hour, fluctuating between extremes of demonstrative high spirits and sullen morbidity. I attempted to fulfil my obligatory post-bereavement pastoral duty towards her, but to little avail, either because of my incompetence, Billie's refusal to be comforted, or her habitual inability to sustain reasonable conversation. We got little further than the usual mish-mash of incoherence, misapprehension, and contradiction. I soon began to suspect that her confusion was clear evidence of some inner drive recently repressed - anger perhaps, frustration, or even - God forgive me - thwarted ambitions. I might have been able to scotch such wild speculations at their inception, had it not been for Billie's oft re-iterated,

"After all I did for him - nothing - not a brick or a penny piece."

Soon there was to come a happy day in the annals of the Newbury tribe. It came to pass that Jake, the elder, gathered his brothers together from field and barn and far away places where they sojourned on that day. Handing to each one of them in turn a handsome cheque, he said unto them,

"A's decided, all by mesel' meynd ye, tae share a big lump o' faather's capital amang ye all. We're all brothers aren't we - well...soort of onyweys. I din't suppose it'll meyake a lot o' difference tae the way we gaws on here, but t'money should meyake better men o' ye all, 'cos neyen o' us hes ivver had much afore."

It was never disclosed however what proportion of Eb's capital Jake had retained, in addition to the entire assets of land, property and stock, nor in what measure he had rewarded each of the lads. And the family instinct for unquestioning obedience ensured that the secret was permanently in safekeeping.

As for Billie, her period of spectacular mourning was of relatively short duration, and in evaporating gave way to a general attitude of petty resentment. Nevertheless she continued to perform her duties to the letter, although it could be said that there was a marked falling-off in her standard of domesticity, and a distinct drop in the level of her 'tender loving care'.

Not many days hence, the children of Ebenezer arose one morning and beheld that the woman Billie had departed, and they were stricken with sore displeasure, for she had, not so much as bidden them farewell. Her room where she had dwelt in peace and prosperity lay stripped of all its possessions, and she had not deigned to leave a forwarding address. And behold on that same day (a co-incidence surely!) the younger son, whose name was Jimmy, gathered all his goods together, and the remnant of his recent inheritance, and with his new car which gleamed like the sun at noonday, had taken his journey into a far country, together with well, one can only presume - that's all.

Chapter 29

NYMPHS AND SHEPHERDS

"Nice long walk'll do you the world of good - benefit to body, soul, and mind I'd say," enthused dear wife Gina, as we stood at the window looking out over the glorious Lyndass valley.

"Care to come with me - sure your body, soul, and mind are equally in need of similar benefit. Lovely walk like that deserves nice company as well I'm sure."

"O, I agree wholeheartedly, I'd simply love to join you, but, duty calls - Ugh. Whoever the fiend was who invented Women's Meetings, to be held on hot sunny afternoons like this should have been burned at the stake," Gina protested. "But duty first I'm afraid, even for poor little me."

"In which case just forget about the walk darling shall we? I'll slip across to Bleabeck in the car as usual. It's more direct, takes up less time, and of course a good deal easier on the constitution. The footpath's really quite a long way round you know, and a bit rough going in places too. And it's such a hot day."

"But I simply insist - you should take that walk, good for you in so many ways. Sorry I cannot come, but tell you what, I'll accompany you in spirit. Now won't that be nice for you - course it will."

I confess that as I continued to look out of the window, across the valley and over the river towards the hamlet of Bleabeck, the prospect of a lone, leisurely walk began to hold out some special attraction. There was an aura of mystery in the scene before me. I felt a strange sense of affinity with Nature's artist who had designed it which seemed to beckon me towards it.

"Alright dear you win, I'll go walkies all by myself. You're quite right you know, I do need something like a solitary walk to unwind me a wee bit."

"You'll need to change your clothes. You can't go wearing all that clerical clobber walking over there on a day like this - you'll roast alive - might tear your breeches as well. No time for propriety or parsonic etiquette or whatever it's called surely. Open-necked shirt and drills would be just right. The village folk will understand...you're maybe the parson, but you're still human, and as likely to get over-heated as anybody else," remonstrated the very practical Gina. "Off you get now, and see you later."

The river ambled lazily under the rickety old iron footbridge, and was crystal clear. At this point, its characteristic verve and dash had deserted it, as it resolved into slow bends and waltzing eddy pools to brace itself for the deep plunge over the rocky falls into the Lyndie Gorge, half a mile further downstream. The mossy turf of the riverside footpath was a deep pile carpet of greens and golds which induced a gentle spring into the step. The rest of the track was likewise lush and unspoiled even where it narrowed through the tangled undergrowth, cut deep swathes through banks of mature bracken, dodged in and out of clumps of low bushes or petered out into wide barren patches. This path was seldom traversed, except by the local salmon poachers who, with their torches and gaffs plied their illicit trade in the dead of night. The balmy air was heavily overloaded with the sweet scents of dried-out grasses and early heathers. The drooping shrubs were too tired to wave a frond. The music-makers whistled a soft symphony, overlaid with piping and trilling solo calls. A myriad insects hummed harmoniously and the nectar gatherers droned drowsily among the undergrowth. The placid river rippled a rhyme over the stones, punctuated at intervals by the percussive plop of a leaping fish. Gradually my enraptured senses were lulled so that my mind wandered carefree, idly drifting... drifting... dri...

"Hey there! Hello dreamer! Got yourself lost then?"

The sharp abruptness of this harsh intrusion, which didn't seem to emanate from any recognizable direction but from everywhere at once, brought me reeling back to earth. But what was it? And why? Obviously but an echo misconstrued, or some mischievous fantasy sprung up from out of the subconscious. I was going crazy? Perhaps the music was mesmeric or there was something intoxicating in the air?

"Where? Where?" I called out jokingly to myself, feeling superficially futile and foolish, "Where? Ha, ha, ha." But then to my utter astonishment methought I perceived a low, dull, husky voice, not my own echo at all, calling back,

"Over here silly... down by river... here... look you!"

Things began to become even worse, for now the imaginary voice turned into an apparition, standing bolt upright on a mound of sandy shingle down by the water's edge. The phantom had form and substance, and although it still seemed rather unreal and exaggerated, the stance induced a flash reminder of the spicy front-cover pictures on certain male-orientated illustrated magazines. As she, or it, swaggered with slow deliberation towards me, my fear that I was hallucinating gave way to a train of unseemly physical observations, my noting in particular that the titillating female attributes on display were in generous and well ordered proportions. The girl's pale blue two piece swimsuit was, to say the least, and in terms of the accepted standards of those days, somewhat risqué. In spite of the conscience battle now being waged between my eyes and my mind, I was intrigued to note that the two pieces did not add up to very much, were close fitting, and immodestly far apart. A quick calculation told me that the lady must have acquired the outfit at some earlier stage in her development. Transfixed by a pleasant blend of shock, surprise and muscle binding fascination, I stood motionless and speechless, as with her slow, rolling gait she continued to move towards me. This was surely no crazy illusion, no product of a disordered mind, but of Nature itself. The spectre turned out to be real, tangible flesh and blood, with most of the flesh on vivid display, and pheromones oozing from every pore. The mobility had melted out from my eyeballs, and I was powerless to stave off the lewd observation that if there is such a faculty as body language, then this girl was singularly eloquent in its application. She would appear to be in her middle twenties, was fairly tall and sported a well cultivated elegance of posture. She had very white skin (almost transparent?) and her face bore faint blemishes from a past history of teen-age acne (not an affliction suffered by ghosts, surely?) Her hair was black, and lank; or was it wet? When she prepared to speak, her large dark eyes cast sly sideways glances, and when she smiled, her shapely lips shifted slightly to the left. She writhed rhythmically as she addressed me in a flat alto voice, and ecstatically stroked her left thigh with her right knee. More fleshly observations taunted me, for this wench was fantastically physical; an exquisite symmetry of soft, smooth concaves and convexes, harmoniously balanced and well held together.

"What a lovely day," she croaked.

"Y-y-yes it s-sure is, act-actually," I squeezed out, managing to wrest my larynx free from its vocal paralysis, "and qu-quite h-hot t-too."

"Very nice though isn't it," the voice coming over like the low notes on a piano struck hard with the soft pedal depressed.

"Yes, very nice... indeed...actually," was all I could muster, and that right bashfully, now convinced that this thing was real.

The cautious preliminaries dried up at this point, and the girl stood closely scrutinizing me with large shifty eyes. It felt like a strip search with a blowtorch. Before I could call up some suitable cue word by which to resuscitate the exchange, I became uncomfortably aware that this nymphatic creature had moved sufficiently close up to me to intriguingly engage my entire field of forward vision. The result was that I could achieve no reaction save a short quivering cough. Then the plucky girl calmly broke the spell,

"Nice day for a bathe... absolutely adorable."

"O yes... sw-swimming... yes... good...you been having a sw-swim?"

"Damn no. A sunbathe I mean silly. Pity to be all cluttered up with lots of clothes on a gorgeous hot day like this. Don't you think so?"

"Sure... yes...of course... you're quite right... actually...what I really mean is—"

"You wish you weren't all cluttered up, that's it isn't it? Such a nice quiet spot this you know, and nobody ever rarely comes down here. So peaceful, and lonesome... I simply love it. Better with some nice company mind you, and... well, you seem awfully nice... awfully nice."

I felt the red pointer on my fluster scale swish round to ultimate, and a hot feeling ran right up my neck and seemed to singe my scalp. Which acutely reminded me of the absence of my clerical collar; that wondrous failsafe device. There are situations when that exclusive implement of dress, although of questionable comfort, is the parson's refuge and strength, and a very present help in time of trouble. It is even more than that, for it at once protects the wearer against crude assaults upon his tender conscience from without, and conceals any residual element of male mischief which may yet lurk within.

"Not at work today then? Day off? Half day perhaps? Lucky you," I succeeded in unscrambling from my blubbering lips.

"Damn no. Not quite anyhow. Call it an extended holiday if you like. All the time in the world I have. But I gets a bit sick of being on me own all the time. I say, isn't it just smashing that you came along?"

"Yes, very nice, at least I'm glad you say so. But it's not my day off I'm afraid... on duty actually...really must be getting along."

"You've got to be kidding. What sort of duty's this? Work you say... over here? What are you - bailiff or summat of that kind? You talk rather posh, don't you?"

"No, not quite. I'm a minister... parson... out of uniform of course, rather like you." How I wished I could take that one back.

"Hell's bells, come off it, you're just trying to tease me. Anyways you don't look owt like a vicar to me, Parson? Phew! Bet you're a right prudie an' all. Are you - really? I say what strong eyes you have—"

"Not exactly... what I mean is...not a prude neither... don't think I am anyway... but I can't help it i—"

"Where's tha funny collar anyways? Vicars wear queer collars don't they? Puts them on back'ards an' all... don't knaw whether they're cumin' or goin... don't knaw theirsel's really do they?" The girl was obviously unimpressed by my claim to clerical status, if indeed that would have meant anything significant to her. It certainly didn't inhibit her all of a sudden.

"Say I bet them collar things gets all hot and sweaty on a day like this - ugh! Must be like stickin' tha head outa t'top of a Turkish bath." And she laughed with some small derision.

"Well I suppose I should know. Yes, quite right, all hot and steamy and stuffy. Always glad to be out of them. Nuisance in so many ways." If by now I had but a modicum of decorum left, this worldly wench's rolling liquid eyes were peeling it off from me layer by layer, and especially as she was now high on mirth. She had just squeezed another slip out of me.

"It all gaws to show," she mused, "a man's a man for a' that eh! And tha's all alike, 'cept for t'clothes, aren't ye now?"

"Well, sort of, I mean not exactly, not always that is, depend—"

"And you all look t'same underneath, when tha's got nowt on at all, and think the same sort o' things in tha heads an' all. And most on ye are like the bairns...

and like nowt better than running around in your birthday suit, sort o' showin' off like."

At this the girl broke into a bout of gravelly earthy laughter which sent swift ripples across every inch of visible flesh. I was at a loss as to how I should follow up that last remark to avoid being misunderstood. I fully realised that it was becoming imperative for me to make a determined effort to divert the alarming drift of this conversation. What could I do, or say, in order to seize and hold on to the initiative? Perhaps, after all, I ought to have taken a tip from the ancient parable and passed this one by on the other side. But she did just materialize out of thin air, didn't she?

"I'm on my way to Bleabeck actually," I blurted, searching for a convenient bolt hole, "I've got to call on someone very special there."

"Someone very special eh? A date I bet... naughty boy." And thus did my first attempt go awry. And yet, I didn't feel the least resentful of her fascinating audacity. Whatever was coming over me? "Did you say Bleabeck?" she quizzed, "Bit of a long way round is it not? What's wrong wi' t'road then?"

"Well, it's an exceptionally nice day, and I had a spot of spare time on my hands. Besides it's so peaceful, and quiet, and secluded over here isn't it, and i—"

"Hey ho. Two minds with but a single thought... I knew it. But it was my idea first wasn't it. But both thinking t'same anyways."

"They say that great minds think alike, don't they," I jested, thus dealing the death blow to my feeble bid for the initiative or whatever, and freedom.

"Hey, we've found summat in common you an' me. I bet we've got loads of things in common if we really got down to it. O I say, am I supposed to call ye 'Vicar', or 'Rev'rent', or 'Father' or summat? Sounds a bit daft to me...'cos you're far ower friendly for that aren't ye. Which reminds me, it's even dafter still 'cos here we are, you and me, chatting each other up like two old pals, and we haven't even been properly introduced. What's your name anyways?"

"Teviot...Don Teviot... haven't lived here long... well, just about a year I think, or thereabouts."

"I like it... Don Teviot... sounds so romantic. Mine's Sal Monaghan. Everybody just calls me Sal... hate Sally, don't you? Horrible. Besides, it's a bit common isn't it?"

"Then how about the full treatment... Sarah?"

"Hell no... Sarah... save me from it." she screeched, dissolving into liquid laughter.

"Well, I agree, it's perhaps a wee bit formal... Sarah I mean. So we'd better stick to Sal, shall we? Anyway I rather like the sound of Sal, it seems just right somehow," and with this near miss I made the startling discovery that I was laughing carefree.

"You like Sal, don't you, just plain Sal. Call me all the nice names you like." she cooed, "Sal included."

"I'm going to stick to Sal - yea. Sort of more... intimate... more... yes inti—"

Fortuitously an eruption deep down in my oesophagus mercifully checked the idiotic slide, and Sal was ready to rush in.

"I'm going to call you Donnie... nice one that... matches Sal a treat don't you think... and they sound just right together don't they. Hey! I've just thought on, I used to have a little Scottie dog called that when I was a kid. Randy little beggar he was an' all - cute little bundle o' mischief, but he was ever so sweet was Donnie. Perhaps all Donnies are alike eh. Know what, in some ways you just remind me of him, you're quite cute, and well... you know what."

I tried hard to appear unimpressed by this frightening speculation, but this girl knew no discouragement. The whole encounter was beginning to shift well over onto the outside of my forte, and yet in spite of my conscious resolve to disengage, my best efforts seemed futile before the onslaught. At the same time I was beginning to suspect that my fascination with this curvocative arrangement of creature delights was tending to outweigh my natural reservations. Why had this subtle teaser so many titillating tricks? And such prowess in the arts of writhing erotica?

"I really must be getting along Sal, duty calls I'm afraid," I spluttered with considerable fluster.

"Duty, what's that? Come off it Donnie boy, nice hot day like this, we like each other's company an awful lot... nobody's in a hurry surely. There's nowt but can wait, I bet. You're just havin' me on aren't you, playin' hard to get stuff aren't you?"

"Well, I suppose there's not really any immediate rush, well not for a few minutes or so anyway...what I mean is...well... I've simply got to go over to the village of course." My resolve was starting to emulate the weakness of my knees.

"Anyway, I've just been thinkin' - what are we standin' here like a couple o' dried up stooks for anyway?"

"Well I really don't know, do you? Well what else is there, except as I've said, better be on my way, not waste any more of your afternoon."

Sal's warm fingers materialised in my right hand, which surprisingly, didn't fall off. I sat down on the grassy ledge near the water's edge beside her large laid out towel and meagre pile of folded clothes. She did not join me there immediately, but stood before me, rather close, her formidable array of physical features totally obliterating my view of the world beyond, leaving me only with the other two members of the dreadful trio, flesh and devil.

"Pity you hadn't brought any swim trunks," she said squirmingly.

"O I do have some you know, but I'm not in the habit of carrying them around with me you see," I addressed to her navel, discomfited by the sense that all my resolve had dissolved.

"You go in stark naked then, do you? You are a one Donnie. I bet you don't swim, anyway."

"As a matter of fact I do - swim I mean - and in swim trunks. Strong swimmer actually... life saving certificate and all that. How about you Sal?"

"Me swim? Water's ower shallow. Who's talking about swimming anyway? Get me swimsuit wet, wash me suntan stuff off. What's wrong wi' just sun bathing anyways? Hot sun on t'skin does quite an awful lot for you... come over all tingly and warm... feel all natural... biological... frisky...nice... real stuff...all ower t'body like." Sal accompanied this intelligence with seductive downward caresses of her ample profile.

"Are you really tingling, and warm, and energetic all over Sal?" I swear that I did not intend that one to come over in that form, or to come out at all.

"Oo-er, that I am. Nice and soft, and warm, every inch of my body." I felt the panic building up inside, and feared it might indicate a rise in the hormone count. This situation was becoming more absurd every time I spoke, yet nevertheless had to be taken seriously. It was imperative that I head off this lecherous female somehow, without disrespect of course.

"Sal my friend look here. I'm sorry, but really I must be going," I announced with wobbly boldness, "time's getting on."

"You're scared o' me aren't you? Poor dear, I think you're trembling."

"It's not that I'm scared of you Sal, or anything else. I'm quite happy just sitting here actually, don't misunderst—"

"What did I tell you, I've got it right, you like me a lot don't you Donnie - I really get you going don't I?"

"Well yes, I suppose I do... I mean you don't ge— well." And before I could turn these maverick jerks into a coherent defence, Sal had flopped herself down close by me. Obviously the time had come for a new ploy, more determined, more energetic. These very sentiments seemed to ring hollow in my mind, for up until now all the advantage had been to Sal, and she was increasing the pressure. What about a spot of sly cunning? Like giving the impression of going along with her, like something underhand, catch her unawares, grasp the initiative? What a sordid train of thought. Worth the attempt, with suitable safeguards.

"Listen Sal, of course I like you, so glad I came over this way today, and that I made your charming acquaintance. I already feel we've known each other for a long time. You're a smashing lass Sal. But we've got to admit, we're still strangers. We perhaps need a bit more familiarity between us." (*O hell where did that one spring up from*?) "What I mean is get to know more about each other. Let's each tell each other a little bit about ourselves shall we?"

Without a second's hesitation Sal launched into her life story as though she was burning inside. She was a native of Lyndassby but had, until recently, worked in London, where everything was fast moving, glittering, colourful, exciting, and above all happy. She had unfortunately lost her job, not through her own fault of course, and was now stuck back here in this lousy, boring hole. Her family were not thrilled to have her home, and openly resented her hanging around them. All of her former acquaintances were either married by now, or had moved out. 'Boys? You must be kidding - seen this lot around here?' She was utterly unhappy and forlorn, and not a little lonesome. She was twenty-five last birthday, but knew that she didn't look it. Sal did not expend any excess of emotion over these disclosures, but rasped them out in a dull, crouped monotone. I never got round to making my contribution, before Sal, in spite of my efforts to coerce the conversation towards subjects of a more general nature, retrieved the initiative and reverted to matters of more immediate concern.

"You said you were going to t'village yonder to see somebody very special. Is she nice?"

"Yes Sal, very nice, and sweet, and pretty, and kind, and—"

"Lot better'n me then?" Why did she have to pout her lips just then?

"Different Sal, that's all, different."

"But not nicer? And you still like me don't you? I'm glad, 'cos you see I'll still be hangin' around here when you come back. You'll not need to be very long will you?" That dark molasses voice again.

"Look Sal my friend. It would sure be nice to find you still here later, and it's good of you to wait, but really I haven't a clue how long I will have to be at Bleabeck, nor even whether I'll be able to come this way back at all."

"That's it then, she must be nicer than me. Special date isn't it? You're a bit of a flirt that's what. Aren't you,— flirt?"

"Sal, let me say, you're simply gorgeous, and it's been just great meeting you here, a most pleasant accident. But you're getting me all wrong, so please listen. I'm on my way to see a very charming little girl, and I love her very much. Her name is Philippa, but she prefers to be called Pippa. She's only nine years-old Sal. She is totally crippled and can't move a thing from her neck downwards. But she makes up for it all with her face. You should see her smile Sal, and hear her chuckle. Somehow she makes all your own troubles melt away. She's a little angel bubbling over with radiant happiness and simple love Sal."

"In that case the kid wouldn't mind waitin' a bit would she? I mean she'll still be around when you get there won't she? She's not going to wander very far is she? So you're not really in that big a hurry to get away are you?" Sal said blandly.

"Her father left home a couple of years ago, ran off with some fancy hussy, and has never been heard of since. Pippa's mother is a lovely soul, sad a bit, and not in the best of health herself."

"Hey. I know what - it's t'mother you've got your eye on, you're after kid's mother, you blo—"

"Sal that's most unkind, it's just not like you at all, and I know you didn't mean it bad. Listen, about Pippa's mother. As I told you, health's a bit shaky and that shows up a lot when she has to push the little girl's wheel chair about, and more especially on the days she has to go out to work. Got to try and make ends meet I suppose, her only source of income. Works up at Matt Torrie's place. Not a fit job for a woman, rough a bit. She get's down in the dumps very often, and thinks she's neglecting Pippa and hasn't enough to give her to make her happy and all that sort of thing. Very tragic Sal isn't it, very tr—"

"How sad. Poor kid," said Sal with no evidence of feeling, "Anyway Donnie you hurry along then and get your job done, and get back here eh. I'll still be hangin' around awaitin' for you." The low pitched voice was flat, and its huskiness made it sound as though it originated from an accumulation of ice crystals. Her cold eyes appeared to have frost in them. I now had little difficulty in bracing myself for a break away.

"Guess I must be going then Sal. Won't mind will you?"

To my surprise, and relief, Sal stood up sharply, leaving behind an outstretched hand, by which she assisted me to my feet with a vigorous snatch. I earnestly swear that I had no deliberate part in the soft, sensuous, full-bodied collision which the action precipitated. Further to my surprise and relief, the brief encounter sent no shock waves vibrating through my system. I however put every resource that system could call up into my endeavour to walk away with cool, calculated, calm. Alas, my legs would not co-operate, and neither would my faculty for concentrating my energies in that direction. I had not proceeded far along the footpath before I was swooning in a pleasing hangover from the feast of carnal delight my eyes had lately enjoyed. Yet surely, such sordid musings were incompatible with my calling, and detrimental to my present errand. On the other hand is not a harmless twinge of the rudimentary instincts perfectly normal in a healthy young male such as me? Surely my present discomfiture arose from the fact that the ethos of my calling conditions an exaggerated guilt response towards any sense impression with sexual implications. And yet, a thing is no less naughty because it's nice, and sensual pleasure, even if it operates but at the periphery of conscious thought, is no less perverse. Nevertheless Sal was right, a man's a Man for all that, and that includes me. The clerical halter about my neck cannot stifle my basic humanity. And what about libido? Good old Freud - liberating, frank, refreshing. Much of what we've been schooled to regard as sin is after all a perfectly legitimate phenomena associated with incidental fluctuations in the cerebral chemistry. But of course there is what we call conscience still to be reckoned with. Yet what is that after all but a conditioned reflex and a do-it-yourself affair at the best of times, therefore never an infallible guide. This inspired bout of soothing self-analysis enabled me to come to terms with my present predicament and move forward with a more confident stride. It also threw me off guard. I had proceeded less than a hundred yards when a powerful compunction crept up on me from behind and swung me completely about to take a look back towards the place where Sal was now sitting bolt upright on her brightly coloured bath towel. The saucy girl affected a lop-sided smile and a slow sensual wave of the right hand. A red hot frisson severely shook my equilibrium and sent my mind back into a whirl. It occurred to me that if biblical precedent is anything to go by, I should have instantly turned into a pillar of salt. No such judgement descended upon me however, neither did my conflicting emotions petrify, and so the dubious moral debate continued. All manner of inordinate affections contended with more chaste aspirations for mastery of my mind, and again the sinews of my lower limbs lost their elasticity. But this bad run of specious reasoning had afforded me no respite or justification, and I turned instinctively to the convenient device of guilt transference. I forced my mind into denigrating the object of my distress. This wily temptress had wilfully sprung this whole fleshy episode upon me. Cheap seducer... common hussy... lecherous cow... mischievous vamp. She had cast a spell, that's what - who said that there are no such creatures as witches or river fairies? And even in this was I not behaving in full accordance with what is called human nature, for it is of the mores of the male of the species to switch accountability over to the woman for any deviation from the path of virtue or honour which he may contemplate. Has it not been so from that primal day in the Garden of Eden, when Adam in his pristine innocence fell victim of the allurements of the scantily attired Eve? And had not our Great Designer stacked the odds heavily against the man? This magnificent diversion towards bible based logic was sufficient to provide a morsel of respite and effect some rapid repairs to my shattered ego, thus enabling me to proceed without caution. A disastrous mistake, for inducing a mood of self-righteous complacency, it laid open my flank to incursion by the paramount sin of sheer, unmitigated pride. With a smug sense of pious content I became profoundly thankful that I had not responded as most other men would have done, given similar circumstances. Pompous Pharisee, male chauvinist pig. The sensation went bad on me, so loathsome that it dried out my mouth. Pride inevitably precedes the fall, and right then an irrational impulse so powerful that I was acting upon it before I could get a grip of myself, stopped me in my tracks and wheeled me round to indulge my wanton eyes just this once more upon this object of rare fleshly delight, the act holding out such rich promise of a fleeting moment of legitimate pleasure. After all surely it would provide an effectual foil to my inhibitions. I was thoroughly mocked, for at this distance a large clump of bracken on rising ground had interposed between Sal and me. But male fantasy is ever ready to compensate, and requires no corresponding factual reality to render it vivid and pleasurable. My errant thought processes went wild with frustration and I pictured Sal's soft curvaceous form, fully reclined on her multi-coloured towel, where she lay in dreamy sun worship, awaiting my return. Another swing of the moral pendulum and I was recoiling at the bitter pain of repugnance. Sad for myself I became sad for Sal. The whole thing required calm, cool, steady re-appraisal. Perhaps I had grossly misjudged her. Any apparent sensuality on her part was but a product of my over-sensitive, or selfish, and biased imagination. Sensuality can be in the eye of the beholder, and the mind is most readily seduced from within. In accordance with the wont of the reluctantly virtuous, I had projected my complexes onto the other, in order to expunge my soul of any guilt in the matter. Perhaps Sal was, after all, but an ordinary country girl who for a season had been over-exposed to the dazzling lights of the big city. Her immature romantic insights had been knocked askew, and she simply could not relate very well to the opposite sex. Poor kid, so naive, pathetic, artless, bored, unsuccessful, attractive. But so lonely - such simple, seductive, loneliness. And regaining some balance I began to regret that I had been so stupefied by the raw presentation of Sal's physical configurations that I had been unmindful of her spiritual dimension. In any event, for some reason best explained by the behavioural sciences, this young minx's unwitting tease game had, as she suspected, got something going in me, unearthed a number of mild repressions, deranged my moral equilibrium, confused my theological concepts, and divested me of every clout of self-esteem, leaving me with no more moral fibre than one of Pavlov's dogs.

Feeling thus I fled from the scene of my humiliation with what I intended to be firm resolute strides. There was now no question of turning back, looking back, thinking back, or of ever straying into the path of Sal or her likes again. Within a short distance however my resolute right foot planted itself on a very unresolute stone and I was sent sprawling into the dense undergrowth. This 'stone of stumbling' left me with no will to struggle back onto my feet, but simply to lie there until I had once and for all resolved this ludicrous situation. From whom was I running away anyway? Surely not from Sal, a mere girl, overtly sexual perhaps, but nevertheless but a simple, gullible creature. Rather from me. Poor miserable fool from whom there was no escape. This wily wench had brought to surface an alter ego of which I was afraid and secretly ashamed? But my respectable conscience was having none of it and my defences soon shimmered back into another bout of fatuous reasoning. Alright, the close proximity of an attractive female in a sparse swimsuit by a lonely riverside on a sultry afternoon had sent my systems whirling. Why make a conflict of that? Perfectly natural - given the circumstances - a spot of innocent lust or a venial slip into pleasurable fantasy are but normal symptoms of healthy male virility. Besides which, I had done nothing improper, not succumbed to anything fleshy, but contained it all within the mind. Except, except - that lust is the seed of transgression, the act in the germ. Did not the Good Lord whom I serve pronounce that evil arises from within and that the desire is as fraught with guilt as the act. Damn Freud! Grief man - not again - we've been over all this lot before. Will this crazy game of seesaw logic not go away.

Just at that point it came. A sudden bolt from the blue which blasted to smithereens the shabby facade of plusses and minuses which had so engaged me. The missing factor. The painful realisation that throughout the whole duration of this disgusting interlude I had suppressed all thoughts which would have inhibited my enjoyment of those titillating moments of carnal mischief. Including my awareness of Gina, the dear wife who is allegedly my whole life. Surely the love which binds should regulate the inner as well as the outer man. And Ordination, that all-binding Sacrament. Are the obligations of this holy vocation to be waived with the temporary shedding of the dog-collar? But for the love of my lovely wife and the grace of God where would I be now? Mercifully I was spared further conflict, for on springing abruptly on to my feet the village of Blaebeck came into view, I saw also that another visitor had preceded me at Pippa's cottage, for Dr. MacLoughlin's big Armstrong Siddely was standing nearby. I met the brusque physician as he left the house and stood by the gate. A hearty conversation ensued, during which, for some unfathomable reason, I slipped in a fleeting mention of the girl Sally Monaghan. The good doctor was in like a flash,

"Och wee Sally. Ye surely dinna ken her diye? I warrant she'll no be a member o' your flock, nor anybody else's for that matter. Braw lassie, but sae damned stupid in lots o' ways. Mind you, yon poor kid never had a chance to be anything other. Dragged up by the scruff o' the neck - quite literally sometimes. Rough lot... shabby a wee bit... auld man liked his ale too much... mother pathetic...awfi lot o' them ye ken...just forget how many."

"You know the family then?"

"Know them - ye can say that again. Now the day yon wee lassie was born - hell of a delivery I mind - Och just forget it. Now as I was saying, this wee Sally... took herself off to London a couple o' years back, and now they tell me she's come back all full o' frills and fancies and swanky talk. Probably went off to try and better hersel', if that was possible. Mind you she's never told anyone what she got hersel' up to down there, but well, knowing the background. All the same I dinna think she'll fit in up here any more, especially with that lot. No a bad looking lassie mind ye, bit anaemic I'd say... had a lot o' growing up problems a few years back... must be about twenty seven now. Pity, sic a pity, if she's got into wrong hands down there... pity."

"But she must have been fairly well grown up when she went away?"

"If she'll ever grow up. Worked up at the Knotty Stowp for a wee while, kitchen and bar, but a bit of a liability ye ken. You've met her then?"

"Well... yes... in some small way... what I mean is—"

"Bit hesitant ye are. Och aye, you've no got your holy eyes on wee Sally have ye? Ye'll never convert one o' that lot in a month o' Sundays."

"No, no. I was just wondering..."

"Wondering what? I'm killed with curiosity."

"Nothing... nothing really... not important actually...just—"

"Pastoral confidences eh? You fellas and your hypocritic oath. Och well nothing to do with me at all. Just didna want to see you embroiled with that bunch, even though you might mean well."

"No nothing like that, nothing at all. Just like you, a wee bit curious."

"Aye, well, so now, what about a far more interesting wee lassie? Young Phillipa in there, you're calling to see her I presume? Not showing any signs of improvement ye ken... not one bit... progressive I'm afraid. Sometimes one fears the worst for her... tragic... tragic. And that poor wee mother o' hers. That woman's worn out with worry and hard work. I tell ye, if I could get my hands on that rotten bastard man o' hers... bloody randy imbecile. Not very professional I know, but by hell I mean it."

I had become well inured to some fairly base notions during the past hour, and therefore this obscene outburst from the doctor didn't shock me. On the contrary, such were my immediate reactions that I earnestly wished that my own professional status had left me free to couch them in similar prose.

"Well, well," the good doctor sighed, "I'll need to be rolling along. And you'd better get yoursel' in there. Got a real fan there ye know. Young Phillipa thinks the very sun shines out o' you. Mind you, I ken ye better eh."

Strange, very strange indeed, but why was it that I recoiled slightly on this last remark?

The hour spent with Pippa was thrilling, and thoroughly therapeutic. Her face radiated with pleasure at my company, and her bright eyes flashed out sweet messages of childish love. The patience, courage, and the irrepressible spirit which this noble child displayed was an inspiration without equal. Time spent in her presence had a rich cleansing effect on the mind and soul, leaving you with your sense of worth dramatically enhanced.

Pippa had a good clear voice, slightly metallic, but perfectly pitched, and a superb gift for song. I used to accompany her on the old harmonium which stood in a corner of the small room which constituted the most part of her world. On occasions when conditions allowed, her mother would undertake the daunting task of pushing her wheelchair up the steep hill out of the village to a vantage point from where to view the surrounding countryside. This was Pippa's idea of Heaven. 'Good God,' I often thought, 'why do you ordain that an angelic little child such as this should suffer thus? Such cruel injustice should not be incorporate in the natural scheme of things. Is there no mercy, no pity, no love out there for this child who will never walk, never run, never skip, never jump, nor climb, nor swim, nor play in the sun among the sweet long grass, never grow up into a mature woman, but for her brief life will be a totally dependent invalid whom few will get to know well enough to love, and many will pity? Where's divine compassion, if such there be? Good God, are you listening?'

As I prepared to leave, albeit reluctantly, a sound of shuffling came from-the direction of the wheelchair, "Hest tha got a kiss for me Rev?" the sweet little face tilted in lovely entreaty. It was but a hasty peck, of the kind which little girls accompany with coy giggles, but it was full of love.

Leaving the cottage I walked home slowly, head bowed, with my mind a turmoil of tumultuous imponderables. Dominant was the thought that though my circumstances were changed, there remained an unknown soldier at work within me who would not be stilled. I took the more direct route home, by the road, and never as much as to cast a glance over in the direction of the riverside path. I must lay that memory to rest. On arrival I was greeted as usual, by Gina's hearty welcome, full of love,

"Had an interesting afternoon darling? My, you do look washed out."

******

On a sunny afternoon one week later to the very day, as I ventured up the main street of Lyndassby, I had the misfortune of encountering the Misses Millicent and Maud Bowran, ex-schoolmistress and ex-Postmistress respectively. Such a meeting invariably entailed a severe test of endurance on my part, including an elongated kerb-side conference on matters past, present, and future, polite small talk, and non-malicious gossip. I had long since expended on them my entire arsenal of ruses and dodges, but was not able to escape from their verbal grip. The dear ladies were sweet in the extreme, but the sweetness was that of honey, treacle, glycerine, and was powerfully adhesive. On this particular occasion, we had done the weather, my dear wife's health, my health, the dear ladies' health in great detail, old Mrs. Donkin's shingles, the new vicar at Keltonthorpe ('doesn't he look old my dear'), Matthew Towson's unexpected passing away at ninety-three, and we were just coming up to 'Aren't the flowers lovely just now' when the whole atmosphere seemed to erupt with,

"Hey there Donnie boy - fancy meeting you here." Suddenly I felt that the only thing which could save me from this hour would be a well-aimed earthquake.

Sally was right upon us, and planted incongruously in the midst of our respectable huddle. Should I formally introduce her, shoo her away, disown her, ignore her, or utilize the rude interruption in a bid to escape from the clutches of the two dear old ladies? None of these alternatives was appropriate or indeed possible, so I simply froze, staring blankly into the grinning face of Sal. That face seemed pale and sallow, yet well formed and quite pretty. Her straight black hair was immaculately groomed, and her perfume was potent as nerve gas. She stood tall and elegant, smartly dressed in a neatly tailored white cotton suit. The streak of forbidden machismo within me went to work immediately, bidding me observe how strikingly Sal contrasted with the two well bred articles of Victoriana from whom I was vainly trying to escape. Chuckling merrily in her wheelchair was dearest little Pippa.

"Sal's my new auntie, and I love her very much. Bet YOU don't know her, Uncle Rev. Auntie Sal's going to take me out every day, aren't you Auntie Sal?"

"Of course I am my darling, of course I am. Every day, up the road, through the woods, over the hills and far away."

There was a living, infectious tenderness in that low, husky voice, and the huskiness seemed to endue it with extra warmth.

"And my Auntie Sal says she knows a lovely quiet spot 'side the river where nobody else never goes, and it's always lovely and peaceful, and warm. And there's lots o' birds and fishes and things. And we can be all by ourselves Auntie Sal and me, 'cos nobody else knows where it is."

"That's right honey - it's a firm date - smashing place, and it's all ours, among the bracken, down by the river." said the husky one.

"And my Auntie Sal says we're going to sun bathe, 'cos I can't swim see, and have picnics, and watch fishes jumpin' and things, aren't we Sal, aren't we."

Just then the dear sisters stepped forward and commandeered little Pippa, whom they would insist on addressing as 'Pippula', and began to engage her in condescending conversation, as was their wont with children. This gave me an opportunity to step aside and speak with Sally more privately. Sally's whisper bore small resemblance to her normally crouped speaking voice, and was designed to ensure that confidences would come over as softly as a clanging cymbal.

"I didn't know that you knew Pippa," I quietly quizzed.

"I didn't know Pippa," she proclaimed, "that is until last week. Better tell you how I suppose, 'cos you're badly mixed up in it all, Of course you are, and you're bound to know why."

"Mixed up - in what? I mean - what the—"

"O come off it Donnie old pal, don't you remember? You see when you left me by the river-side last Wednesday remember - well I put my clothes back on and—"

"Shshshshshshshsh... Sal!"

"Well as I was saying, I got back into my things, and just didn't feel like sunbathing any more - I was that upset you know. I was, right upset, about what you told me about t'little girl and all that. I just lay there on me back like I was, starin' up at t'sky for a gay long time. Then I had a good cry... I did... I cried me bleedin' eyes out..."

Then I got up, and followed you, a long way ahint on you, but I nearly caught up on you 'cos you were agoin' so very slow. But I saw where you went to and I waited aback on a tree. Then you came out of th'ouse, I went and knocked on t'door and asked about Pippa, and I said I was a close friend on yours. Then Audrey, that's Pippa's mum you know, asked me in to see her. We had a great time the three on us I tell you, some tea, and some great times since an' all. And we're going to have some great times in the future an' all, I tells you."

I moved my lips, but no words would form.

This ordinary country girl, with languid eyes, luscious lips, and contours which would halt a marching army in its tracks, simple, uncultured, unsophisticated, had once, in all innocence almost incited my soul to rebellion. *Femme fatale*? Salacious Sal? Or - 'Angel unawares'?

"Well, here we are, ready to go now darling, got to go up to t'shop for lotsa sweets haven't we." Sal's voice had sweet music in it.

What looked like frowns of disapproval and disgust were exchanged by the two sisters, then aimed directly at Sally so as to glance off towards me. An awkward stillness followed, when I fancied that even the sparrows had ceased to twitter. It was only at that moment that I realised I was gently holding Sally's hands.

"O...phew... well... cheerio ladies, so nice to see you...lovely day. Now if you'll excuse me, I'll need to help push this heavy little monkey up the hill to that sweetie shop... Bye."

"Oo lovely. It'll be easy with you two pushing me together won't it. And you can both share my sweets with me. Can't he Auntie Sal."

My task accomplished, and sweets awarded, I turned and walked slowly home, a very sore chastened young minister - but a happy one.

"Had an interesting afternoon darling?" Bless you Gina!

Chapter 30

ARCHIE'S ANIMAL

Young Archie Trewitt was a scatterbrain. Only such a being would purchase so mighty and fearsome a machine as his motorcycle, when he himself stood but five feet one inch tall and weighed in at every ounce of eight stones. The said iron horse was a flashy exuberance of chromium plating and cerise enamel, with everything near expired with age and unfair wear-and-tear. At least, all except the flashiness. The great hulk sported the prestigious logo of 'Royal Enfield' emblazoned on either side of the saddle tank, and on a tattered blue pennant affixed to the tip of the front mudguard. The exact power rating was one of the machine's many imponderables, but my rough guess would be in the region of 450cc. Mind you, the blast from the large fishtail exhaust pipe was strongly suggestive of a horsepower running into thousands. The general impression given by the machine, even when merely standing idle on its support stay, was that of a large untamed stallion poised for a sudden bolt of mad fury.

It was no surprise therefore, that the undersize Archie was somewhat wary of the brute for the first few weeks of his proud ownership of it. He would often be seen traversing the gutters in bottom gear, keeping close to the grass verge at all times, so as to minimise the effects of a highly probable tumble. Enlightenment, confidence, bravado, or by any other name, seemed to come to Archie quite suddenly one day, onward from which there was no holding him back. Some men are born stunt riders, some acquire remarkable skill as stunt riders, and others have stunt riding thrust upon them. When Archie practised solo, on a local patch of barren moorland of course, it was difficult to assess which of these categories applied to him. There was never before in the history of cyclopedic locomotion, a rider so agile as he in executing the deft manoeuvre of letting go of the handlebars, and affecting a swift backwards leapfrog over the pillion at the slightest threat of a mishap. By some unknown providence, Archie and his red and chrome monster survived many tumbles, scrapes, and collisions. Several of the brave men of Lyndassby had in turn undertaken to give Archie some practical instruction, which of course entailed accompanying him per pillion. None was known however to have repeated the gesture after the first session. There was the occasion when I chanced my luck. After a few breathless hundred yards, Archie mounted and 'negotiated' a steep embankment at a death or glory slant, with one hand off the handlebars grappling with the gear lever in obedience to my mistimed instruction to 'Change into top...NOW', which mercifully he failed to achieve. That is until we were back on the level, or otherwise I might have suffered a far worse indignity than being deserted by a swiftly departing pillion seat, and left spinning on my posterior. Eventually, after many weeks of thrills and spills, during which Archie and his intrepid accomplices were oft in danger, oft in woe, our hero was sufficiently confident, although by no means competent, to take to the road, and instigate a new era of fear and terror in the fair land of Lyndassby. Most people were grateful that the machine conducted its business in so noisy a fashion, for this gave sufficient warning of its imminent appearance to enable the necessary precautions to be got under way. To the astonishment of all and sundry, Archie passed his driving test at the first attempt. Rumour established that the examiner was blind drunk, terrified out of his wits, or simply had no wish to run the risk of having to bring Archie back for a repeat performance.

At Archie's generous suggestion, I borrowed the machine on an occasion when my old car was indisposed. In my time I had flown, parachuted into enemy territory, gone through the rough in tanks, been tossed for days on choppy seas, and riding horses from childhood, but never had I experienced so terrifying a journey as my eight mile trip to Threckleby. The ordeal was akin to a ride on a bull camel gone berserk with its tail on fire. The front tyre was half deflated and making a frightening flapping sound, and the front suspension was partly adrift and rattled ominously. Together they ensured considerable steering difficulty. The gear lever, a hand operated device on the right side of the petrol tank, sent crippling vibrations up the arm each time you took hold of it, the sensation greatly enhanced by the fact that the ball-knob which normally would absorb such shocks, had been lost from the top of the handle. There was so much slack in the clutch cable, that gear changing was always a chancy business. Mind you, Archie had previously informed me that this model was fitted with a 'crash gearbox'. There was so much lee-way on the main drive chain that each time the engine was throttled up (and this could only be accomplished in jerks) the resounding slap shook the entire machine from end to end, and the rider throughout his total anatomy. The heat in the vicinity of the knees and lower legs was almost unbearable. The acrid smell of oil at boiling point, and pungent evidence of leaking petrol somewhere along the line induced a dread like sitting astride a time bomb. The exhaust report was, as aforesaid, so all pervading that it seemed to be coming from and going to everywhere at once. Then there was the small matter of the brakes. They didn't work. The front one had a broken wire, and hard pressure on the foot lever would only produce a shrill metallic scrape in the region of the rear wheel, but otherwise have little noticeable effect upon the overall volition of the vehicle. Whoever sold that infernal contraption to young Archie Trevitt should have been charged with culpable homicide. Indeed they might well have been, as the following episode might show.

It so happened, that aided and abetted by several others like-minded, I had persuaded Archie that the performance of his beloved steed would be greatly improved by a general overhaul, and that Mr. Ben Backnall of Rooksdale was the right man to do the job. The day came when my young friend set off to deliver the machine to the garage, with me accompanying him from some hundreds of yards to his rear in my spritely MG Midget, in order to bring him back home to Lyndassby. That journey was, to say the least, a hair-raising experience, the effects of which have, quite literally, never departed from me. I deliberately maintained what I considered to be a discreet distance between Archie and me, not only for the sake of safety, but because I was a reluctant witness to the road rodeo going on ahead of me. The numerous twists and turns, rises and falls of this particular section of highway nevertheless gave me cause for considerable anxiety, and extreme caution. My quarry would temporarily disappear from view on occasion, so that every time I broke out into the open, it was with some trepidation, and sometimes shock. Archie would always be driving too close to the rough edge of the road, too fast on the bends, erratically on the straight, and in all circumstances unpredictably. And there was the persistent fear that, even if the rider did possess the necessary skill to carry out an emergency manoeuvre, the old machine was not capable of the appropriate response to what would normally be called controls.

At last the top of Scraugh Fell came into view, and this offered some small consolation. Except for a double twist near the bottom, the road from here onwards included some long straight stretches, affording for the most part a clear line of vision. There were neither walls, fences, ditches, nor any other allurements, and on either side were wide grassy verges. Young Archie however confounded my best anticipation by converting the pleasing prospect into the most frightening display of cyclobatics I had ever beheld. With some urgency I decided to try and close in and caution him. But how? I could sound a few blasts on the horn, except that the deafening din issuing from Archie's pounding machine would render that impracticable. Moreover, knowing Archie's turn of mind, I realised that he was fully capable of interpreting the gesture as my signal to him to put a move on. I finally opted for following a little more closely than hitherto, if only to prevent him slipping away from sight and range, which I considered he couldn't do, for his old crate must surely be running at optimum speed and durability. After a gradual straight descent of almost one mile, the hill levelled out before presenting a steep plunge and a pair of narrow bends a few hundred yards before entering the small village of Crosby Kirkbridge. It was during these hazards that I temporarily lost sight of Archie once more, as he roared furiously round the left-hand bend ahead. Some instinct switched my reactions over to 'Danger' but too suddenly, and too late. Archie was off, spread-eagled among a dense clump of heather and gorse.

The motorcycle had written itself off against some large roadside boulders, and lay distributed in a smoking shambles across the narrow road, directly in my path. My violent swerve did not pay off. My mighty thrust upon the brake pedal rendered the car airborne for some yards, before she plunged over the left side embankment, heeled over onto her side, and tipped me overboard before making a second roll across my entire body, coming to rest with the engine roaring and the rear wheels madly thrashing the air.

The pain in my legs and back was excruciating, and an odd feeling of vagueness occupied the space where my head should be. The first mortal I was aware of was a very pale-faced and shaken Archie, trembling violently and leaning over me, frantically muttering, “Tha’s alreyght now...la’al car’s gittin itsel’ brok up a bit, but tha’s alreyght now.” Two swarthy hill shepherds appeared from nowhere, and raised up the inverted car with their bare hands, while a very large woman materialised to ease my trapped legs from underneath. Within minutes people were scurrying out from the village, and there was loud shouting and the barking of many dogs. Twice a battle casualty during the recent war, I had previously suffered the pain of shattered bones, and raw open flesh, but never anything so intense as during those first few moments of rescue. The law was on the job in a remarkably short time, in the long, lean person of Police Constable Jack Withenhurst who, conveniently, lived nearby. A man who could always be relied upon to make a rapid assessment of any situation which required the offices of the ‘long arm’, and regulate his priorities accordingly, he decided to forgo the customary formularies and seek urgent medical assistance. This was before the days of police personal radios, and what was worse, the constable’s house telephone, incidentally the only one in the village, was out of order. So it was, that the valiant lawman shot off with incredible velocity on his elderly motor cycle, in the direction of the small market town of Rooksdale about two-and-a-half miles away.

Meanwhile back at the scene of calamity, the locals were doing their best towards my comfort and well being. At very brief notice, the dour Percival Bramthwaite had presented himself, to be of any professional assistance. Now Percival, a very kind-hearted and well-meaning fellow had a self-confessed talent for leadership, and was thus prone to take complete charge of any situation he should chance upon. He was at once the local joiner, jobbing builder, painter and decorator, general Jack of all trades, and, in accordance with common rural practice, undertaker. He arrived on the scene in that curious vehicle, of uncertain vintage, which served as transport concomitant to all of these trades. The said automobile, a Morris Commercial, probably originated in the mid-nineteen thirties, when it was said to have been either a baker’s or a butcher’s delivery van. It was known to have done gallant war service trailing a pump for the Auxiliary Fire Service, although it had never been called out. In latter years, by the addition of two side windows, and various other impedimenta, it had attained its present status. By pure chance, it just happened to be painted black.

“Aye, Mr. Bramthwet hes a grand moatha car there. Just weshes it down a la’al bit, and puts sum leaves and bracken up on th’top, and a few fluers inside, and she's a grand 'earse, that she is. Aye, she's teyen a gay lot o ' good foalkes for t'last ride that yan hes," Old Sammy Smith once confided to me.

The grisly sight of my right foot rotated half-circle backwards, some jagged bone ends protruding from my shins, and blood all over the place caused awesome confusion amongst the men, most of whom felt helpless to do aught but stand around like a burial party, uttering sporadic comments like,

"Airrrghh... bad job 'appen, bad job, aye. Reckon t'poor youth's gawin' tae loss ya leg... mebees beyth... aye... reyght feyet's just hingin' be bit o' skin onywees."

"Airrrgh...his he-yad's what I'm worrit about... lossin' mare blood there than's guid forrim... must be big hole or summat sumwhere 'appen."

"Maggie Tuppenam says t'steerin' wheel was all pushed inti 'is chest. Reckon if he was yan o' my beasts, t'knacker would've been on t'job afore now... airrgh... leyeks gayly bad...aye."

At last, thank God, the women to the rescue, with their calm, cool efficiency. I heard the soft voice of Minnie Carter, bless her,

"Fetched tha sum tea luv... but here git this down ye fust... drop o' brandy... dae tha t'world o' guid it will. I knaws thee and tha chapel foalkes din't alweys believe in drinkin' or owt leyke, but 'appen din't believe in gittin' theesels hurt neither. Onyweys what's gawin' on here's mare important than gawin' tae chapel and all that." Minnie heaved her massive thorax and appendages in a chuckle of wheezy laughter which was prescribed to cheer me up a little.

I sipped the deadly stimulant, every drop, and the cup of sugary tea which followed. All wrong I knew, clinically speaking, for there was evidence of haemorrhage. But it was healing magic, and especially when it was accompanied by the slow caress of my cold, clammy forehead with rough fingers that were more accustomed to pulling udders twice a day than to administering succour to an injured motorist. Thus fortified I found voice,

"First aid... first aid... please... think I'm hurt somewhere."

Now a cow in a bog, a 'kessened' sheep, or a horse with broken wind, and these good people were instinct with practical knowledge as to how to proceed, but a parson 'all brok tae bits under his motor' was quite a different matter. There was plenty of conversation going on by now, although the only words I could discern seemed to refer to 'gittin' that damn moatha-bike off t'road afore we gits another bang-up'.

"Please get me off this rough ground somebody... please... no... please... don't try to drag me... something flat... rigid... door or something... please," I gasped in excruciating pain.

Hearing this, the ever ready Percival leapt into action, and with long urgent strides hastened to his van. In a short time he returned bearing a stout six feet by two feet piece of timber.

"Me layin' owt booard, champion for t'job. Can strighten 'im out and keyep 'im nice and stiff on this." The jolt from this suggestion broke something loose in me, notably my voice, and I was able to scrape,

"But ah's not de-ad yit Percy...not de-ad... not quite ready for tha yi...not yet... not y—"

The laughter which this set up among the group of men standing over me was the best piece of resuscitation I had received thus far, apart from the brandy of course. Then came bad news. The doctor was away on his holidays, and his locum was out attending another emergency somewhere over the fell, and could not be tracked down. Noise from afar signalled the return of P.C. Withenhurst, who during his absence had been by no means idle. When his faithful old Coventry Eagle two-stroke plopped to a reeking halt alongside where I lay, the pillion rider turned out to be no other than the local, indispensable, indefatigable, indestructible, infallible District Nurse Aylene Hadley. A local baby had fortuitously elected to be born at just about this time. Miss Hadley was a lady of formidable proportions and indomitable will, who in any circumstance of good or ill, invariably got her way. No useless preliminaries for this super-nurse, for hardly had her feet touched down and she was into action. Delivering a stern lecture to the menfolk, she severely reprimanded them for having moved me without her consent. Much to my dismay however, she did approve of the board, obviously not being aware of its origin or its normal function. Deftly she snipped away as much of my trousers as she dared, public decency taking precedence over medical expediency, and then mopped up the bloody mess from my legs, face and head.

"Ah Mr. Bramthwaite, I'm so glad you're here. Now look, we're going to need a box. Have you got any tools with you? Ruler? Tape-measure?"

"Alweys carry them wi' us Nus 'adly, Aye. But 'e says he's not agonna tae dee Nus... not yit onyweys... aye."

"A box splint you silly man, to put his smashed-up leg in, to immobilise it. Come on now, hurry up man. And what are you lot sniggering at?"

A funereal atmosphere came over the place as the nurse went about her healing work, cleaning, dressing, comforting and supporting. A hypodermic needle thrust deftly into my buttocks sent Charlie Bland down in a dead faint. Gently but firmly the skilful hands manipulated the mauled limb into Percy's hastily fabricated box splint, then held it still whilst the canny craftsman screwed down the top piece - displaying his best coffin-lid technique.

"Thank you Percy, and well done. Now we'll need some more splinting of sorts, there's lots more breaks I fear. So please see what you can bang together for us. And you ladies, a blanket or two please. O and hot water bottle - he's going into shock I'm afraid."

I became aware of the sound of Percy's hammer tapping out its sharp staccato somewhere in the distance. Then the policeman's motorcycle was started up, belching over me a cloud of reeking smoke as it ticked over erratically. There came a confused sound of many agitated voices and I began to feel myself losing hold as the noises ran together into a mad crescendo... guns... short-range... coming closer...rat-a-tat stutter of a Mauser - not far off... getting nearer... closer... closer... and that infernal shouting...raucus... guttural... shouting... shou..."

"Aye...aye... ayah... 'saapen gitten esel a grossen smashen uppen thissun... ayah... ja whol... ja whol..."

"Er blutet viel...kouldntt ot gitten much warser... warser... wasser... wasser-schnell... schnell... hell... bluddy hell... hey Medic... here sharp."

"Is he goin' tae be alreyght Nus? Nus... Nurse... Nur -"

"That you Margaret... bless you...knew you'd be around...sweetest girl... favourite nursey... love you... your hand... han—"

"Alright Donny boy, alright... where... wher... wo... haben... sie... die schmerzen...schmer...zzzz—?"

Now the blazing sun was burning my face relentlessly, but I couldn't move my head to turn aside, and my nostrils were full of burning hot sand. A trickle of fresh warm blood ran down my neck and coagulated among the hairs on my chest. I put my hands up to my eyes to try and make them see, but the blood which had collected in the sockets welled over, mingled with the desert dust on my face and set hard. The pain in my head was unbearable.

"Sorry about the needle mate... blunt as hell... been stickin' it into fat arses all day. There that should fix you up. Hey driver... here."

"OK Lieu, it's OK now... that was field Medic...patched you up and all that. This is Steadman here... you know... driver... Jeep's had it sad to say... soon get you a new un though... just waitin' for t'blood wagon to come up... blut... wagen... blut... Jemand soll den Blutwagen holen—"

"Still there Margaret... still... th—" my voice and my ravings were suddenly swallowed up in the deafening roar of engines.

"Achtung...achtung...Schpitfire... Schpitfire... schpthigher... bit higher...up a lal bit... higher... steady... now forrard...not sae rough on'im lads, he's hu't a bit 'appen... that's it." Bright buttons and a shiny helmet appeared in my now partly cleaned up eyes and a cruel hard face glowered into them. "You stinking rotten Nazi, get your filthy hands off me... if I could get at you... you lousy bas—"

"Alright me lad, now just ye calm theesel down a bit. Been hevin' bit of a rough time eh. It's only Withenhurst 'ere... poliss. Got ye nicely trussed up in ambulance here... soon be OK... OK... OK... Tobruk... Tobruk...broken out o' Tobbruk... A... uk—" and all went dark and silent.

When I regained some element of consciousness I guessed I must be either in Heaven or somewhere closely akin to it, for the gentle touch of the warm hand that was stroking my forehead bespoke an angel, and the soft soothing voice in my ear was vaguely familiar and full of love. My eyes had clouded over again and the voice had a thousand echoes.

"No darling it's not Margaret I'm afraid. She was years and years ago, whoever she was. Sorry darling, but it's only Gina. Now you're going to be alright 'cos I'm right here beside you, and I won't go away, ever. Mr. Bramthwaite fetched me in his - er - van. No darling you're not in the van this is the county ambulance. They're taking you to hospital. Nurse is here with us - no, darling not Margaret, someone else. Gosh Donny I think you smiled there, good work. Now just you have a little sleep... I'll still be hanging around."

I tried hard not to fall asleep, but that field Medic and his bent needle had done a pretty thorough job. I was scared of the possibility of relapsing into the dreadful delirium I had lately suffered, wherein my subconscious mind had become entangled in a conglomeration of unpleasant memories of a former mishap in the Western Desert, which were now presenting as current experience.

Archie was a born survivor. It turned out that he had by chance chosen precisely the right moment to abandon his charger and leap blindly into space, for it landed him with nothing worse than some severe bruising and a broken collar bone in a dense mass of moorland vegetation. Archie was shockproof, after a fashion, for like all other impressions, this one also was somewhat delayed in taking effect. The great Royal Enfield had continued on automatic pilot for twenty yards or more before converting to scrap iron by some roadside rocks. The little yellow MG was also a survivor, for it seemed to have brushed this one off as just another incident in its long career of ups and downs. After PC Withenhurst and three burly shepherds had rolled her back onto her wheels, merely to restore her dignity of course, they stood back in utter amazement. Apart from a torn off windscreen, she had suffered but small hurt, and the enterprising Ben Bracknall was soon on hand to tow her in for overhaul and, so he boasted, for inevitable re-sale.

"That parson fella'll not be wantin' this yan ony mare, or ony other moatha-car neither. T'wife'll not be wantin' much for it neither... think I've got me eye on ya buyer."

The last word however was with the highly proficient Constable Withenhurst, who for many weeks to come would be declaring to all and sundry, o'er hill and dale, in village and market, and all places where people gathered,

"Aye, I tells tha, if t'pethrol tank hadn'ta been nearly bone dry when he cowped t'la'al yilla car ower t'bank, this story meyght hev had a far diff'rent endin', that it would, Aye, aye, aye"

"Aye?"

"Aye!"

Chapter 31

A BRIDGE IN TIME

"Tell me more about Nijmegen," said a still small voice close to my ear.

"Damn it," I thought, "dreaming again, and as always angels, pretty girls, shapely nurses."

"Come on Mr. Teviot I'm sure you heard me - NIJMEGEN," the voice was louder now, emphatic, and I felt myself becoming agitated and afraid.

"Don't you worry love," I heard my own voice saying, "you're going to be alright... we'll take care of you... soon as we get these b—s cleared off this bridge... now keep down... won't let them hurt you... down now... down... won—" A soft cool hand adjusted a bandage on my face and stroked my hair, causing me to open my eyes slightly, "Good grief, right on it... middle... never get back... got toooooo—"

"Right over it my dear, we're right over it...we're alright... right out into the clear." The cool hand was still on my head and I opened my eyes wider. I found myself looking straight up into the sky, through massive girders, silhouetted against a blaze of aerial shell bursts and fire flashes.

"Hell we've got to get off here... come on... she might go up any minu—"

"Steady love, steady. Anyway it's not the bridge you're looking at, it's your frames, We've got you all trussed up you know, for your own good as well, jumping about like that." Locating the voice, and turning my head, I looked into the smiling face of a young nursing sister.

"Phew - how long have I been in this mess? Thought I was i—"

"Don't know precisely, for you seem to have been well and truly over at Nijmegen in Holland off and on for the past seven hours that I know of. We'd better tell that lot down at Theatre to give you a lighter whiff next time eh!"

"Did I hear you mention Nijmegen, Sister, or am I going dippy again?"

"No you're not going anything...Cyclopropane you know...does funny things to folk. Yes, you probably did mention Nijmegen, come to think of it. You certainly talked about it plenty, and said some pretty unrepeatable things as well. Won't go into details about that though - keep our little secret shall we. Sat with you most of night you know."

"And I kept blabbering on about Nijmegen? Was there you know... few other chaps as well of course. That bridge - messy business - would like to forget that lot, I really would."

"I know - I know - all about Nijmegen. Upset me a bit, but glad you talked about it all the same...kind of relief actually...felt I was right there with you. You see Mr. Teviot, Bill died on that bridge... my husband. His mates told me all about it afterwards."

"I'm so dreadfully sorry Sister. It's all so sad, so tragic," I said with a weakening voice, and at the same time taking her hand into my limp fingers, "And here I am, a complete stranger to you, absolutely from out of the blue, and well, it's just possible that I may have been right close to your Bill whe—. Look Sister, please forgive me, I'm not yet fully responsible for what I'm doing or saying at the moment... as you say, post-anaesthetic and all that. By the way, what was his name?"

"You're no stranger to me soldier boy, not from this very moment anyway. You brought him back all so close to me. Bill Reynolds was his name, Royal Engineers. So sorry to be acting silly like this, but you see the pain won't go away. I know you'll understand, I just know you will. Anyhow, I'll just slip away now and make us both a nice cup of tea eh."

"By the way Sister Reynolds, before you go - because I still think I'm just dreaming all of this - what's the score? I can't seem to be able to move a thing."

"And by the way, just to you mind you, 'cos you're very special, it's Gladys. Make sure you always whisper it. And as for you Don - can call you that can't I? - a broken bone here and there, bit of damage to some of your works inside, slight face-lift. O yes, and a spot of concussion. Otherwise, we're OK, we'll survive. Shouldn't go round all-in wrestling with fast sports cars you know, or you might get hurt one of these days you know. I'm told your car got a bit bent in this one, thought you might like to know. Now just you forget all about Nijmegen and nasty things like that, and I'll go and fetch that tea."

"Alright Sister I'll try. And I promise, I'll hang around - won't wander off very far. O and just one other thing before you disappear. You didn't come in with the concussion did you, or the gas or whatever? I mean, you are real aren't you? Not a kind of hangover? Gladys."

That post-operative encounter with the tragic young sister started me off on a period of serious reflection which was to persist for the greater part of my ten weeks spent in the County Hospital. Weighted and trussed in skeletal traction, I lay on my back, occupying a large proportion of my time in filling the blank white ceiling with a riot of memory pictures. It was sometimes a pleasant experience, except for those grim occasions when relapses into drowsy delirium brought on a time warp, and I would re-live dark experiences from wartime days. At such times, the sweet ‘Sister Nijmegen’ was quickly on hand, with cool hands low soft voice, and re-assuring words.

I received so many visitors during those few weeks, that at one time it was rumoured that ‘yon yan wi’ all t’strings and weets and whatnot on ‘im meyest be summat special, gittin’ all them foalks around. And that Sister fetchin’ flooers for ‘im, and sittin’ aside him for la’al while ivvry day afore she gaws off duty.’ Then there was considerable curiosity about yon bonnie young lass who used to visit him on most afternoons. It was well known that she was conveyed from Lyndassby by a different young fella every day an’ all - lang trip that. Most of my fellow inmates however simply assumed that Gina must be my younger sister, a niece, or even a daughter. But all the same, somebody should be keeping an eye on her, with all those young chaps hanging around. Gina’s volunteer escorts, all obviously farmers, almost inundated me with daily offerings of fresh eggs, farm butter, and one even managed to smuggle in a bottle of his Mum’s celebrated hay-time wallop. It was further rumoured that I must be very good, singularly bad, or notably rich, otherwise why the constant attention I was receiving from visiting clergy? Concerning these well- meaning brethren, I must confess that there were times when I found their pious solicitations and cultivated bedside manner a trifle irksome in a circumstance where ordinary friendship would have sufficed. Within this context it so happened that on one afternoon Gina and her ungainly driver escort, followed closely by the Roman Catholic priest, a vicar and his curate, and two sombre non-Conformist ministers all seemed to be heading for my bedside simultaneously. As they drew near to the tightly drawn curtains a gap appeared from within, through which emerged a rather harassed doctor, a fussy sister, one male nurse, two auxiliaries, and a trolley bearing a figure, prostrate and pale, bereft of weights and pulleys and all other medico-mechanical paraphernalia. As though by some common instinct the holy group switched into processional mode and followed the trolley and its entourage solemnly down the middle of the ward. Deep silence fell over the place, and as the procession passed by, visitors respectfully rose to their feet, other patients looked on gravely, and the faithful crossed themselves. On reaching the door, the ‘corpse’ raised up its head and cried out, “Right turn for the morgue.”

“Theatre - secondary haemorrhage - everything’s alright - no worry - that parson’s a scream,” a bemused student nurse re-assured.

The weeks spent in Ward 3 Major Surgical dragged on, accompanied by some pain, apprehension, and repetitive ward routine, and for me very frustrating, for I was immobilised on my back in a form of gantry which must have shared some patent rights with the mediaeval rack. “You’ll just have to learn to lie still, stop complaining, and concentrate on getting better,” a middle-aged sister of the battle-axe breed commanded me each morning. There were compensations of course. For anyone who would care to laugh at life and cultivate some indifference to his current predicament, life in the typical hospital ward provides ample scope for entertainment and education. It throws together all sorts and conditions of men; sickness and hospital pyjamas are great levellers. My nearest neighbours, as well as myself of course, were by no means exceptions to this rule. Some alas were significant chiefly by virtue of their perversity. The bane of my life was the retired engine driver fellow two up from me, who each night would die from 10-00pm until 4-00am, all the time snoring tortuously. With unfailing punctuality he would awaken at this unseemly hour and arouse the entire ward with his pitiful cries for sleeping tablets, a urine bottle, and his feet tucked in. And there was next to him old Charlie, who would collar anyone who chanced to be passing by his bed, and afflict them with his ten minute set-piece, that being a lurid account of his recent bladder operation. Ward 3 was a long stay surgical ward and consequently contained a proportion of 'up-patients', all of whom were very supportive of their bedfast colleagues, in addition to which they likewise provided their quota of human interest. Like the bragging parvenue with neither brains nor breeding but much business success to his discredit, and the over-weight machismo maniac who would hail his disgusting habit of making verbal passes at passing nurses as express proof of his superior sexuality. One of the worst dreads was to have the vociferous Billy Cass draw a chair up to your bed and assail you with a session of his persistent war talk, that was until it was revealed that in actual fact Billy's entire war service consisted of his being the obscure, sole ARP warden in a remote hamlet tucked away amongst the Cumbrian hills which even the eagle eye of the Luftwaffe had never succeeded in locating. Obliged to alter his tack, he then took to making snide comments upon the lingering guilt of those who took innocent lives during the course of the recent war. An unfair charge of course, which was amply dispatched by the ex-bomber pilot in Bed 14 who pointed out that the bitterest irony of war is not only that the innocent are killed, but the innocent are called upon to kill. There was the unforgettable Michael, a pathetic little man who never had any visitors, and his bed, being No.1 and tucked away behind the door was frequently passed by unnoticed. He was well accustomed to such treatment for he was a vagrant, and victim of a hit-and-run motorist. If ever a man was in need of a Good Samaritan, it was old Michael. Some of the fellows were a sheer delight to have near. Like the lively Geordie chap from the adjoining ward, whose daily greeting was "Ony on ye waantin' owt dun for ye noo? Bottle? Bedpan? Pint o' Newcastle Broon Ale? Yor aall ower weel off in heor, that's whaat." Geordie's verbal acrobatics, oral contortions, and astringent phrases were not only an object lesson in linguistics; they were an inspiration. And to this day I cherish the memory of the tall, softly spoken retired schoolmaster who would sidle up and sit by my bed in the evening. He pondered much, and talked sparsely, but each time he spoke, words of wisdom fell from his lips like precious drops of some rare essence from a magic still. And meanwhile, throughout these days, what was happening to the pitiful object in my bed? As well as providing his full share of surprises, shocks, and amusement, he was improving his education, and one hoped, undergoing a healing process in more than his smashed up body.

Set daily routines became particularly amusing, chiefly because of their unvarying predictability. The Matron's arrival in the ward at prompt 9-00am ('Kit Inspection' we called it) was a typical exercise in perfunctoriness. To the flurry of skirts and the crackle of starch, she would lead her patrol through the ward, pausing briefly at the foot of each bed, where she would flash a synthetic smile, pronounce a toneless "How are you? Well I hope - very good." Then she would turn with a swish and move on to the next bed for a repeat of the performance. Finally she would abruptly disappear into the corridor, and the 'All Clear' would be sounded. Occasionally a Consultant would appear, surrounded by a servile cluster of bemused satellites, with a string of bewildered vassals following on. If you were sufficiently spectacular, of rare physiology or special clinical interest, he would pause by your bed, gather his entourage about him, and address them at length in an unknown tongue. An underdog would be commanded to test your bones for soundness, another to palpate your flesh for tenderness, and a third to ask you in baffling terms how you were feeling. Then with each one in turn, the Great One would openly discuss your clinical data and your prognosis until you were left wondering whether or not you were still a conscious living organism. The male nurse was a magnificent fellow who had a distinguished war record with the R.A.M.C. All was well with him, except that he seemed to recognise only two categories of the healing art - kill or cure - and at times it was not easy to discern which of them he was administering. On the whole however, the nursing staff were angels, and one would have been thoroughly unnatural if he hadn't fallen madly in love with each one of them in turn.

Regretfully, there was one important feature of ward life which turned sour on me. It was the pastoral performance of certain members of my own fraternity, who, devout, diligent and well-meaning though they undoubtedly were, left some ambiguity as to the motivation behind their ministrations. On entering the ward, the clergy of various denominations would home in on their individual charges, courteously ignoring all other frail mortals, and politely acknowledging one another with pious nods and ambivalent smiles. Even as the custom of the day dictated, religious segregation was the accepted norm, practised with guiltless impunity, and ecumenism was still at the foetal stage of development. Apartheid is a terrible thing in the world of the spirit. I confess to some shame and embarrassment over a brash young blood clad in an incongruous assortment of sporty attire and psuedo-clerics, who gave the impression of being possessed by either a warped evangelical fervour or a vividly imagined sense of humour. Crashing into the ward with four-fifths of his boyish face swathed in a clownish grin, he would lift up his nasal voice and call out, "Hands up any lost sheep or Methodists." To his credit however, one would add that this is the nearest approach to practical inter-church relations we ever witnessed. The top prize should be awarded to the resident Church of England chaplain who used to send a very junior student nurse around the beds each Friday to gather up the names of 'Anglicans only' for weekly Communion ('Only does church ones you know'). On one day a visiting Roman Catholic priest caused an undignified furore in the staff room, having previously entered the ward to find that one of the faithful had inconveniently died at very short notice some twenty minutes beforehand. At the time only a Baptist minister was present, and this good brother had been urgently implored by the relatives to say an appropriate prayer. Presumably the great issue at stake was that the patient in his dying moments, hearing only that alien voice and therefore missing out on the application of the proper oracle, had irrevocably jeopardised his acceptance for immortality by presenting himself at the heavenly gates on a wrong ticket. Sometimes one would be included in the random selection to be called upon by one of the official senior clergymen, who would pause by the bed, introduce himself with some sanctimonious small talk, then intone over your feet the Prayer for The Sick and Afflicted from his shiny black book with purple ribbons sticking out, before cutting you short mid-sentence with an 'Amen' and a 'Hrumph' and creeping up on his next victim. Some of these crusty old clerics dispensed their pre-packaged ministrations with no more spontaneity than a tired nurse doing her routine evening sleeping pill round. Then there were the diffident ones, who addressed you with their eye-balls turned upward, confidingly in a mysterious low whisper, and before departing fortified you with the Twenty-Third Psalm. We sometimes had to endure the new vogue hail-fellow-well-met variety; automatic talking machines merrily dispensing spiritual placebos and moral tranquillisers from their seemingly inexhaustible supply. Most dreaded of all, and hardly deserving of mention, were those dishonest, pathetic purveyors of sugary anodyne, who left you with but an exaggerated sense of the seriousness of your indisposition. My observations from my bed may seem somewhat unfair to the elder clergy, many who had remained in their stations because of the exigencies of the war and its aftermath. And yet try as I may I could not rid myself of the painful conviction that here was no place for weary old fathers who seemed to subsist on a drip-feed from the Book of Common Prayer, or rest in the glories of a past age of popular dissent. Once more I was maybe unreasonably prejudiced, being held rigid and miserable by my surgical ironmongery. Surely a hot-bed for quick growing cynicism!

There were the bright spots. Like when two neat nuns came in each Friday and whispered sweet solace to the elderly faithful. Their processed personalities and sanitized smiles however seemed to arouse little in the rest of the men except pity - or lust. My Catholic neighbour would refer to them as the 'immaculate virgins'. The ministrations of the official clergy were supplemented by clutches of stern-faced deviants who would infiltrate the ward, usually passing themselves off as 'hospital visitors'. Chaplaincy in hospitals was not very strictly regulated in those days. I suspected that the primary motive of these people was to compensate for the errors and shortcomings implicit in the witness of the mainstream churches. Such an one would materialise at your bedside and launch into a spiel which was as predictable as the familiar 'Temperature-Pulse-Respiration-Have your bowels moved today?' routine. Life was evil and uncertain, death was inescapable, Hell was nigh, a place in Heaven was prepared for those especially chosen, and he or she, who had been sent to declare it unto you, had been singularly blessed with the custody of the whole, unalterable truth. Further down the scale (or up?) were the shady dealers in celestial logarithms, whose wild theological speculations, scriptural permutations, and eschatological predictions made you want to scream for morphine. Benign old gentlemen in dull clothes, accompanied by kindly ladies with pastel shade personalities, would dispense 'spiritual comfort' and leave on your locker a pile of lurid tracts which generally assumed that you were at death's door, your soul was in grave peril, and so was their's if they didn't warn you. Gospel cheap Jacks would arrive now and again, with their special offers of glory on the strength of nothing more sublime than a hymn, a prayer, and your signature on a little coloured card bearing the title 'My Personal Decision'. Bands of self-styled evangelicals would bring along their captive teenagers to serve up their off-the-shelf 'personal' testimonies, usually in the evenings. The undisputed favourite however was the small band of Salvation Army Songsters, led by their young lady Lieutenant with model proportions and a close-fitting uniform. Eventually I was loosed from my worst bonds and promoted to wheelchair transport. I was thus enabled to attend a church service. As it would be 'chapel' an official invitation to me was considered to be appropriate. My first sight of the congregation called to mind the New Testament image of Our Lord standing on a Galilean hillside surrounded by the sick, the halt, the maimed, the blind, and the washed-out dressing gowns in which the people were clad added a distinctly Eastern flavour. Otherwise it was a very mixed crowd of all sorts and conditions of women and hymns ancient and modern. A portable harmonium on shaky legs and reminiscent of a coffin on pre-burial display, was produced and played by a spindly youth with severe acne. The service, although a hotch-potch of unrelated items was nevertheless a welcome break from the life of the ward, and the hymn singing was a tonic. We were not informed which denomination had spawned the preacher, which was just as well, for we did have to endure twenty minutes of his periphrastic perambulation (I believe they are called sermons in some circles) as he roamed his tangential way to an indeterminate inconclusion.

It should be emphatically admitted that the cases cited here were but notable exceptions, to which in my state of ill health I was particularly susceptible. On the whole, the patients were most grateful for, and tolerant of the kindly attentions of the churchmen, of all shades. For my own part, I was in total sympathy with the clergy, for surely it was because of conscious shortcomings in my own ministry that I so readily made sport of theirs. These men were, after all, but slaves of the system, who were not necessarily acting in accordance with their own individual lights, but merely conforming to convention. There may have been others among the visitors, equally well meaning, but crudely opportunist, or who were motivated by frenetic fears of the unknown or unknowable. In my better moments I longed that this period of unbridled negativism would clear the way for new vision and firmer resolve in my own ministry forthwith. I had originally intended my mischievous observations to be for self-amusement only, such is my natural pre-disposition, but they back fired, and initiated further sad pre-occupations. I would sometimes note with absorbing interest the activities of those visitors to the ward, family and friends, who arrived each day bearing nothing more sublime than the ordinary human qualities of loving concern, good cheer, and grapes. Sometimes it would start up a depressing train of thought. Young, radical, unsacerdotalist that I was I wondered what special virtue, extra to these family gifts of such great therapeutic worth, were exclusively the prerogative of the official pastoral visitor, for surely nothing could be more holy than these things. Trying to be utterly realistic I questioned whether there was a mystical sacramental grace which could only be appropriated through the medium of certain symbols, rites and rituals, and dispensed exclusively by a priestly elite who, on the authority of the church were divinely endowed with some esoteric quality which is not available to common mortals. Such were some of the rebellious ravings troubling the mind of a young cleric at the beginning of the road, caught up in too rapid a transition, who now given much time to think, was terrified at the prospect of disillusionment. Yet surely this period of separation and immobility would be destined to piece together far more than my broken bones and shattered works, and enable me to try and set my major priorities in good order. I would lay hold on lessons upon which I would never turn my back. I had 'seen oursel's as others see us'.

******

It had been a cheerless day, by now I was growing weary of persistent pain and frustration, and was trying to fight back the onset of a mood of deep depression. I hoped that no-one would come to visit me on that afternoon, and that none of my ward mates would come over and sit with me, for I wanted to remain miserable. But it was not to be, for standing at the foot of my bed, peering through my tension cords and plaster casts, cap at a rakish angle, beaming a rosy-faced smile, a brown paper bag of eggs held out precariously toward me, was my friend Jimmy Guthrigg from the far reaches of Scarston Moor.

"Howistha lad... tha's gittin' theesel' inti a gay scrow there 'appen...what've they been deyen' tae tha then? Here, where can I put these? Tha's got ower mony floo-wers on that locker there... they must be thinkin' tha's a'riddy dey-ad or summat. Here where can I put these eggs? Me Leghorns laid them special for tha. Hey Miss... Nuss... put t'minister's name on this lot, and mek sure naebody else gits them - I've put poison in t'lot."

"Well Jimmy lad, howistha theesel? How nice tae see tha. Whatever's brought you right down here?"

"Fust and foremeyest, tae see thee and mek sure tha's behavin' theesel proper leyke... not runnin' off wi' ony on these nusses or owt...'appen tek mare than a few brokken bones tae keyep thee in order I reckons."

"That's what all this lot's about Jimmy," I said, pointing out my miniature shipyard.

"O aye, and whilst I'm ower here... hev tae gaw and see about yan of yon la'al grey Ferguson tracthors they're all gittin theirsel's. Got tae keyep up wi' times, hest tha not. Thowt tha meyght gi' us a la'al bit o' advice or summat - knaw what I mean leyke. Aye - TE20's what tha calls them - grand machines."

"But I'm not an expert on tractors Jimmy. On nurses neither for that matter, all models."

"Now just tha meynd what tha's sayin' about nusses. I forgat tae tell tha, I've fetched tha wife ower wi' me, and she says tae tell tha she'll be a-cumin' tae see tha when she's finished her shoppin... naebody tae keep her in order amang t'shops now 'appen, eh."

"That's jolly sporting of you Jimmy, you're a real pal, to us both."

"O aye, and seein' as tha's all trussed up like a bale o' straw and not gittin' about ower weel, I'll tek her out for a bite o' tea meesel'. Knaws a good spot ower be t'Mart... alweys gits a good fotherin' in there. Then I'll tek her back hoame for tha...doesn't seem tae be ony rooam for her in there aside o' ye."

"Thanks again Jimmy, I'm sure Gina will appreciate that. But getting back to the business of tractors, I'm no expert on such things."

"Tha's a bit of an expert on ivvrything... knaw what I mean... lot o' good money tae be puttin' out all at yance. Just wonderin' if I was deain' t'reyght thing, or it's just me fancy...knaw what I mean leyke."

"You're really wanting that Ferguson Jimmy Guthrigg aren't you? So just you stop kidding yourself, and trying to kid me. You've already got it all worked out haven't you, and all the good, sound reasons why you've simply got to have it. There's one small matter though. You have I hope reckoned on in your economic research, that is to make the proposition a worthwhile practical one, all that extra gear, and extra cost that goes along with the Ferguson."

"What did I tell tha? Real expert tha is - thinks of ivvrything. Aye well, I've thowt o' all that an' all, and wucked it all out."

"And what did I tell thee Jimmy? Tha mind's pretty well made up isn't it. Just asking me to make yourself feel better, or perhaps cheer me up eh."

"Well as ye knaw, me oily owld Field Marshall's just about clapped out. Well nigh shaks t'life out o' me that yan. Me faather had it lang time afore he passed away, wucked a lot o' owertime during t'war an' all. Startin' tae cost ower much just tae try and keyep it gawin. But ye see, I just wanted tae meyeke sure I was daein' reyght, and it seems tha thinks about t'seyame as me be t'looks on it."

"Using me as a kind of rubber stamp eh, or perhaps to carry the can if things turn out wrong. T'minister said it'd be alreyght 'appen."

"Nay nowt leyke that. Ye see, there's summat else - t'weyfe. She keyeps on at me 'cos there's a lot needs done about th'ouse. And there's t'coos, hev tae build up bigger spread tae mek owt on 'em, t'way things are nowadays, and worse than that there's th-"

"I know Jimmy, I know. You smaller hill farmers have really got your work set out these days. Things just ain't what they used to be, they're not. You've simply got to keep up haven't you or you - go down."

"What would tha dae, if tha was in my situation then?"

"Unfair question, for I could never be in your situation. I'd have gone under ages since if I had been. Nevertheless, for what it's worth, I'd say just you carry on, and do what your better judgement is obviously telling you to do. Go out and order that Ferguson man - now. It'll pay for itself in no time in increased efficiency and lower running costs, that to be sure. Go on, take the plunge Jimmy, like every time you drop a seed into the ground."

This strain of conversation was no new experience for me. Many of my farmer friends were facing considerable problems over the post- war economics of farming, with unfamiliar regulations, guidelines, and quotas, and the new and baffling world of accounting and form-filling. I had often become embroiled in their administrative tangles, and was gaining a reputation as 'a very present help in trouble'. I was frequently being dragged into the composite role of accountant, counsellor, secretary, and consultant engineer. I soon found that there was much more to being a country pastor than preaching and praying.

Eventually Gina arrived, flowers in hand. She looked absolutely radiant as she moved down the middle of the ward with stately rhythmic steps, her face aglow with her girlish smile. Jimmy chose the moment to leave, rather hastily, and presumably to go off and order his new tractor before any unwelcome impediment should come into mind.

"New tractor," exclaimed Gina, "Should rather be doing something about his old Standard car I reckon. Lucky to have got here... falling apart it is...and the vibration and din... worse than ours. Sorry dear."

"These younger farmers are having some big problems re-adjusting their priorities I'm afraid. As well as fields, barns, machinery, and livestock, they've got wives and families and homes to consider."

"Good point. Houses for instance, centuries old most of them, and pretty dilapidated too...no comfort, crude and inconvenient, hard work. The wives need to move with the times also you know, and have every right to do so. Just look at poor Edna's kitchen range. Did Jimmy mention that?"

"Aren't we lucky we're not farmers just starting up darling? We've maybe got no money, and have our share of hardships and anxiety, but we do have so much else to be thankful for, haven't we."

"S'right Donny boy, so much else. All those lovely people around us. This heavenly place to live in, mountains, rivers, trees, and wide open moors. And to cap it all, the certain prospect of an exciting and adventurous future together."

******

Jimmy returned sooner than expected, with a ten-acre grin on his face, by which I gathered that he had done the awful deed. Come to think of it, he had done a great deal more, for his visit coinciding with that of Gina, had come not only as a timely blessing but the harbinger of an extraordinary switch of direction. The morbid thoughts and dismal prospects which had troubled me for many days gave way to happier considerations. Jimmy had brought in with him the aura of the high fells, wide open heathland, craggy valleys, tumbling streams, meandering river, kindly rugged people and golden friendship. Then Gina had added the priceless ingredient of flawless love. And when the bell rang, and the visitors departed, the inspiration remained. I fell into a deep meditative mood. There was soul therapy at work. Was it really but twenty months since I had arrived at Lyndassby, raw, inexperienced, self-confident, and over-zealous, equipped with nothing more sublime than a recent theological degree, and a knowledge of life derived out of six-and-a-half years as a fighting soldier? I now began to realise that it was out of the solid stuff of which the affections, relationships, and trust of these Pennine people was made I would build the foundations of the long ministry in the wide unknown which yet lay before me. I began to take stock, so far. Receiving shattering confidences without outwardly wincing, dismissing unsubstantiated rumours without betraying partiality, listening eagerly to tales of guilt and woe yet resisting summary judgement, sharing remorse without remonstrating, reconciling the irreconcilable, breaking down intransigence with patience rather than force, carefully discriminating between the factual and the fanciful, accepting in mutual trust bilateral or counter-poised secrets in painful silence, remembering at all times that the line between absolute right and absolute wrong is not always clearly definable; and all of this without an outward trace, or inward feeling of pride, arrogance, or patronising pity. All of this, and much more, was part of the minister's lot with which these dear people helped me to come to terms. The good minister meets people at the level of the soul, his own as well as theirs. In those days many people still tended to take to the minister who had earned their trust, personal matters for which they now relate directly to a doctor, consult a psychiatrist, see a social worker, or fly for tranquillisers. They still saw their moral lapses as sins. It was no wonder that our arrival at Lyndassby had presented us with a thousand cultural shocks. None of the classical applications stockpiled in my years of training was to avail much in the nitty gritty of real life, or in providing practical proficiency in coping with typical human situations. People are not so easily typecast or categorised as I had been taught to anticipate, nor are there any standardized reactions to a given situation. The theory of conditioned reflexes should be confined to where it belongs - the lecture room or the clinic. Every human personality is highly prone to springing its shocks and surprises, for in each one of us the proverbial wheat and tares flourish side by side, albeit in varying proportions. The minister therefore commonly operates within a one-to-one situation, where there are as many variants as there are members of the human race, and where, so far as he may be concerned, there are no precedents. Secretly there lurks in the background of his every endeavour, his hard personal struggle with that ever-present irrepressible quantity - his own human nature. He is often placed into a position where he is made ingloriously aware of his deficiencies in such elementary virtues as patience, humility, unselfishness, for which there is no theoretical answer, and no safety net should he chance to stumble. His pastoral duty is supremely a work of inter-action in which he must never exceed his half share, be over patronising to the simple, condescending to the humble, nor toadying to the mighty. And when, as is sometimes his lot, he is entrusted with much, he must trust much in return, and be ever mindful of how dreadful his responsibility may be.

How long I pondered I did not know, although I was surprised by the arrival of the evening 'pill wagon' - "No aspirin or No.9's thank you." My quiet thinking had been a splendid tonic for the ego. On balance however I was compelled to remember that there had been periods of grave disillusionment and frustration, when my self-esteem, sense of vocation, and even my personal faith had been severely tested. I had more than once found myself in that dreaded make or break situation and teetered on the brink of disaster. Perhaps this had been all to some good purpose, if only to lead me out of my acquired war aggression and towards the nurturing of those human graces more needful to my task. No man has sat wearily through the long silent night watches with a dying friend and come out unscathed, nor listened to heart-rending disclosures of guilt and remorse, and gone unmoved. To be called upon to relieve despair and feel inept and inadequate, to be witness to earnest faith that has to go unrewarded, the prayers of the faithful unanswered, the suffering of the righteous and the triumph of evil, and have no logical answer nor comfort to give; to be expected to proclaim the universal love of an Almighty Father with heart-felt conviction at the end of a week of calamity, without being overcome by a crippling sense of hopeless futility; these are but some of the dilemmas with which I was already having to learn to cope, for they are part of the pastor's stock in trade. And there were more: To hope against the odds, to trust in the face of inevitable defeat, to refuse to issue false comfort, even if it entails admitting to ignorance and suffering loss of face, and to be entrusted with tragic confessions without either bluffing to assuage them, lying to conceal them, or appeasing to forget them. There is no professional code nor any intellectual aptitude that is sufficient to resolve such situations. You are out on your own, but for the grace of God, your individual integrity, and not least, the loving patience and understanding of your partner. Fortunately, however, there had ever remained open to me one essential escape route, which despite my blunders, faults, and foibles, had often preserved me from dismay, and saved me from catastrophe. I had been given a sense of humour. To see the farcical in a circumstance which should otherwise plunge you into the depths of dire despair; to match your most debilitating misgivings with an irrefutable optimism; to manage a smile when your heart is broken; these are the indispensable tools of any who would undertake the cure of souls. And while such qualities may not alone denote an excess of fortitude, their application will certainly keep open the channels by which strength is communicated. If you can laugh at yourself, it is easier to laugh with others. And to cry for them.

These things and more I pondered, and pondered, over and over in my mind, until they burned into my soul. Over and above it all there came a profound feeling of relief that, right at the beginning, I had been, thrown in at the deep end. Some baptism! Above all there was my profound indebtedness to these wonderful people of the fells and valleys of Lyndass who, perhaps inadvertently, by being simply their own good selves, had conducted me safely through my sound schooling. Or, to change the metaphor - a time of crisis, transition, and a perilous bridge crossed.

"O hello sister - dear Gladys. Sorry, I didn't notice you standing there. Day dreaming I'm afraid... lost in thought. Been there long? How nice of you to come, and how wonderful to see you."

Chapter 32

UNTO JOY OR SORROW GROWN

After ten long weeks in hospital, and a long period of convalescence which included some months of rigorous outpatient rehabilitation, I was turned out to face an uncertain future. Both of my legs were rigidly callipered from toe to thigh, and the prognosis was not encouraging. Consequently I became heavily dependent upon the concern and generosity of other people. In this matter the kindly Pennine folk excelled, going to such typical measures of practical consideration as to modify the seating arrangements in cars, like dismantling a front seat to accommodate my temporarily jointless legs. From now on my journeyings, whilst rich in rugged companionship were nevertheless fraught with secret sadness. There was the lingering fear that never again would I traverse those rough and lonely roads, except as a grateful passenger, cycle along those narrow country lanes alone with my cares, walk the lush fields and pastures and feel the slither and slosh of fresh cow dung under my feet. Never again could I stop off to stand alone and spellbound on a high fell summit or isolated rocky crag and gaze in silent wonder at the paradise below. No more would I do battle with the wild elements, take on the challenge of raging blizzard or furious gale, and win through. Then there was my most acute sorrow; for never again would I revel in the invigorating slipstream sweeping over the windshield of my little yellow MG Sport, thrill to the music of her friendly snarls or the deep aggressive roar of her murky exhaust, all making me feel that so long as she and I were together, all power was mine, and the world was at my feet. For alas she was no more. The little car had wondrously survived the crash which severely injured me, and according to promise Ben Bracknall of Rookside Garage had restored her to full vigour and glory. Then, at Gina's request, for we were totally broke, he had put the car up for sale. To the great consternation of all, Archie, the notoriously mad motor-cyclist whom it was known had initiated the said crash, purchased the faithful MG on the safe pretext that 'fower wheels are 'appen a lot mare safer than two'. Within a few weeks, Archie had totally written off our pride and joy in a high-speed head-on collision with a massive roadside boulder in failing to negotiate a turn near the summit of Blackrock Fell. And what a ghastly co-incidence it brought about, for the scene of the tragedy was but a few feet of the point where the prim Miss Victoria and I had foundered on that never-to-be-forgotten Winter's night some few months before. Sadly, Archie had not lived up to his reputation for agility, and neither had the usual guardian angels been on hand to ensure his survival.

A time came when the supreme church authorities, deeply enclaved in our distant Capital City, sent forth a decree that young Teviot should be instantly recalled from darkest Pennine country and posted to what in their profound wisdom they termed 'a more compact, conducive, and agreeable environment' in the South of England, this being more 'compatible with his present state of disability'. Soon, so very soon, Gina and I were callously uprooted and sent on our way, dejected and sad. It was surely of the utmost irony that those who were delegated to attend to our final departure were none other than that same dear couple who had welcomed us on our memorable arrival at Lyndassby only two years before. By this time we had ascertained their rather enigmatic relationship, and now knew that Doris was not, as we had initially supposed, either Harry's wife, sister, nor daughter. She was nobbut his loyal housekeeper of long standing - 'had 'er syne she was nae mare than a la'al lassie' was the common local designation. Not always a safe one however, it being capable of divers insinuations. And was it but a co-incidence that to transport us to the main line station some twenty-three miles away was the indomitable Josh Wyatt, who on that day of our arrival had been the first member of that beloved fellside community to greet us, with a lusty handshake and 'Sum eggs for t'la'al weyfe's tea and sum pethrol coupons for tha la'al yella car'? Thus it was that on a fateful late-August day in the year nineteen-hundred-and-fifty-one we set out, back along the road by which we had come. The friendly moor now treated us to a nostalgic re-run - in reverse. There was stretched all around us that vast undulating panorama, variegated in multiple shades of green, richly dappled with limitless acres of full-blown heather, beribboned with the deckle-edged narrow white trail, twisting and turning, rising and dipping, out from where it had lost itself among the gentle folds of the hills in the purple distance behind. There were no fences by the roadsides, nor any kerbstones, and at frequent intervals wide strips of vegetation had invaded long stretches down the middle. In the near distance, rugged dry-stone walls struck irregular patterns up and over the fells, giving the entire vista an aura of unorganised splendour. The ubiquitous sheep perpetually engrossed in sideways chewing would raise a head, waggle an ear, or twitch a nose disdainfully as we passed, and all without the slightest interruption to the movement of the mandible. At times our passing would raise a curlew, piping frantically, or give a pair of lapwings cause to harry us from overhead.

A panicking flurry of grouse would explode out of a patch of bracken by the roadside, with loud 'crrrucks' and thrashing pinions. There were of course the rabbits, scores of them to the mile, recklessly skittering over the road in every direction and scurrying about the verges. A dull thud from the front of the car indicated that one unfortunate creature had got its timing wrong, bringing from Josh a broad grin and the casual observation,

"Another yan for t'poliss's dog's dinner 'appen."

We tried hard to force the appropriate laughter, but it came out with a patronising sound in it. There was little sustained conversation and Josh seemed content to assume that perhaps the heat was making us drowsy, or that we were unduly tired. But we knew better and that it was because thoughts which flooded our minds came up with no words attached to them. The mournful drone of Josh's old Morris Ten-Four saloon, as it toiled up the long ascent away from the lovely Lyndass Dale, added a further element of pathos to the situation, as though the faithful old girl was in deep sympathy with our own unwillingness to depart.

"Stop Josh - please - just here," Gina suddenly called out, "and could you turn her about a wee bit - just a wee bit - please Josh."

We had reached the top of the escarpment. Helped out of the car I stood with Gina, and gazed enraptured. There came over us a solemn stillness, after Josh, picking up the special significance of the moment, had stopped the throbbing engine. A curlew piped overhead and a flight of lapwings wheeled away into the distance. Down below and far beyond stretched out the magnificent valley. In the clear light of the morning sun, nestled about an acute curve in the glistening river, between two gently rounded massives shimmering in the pale blue haze, lay Lyndassby. The sheer magic of a similar moment but two years ago returned, but now it was touched with the sadness only known to disappointed youth. Even yet, the ingredient of sacredness remained intact, and indeed enhanced by dear memories. Vividly there came to my mind a prayer of an old friend;

When we feel all is lost,
every aspiration has come to naught,
and every effort has been in vain,
may we remember You O Christ,
on your Cross,
with - nothing.

"Thank you Josh - the circle's complete - let's be on our way."

And thus saying, all of Gina's radiant sweetness went into the gentle kiss which she planted on that big tough farmer's cheek.

* * * * * * * * * * * *